Y0-BDJ-023

to Debbie
Hope you love it.
Sheila Lowe

WHAT SHE SAW

BY SHEILA LOWE

SUSPENSE PUBLISHING

WHAT SHE SAW
By
Sheila Lowe

PRINT EDITION

* * * * *

PUBLISHED BY:
Suspense Publishing

Jacket design: Lyn Stanzione

Second Edition

ISBN-13: 978-0692283462 (Suspense Publishing)
ISBN-10: 0692283463

ALSO BY SHEILA LOWE

Poison Pen
Written in Blood
Dead Write
Last Writes
Inkslingers Ball

Non-fiction

The Complete Idiot's Guide to Handwriting Analysis
Handwriting of the Famous & Infamous

ACKNOWLEDGMENTS

With grateful thanks to the usual suspects, who comprise the best critique partners in all the land: Bob Bealmear, Bruce Cook, Gwen Freeman, Barbara Petty, Raul Melendez. As always, Dr. Doug Lyle provided helpful insights on medical issues, Suzanne Bank in matters of interior design, and George Fong whose generous sharing of his FBI expertise made all the difference. Add to that esteemed crew Jane Myers, who answered my questions about the mental status exam.

Thanks, also, to Kristen Weber, my former editor at Penguin, who still has important comments to make on my work. And a special nod to the early readers who caught my errors and reminded me not to rush things at the end. Thank you Bob Joseph, Jackie Houchin, Becky Scott, and other indulgent friends.

PRAISE FOR 'WHAT SHE SAW'

"Sheila Lowe's *What She Saw* is a gripping, psychologically astute thriller, with a sympathetic heroine and enough suspense to keep any reader turning the pages!"

—Dennis Palumbo, licensed psychotherapist and author of the *Daniel Rinaldi Mystery* Series

"Lowe spreads the mystery out one delicious morsel at a time. Both her characters and her plot are flawless."

—Peg Brantley, author of *Red Tide* and *The Missings*

"From the foreboding opening chapter to the explosive climax, the reader will experience non-stop anxiety about who this woman is and what jeopardy is about to engulf her."

—Jackie Houchin, reviewer

"Twists and turns, a riveting tale of suspense that will keep you on the edge of your seat."

—Connie Archer, national best-selling author of *The Soup Lover's Mysteries*

WHAT SHE SAW

BY SHEILA LOWE

ONE

The first thing she noticed was the sound. Steel wheels rolling on rails, thrumming in time with her heartbeat. Instinct whispered that if she could only screw up the courage to pry open her eyes, she would see the world hurtling past with the breathless rush of a roller coaster. But that kind of courage had deserted her.

How long had she been sitting upright, hands clasped in her lap, knees and ankles pressed together as tightly as if they were bound? *Hours? Days?*

It would be so easy to pretend she had the answer; to continue drifting on a sea of passivity and give in to the lethargy that threatened to consume her. But somewhere deep inside, a voice insisted, *You have to come back.*

Leave me alone.

Even in her head, the protest sounded weak. She sighed, recognizing that she had no choice but to accede. And once she came to that understanding, a gradual unraveling began, thread by delicate thread, of the veil that separated consciousness from the abyss.

With consciousness came a sharpened awareness: refrigerated air on flesh stippled with goosebumps. At least her sensory perceptions were in working order.

She began to take inventory. Olfactory: the ropy odor of a pot smoker somewhere nearby—check. Hearing: Valley Girl chatter behind her—check. Taste—the dregs at the bottom of a Mezcal bottle were less toxic than the inside of her mouth. Check.

With just one sense left to test, a sudden primal fear brought the self-inventory to an abrupt halt. *Don't open your eyes. The truth is too grotesque to name.*

But when the raucous blare of the train's horn rudely snatched away the choice, her eyes flew open of their own accord. It took only a split-second to squeeze them shut again, but a split-second was time enough to absorb the sight of gauzy mist floating above grey, choppy water.

Words that failed to attach themselves to any personal meaning filled her brain.

Ocean. West Coast. United States. Pacific.

A thousand desperate questions tried to form, but she pushed them all aside, listening instead to the voice, which began to whisper instructions: *Breathe. Relax. Focus.*

Five times...ten...fifty, she mouthed the mantra until the outside world receded and the abyss welcomed her back.

A loud clanging jerked her awake once again as the train thundered across a railroad crossing. She pressed her cheek against the cold window, straining to see up ahead. No point in trying to keep her eyes closed anymore.

How long had she been unconscious this time? Long enough for the scenery beyond the window to have changed. Scrubby weeds and dirt had replaced the ocean. Beyond the tracks, patches of dense fog brooded low to the ground, like a ghost cat on the prowl...an eerie landscape where anything might be lurking.

There was the coastline again; there, a neat patch of yellow rental umbrellas and beach chairs lined up on the sand; a long wooden pier jutted out over the ocean.

Rounding a bend, the train slowed for a truss bridge that had been used as a canvas for some urban artists' particular brand of graffiti. Then the sand-colored walls of a hotel came into view on the promenade, with a sign identifying it as the Crowne Plaza.

Vaguely aware that her fellow passengers were beginning to stir, she arched her back and wiggled her toes inside her shoes; stretched out the kinks in her legs as the conductor announce the next stop: Ventura Station.

At the far end of the carriage the EXIT sign beckoned.

Like a prisoner whose cell door has unexpectedly swung open, she lurched to her feet and stepped into the aisle.

Everyone thinks you're crazy.

That's because you are *crazy.*

Faltering, discomposed by the new murmuring in her ear, she gave her head a sharp shake. But instead of ceasing, the insidious whispers morphed to a loud buzz, exploded into a harsh cacophony.

She reached out, grasping at the closest seatback, swaying with the motion of the train, and attempted a few unsteady steps forward before slumping into an empty aisle seat, gulping like a landed fish. Her hands were slick with sweat.

A voice—not the one in her head—an elderly male, said, "Are you okay?"

Ignore it. You're hallucinating.

"Miss? Do you need help?"

Sane people don't act like this.

A hand touched her shoulder. "I'll call the conductor. You don't look…"

Not a hallucination. Twisting her head sideways to look at him, she pasted on what she hoped would pass for a smile, though she suspected it emerged more as a grimace. "I'm fine. I'm fine."

"You sure? I'd be glad to…"

"No," she cut in more firmly. "I'm fine."

The truth was her skin was hot and tingling and she was shaking like a dry drunk. A completely inappropriate giggle slipped past her lips. An image had flashed in her head: a chorus line of pink elephants in tutus.

The man gave her a look of concern, but sat back in his seat across the aisle without further comment. She could feel his eyes still on her, and the scrutiny made her uneasy.

She pushed herself to sit up straight and began to count silently, focusing on each number through sheer force of will as if it were a buoy to cling to. By the time she reached thirty, the din in her head had begun to subside and her breathing leveled out.

You can do it. You can do it. You can do it.

What am I? The goddamn little engine that could?

Watch your language!

Shut up.

She pulled herself to her feet again, determined she was going to shut out the voice, and resumed her march to the EXIT sign—a tightrope walker on a high wire who must reach the termination point without losing her balance. Ahead of her the carriage bent and elongated; a hall of mirrors stretching to infinity.

She passed the Valley Girl still yakking on her cell phone. Passed the pot smoker, who tipped his chin at her as if to catch her attention. The sickly sweet odor of marijuana wafted off him, like the dirty cloud hanging over Pigpen's head in a Charlie Brown cartoon. Refusing to change her focus, she ignored him and continued on her way as if she were just a normal person on a train, preparing to alight after a normal journey.

Except this was no normal journey and she was no normal person.

By the time the train ground to a halt she had reached the exit. The carriage doors slid open and travelers maneuvered past, debarking around her. Yet, she found herself unable to follow them, staying where she was, fingers wrapped around the handrail as if permanently attached.

New passengers climbed aboard. Then a conductor was heading her way. She could already read the questions on his face: Is this your station, or are you staying on the train? Where are you headed? And the one he would leave unspoken: What are you doing, standing on that step?

Her need to avoid those questions was stronger than her need to remain in the relative safety of the train.

Three—Two—One—Go.

As soon as her feet touched the platform she turned her back on the conductor and walked briskly in the opposite direction.

The station, a mere strip of concrete 50 yards long; nothing more than a couple of benches, an electronic ticket machine, and a sign reading "VENTURA." She hurried to the end of the wrought iron fencing that separated the tracks from the street.

"You're late."

She swung, breathless, to face the man who had spoken the

accusation. Not much taller than her, wearing short-sleeved shirt and slacks, he was slight in stature. He didn't look particularly threatening, but it was with an odd sense of relief that she realized his scowl was directed, not at her, but the Valley Girl.

"Oh, like I was driving the train or something," the girl retorted, earbuds still plugged in. "It's only five-thirty anyway. We're not all *that* late."

They hurried off and climbed into an SUV parked at the curb. As she watched them drive off, behind her, the train's engine began to rev. At the same moment, a sudden sharp breeze sprang up from the ocean, nipping at her bare arms, reminding her that she had no jacket to cover her thin t-shirt.

No purse, either, she realized in confusion. *You don't get on a train without some means to buy a ticket—cash, credit card—something...* She jammed her fists into the pockets of her Levi's clawing at the denim; first the front, then the back. No ID. Nothing but lint. Not even a dime hiding in the seams.

How could you be so stupid?

Whirling, she dashed back onto the platform, but the behemoth was already on the move.

"Hey!" she shouted, running alongside the train, heedless of the massive wheels turning mere inches from her feet. Her fist beat uselessly against the siding. "Hey, wait! Wait!"

The last compartment lumbered past, forcing her to jump back as the train picked up speed, watching in dismay as it disappeared from view. *What now?*

Alone on the platform she turned in a slow circle, taking in her surroundings. Across the street was a huge empty field of concrete, a parking lot that, according to a marquee on the corner, served the Ventura County Fairgrounds. To her right, the road that ran alongside the railroad tracks dead-ended.

Fighting back tears, she bit down hard on her lip and turned left, walking away from the station. And as she walked, the thing that had been clamoring at her all along struck her with the force of a body blow: the terrifying truth that refused to be silenced; a truth she had been warding off since the first inkling of consciousness on the train. A truth from which she could no longer protect herself. And with that emerging truth, the question to which she had no answer: *Who am I?*

TWO

The street sign read 'Harbor' on the Amtrak side and 'Figueroa' as the cross street.

The names meant nothing to her; she might as well be on Mars. Questions reverberated in the vacant space where her identity should have been.

What was I doing on that train?

Where did I travel from?

Where do I live?

What day of the week is it? What month? What year?

Omigod, why can't I remember anything?

It was light now, but in a couple of hours it would be dark and cold. What then? Was it safe to sleep on the beach? What about the tide? Would it cover the sand and rocks, leaving no place for someone lost and alone with no place else to go?

The voice mocked her.

You're not going to get any help standing here, dumb shit.

She turned on Figueroa, where two highway overpasses spanned the small, empty street. Etched in the concrete was the word DOWNTOWN. Maybe she could get some help if she headed that way. Or maybe by the time she reached 'downtown' a brilliant idea would have inspired her and she would know exactly what to do.

A pair of long mesh screens stood beneath the overpasses,

which would otherwise have been dead space. At some other time it might be interesting to examine the colorful children's drawings posted there, but this was not the moment. The unnerving sensation of being watched was giving her the creeps.

With a furtive glance over her shoulder at the lengthening shadows already falling across the empty sidewalk she scuttled past the first screen. She had made it halfway past the second when she heard a coarse laugh.

"Hey, sweet thing; you friendly, honey?"

Like a puppet on a string she jerked to a halt. Her imagination had not been playing tricks. She could *feel* them sniffing her vulnerability: two men sprawled on the incline, half-hidden behind the screen.

The scumbag who had called to her rubbed his fingers together, as if suggesting a financial transaction. "Come on over here, girlie."

The second creep hoisted his can of Budweiser in solidarity. A scattering of battered empties lay between them. "Yeah, cutie pie, how about it?"

Why couldn't she make her feet move? Her brain was sending commands to her legs, but fear had completed its circuit and shut down her ability to respond. An angry retort stuck to her lips: Do I *look* like a hooker?

A pulse bumped hard in her throat. *Oh God, am* I?

Scumbag number two stuck out his tongue and wiggled it at her, like some obscene species of overgrown lizard. The other, more aggressive, pushed to his feet and began to stagger down the hill making wet kissing noises that caused the bile to rise in her throat. His hands, outstretched like claws, were aimed at her breasts. "What's ya' name, cutie? C'mere…"

He was close enough that she could smell the beer on his fetid breath. All at once he halted, staring over her shoulder. For an instant his eyes widened. He swung on his crony and hissed, "Hide that shit, dude."

Moving with the urgency of a man on fire, Scumbag Two shoveled empties under a bush, whatever fantasies he'd had of a hook-up vanishing as fast as the beer cans.

A half-second later, when a black-and-white patrol car pulled to the curb, she knew she ought to be grateful for the intervention.

But for no reason she could identify, she was not grateful at all, and for a tense moment her paralysis remained.

One hand rested on his nightstick as the patrolman climbed out of his vehicle, ignoring their protestations of innocence as he sized up the two scumbags. The cop turned to her, his square jaw jutting. "Is there a problem here, miss?"

She opened her mouth, but her voice seemed to have deserted her as completely as her memory.

"Miss? Are you—"

"No," she managed to gasp. "No problem."

Without stopping to question why his appearance had shaken her more than the threat from the two men, she spun on her heels and started running back the way she had come, tearing up the sidewalk like a witless thing pursued by a pack of the undead. The cop yelled something, but it didn't matter, she had no intention of stopping.

At Harbor Boulevard, turning away from the train station, she ran until the air was rasping in her throat and painful shin splints forced her to flop against a wall, panting.

Trying to catch her breath, she rummaged in her mind, frantic for something to hang on to, some morsel that would provide a clue to who she was, where she belonged—*anything*. But a memory as empty as her pockets had nothing to give.

What if those men had raped and killed her? When her body was found, no one would know who she was. *She* didn't even know who she was. But something else nagged: the appearance of the policeman had completely and irrationally unnerved her.

Why? Why? Why?

The closest public building appeared to be the Crowne Plaza. She started walking towards the hotel, about a quarter-mile away, rehearsing what she would say to the smartly-uniformed clerk she imagined would be manning the front desk. *I have no money and I don't know who I am*. In a burst of harsh reality she saw her circumstances for what they were. Would that front desk clerk look at her worn Levi's and scuffed running shoes and take her for a homeless person?

They would certainly call the cops to haul her away to a

psychiatric hospital. Was that why the sight of a policeman had scared her so badly? Maybe she was an escapee from a mental institution.

By the time she reached the hotel's front door, her resolve had melted like ice cream on a hot day and she had talked herself out of entering.

What now?

She was still searching for an answer when a group of tourists following their guide filed past her to the crosswalk in front of the hotel. Obeying a sudden impulse, she attached herself to the end of the group and crossed the road with them. Chattering among themselves, no one seemed to notice her as the group continued its trek up California Street. She let them go, lingering on a pedestrian footbridge, mesmerized by the traffic speeding on the road below.

The 101.

The words flashed in her head with a little thrill of recognition. A small victory. She had conjured up the slang name for this segment of the interstate highway. She knew *something.*

But it took only a moment for the excitement to fade. She was still the same nameless nobody. All of those people actually *driving* on the highway—those people in their Mercedes' and Toyota's, their trucks and motorcycles—they all knew where they were coming from, where they were going.

Was anyone wondering where *she* was?

A sudden flurry of sound made her turn as a crow alit on the guard rail only a foot from where she stood. The sharp black eyes seemed to bore into her soul, as if it could read her despair and found her wanting.

The big bird looked straight at her for a long moment, then, with a flap of its powerful wings, rose gracefully into the sky, circling away on an updraft.

How wonderful it must feel, she thought, watching the crow disappear into the clouds. What if you could spread your arms like those wings. You could lean over the edge until you were soaring on the wind…

As the image formed in her mind, her arms stretched out to her sides. Her left foot lifted onto the ledge and she started to lean…

...A passing motorist blew his horn.

What the hell are you doing?

She was well aware that the voice was in her head, but it was loud enough to jar her back to reality. Appalled by how close she had come to following that insane urge, she flung herself to the far side of the walkway and sank to the edge of the curb, trembling violently.

Am I suicidal? Dear God, what happened to my mind?

The questions replayed over and over. Maybe if she concentrated hard enough, she would get some answers.

The answer is, you're nuts.

That can't be right.

Nuts.

Once her hands had stopped shaking and her heart rate slowed to something resembling normal, she got to her feet and debated where she might go next. Having no better ideas, she decided to follow California street in the direction the tour group had gone.

The strobe in her head started flashing again when she crossed Thompson. Names of what she somehow knew were local businesses clicked into place: the white building with rust-colored awnings was the Hamburger Habit. Beyond the Habit was Clark's Liquor. Right after the liquor store, a small rectangular building constructed of red brick was home to the Bombay Bar and Grill. The thump and strum of a live band reached her while she was still passing the liquor store.

The sound of rhythm-and-blues spilling into the street drew her. She paused to watch the band performing on a tiny stage in the Bombay's front window. The husky-voiced singer was named Joe Wilson, and the song he was belting out was called *Bad Behavior*. That piece of information earned a triumphant little fist pump just before misery overwhelmed her again. How could she know these trivial things but *nothing* about herself?

More pressing was the setting sun, whose dimming rays were rapidly bringing dusk.

What the hell *am I going to do?*

"Jen! Hey, *Jennnnna!*"

She paused mid-step at the man's voice behind her. She knew, of course, that he could not be yelling at her. But the voice came again, louder, more insistent. "*Jenna! Wait up!*"

Fully expecting to see someone else responding to him, she turned. A man was standing outside the Bombay's door looking directly at her, his palms upturned in a question. She quickly took in the shaggy black hair, the t-shirt and surfer shorts on the lanky body. Thirtyish, she guessed, breaking out in a cold sweat of hope as he jogged nearer.

"Hey, chicklet, what's the rush?"

Nothing about him felt familiar, but she was too elated to care. *Someone knew her.* She had a name. He'd called her Jenna. She tried it on for size and found it slightly uncomfortable, like a too-tight pair of high-heeled shoes. But she clung to it, fearing he would take a second look and utter an embarrassed: *Oh, sorry. I thought you were someone else.*

"What's up with the haircut?" he asked, appraising her. "I almost didn't recognize you."

Her hand went up and raked a mass of thick locks cut boyishly short. She opened her mouth to tell him that she had no idea who he was, or even who *she* was, but the words refused to come out.

"Uh, thought I'd try a new look," she heard herself say. Her voice felt rusty, as if it hadn't been used in a while.

"It's cool," he told her. "Just…different."

"Thanks, I guess."

"So, where you been, chicklet? You didn't get that bug, did you?"

Rule Number One: Tell the truth whenever possible.

And when it's not possible?

Lie like a mutha.

Where did *that* come from?

She pounced on the convenient excuse he had provided. "Yeah, I was pretty sick; really out of it." Being down with a flu bug sounded a lot better than *riding around unconscious on a train.* It had come out so easily. Did that mean she was an accomplished liar?

He nodded sympathetically. "You shoulda called me. I would've fixed you some soup." Then he grinned. "No, I wouldn't. I'd be a fucked-up nurse. But I coulda picked you up something. … Hey—are you okay?"

He had caught her staring at the artwork on his black t-shirt: a tortured stone angel, crimson lips dripping blood, a Rorschach splash polluting its robes. She pulled her eyes away and shook her head. She had to tip her face up to look at him. "Still not feeling so great."

"That sucks. So, I guess I'll catch you later, then." He started to turn away, then wheeled back. "You need help with that flat tire?"

"What?"

"I noticed your ride's out of commission. If you want, I'll change the tire for you."

Hardly daring to believe it, she rapidly digested what she had just learned: He had not only supplied her with a name, but he'd told her she owned a car. He also knew where she lived, which was volumes more than she had known five minutes ago.

"If you wanna call in late to work tomorrow," he added, "I'll do it in the a.m."

Sure. I could call in…if I had a phone and knew where I worked.

"That's great, thanks," she heard herself say.

"Okay, cool. You want a ride home?"

For the first time, she smiled. "I'd love a ride home."

Oh, that's really smart, "Jenna." *What are you gonna do when you get "home?"*

Figure it out later. At least I'll know where I live.

And you're gonna get inside, how?

Shut up! Figure. It. Out. Later.

The conversation inside her head had diverted her attention and she'd missed what the man said. He put a hand on her shoulder, looking at her with speculation in his dark eyes. "Don't take this the wrong way, but you look kinda sick, chick. Let's get you home."

He guided her to a parking structure around the corner on Santa Clara. When he pointed his key fob at a big black Dodge Ram, for a nanosecond Jenna—she had accepted the name as her own since she had no other and he seemed so sure that's who she was—questioned the wisdom of getting into the vehicle with a stranger. But in a world where *everyone* was a stranger, herself included, and with no ID or money, she could think of no better alternative. One thing she knew for certain, turning herself over to the police was *not* an option.

Besides, this guy already knew where she lived, and he was acting like they were friends. He opened the passenger door and boosted her into the cab as easily as if she was a child.

"Just toss that on the floor," he said, referring to a thick manila envelope resting on the passenger seat.

She picked up the envelope, and as he circled around to the driver's side, read the name scrawled in black marker across the front. "Zach," she said softly.

He shot her a cheeky grin as he climbed in and fired up the engine. "That's ma' name, don't wear it out."

"It suits you," she said, sneaking a glance at his profile. She thought he looked a bit like Keanu Reeves.

"So you always say." He drove down the ramp and made a left. "Hey, what happened with Mr. Mystery the other night?"

Her stomach twisted into an acrid knot. What was he talking about?

"C'mon," Zach prompted. "Give it up. Tell your Uncle Zachie."

Why don't you just tell him the truth?

No!

The corner of his mouth quirked upward. "You sure that guy exists?"

"What—what do you mean?"

"I keep waiting to see him, but..."

She reached into the darkness for an answer; didn't find one. "It's, uh...it's complicated."

"Riiight." Zach threw her a sidelong glance. "Okay, no more tough questions."

She sat back, trying to read the street signs as they passed. He'd hung a right on Chestnut and a left onto Thompson, a wide boulevard that changed in character as it meandered through the beach town of Ventura. Plaza Park, where children scrambled over playground equipment. Old growth trees, modest houses, a few custom homes. Café Nouveau, a veterinary hospital, a used car lot.

Less than five minutes after they left the bar, Zach slowed and flipped his left turn signal. He drove into an alley that ran alongside a small apartment building—an attractive Spanish casa—and braked at the four-car carport in the alley. Three spaces stood empty, the fourth was occupied by a Nissan coupe whose front driver's side tire was puddled on the ground.

Seeing it, something dark flashed across Jenna's vision. The flat tire was somehow connected to the black hole of her memory. She knew it, and the knowledge terrified her.

"Probably ran over a nail," Zach said, not noticing the shudder than ran over her. "That friggin construction across the street. You got a good spare?"

"I—I'm not sure." She opened the door and jumped out of the truck. "Thanks, Zach."

"No problemo, chicklet. I'll be down in the morning to take care of the flat."

He scrunched down in his seat and gave her the squint eye. "You *sure* you're okay? You look kinda—what my grandma calls 'peaky.'"

"Really," she insisted. "I'm good. Thanks for the ride." She wasn't going to admit that her head was spinning yet again and she was sick to her stomach.

There were no numbers, no indications on the carport that indicated to which apartment the Nissan belonged. Jenna followed Zach's truck back out of the alley and down to the bank of mailboxes she had noticed on the sidewalk.

A label maker had been used to emboss a first initial and last name on brown plastic strips on each of the boxes, and she took her time examining the names. Apartment one and two both had J names: J. Kroh and J. Marcott. Apartment three was Z. Smith—apparently Zach was her upstairs neighbor. Number four was R. Mendoza.

She rolled the J names around in her mind a couple of times to see whether something stuck. *Jenna Kroh. Jenna Marcott.* Not a twitch. That her choices were limited to the two ground floor units simplified things, but which one was home?

Following her gut, she walked through the alley, avoiding looking at the Nissan with its flat tire, and went around the back of the building to the rear apartment. Reaching over the wooden gate in the stucco wall she lifted the latch and entered the pocket-sized yard.

No certain memory told her that she had chosen the correct unit, but she knew right away that she had. It was the garden gnome that did it; a foot-high statue on the front porch next to a terra cotta planter filled with geraniums. The paint on his tall red hat and white beard was faded and chipped, as though he had been guarding the door for a long time.

Led by an overpowering sense of recognition, Jenna tilted the gnome on end and reached into the opening on the bottom. Felt no surprise, only satisfaction when she gave the little man a shake and the key fell out into her hand.

THREE

This is ridiculous. Go the hell inside.

No!

What's wrong with you?

I'm scared to.

Stupid. You can't stand out here all night.

Whose pernicious voice was that, deriding her without mercy, picking at her every thought?

She had to psych herself up with a couple of deep breaths before unlocking the door onto silence and shadows. Nudging it open with her foot until she could see straight through to the far wall of the living room, she called out a hesitant, "Hello?" When no reply came after a thirty second silence, she took a cautious step inside.

The apartment smelled slightly stale and closed up, but what she had been expecting—the stench of death—was absent. From what she could see, there were no signs of a struggle. No bloody fingerprints marring the café au lait walls, no monster waiting to attack her with razor-sharp claws. Letting out a little sigh, she closed the door behind her and looked around.

To her left, a tiny strip of kitchen boasted a stove and refrigerator, a microwave on a wooden stand next to the empty sink. No dirty dishes had been left in the sink or out to dry on the well-scrubbed counter.

The apartment was small and inexpensively decorated.

"*Furnishings by World Market*." She said it aloud, mildly pleased to have identified *something*, even though it was just the name of a quirky chain store. Jenna toured the living room feeling like the stranger she was, touching things, hoping to recognize something the way she had the garden gnome. She deliberately ignored the closed door to her right.

Placed at right angles to the loveseat was an overstuffed chocolate leather armchair. She could easily picture herself sitting there, huddled under a blanket on cold nights with a mug of cocoa and a good mystery novel. Her approval did not extend to the big coffee table that squatted like a metal toad between the chair and loveseat. Had she *chosen* that ugly piece of furniture?

There wasn't much more. A square of black walnut for the dining table, two matching chairs and cheerful batik cushions. A bookcase, its shelves bare, stood behind the dining table. A sliding glass door led to a walled patio with just enough space to accommodate a chaise longue.

Stacked in the corner, each sealed with a perfectly straight line of packing tape, were four large cartons. Had she recently filled them with books from the bookcase preparing for a move? Or were they waiting to be emptied? Something stopped her from ripping them open.

With the exception of the coffee table, she liked everything she saw, but the liking was objective. She wanted to feel that she *knew* it.

Her eyes went to the closed door.

I don't want to see it.

You can't stand here forever.

Maybe I can.

Just do it.

Jenna had run out of excuses.

The sight of the pristine white comforter on the neatly made double bed hit her like an electric shock. Where was the corpse she had *known* lay behind that closed door? Where was the blood?

Jenna grabbed the pillow shams from the bed and tossed them to the floor, hellbent on finding evidence that she had not been hallucinating some terrible crime. She dragged off the comforter and shoved it to the corner in a heap. Even the sheets, tucked as tight as a tourniquet, surrendered to her frenetic deconstruction.

But when she was done, the mattress was as spotless as the linens she had ripped from it. There were no faint stains to be seen; no sign that someone had attempted to scrub away the evidence of savagery.

Bewildered, she went back over everything that had happened since coming back to the real world on the train. The pot smoker leering at her. The creepy men under the bridge. The cop. Zach. They were all real—*weren't they?*

How could she be sure when the dividing line between what was and what might not be had become so blurred?

Who the hell am I and what have I done?

She took a long, careful look around the room, noting the computer desk on the other side of the bed. All she had to do was walk over and switch on the CPU. A computer was bound to contain information that could tell her about her life. But the prospect unleashed a flood of renewed dread that was not in her imagination.

Turn it on!

Not yet.

You are so chickenshit.

There's something I have to do first.

Arguing with herself that she wasn't just making another excuse to delay what had to be done, Jenna took a deep breath and closed her eyes, reaching up in the way a blind person might, touching the landmarks of her features with her fingertips. The skin was firm and young, the cheekbones prominent.

That was the first step. Next, she moved to the bathroom door and took two more deep breaths, then crossed the threshold.

Looking back at her from a wide mirror that ran the length of the wall was a waifish young woman with short honey blonde hair. Pretty enough, if wide, pain-filled eyes appealed to you. What was behind the anguish reflected in those cool blue windows to her soul? Her mind skittered away from the question as fast as a cockroach exposed to a sudden beam of light.

Petite, perhaps five-three or four, she estimated her age as early twenties. She took careful stock of the person Zach had identified as Jenna, gazing at her image for a time. Her skin was pale, as if it had not seen much sunlight in recent days. Maybe she had not been lying when she told Zach she'd been sick. Maybe an illness had stolen her memory.

Maybe… For the space of half a breath, her image seemed to shimmer and dissolve. Pain exploded in her head and a high-pitched whistle filled her ears. The edges of her vision darkened. The world tilted.

Jenna groped for the edge of the vanity. Afraid she would lose consciousness again, she lowered herself to the lip of the bathtub and leaned forward until her head was between her knees. Battling to keep her wits, trying uselessly not to think about what she had seen lurking behind her in the mirror—an immense faceless figure.

After the room had stopped revolving, Jenna slid the shower curtain open and checked, just to make sure the monster wasn't hiding there.

Am I batshit crazy?

Maybe.

Okay, then. Time to get better acquainted with the crazy lady.

Like the kitchen, the bathroom was spotless. Lemon yellow towels on the wall rack were folded into perfect rectangles. The pump on the bottle of liquid soap was as fresh and un-caked as you'd find in a hotel room.

I may be crazy, but at least I'm a clean kind of crazy.

She started with the medicine cabinet. No matter how insignificant the contents—peroxide, Band Aids, lip balm—they were pieces of the puzzle that made up Jenna Marcott.

In the top drawer of the vanity was a toothbrush in a travel holder, a man's electric razor, and an unopened packet of birth control pills. She slammed the drawer shut, alarmed by the new questions the items raised, no longer certain she wanted to continue her search.

Maybe if she just laid on the bed for a while she would go to sleep and wake up remembering who she was. Or, maybe she would wake up and find herself on the train again, stuck in a loop like Bill Murray's character in *Groundhog Day*, waking up in precisely the same circumstances, day after day, month after month.

How can I remember an old movie but not my own name?

The bedroom closet held a rack of stylish business suits, blouses, pants and tops, and 'dressy' dresses sorted according to color. Jenna was a neat freak.

At the back of the closet was a man's suit, size 42 Long. A dark charcoal, single-breasted Zegna, with a maroon silk tie tucked into the pocket. A soft Egyptian cotton shirt in the lightest of blues shared a hanger with the jacket. Zach's Mr. Mystery apparently had good taste.

Where is he?

Someone accustomed to leaving his clothes at her apartment must want to know if something had happened to her.

Unless he already knows.

Did he have something to do with it?

Shoving aside that question along with the other pile of things she didn't want to think about, Jenna turned to the lowboy chest of drawers. T-shirts, Levi's, and sweaters in neatly folded blocks. A pale blue sweater drew her and she pressed her nose into the soft cashmere. Something about the faint flowery scent that clung to the wool made her want to weep. Pulling it over her head, she hugged herself, comforted by its warmth.

The stylish zebra print clutch purse that she found on the floor of the closet held blush, lipstick, a small palette of eye shadow—all high end products—new-looking in their containers, although they had been used. A small wallet with ten crisp twenty dollar bills folded in precise halves was also included in the purse, it seemed high as far as walking-around money was concerned. Had she withdrawn it from the bank for her train trip?

So how did you pay for the train if the money is here?

There was no shortage of plastic, either. MasterCard, Visa, bank debit card, Barnes & Noble membership card, and an upscale dress shop card. All embossed with the name Jenna Marcott.

Seeing the neat signatures written across the magnetic strip on the backs of the cards felt weird and creepy. Her signature was just one more piece that had broken off with her memory and was now as alien and disembodied as everything else in this waking nightmare.

The driver's license yielded significant information: her birthday was January 1st, with the renewal due next year.

I was born on New Year's Day.

I look younger, but I'm twenty-seven.

The face in the photo, which according to the date on the license was taken four years earlier, was slightly fuller. The hair was shoulder-length, but she had no trouble recognizing the girl from the bathroom mirror. The address came as a surprise: Speedway Avenue in Marina del Rey, not Thompson Boulevard in Ventura.

Marina del Rey.

A mental vibration hit like a small quake: a three-story apartment building, with a pink and beige color scheme. Marina del Rey was in Los Angeles County, about sixty miles south of Ventura, which explained the moving cartons. How long ago had she taken possession of this apartment? Just one more question with no answer.

A key ring in the purse had a key to the apartment door and a car key. There was also a small silver key with a round head that might open a suitcase or file cabinet. The last was stamped with the words "Duplication Prohibited."

According to a laminated photo ID badge in the purse, Jenna Marcott was an employee of BioNeutronics Laboratory in Oxnard.

She dropped the lanyard over her head and let the badge slide down between her breasts, then shut her eyes, waiting for another image like the one she'd had of the Marina del Rey apartment.

She waited for a long while, but nothing came.

The badge suddenly felt like it weighed a ton. Jenna ripped it off and hurled it to the floor, as if the act of rejecting it gave her some kind of power.

That was a sick joke. She had about as much power as a newborn kitten. What in the name of all that was holy had so completely ripped away her past? Tears welled up and spilled over her cheeks; a trickle at first, then a torrent. She wept for her lost self, for the part of her mind that must have been filled with twenty-seven years of memories. Would she ever get them back?

Can you grieve for something you don't remember having?

She wept until her eyes were swollen and there were no tears left.

After splashing cold water on her splotchy face and patting it dry, Jenna gave herself a pep talk and returned to the task of exploring the purse. She had a safe place to stay. That was enough for now.

The last remaining items were a folded piece of graph paper and an appointment reminder card for Jenna Marcott to meet with Zebediah Gold, Ph.D., Psychologist, on August twenty-ninth at three p.m. in Venice.

You don't have to be crazy to see a shrink.

But it helps.

On the graph paper was a short message scrawled in bold black ink:

I'm warning you, Jen, back off. Now!!! You've got to give me more time.

Back off from what? Time for what? There was no signature. The writer must have expected her to recognize the handwriting, which of course she did not.

Maybe she had talked to Dr. Gold about this vaguely threatening note. Maybe the appointment had not already passed and he could tell her who had written it. Her eyes shifted to the bedroom doorway where the computer was still waiting to tell her what day it was…and so much more.

You have no choice.

I know.

The fear still reverberated in her bones, but her need for information was too powerful to ignore any longer.

Jenna seated herself at the computer and leaned down to power up the CPU under the desk. Near the edge of the metal keyboard tray, her eye caught on a reddish-brown patch the size of a quarter. It seemed to pulse and glow like neon.

The breath whooshed out of her lungs so fast she might have been sucker-punched. The whistling shrieked in her ears…the world faded to black.

FOUR

Her eyes opened onto darkness so dense that for a terrible moment she was sure that she had lost not only her memory, but her ability to see. Then, thankfully, her pupils dilated and shadows morphed into the familiar shapes of furniture. A slice of moonlight shone in from under the window shade above her. She was lying on something cold and hard, the back of her head tender where it must have hit the floor when she passed out.

Was she still in the apartment? Or had she gone to some other place? Reaching out her left hand, her fingers came in contact with fabric. The bed skirt.

Still in the apartment.

Time and space seemed mutable, unsure. Groggily trying to work out how long she had been unconscious, Jenna got slowly to her feet. She fumbled her way to the nightstand across the bed, switched on the lamp and looked around.

What the hell happened?

The stain on the keyboard tray.

I didn't hallucinate that stain.

True, the stain was not the river of blood she had expected to find. But it was evidence of—*what?* The question hung there, mocking her. Not rust, not paint. Where had that spot of blood come from? She stared across the bed as if the computer were some kind of malevolent transformer, a robot that could unfurl wings and fly across the room to attack her.

Whose blood is it?

Jenna pushed up the sleeves of the sweater and examined her hands and arms, rotating them so she could see for herself that the smooth skin had no cuts or abrasions. She checked her neck in the bathroom mirror. Shrugged out of the sweater and t-shirt and inspected her torso, pivoting and stretching. She stepped up on the lip of the bathtub and contorted her torso to view in the mirror the unmarked flesh of her back. She kicked off the tennis shoes and stepped out of her Levi's. No cuts or bruises marred the pale legs.

For just a flicker, as she stood shivering in her underwear, she considered running upstairs to Zach Smith's apartment and banging on his door. She would tell him the truth and he would— No. This was not the sort of truth you could share with just anyone.

She dampened a paper towel in the kitchen and took it to the computer. The small act of scrubbing the stain off the drawer lessened its initial impact and made her feel a tiny bit better. But she took care to fold the paper towel inward so that she could not see the transferred blood, before flushing it down the toilet.

Jenna booted up the computer and saw with relief the date at the bottom of the screen. Her appointment with Zebediah Gold, Ph.D., was scheduled for tomorrow afternoon. Almost today, in fact, according to the computer clock—it was a few minutes before midnight. She had been unconscious for more than five hours. Had she gotten up and gone somewhere else during that time? Engaged in some activity that she'd now forgotten? No. Waking up in the same spot where she'd blacked out convinced her that she had not moved an inch during those hours.

The Documents folder was empty, as were the Email Inbox, Outbox, and Sent folders.

Where are my emails? My data files?

She raced through possibilities, clicking from one folder to another, rooting around for any sign that the computer had ever been used. Maybe it was brand new and she hadn't yet saved any personal files. That her computer was as bereft of information as her own memory just didn't add up to coincidence. Maybe it had suffered a viral attack that wiped out everything on the hard drive.

Or...maybe everything on it was deliberately erased.

On top of the monitor a web cam stared back at her like an evil eye. There was no light on the camera, which indicated that the software that would visually connect her to another computer was turned off. But it *felt* like it was looking right at her, spying on her movements. She reached up and unhooked the device, laid it face down on the computer desk; then, in a burst of overkill, bent down and unplugged the USB cable.

Riffling through drawers of scrupulously folded sleepwear, Jenna felt like an intruder in somebody else's life. It would not have surprised her had someone unlocked the front door and marched right in, demanding to know what she was doing there, pretending to be Jenna Marcott.

Did the man Zach called "Mr. Mystery" appreciate the black silk stockings, the sexy push-up bras, and the barely-there thongs? She wondered when they would meet, and what she would say when they did. *Hi, honey. Did you have anything to do with my amnesia?* With the suit in the closet being the only male garments in the tiny one-bedroom apartment, he obviously didn't live with her.

On the bottom of the special lingerie drawer a flat package loosely folded in brown paper had been sealed with adhesive tape. Reaching for it, Jenna quickly dropped it back in the drawer, stabbed by something sharp.

She stared at her fingertip where a red balloon blossomed. Acid surged into her throat as she made a dash for the bathroom. She retched until the dry heaves left her clammy-skinned and quivering.

With a pair of tweezers she found in the medicine cabinet, Jenna worked the glass splinter out of her finger. The cut burned like fire. She held her finger under the faucet until the water ran clear, then put a bandaid around it, asking herself why the most insignificant spot of blood left her completely unhinged.

Jenna carried the package to the kitchen with care, wondering what she would find inside.

What if it's a can of worms?

You want to know, don't you?

I don't know. I don't know.

You have to open it.

Yes.

She opened it over the sink in case there was more glass in the package. Inside was a splintered wooden picture frame, its cardboard backing, and a color photograph that had been ripped into several pieces.

Her heart sped up as she spread the torn pieces out like a jigsaw puzzle on the dining table, shifting them around until she located the ones that matched.

The size 42 Long suit.

Zach's 'Mr. Mystery,' she was pretty sure. Dwarfed by his height, Jenna stood beside him in the picture with his arm draped possessively around her shoulders. Even with a jagged tear through his face, the man had movie star-quality looks. Soulful brown eyes you could drown in; dark hair threaded with silver, trimmed close to his head. The slight growth of facial hair gave him the look of someone on vacation who hadn't needed to shave for a few days.

Though he was clearly older than Jenna by more than a few years, they made a striking couple by any standard. In the strapless black evening dress, with diamond studs sparkling in her earlobes and a matching pendant resting against her throat, Jenna had to admit she looked stunning.

Had she had been trying to close the age gap by sweeping her hair up into the sophisticated 'up do'? When had she cut it short? Judging by Zach's surprise, pretty recently.

When did I look that happy? How long ago?

The photo could have been taken anytime—last week, last year. She had no way of knowing. She gazed at it for a long time, trying with all her might to recognize the man. In the end, she had to concede that at this moment, she would not have been able to pick him out of a crowd.

The dark, soft-focus background looked like it might have been taken in a bar or restaurant. Her photo 'self' smiled up at her companion with an intensity that bordered on obsession. Had she been too adoring, too clingy, causing him to dump her? Was that why she had destroyed this beautiful photograph? Or, had he cheated on her?

What could have driven her to destroy what, by all appearances, had been a happy memory? What had wounded her so deeply that she had destroyed not only the photograph, but the frame, too? And why not just throw the picture away, instead of saving all the broken pieces in the drawer? Just more questions to add to the mounting catalog of: "What Jenna doesn't remember."

It was after one a.m. when she returned to the computer and opened a browser, googling "Causes of Amnesia." Wikipedia came up first, listing a wide spectrum of causes beginning with head injury; "e.g., a fall, a knock on the head." She read on. Dissociative amnesia had a psychological cause and resulted from repressed memory about a traumatic, possibly brutal event, such as rape.

Dissociative fugue was also caused by psychological trauma; "usually temporary, unresolved, and therefore may return." As her gaze traveled over that section, one phrase in particular caught her eye: "one or more episodes of amnesia in which the inability to recall some or all of one's past, and either the loss of one's identity or the formation of a new identity occur with sudden, unexpected, purposeful travel away from home." But that condition was rare.

It might be rare, but here I am, proof that it happens.

The Mayo Clinic's website had a section on transient global amnesia that gave her hope: "your recall of recent events simply vanishes, so you can't remember where you are or how you got there. Episodes are usually short-lived, and afterwards your memory is fine."

When? When will my memory be fine? How long do I have to wait?

She googled herself next and learned that Jenna Marcott shared a name with a junior at a small college in the East. The other Jenna had pages on MySpace, and Facebook. She had a gym membership and played tennis. There were scads of photos posted of a tall, willowy, redheaded Jenna Marcott, but no references to a diminutive blonde in Ventura or Marina del Rey.

FIVE

The persistent chiming of the doorbell woke her.

Her mind still halfway stuck in a bad dream, she blinked at her surroundings, trying to figure out where she was. In nothing flat, the shock and confusion came crashing back. The train, Zach, the apartment, the torn photograph...she was Jenna Marcott, lying on top of the bare mattress in her bedroom, legs tangled in a sheet.

Right away she knew that her memory remained a blank slate; her hope of waking up with her life intact dashed. It seemed peculiar when she had lost so much to feel so profoundly grateful that she had managed to at least retain the memories of the past few hours, if nothing else.

Far from ready to face another day of amnesia, Jenna dragged herself out of bed and went to the door, expecting to find her upstairs neighbor on the porch, ready to fix the flat tire on a car she did not remember owning.

But it was not Zach's cheeky grin that looked back at her when she opened the door a few inches and peeked out. The man on the porch was probably Zach's age and height, but his watery blue eyes and thin lips, dirty blond hair and scruffy beard, ended the resemblance. Skinny, maybe thirty pounds less than what should be his best weight, he huddled in a dark green field jacket as if the temperatures were midwinter, rather than end of summer, a backpack slung over his shoulder.

Something about him seemed vaguely familiar, but Jenna couldn't imagine he was someone she might choose as a friend.

You have no idea who you would choose as a friend.

No, but…

He gave her the onceover with a casual eye. "Hey, you're here."

Flashback: The pot smoker on the train. *Pigpen.* The smell still clung to his clothes.

Jenna stared back at him, baffled by his arrival on her doorstep. "What do you want?"

"Hey, take a chill pill; I'm doing you a favor." He swung the backpack off his shoulder and held it up for her inspection. "This is yours, right? The tag has this address."

An immediate pulse of recognition made her reach for it. "Oh! Thank you, I really appreciate—"

"You're lucky they didn't explode it," Pigpen interrupted, letting the backpack drop to the ground by his foot. "Bad idea to leave a bag on a train these days. You coulda got arrested."

"If you saw me leave it, why didn't you say something?"

"Tried to, but you wasn't about to give me the time of day. I was gonna keep it, but then I figured, you know, do a good deed, help us both out." He turned and spat into the pot of geraniums next to the door.

Jenna leaned down to pick up the canvas bag, but Pigpen nudged it aside with his foot. "So, how about a reward for being a good citizen?"

She glared at him. "I don't mind giving you some money, but that's *my* backpack. Are you holding it for ransom or something?" Her voice rose with indignation.

Upstairs, Zach's screen door opened and he leaned over the low stucco wall. "Hey, what's up?"

Pigpen craned his neck to look at him. "Get lost, dude," he said rudely. "Fuckin' butt out."

Zach's eyes narrowed. All of a sudden, he was no longer the easygoing neighbor who had given her a ride home the evening before. He had acquired a distinctly menacing presence. Pigpen, who looked as though a strong wind could blow him across the road, would be no match.

Zach started for the stairs. "Yeah? Well, fuck you too, asshole."

Jenna had assumed he was a good guy, but she reminded herself that she didn't know him at all. Anyway, their pissing match meant nothing next to her. Finding the clues to her lost identity that must surely be in the backpack was all she cared about. "He's just dropping something off for me," she broke in. "It's okay."

Zach halted, but even with the flight of stairs between them, Jenna could see the glint of a threat in his eyes. His gaze bored into Pigpen, but he addressed her. "Call me when you're ready."

"I will, thanks."

"Dickwad," the pothead muttered, turning his back on her neighbor. "Let's do this before that motherfucker gets crazy."

"Wait here." This time, Jenna snatched up the backpack and slipped the strap over her shoulder, an act as natural as if she had done it a hundred times before.

"Hey," Pigpen called after her as she closed the door in his face. "Anyone else woulda kept it."

She carried no illusions about him having helped himself to whatever money or anything else that might have been in the bag, but that was of little consequence. Getting the backpack was like every birthday gift and ten Christmases rolled into one; one more slice of her life had returned to her, and that gave her hope for more to come.

Cradling it as gently as if it were a baby, Jenna set the bag on the armchair and took a twenty from the billfold in the zebra purse. With her small stash of resources, that was as generous as she could afford to be.

She offered the money to Pigpen. "I appreciate the good deed."

He looked at the twenty and snorted. "That's all your shit's worth? I shoulda just sold it."

"Take it or leave it," she said, starting to withdraw the hand holding twenty.

He grabbed the bill with a shrug and turned away. She watched him slouch to the gate, where he wheeled back around with a salute.

"Nice doing business with ya, Jessica."

SIX

Jessica?

She wanted to yell at him to stop, to demand that he come back and explain himself, but the words froze on her lips. *My name is Jenna Marcott. The mailbox says so. Zach said so. My driver's license says so.*

Who is Jessica?

She locked the door behind her, deciding that Pigpen's parting words were nothing more than pothead confusion. The backpack waited on the armchair to be explored.

An unexpected lump caught in her throat as she ran her hands over the pink and green floral stitching. The feeling was less recognition than *knowing.*

As Pigpen had said, there was a luggage tag attached to the strap. Reluctantly, she read the card in the plastic window: "Jessica Mack" and the Thompson Street address.

Who is Jessica Mack, and why is her name on my backpack?

The fact that Jessica Mack and Jenna Marcott shared the same initials was not lost on her. She pressed herself into the cushions of the armchair as if they could provide protective armor against any new assaults on her psyche.

In the outside pocket she found an older model mobile phone. That meant stored names, phone numbers, text messages, maybe—vital data for someone searching for memories. But when she went to power it up, the phone was dead and there was no charger.

Note to self: find a Radio Shack and buy a charger.

The J-shaped key ring held a house key that did not fit the apartment's entry door. The car key was for a Honda, not a Nissan. There was a mailbox key and a couple of others she could not identify. Nursing an urgent desire to find that would jog her memory, Jenna unsnapped the closure.

Inside was a jumble of clothing: a couple of black t-shirts, skinny-leg black Levi's, a sleep shirt much like the one she was wearing, thong undies, and a bra, size 34B. The thought of Pigpen digging through her stuff made her cringe. Everything would have to be washed before she could put it against her skin.

Tucked under the clothing was a clear plastic bag containing a travel toothbrush, toothpaste, and comb. Feeling lucky that Pigpen had left anything for her, she added the $67.53 she found on the bottom of the bag to the money in the zebra purse. At least she had enough cash to keep her going for a little while.

There was an ATM card with the name Jessica Mack, and a California driver's license with her photo and the same name and an address in Escondido.

An image flickered: Amtrak station. Running in the dark. Leaping across the yellow 'caution' line at the curb of the platform. Boarding the train just as the doors were closing. Dropping into a seat next to the window as the train began to move. Chugging past a sign on the platform…spotlights pointed at the station name: white lettering on a blue background, Solana Beach. Then, like a puff of smoke, the image was gone. But it was *something*. She had remembered getting on the train in Solana Beach!

So what? the voice in her head taunted. *How much more do you really know than you did before?*

"If that memory came back others can, too!" she argued aloud, then felt foolish.

Taking the driver license out of the purse, she placed it on the table next to the one for Jessica Mack and compared them. The vital statistics were identical, and in both pictures her hair was longer. Why did she have two driver's licenses with two different names and addresses?

Am I a crook? A drug runner? A spy? What other professions would call for dual identities but the ones on the wrong side of the law? Remembering the cold fear from yesterday when the patrolman had showed up under the bridge sent a fresh ripple of unease through her.

There was another possibility: what if the man in the broken picture frame was stalking her and she had to change her identity and move away to avoid him?

Holy shit.

She worked her way through the scenarios and reached two solid conclusions: she was running from something or someone; and *something* had caused her memory to shut down.

Maybe the two *somethings* were one thing.

No telling how long it had been since she had last eaten and she was famished. A cursory search of the pantry yielded an unopened box of stone ground crackers, a plastic container half-filled with trail mix, and a Trader Joe's bag of dried apricots. In the almost-bare refrigerator she found Greek honey yogurt, a bottle of unfiltered apple juice, a block of plastic-wrapped cheddar cheese, and a bag of apples in the crisper drawer. Health foods.

Am I a vegetarian?

Don't know, don't care.

She would have eaten a whole cow if one had been in the fridge. Tearing open the crackers without regard to keeping a neat fold at the top, she attacked them with the appetite of a starving child. Even as she pulled a knife from the wooden block on the counter to hack off a chunk of cheese, she was already cramming a dry cracker into her mouth.

When she had finished her makeshift meal, the kitchen was no longer the immaculate area scrubbed spotless enough to perform surgery. Along with her memory, the neat freak had disappeared.

The Nissan was covered in a film of dust. Today was Monday. How long ago had she boarded that train in Solana Beach? And for that matter, what had she been doing there?

Zach said nothing about Pigpen as he walked her around to the carport and inspected the flat tire, and Jenna did not volunteer a reason for the pothead's visit. To explain about her backpack would mean admitting that she had foolishly left it on the train, and since she had no explanation for that, keeping quiet seemed the most sensible route.

"Pop the trunk, chicklet," he said. "Let's get this baby up and running."

Jenna stood by the rear fender and watched him work. "I have an appointment in Venice this afternoon," she said. "I hope the spare isn't one of those little donut things."

The words about spare tires had come out of her mouth without a thought. How ironic that she knew how to function in the world, yet knew nothing of her own history...her own desires.

Zach removed the floor mat and pulled back the cover. "No worries, it's full size." He grasped the tire with both hands and jerked it out, then reached back in for the jack. Setting it on the ground, he hiked a dark brow at her. "Do you always keep a camera under your spare tire?"

"What are you talking about?"

He reached back into the wheel well and came out with a small camera bag.

"I have no idea what it's doing there," she said, trying to hide her excitement. Photos would give her some idea of her existence prior to her sojourn on Amtrak and could perhaps provide important clues to who she was. And maybe who Jessica Mack was.

She reached for it, but Zach unzipped the bag and took out the camera. "How about letting me borrow it?" he asked. "I'm running up to the mountains later, and you obviously aren't using it—"

"Sure, just let me see what's in the memory."

Disregarding her outstretched hand, Zach pressed the power button. Jenna could see the digital screen light up. "Hey, give it to me! There might be private stuff in there."

"You and Mr. Mystery doing the nasty?"

The blank space in her life where "Mr. Mystery" fit in didn't feel funny, it felt ghastly and empty. "Give it to me, Zach!"

Zach's grin dropped away. He handed over the camera with a slight shrug. "Okay, sure, whatever."

"I'll download the pictures to the computer, then you're welcome to take it," said Jenna.

Inserting the memory card, she plugged the adapter she'd found in the carrying case into an empty USB port on the computer. The drive window came up and she dragged the photo folder onto the screen, impatient for the thumbnails to open.

The folder held only eight files.

Her heart sank. Every time she thought she was getting somewhere, she drew a blank.

The first was a shot of a piece of paper on a desk, but the hand that snapped the photo had been unsteady, the image too blurry for Jenna to read it.

The next file was an image of the same desk, the same document, but when she moved the slider on the magnifier icon, the enlarged words were crystal clear. Her stomach constricted. The printed notations on the screen were written on graph paper like the note she had found in her purse.

Fetching the original note, she compared it to the one on screen. She was no handwriting expert, but she was pretty sure both had been written by the same hand.

The paper in the photo appeared to be a list of notes:

unique vibrations (3.50HZ, 5 milliwatt) ->
monitor ->
alter frequency ->
stimulation ->
spikes ->
= desired effect

The next image was a close-up of a square object, colored threads protruding from it like the long legs of a spider. But when she enlarged it, she realized that what she was not seeing was not threads, but wires. A microchip.

In the next image, a penny had been placed beside the microchip as a sizing tool. The penny was several times larger than the tiny chip.

The remaining files contained pictures of an electronic tablet lying on a shiny black surface taken from several different angles. The file dates indicated that the photos had been taken a couple of weeks earlier.

She returned to the carport with the camera to find Zach

finishing up, wiping his hands on an old towel. The flat tire lay on the ground. He shook an unruly lock of black hair out of his eyes and grinned, irrepressible. "You delete all the dirty pictures?"

Jenna gave him a big smile. "Sorry, but there's nothing the teeniest bit exciting."

He feigned disappointment. "Damn, I was hoping..."

She touched his arm. "Thanks for all your help, Zach. You're a lifesaver."

"What are neighbors for? I'll get this one fixed for you." Hefting the flat tire, he carried it over to his pickup and heaved it into the truck bed where it landed with a clatter. "Hey, you wanna hang out after you get back from Venice? I rented a couple of flicks."

His manner was casual, but Jenna had an intuition that something else hid behind the invitation. Something that might be interesting to explore sometime, but not tonight. After her visit with Dr. Gold, she didn't know whether she would be in the mood to watch movies and socialize. And there was still the issue of the Mr. Mystery to solve.

SEVEN

Zebediah Gold opened the four-drawer cabinet in the locked closet where he kept client files, and retrieved Jenna Marcott's file. He carried it to the low-slung armchair and flipped it open to review the notes he had written about his next appointment.

Starting with the intake sheet, he got down to the business of refreshing his mind regarding the Marcott girl. *Woman*, he reminded himself—she was closer to thirty than twenty. But he hadn't forgotten the vulnerability that came off her in waves when she had arrived for her one and only appointment. Small and slender, she weighed maybe ninety-eight pounds with boots on, which added to the impression that despite her chronological age, she was little more than a girl.

Since that day a couple of months ago, Jenna Marcott had made and broken several appointments, always canceling by voicemail at an hour when he probably wouldn't answer the phone anyway. After each cancellation, although Gold had not required it, she'd sent him a check to cover the appointment along with a note of apology for wasting his time.

He hadn't heard from her in more than two weeks, when out of the blue she had phoned, swearing that if he would give her one more chance, she *would* show up; she really, really needed to see him.

It was Gold's philosophy that when the client was ready, she would keep her appointment without him having to apply pressure. So, once again, he had mailed her an appointment confirmation card and hoped that this would be the time of their next meeting. That the young woman intrigued him was undeniable. He was still scratching his head over her abrupt departure from that first appointment.

He thought about it for a while, asking himself what it was about her that had particularly caught his attention. The fact was all of the clients he saw these days were worlds apart from the mentally ill offenders he had treated in maximum security prisons over much of his career. Since taking semi-retirement and moving to a guest house in Venice Beach a few years ago, he saw carefully selected clients by referral only, and those were ones he believed would respond to short-term therapy. He hadn't had the luxury of choice in his prison work.

He'd felt there was something different about Jenna Marcott. It wasn't a sexual attraction or he would have immediately referred her to another therapist. But there was something he couldn't quite put his finger on, a vulnerability that made him want to protect her. He knew he would have to monitor himself and make sure that he crossed no boundaries in their doctor-patient relationship.

Jenna had come to him by referral from his friend and colleague, Claudia Rose. She'd met Jenna while working at a pharmaceutical trade show in San Diego. Claudia was a professional handwriting analyst who had been hired by a major drug company to demonstrate her craft for visitors to their booth.

Squinting to make out his own odd brand of scribble, Gold re-read the notes he had written on the intake sheet after the appointment:

JM at trade show w/boss.

Claudia analyzed her hw. JM, unfam. w/handwr. analysis, IMPRESSED.

Confided unspecified "serious problem," Claudia ref. to ZG

Gold's recollection of Jenna's single session was that she had reminded him of a young Princess Diana in the way she glanced at him shyly from under her lashes as she slipped past him into his office. She had taken her time getting settled on the couch, fussing with her clothing, picking at the hem of her crisply pressed blouse, pinching the knife-sharp crease of her slacks between her fingers. She had shifted her purse several times before putting it in its place next to her.

At last, when she was satisfied, Jenna became motionless, hands clasped in her lap. Her stillness seemed to be an off-key note, completely the opposite of her earlier fidgeting.

Anxiety, Gold surmised, evaluating every movement she made, every word she uttered. He took note of how stiffly she held her thin shoulders, as if she'd left the hanger inside her blouse.

He gave her the little speech he was required by law to give: Everything that passed between them was confidential unless she gave him information that indicated she was planning to hurt herself or someone else. She had listened quietly, then signed the form that stated she understood and agreed to the terms.

Gold was aware that she was waiting for him to begin, so he asked his standard opening question: "How may I be of help, Jenna?"

Her silky blonde hair fell forward, hiding her face like a partially drawn curtain as she looked down at her hands. Gold could see her lips working, seeking the right words.

After several seconds she gave a little sigh of resignation and shook her head, speaking in almost a whisper. "I shouldn't be taking up your time. Nobody can help me."

Nobody can help me.

This was far from the first time that Zebediah Gold had heard those desolate words in his practice of psychotherapy, but the anguish they conveyed never failed to evoke his deep compassion. He leaned forward, resting his elbows on his knees so that his client could sense his genuine interest in her plight. "It sounds like you're in a lonely, scary place, Jenna. But you came to see me, so I believe there's a small part of you that hopes I *can* help."

She began to stroke the zebra-striped fabric of her purse as if she was petting a cat. "No. I shouldn't have come."

"I've been in this business for a very long time," Gold said. "And what I've learned is this, there's a solution to most problems."

"Not this one."

"Even this one. We'll work together to find the right solution."

She looked up, her lips twisting with doubt. "But you don't know what my problem is yet."

"Even so." Gold considered whether, with that level of hopelessness, she might be suicidal. Following his intuition, which had been honed over a forty-year career, he asked, "Jenna, has someone let you down who should have been there for you?"

At his words, she drew a sharp breath and put her hands out in front of her as though she felt the need to defend herself. Gold noted they were trembling. Her shoulders shook, too, with the effort to control her emotions. How tightly she was strung. He stifled an entirely inappropriate urge to gather her into his arms the way a father might a small child, and assure her that everything was going to be all right.

Jenna's hands dropped back into her lap and she locked her fingers together, one thumb rubbing the other with enough vigor to chafe the skin.

"Why don't you tell me what's making you afraid, Jenna?"

She looked up at him. "Have you ever betrayed anyone, Dr. Gold?" Her answer seemed a non sequitur.

"I hope not. I certainly have never intended to." Seeing tears come into her eyes, Gold took the box of tissues on the table between them and offered it to her, noting that even in her distress, Jenna folded her tissue with great care, lining up the ends.

She dabbed at the tears trickling through her lashes. "I really thought he would protect me," she said. "But now they're going to kill me. He wouldn't—" she broke off.

Gold didn't allow the surprise to show on his face. Adjusting his impression of her, he evaluated the possibility that she might be delusional. She seemed reasonable enough, but delusional people often did. "That sounds frightening," he said, leaving her space to elaborate.

Jenna plucked another tissue from the box and delicately wiped her nose, then folded the soiled tissues twice more before depositing them into her purse and snapping it shut. She looked over at him and all at once something in her eyes seemed far older than her twenty-seven years.

She spoke softly. "I'm in big trouble, Dr. Gold. I've become a danger to someone very powerful and I—" She broke off and stood up, giving him no chance to protest, and hurried to the door. "This was a mistake. I'm not going to put you in danger, too."

EIGHT

Following an instinct, Jenna left the 101 at the Las Posas exit, opting for the coastal route over the freeway's endless sea of brake lights.

Miles of farmland stretched as far as she could see; rows of stooped migrant workers in broad-brimmed straw hats picked strawberries. She drove parallel to green fields and brown fields, past a lot of nothing, until she began to question the instinct that had lured her off the freeway. But ten more minutes of driving south and the brown hillsides swelled in front of her. Soon afterward, a green highway sign pointed to State Highway 1.

PCH, she said aloud, automatically identifying the name the locals gave the Pacific Coast Highway. Taking the entrance marked Malibu and Los Angeles, she drove past the Point Mugu Naval Complex, crossed the bridge over Mugu Lagoon, and soon rocky crags rose on her left. On the right, the road dipped so close to the ocean that she almost believed she could reach through the window and wet her hand in the sea spray splashing against the rocks.

Unaccountably, her spirits lifted and she was tempted to stop at the side of the road and soak it all in. But her foot stayed pressed on the accelerator. She had an important appointment to keep.

Jenna had been expecting an office building, but Dr. Gold's address brought her to the corner of a street located in the middle of a neighborhood of sizeable homes. The street number on his card was followed by '½,' which confounded her until she understood that his office must be behind the Asian-style dwelling surrounded by a tall cedar fence.

She drove around the block twice, looking for a parking place, but vehicles were jammed nose to tail. Space was at a premium in Venice. Her eyes darted from one side of the narrow street to the other. You could stand on one sidewalk and touch the other without much of a stretch. There was nowhere to shoehorn the Nissan and without parking she would not be able to keep her appointment.

Her respirations turned shallow, came faster as she visualized a lifeline slipping away. What if the doctor had the answers she needed?

If she could just get enough air—why couldn't she catch her breath? Her chest felt compressed, as if something physical blocked her from filling her lungs.

I'm having a heart attack.

It's a panic *attack, stupid.*

Shut up, I knew that.

She gripped the steering wheel harder. The lack of oxygen was making her lightheaded. The buzzing started in her ear. She hadn't noticed it since the train, but the angry wasp now took up residence with a vengeance. And behind it, the ever-present voice...

Crazy. You must be crazy.

No I'm not!

Yeah, yeah.

This is ridiculous. I can't *be this much of a wimp.*

Making sure there were no vehicles behind her, Jenna brought the car to a stop in the middle of the road. She shifted into 'park,' then bowed her head against the steering wheel and began her mantra.

Breathe.

Relax.

Focus.

Repeating the words over and over helped her to slow her

breathing. The buzzing receded.

She took a look around, thinking rationally now, and realized that she was right around the corner from Dr. Gold's address. Her state of anxiety had prevented her from seeing the alley that ran behind the house. Steering into it, she immediately saw a sign on a garden wall that declared the marked space "Reserved for Clients of Dr. Gold."

Jenna switched off the engine and checked the dashboard clock. After all her attack of nerves, all the pissing and moaning, she was a half-hour early for her appointment.

She stepped out of the Nissan into an afternoon made grey and damp by the low layer of marine clouds and exited the alley, glad of the time to gather her thoughts before her meeting with the psychologist.

A couple of blocks walk took her to a street called Electric Avenue. That set an old song echoing in her head: *We gonna rock down to Electric Avenue, and then we'll take it higher...* Did the song have any special significance? Without context, everything or nothing *could* be significant.

She crossed the street, turning onto Abbot Kinney. Jenna peered into the windows of boutiques, antiques stores, a new age bookshop with the enchanting name of Mystic Journey, feeling anonymous as she hurried past, pretty sure she'd never been here before.

How would you know, when you've no idea where you've been?

She stopped at Jin's Patisserie and sat on the patio drinking jasmine tea, trying to ignore the gnawing dread that at ate her. What if Dr. Gold couldn't fill in the blanks? Would he know about Mr. Mystery and why she had kept the torn picture and broken frame? And who was Jessica Mack? Why was her face on Jenna Marcott's driver's license?

When her cup was empty and she'd paid the bill, Jenna retraced her steps to the house where Dr. Gold resided and saw clients. Entering from the street she passed under a roofed gate into a manicured Japanese garden. A small signpost embedded in a clump of temple grass pointed to Dr. Gold's office.

Tension had heightened her senses. The plaintive strains of wind chimes jangled too loud in her ears; the vivid spots of color hurt her eyes. She paused at a miniature bridge that spanned a lily pond, staying just long enough to whisper a request to the stone Buddha kneeling in prayer under a Japanese Black Pine: *Please let Dr. Gold help me find my life.*

Following the path of smooth, round paving stones, Jenna arrived at a charming guest cottage behind the main house. The door opened as she approached and a tall, lean man stepped outside. Late sixties, he wore the kind face of a favorite uncle with a trim white beard and thinning sandy hair. His casual dress—a linen pullover shirt and khaki shorts with sandals—seemed odd for a therapy session, and immediately put her at ease.

"Dr. Gold?" Jenna asked. Seeing a glimmer of surprise cross his face, she immediately realized her error. He had expected her to recognize him, as he recognized her. This was not their first meeting. Her heart rose—he knew her; he would know how to help her.

Brushing off the gaffe, Zebediah Gold stretched out both hands with a welcoming smile. "Hello, Jenna, I'm glad to see you again. I like your new hairdo."

She allowed him to take her hands in his warm, bearlike paws. "I—I parked in the space around back," she stammered. "I hope that's okay."

He smiled with straight white teeth and she detected the faint scent of mint on his breath when he bent down and gave her shoulders a quick squeeze. "It's fine. Let's go around to my office."

Stupid! You're supposed to know it's okay.

The gentle sound of water trickling through a series of suspended bowls followed them inside. Jenna's first impression upon entering the psychologist's office was that it resembled a sort of shrine. Dim light filtered down through the skylight, bamboo shades over wide windows were lowered to three-quarters, and a bamboo-filled urn decorated one corner. In the other, a Laughing Buddha stretched his arms joyfully, hands open wide to the heavens. A great deal of care had been given to creating this simple, tranquil space.

Dr. Gold took the chair that faced the door and left Jenna to choose between the couch and two comfortable-looking armchairs. A low table stood between them, providing a sort of barrier that allowed her to maintain the illusion of protecting herself. *Against what?* In this room, at this moment, her defenses seemed ridiculous and unnecessary.

As soon as she took the chair opposite him, Jenna could feel her body respond to the setting. Her muscles began to relax and for the first time since waking up in this alien world, she could inhale a full breath without any effort. In spite of herself, the stiffness in her neck and shoulders began to drain away.

Dr. Gold was quiet, giving her time. Though he was subtle about it, Jenna was keenly aware that he was watching her wrestle to find the right words to begin. On the drive down to Venice she had rehearsed her story over and over, but now, facing him across the table, all the clever phrases that had sounded so logical and easy in the car had deserted her.

As she was starting to feel uncomfortable, Dr. Gold spoke up. "I know it wasn't easy for you to come today, Jenna," he offered. "But you're here, and that's a big step."

She pounced on his words, got lost in them. What had happened during their last session to make him think it would be difficult for her to return? Her eyes drifted to the Zen garden on the table: a few polished pebbles sat beside a tiny mud man with a long white beard. Someone had raked the sand into concentric circles. His previous client? She leaned forward to pick up the tiny rake.

Dr. Gold is sort of Buddha-like, if not Buddha-sized—he's in good shape—but the way he sits, he looks so...serene...he...

"Jenna?"

She dropped her hand and sat back in the chair, worried that her mind had wandered too far for too long.

"You're pale," he remarked. "Are you all right?"

"I've been—sick," she said, resurrecting the excuse Zach had given her. "I—I've had the flu."

Why don't you just tell him the truth?

Not yet!

"Would you like some tea?" he offered.

"Yes, please." The words came out automatically. She didn't really want more tea, but the mundane chore would buy a few extra minutes if nothing else.

On the table was a cast iron tea pot on a trivet and two mugs. Dr. Gold's hands made the pot look ridiculously small as he poured and handed her a mug.

"This feels good," she said, accepting it. "It never did warm up today."

"So aside from the flu, how have you been, Jenna?"

"Uh—Um..."

Dangerous territory.

"I was concerned after you left last time, and then cancelled our appointments."

His kind eyes probed, but she had no answers to give him. What could have made her leave her last appointment? Cancel appointments? Why had she been stupid enough to think she could come here and pretend she could just pick up from where they had left off, when she hadn't the vaguest clue where that was?

Tell the truth whenever possible.

"I don't know what to say."

Dr. Gold steepled his fingers under his chin. He clearly wasn't a man given to rash pronouncements, and he looked serious enough to frighten her. Jenna wrapped her arms around herself in a hug, insulating herself from whatever would be said. Maybe she should just get up and leave now, the way he said she had before. But she waited too long; his next words riveted her to her chair.

"I'd like to hear why you think someone wants to kill you."

Tea splashed onto her Levi's and she set the mug on the table with a trembling hand. "*What?*"

Dr. Gold handed her a cloth napkin. "You talked about someone wanting to kill you, Jenna. Please tell me about that. Who are you in danger from?"

"Dr. Gold, I—don't exactly know how to..."

Could she trust him? What if he didn't believe her? What were the chances he'd have her committed to a psychiatric hospital if she told him the truth? Was that even an option? She had no idea.

As if he could read her thoughts, the psychologist caught her gaze and held it. "Jenna, remember what I told you on your first visit? Anything you say here is confidential unless you tell me that you have definite plans to hurt yourself or somebody else. Do you have any plans like that?"

"No! I don't have any plans. I—"

"*Confidential.* You're my client. I'm not going to reveal anything you say to anyone without your express permission."

Everything about him invited confidence, but she kept picturing herself in a straightjacket locked up in a psych ward. The volume of the buzzing intensified. She could barely hear her own thoughts as she spoke over the irritating sound, hoping her voice wasn't too loud. "Do you remember what else I said about—about—what you just said? Please tell me. Please."

He paused before answering, as if reluctant to repeat it. "You said that you were a danger to a very powerful person." It must be his therapist's training that despite the shocking words he had just delivered, his expression never changed.

"Danger to a powerful person," she echoed.

Why would a powerful person want to kill me?

Had that person already made a failed attempt, leaving her with the amnesia she now suffered? *What happened to me?* She clawed at the emptiness where the memories should have been.

The psychologist's quiet voice nudged its way into her thoughts. "Has someone actually said they wanted to hurt you, Jenna?"

She cleared her throat, digging deep for courage. She would need every bit she could muster if she was going to tell him the truth. "What do you know about me, Dr. Gold?"

He gave her a measured look. "Since we only had that short session together, I don't know much. but as I explained to you before, if you are in any danger, I have a legal obligation—"

That the psychologist did not hold the key to her condition after all had the effect of a bucket of icy water thrown in her face. Dr. Gold was not going to be able to help her. The Buddha had ignored her prayer and she was, yet again, shit out of luck.

The familiar dark cloud of despondency descended.

Jenna picked up her mug and pretended to sip tea, trying to fit the puzzle pieces he had just handed her with what little she already knew. "All I told you was that someone powerful wanted to *kill* me? I must have said more than that. You've got to tell me everything. *Please.*"

"Jenna, I can see you're distressed…"

"*Distressed?* Distressed doesn't begin to cover what I am."

"What word fits better?"

"What?"

"What word fits better than 'distressed'?"

Making up her mind, Jenna set her mug back on the table. "Amnesia."

"Amnesia?"

"The truth is, Dr. Gold, I don't remember coming here before. The *whole* truth is, I don't remember *anything*. I don't know who you are. I don't know who *I* am."

And she let it all out, everything she'd experienced since arriving at the Amtrak station in Ventura less than twenty-four hours ago. It didn't take long; there was precious little to tell.

He listened without interruption, and she got the impression that her tale was far from the strangest story he had heard in the pleasant room. When she came to the end he simply asked, "You're not aware of anything that might have triggered the amnesia?"

"Like what?"

"A bump on the head, an illness?"

"No, I don't remember *anything*."

"Have you checked for any lumps or bumps up there?" He tapped his head.

"I checked my whole body. There's noth—" She broke off. *Stupid!*

Last night she had examined most of her body, but now she realized that she had left out the most important part. Touching her fingers to the top of her head, she began to rake them systematically through her hair. Below the crown, roughly parallel to her left ear where the horrid buzzing originated, she detected a slight ridge, an irregularity in the skin.

"There's something here," she said, her eyes locked on to the psychologist as if he was now offering her the lifeline that she had earlier watched float away. "There's something…I need you to tell me what it is. Please? *Please?*"

When he hesitated, it crossed her mind that he might view it as inappropriate to put his hands on a client in such an intimate way, but she couldn't care less. She needed to believe that Dr. Gold understood the urgency that drove her.

Without giving him time to refuse, she left her chair and crossed the two steps to where he sat. She knelt on the reed mat at his feet and bent her head, parting her hair where she had felt the ridge. She clutched his hand and guided it to the spot.

For a large man, his hands were remarkably gentle as they ran over her scalp. "There's a contusion of some sort, a scar, maybe." He gestured for her to return to her chair. "Does it hurt?"

"No, it doesn't hurt. It's actually kind of numb." With the knowledge that her memory loss more than likely had a physical cause, it seemed as if a pressure valve released a little bit.

"It seems to be healed, so I doubt it's terribly recent."

The valve tightened once more. "You're saying I could have been walking around like this—not knowing who I am—for weeks? Months?" she cried. "I'm a ghost. I don't exist!"

Dr. Gold put his hands up in a calming gesture. "I know it must be extremely difficult for you, Jenna, but we're going to work through this together."

"How can you help me if you don't know anything more than I do?"

"I'm going to find a way to help you. You're not alone."

"Maybe I was attacked! If someone was trying to kill me, maybe they hit me over the head. That could make me lose my memory."

That doesn't explain why I'm not dead.

"That's one of several possibilities," Dr. Gold allowed. "Or it could be a surgical scar. Or the scar might have nothing at all to do with your amnesia. Amnesia can be caused by many different things."

"Maybe I had surgery for a brain tumor and after I left the hospital—" Without warning, the dark thing came flying at her—a vision—and with it a crushing panic that penetrated every part of her being. What was it? If only she could see…

The edges of her vision softened, dimmed. The whistle replaced the buzzing and she moaned softly, anticipating what was coming.

"Jenna?" Dr. Gold's voice came from far away. "Jenna, put your head down. Put your head between your knees."

She could tell that he had risen from his chair because she felt pressure on her shoulders as he told her to lower her head.

Gone.

NINE

When she came to she was slumped in her chair, a damp paper towel draped across her forehead, agitated because she didn't know how it had got there. She looked for Dr. Gold and found him pouring a glass of water at a small sink across the room.

He brought it to her and helped her drink. "How are you feeling?" He asked in a voice full of concern.

She handed him the paper towel. "Kind of weak. How long was I out?" Something in his expression alerted her. "What? What happened?"

"Well, sweetie, you went *somewhere*, but you weren't exactly 'out.' Do you remember anything?"

"No. Everything went black. What—what did I do?"

"You were mumbling something, like talking in your sleep. But it wasn't lucid enough that I could tell what you were saying."

"Is this what my life is going to be like?" Jenna cried. She pressed her hands to her face, feeling ashamed of her blackouts, as if she had some control over them, hating that she did not. "How can I ever go anywhere, do anything?"

"We've only just started; don't give up yet," Dr. Gold said, lowering himself into his chair. "I'd like to call paramedics to check you out."

"No!" Paramedics meant the hospital. The prospect was upsetting to her in the same way the appearance of the cop had upset her the day before. She flashed on herself in a hospital gown, begging to go home. Was it an actual memory, or simply her imagination? She wanted to rip her head open, reach inside and shake up her brain.

Despite knowing that Dr. Gold could see right through her, she sat up straight, and lied. "I'm fine. Truly, I am. I'm fine."

He shook his head. "I can't let you drive like this."

"I just need a minute. If you have another appointment, I can go sit in my car."

"I don't have another appointment, but what you need is a full work-up. It's important to rule out the possibility of a neurological disorder being the cause of your symptoms."

"If you call the paramedics, I'm leaving now." Jenna started to rise from the chair, but giddiness dropped her back down. "No paramedics. No hospital." She knew her voice sounded weak, but she was bent on following through on her threat.

Dr. Gold looked unhappy, but he showed her his palms, giving up the argument before it could get started. "Okay. Okay. You didn't actually lose consciousness, so you have the right to refuse treatment. And I'm still bound by confidentiality if you're sure you don't know who was threatening you. But I'd like to perform a mental status exam to—"

"I'm not crazy!"

Are you serious? You're batshit crazy.

"I know you're not crazy, Jenna, it's just to help me determine the extent of your memory loss. I promise, it's quick and easy." He reassured her with a smile. "And if you don't want me to call the paramedics…"

If it would keep her away from the hospital, she would do anything he asked.

As he had promised, the questions were easy and she aced most of them: Where are you right now? What's today's date? Who is the President of the United States? What's your name?

"How can I know the president's name but not my own? I only know what the driver's license says it is. And there are two of those."

"Don't give up, Jenna. Are you ready for the next series of

questions? Tell me the months of the year in reverse order."

Easy.

"Can you tell me your favorite movie?"

Blank.

"Tell me what you're doing here."

"I found an appointment card in my purse. I assumed it meant I had an appointment for therapy, so here I am."

"Okay, good. Now, can you tell me what you think just happened a few minutes ago?"

She thought back to what they had been discussing. "We were talking about what might have caused my memory loss," she said slowly. "I thought I passed out, but you said I didn't. Then I came back."

His eyes creased at the corners when he smiled, and she felt as though she had earned a merit badge. "You did very well, Jenna. There doesn't seem to be any major cognitive impairment—you understand where you are in space and time. It's the factual information about your life that seems to be inaccessible. And that's why a neurological exam would be helpful, to provide a baseline."

"Dr. Gold, I don't know why but I *don't* want to go to a hospital. At least, not now."

"I understand that you're afraid of hospitals and police. But realistically, we need to contact them. We have your name, your address." He corrected himself. "Names. Both of them."

"I'm probably a criminal," she said miserably. "I have two different names, two driver's licenses. That doesn't look good, does it? It implies something shady."

"You don't know that. There could be another explanation."

Wrapped in her escalating anxiety, she scarcely heard him. "What if I go to the cops and they lock me up for something I can't even remember doing? Or, what if I did something so awful that I *wanted* to forget it? Maybe we should just leave it alone."

"Whatever we find, we can work this through, Jenna."

"Or Jessica." She looked away, afraid to meet his eyes, avoiding the questions that she was certain must be there. "Why do I have an alias if I haven't done anything wrong? Maybe there are *more* names and addresses that I haven't found yet. Maybe that's why

I'm afraid of the police."

Gold held up one finger, halting the rapid flow of words. "I have an idea. Do you remember Claudia Rose, the woman who referred you to me?" He made a wry face. "Forgive me, of course you don't. She's a handwriting analyst you met at a medical convention a few months ago in San Diego."

"A handwriting analyst?"

He told her what Claudia Rose had said about their meeting.

"I must have been living in Marina del Rey then," Jenna mused, remembering the address on the driver's license she had found in the zebra purse. "I wonder how long ago I moved to Ventura. There are unpacked boxes in my apartment."

"When you came to see me last time, you were living in the Marina. That's where I mailed the appointment card. It must have been forwarded by the post office."

"Maybe I moved to get away from the person who wanted to kill me."

"Another good reason to consult the police."

"But I have no idea who that person is. For all I know it could be you!" She could tell he was dissatisfied with her response, but he let it go.

"I mentioned Claudia because she's connected to a detective at LAPD who I think could help," Dr. Gold said. "If you would give me your permission, I'll ask if he can make some informal inquiries. You would have to sign a waiver that allows me to talk to Claudia about you."

"But if I did commit a crime and he finds out, wouldn't he have to turn me in? Are you *sure* that's what I ought to do? And what about the 'powerful person' who wants to kill me? Or do you even believe that? Do you think it's just a fantasy, part of the reason I have amnesia?"

"If we're going to find out what happened to you, we have to start somewhere." His voice was soothing, but she noticed he hadn't given her a direct answer.

She released a long sigh. "I know, but the *police*…"

"There is one thing we could try first."

"What?"

"It's sometimes possible to recover lost memories with

hypnosis."

"Would *you* hypnotize me?"

"Yes. I guess you don't remember whether you've ever been hypnotized?"

Jenna shook her head. "How would it work?"

"If your memory loss is connected to a traumatic event, or events, the memories still exist inside your brain, but you've blocked them out—in effect, buried them. It's called dissociative amnesia. That's different from the type of amnesia caused by organic brain disease or physical trauma, where the information is lost. In that case, hypnosis wouldn't help."

"The scar on my head proves *something* physical happened to me."

"That's true, but that scar may or may not be related to the amnesia. There are no guarantees that hypnosis will work, but we can try it if you like. It may help you remember what happened."

"Can we do it right now?"

"You're my last appointment this afternoon, so if you feel ready, yes, we can."

"I'm afraid, Dr. Gold. What if—"

"It will be like watching a movie, not quite like you're actually experiencing the events again. First, I'll help you to relax and give you a safe place to recall those memories into your conscious mind. If you feel uncomfortable, you can indicate it to me and I'll bring you right back to full consciousness. You will be in complete control at all times."

"Okay. What do I have to do?"

"Lie down on the couch with your head on this side. I'll put on some relaxing music and, while I'm doing that, you can begin to focus on your breathing. Close your eyes and breathe in through your nose to the count of five, hold it for three, then breathe out through your mouth for five. Listen to your breaths."

Jenna slipped off her shoes and stretched out on the couch, resting her head on a small throw pillow and wriggling into a comfortable position. The cushions were soft and puffy, easy to relax into. As she closed her eyes and began to tune in to her breath she could hear the sounds of a CD drawer opening and closing.

A few seconds later, the muted clang of a gong reverberated

through the room; then another in a different key, then another. In their echoes, the haunting melody of a wooden flute reminded Jenna of the wind chimes in the garden knocking together in the breeze.

Dr. Gold spoke quietly from his chair. "Take a deep breath and think of something beautiful, a rose perhaps. First see the bud, then let it slowly open, watch the petals unfold…

"Now exhale slowly, allowing yourself to go deeper into relaxation. Know that you can open your eyes at any time, but because it feels so good and you are so relaxed, you prefer to keep them closed." He was quiet for a few breaths, giving her time to follow his instructions.

He began to speak once more. "I want you to visualize yourself at the top of a flight of steps. I'm going to count backwards from ten and with each number, you will walk down those steps. With each step, you will become more and more relaxed…going deeper and deeper."

He started to count and she imagined herself descending a basement staircase. In her mental image she looked down and saw that she was wearing athletic shoes—white, with hot pink accents. Had she really worn shoes like that sometime, or…?

"Ten. Nine. Eight. Deeper and deeper…"

Her eyelids began to feel heavy, her limbs made of lead. Down one wooden riser at a time. Down, down.

"Seven. Six. Deeper still…"

Jenna considered moving her fingers just to prove to herself that she was still in control of her body, but they were too heavy to bother making the effort. She sank deeper into the cushions, imagining them molding themselves around her shoulders, her hips, her calves.

The psychologist's voice faded, then returned. "Let your mind wander in the quiet serenity and peace. Let yourself go deeper and deeper into relaxation and know that you can return to this peaceful place any time you want."

She felt wonderful, relaxed and decompressed, as if she had moved out of her body and was floating on a sea of well-being.

Dr. Gold's voice intruded on the peace, "Now we're going back to a time you can remember."

Her emotional mind wanted to resist his instruction, but the logical side argued that this was what she had come here for. She must go where he was leading her.

"....as if you're watching a movie. Go back..."

His monotone droned softly, but Jenna was no longer listening. Behind her eyelids a glittering curtain of rain sluiced down a car windshield. It was nighttime, and she was a passenger on Interstate 5.

She recognized the segment of highway as northwest of the Central California town of Fresno. As if witnessing the scene from a distance, she observed with detached interest that the vehicle was traveling too fast for the bad weather and mountainous terrain. Her eyes followed the wipers slapping noisily back and forth on the windshield.

She noticed the sour fruit odor of alcohol, faint but unmistakable. A cold shiver ran through her and she turned her head to the driver.

A man's strong hands gripped the steering wheel. Black hair curled over the collar of his leather jacket when he checked the left lane over his shoulder.

Who is he?

You know.

No.

"Slow down," she urged in a voice that sounded as if it was running in slow-motion.

The driver swung on her, animosity sparking like a road flare in his eyes. His lips curled into a sneer. "Fuck you."

She reached out to touch the soft leather of his jacket. "Please, slow down!"

He tore his arm away and balled his hand into a fist. "You have no clue what's going to happen to you, do you?" She recoiled against the car door, waiting for the fist to slam into her. "*Please*, stop it."

Was it the trance body that was trembling so violently, or was it her physical body back in the real world? She was as cold as if she'd jumped naked into a snowbank.

The driver ground his foot down on the accelerator, causing the car to skid slightly on the slick road. His voice rose to a roar.

"What the hell do I have to lose? Tell me, Jessica! What do I have to lose?"

"You *know* the answer."

Dr. Gold's calm voice intruded into the scene. "It's just a movie, Jenna. You're completely safe."

I'm not Jenna.

"Tell me what you're seeing, Jenna."

Not Jenna. Not—

"I'll fuck you twice, bitch. I'll take you both with me." He was shouting at the top of his voice now. Flecks of his spittle sprayed her skin. She imagined that if it were lighter outside, she would see the veins bulging in his neck.

He gave the steering wheel a twitch, fishtailing them into the right-hand lane and for a few seconds they were only inches from the long, steep drop that she knew was out there. She hooked her fingers around the armrest and clung to it. "Please…don't…"

From the backseat came the cries of a small child. She wanted to cover her ears and pretend she couldn't hear, but the cries pierced her heart.

A movie. It's only a movie.

A big rig lumbered up the steep grade, its headlights lighting up the car as it moved into the next lane and passed them. Her driver—she stubbornly refused his name—accelerated, surging up on the bumper of a slower moving Suburban ahead of them. "Get the hell off the road, asshole!" he shouted, as if the Suburban driver could hear him.

The crying in the backseat grew louder. The driver shot a poisonous glance at the rear-view mirror. "Make that noise stop *now*, Jess, or I will."

That was when she felt the first tremor of real fear. The healed bones in her wrist were proof that he would follow through on his threat. She had shielded him then, telling emergency room personnel that she'd fallen. If only she had stopped believing him sooner when he swore he loved her enough to stop drinking; when he'd promised everything was going to be happy again. If only…

None of that mattered now. Hating herself, Jessica unclasped her belt and twisted awkwardly to kneel on the seat. How could she have exposed him to this kind of danger? Filled with self-reproach, she took hold of the little hands that reached out to her.

She told him he was a good boy and that she loved him. Wiping the tears from his flushed baby face with her fingertips, she promised that everything was going to be fine.

The howling quieted to a whimper. He was as safe as she could keep him for now. She was wriggling back into her seat when the Suburban came alongside them and passed on the right.

Her driver hit the gas and caught up with the other vehicle. Indifferent to the freezing rain that lashed her face, he lowered Jessica's window with his control panel, bellowing across her, hurling profanities at the other driver.

She started praying then, making all the promises that hopeless people make when there's nowhere left to go.

I'll be stronger. I'll do anything you want me to. Just keep us safe.

"Jenna..." Dr. Gold's distant voice.

Not Jenna.

"...just a dream."

The tires were hydroplaning on the rain-saturated road. They swerved toward the Suburban, avoiding a sideswipe by a hair's breadth, then veered back into their lane, chased by the long blare of an angry horn.

Suddenly, the rear bumper of the big rig was right in front of them, brake lights glowing like demonic eyes.

"Watch out!" Jessica cried, working her seatbelt clasp.

Her driver spun the steering wheel and at the same time jammed on the brakes. The car slid on the wet pavement toward the embankment.

They were suspended in space. Jessica's head slammed into the roof, then smashed against the windshield.

rolling and rolling...

baby crying...

cold rain...

silence.

TEN

Claudia grabbed an Amstel Light from the refrigerator and waited for Joel Jovanic to shrug out of his jacket before she handed it to him. Taking his discarded coat, she draped it across the back of a kitchen chair.

With the beer bottle in one hand, Jovanic wrapped the other arm around her waist and kissed her thoroughly. "I think I like this. Does it come with a pipe and slippers, too?"

Claudia gave him a sly smile and shimmied her body against his. "It comes with whatever you want, Columbo. I need a favor." Stepping back, she slid into the breakfast nook, inviting him to join her.

Jovanic took a long pull on his beer, put the bottle on the kitchen table, and followed her with a small groan. "I knew it was too good to be true. What do you need?"

She told him what she knew about Zebediah Gold's client, Jenna Marcott.

"You referred her to Gold? What was your impression of her?"

"You know how those conventions are. It was three months ago and I talk to hundreds of people at those things. One thing I do remember is that when I told her what her handwriting said, she got all teary eyed. She said that I'd told her things no one else knew about her." Claudia paused to smile. "People say that kind of thing to me all the time, but this girl seemed *really* affected. I wanted to spend more time with her, but there's never any extra time at those events."

"Why did you refer her to Gold?" Jovanic asked.

"She said she had a serious problem and needed help. And I liked her. She seemed, I don't know—kind of lost."

"And you're a sucker for little lost lambs," he remarked with an indulgent smile.

"Well, she did call Zebediah, so something I said resonated with her."

"Do you still have her handwriting sample?"

Claudia shook her head. "The client kept all the samples for marketing purposes."

"How likely is it that they still have them? Would they let you see them now?"

"It'd be easier just to get her to write a new sample. The one at the convention was just a couple of lines and a signature. Not adequate for a proper analysis."

"Easier, yes, asking for a new one…but she might change her handwriting if you ask for it now."

"Why would she do that? What would be her motive for disguise?" she asked.

"To support this tale she's told your buddy Gold. Could be total bullshit. The first sample would show her natural self, right, GraphoLady? Isn't that what you've always told me? The best sample is one that's not written for the purpose of analysis?"

Claudia opened her eyes wide in mock surprise. "Wow, Columbo, I'm impressed. I didn't know you were actually listening."

He pressed his hand to his chest, pantomiming hurt. "I'm cut to the quick. I just happen to listen to every word you say."

"Of course you do." Leaning across the table, she offered a kiss. They had both reached the end of a long day, and his stubble was like sandpaper against her chin.

Claudia said, "If I ask her to write something now, it's true she'd be more conscious of what she's writing. Still, I can't think of any reason for disguise."

"It would be better to have more writing to look at."

She nodded. "Yes, of course. I'll call the client and ask if they kept them on file. They can either have the sample overnighted, or I'll head downtown to their office and sift through them to find Jenna's. At least, that was the name she was using when I met her."

"That's my point, babe. What's up with the Jessica Mack alias?"

"Hey, Detective, I realize that *Skeptical* is your middle name, but we don't know it's an alias."

"What do you call it when someone has two completely different IDs?"

"Maybe she's DID."

"She's what?"

"Dissociative Identity Disorder: AKA, Multiple Personality Disorder. You know—when different personalities live in one person's head, but they have independent lives; they don't know about each other."

"You think that's real?"

"Psychologists are still arguing about it. Some are adamant that it is a very real condition; but there are those just as adamant that it's a total fabrication. I once testified in a murder case where the client claimed to be DID."

"What happened?"

"He was charged with hacking his wife to death with a bolo knife. The prosecution had a mountain of evidence, but the defense brought in the defendant's minister and a bunch of people who swore up and down that he was just a mild-mannered store clerk who wouldn't hurt a fly."

Jovanic snickered. "Yeah. All defendants are innocent. Just ask them."

Claudia shot him a look. "You're jaded, honeybun. The judge ordered a psych eval and, in the end, even the court psychiatrist concluded the guy was DID. The defense was claiming the murder was committed by one of his alters—that's what the other personalities are called, alters."

"So he used the SODDI defense."

"The what?"

"SODDI—Some Other Dude Did It. But you're saying this time, that the "other dude" was actually living inside the scumbag on trial?"

"Well, yeah. The attorney gave me a stack of handwritings the client purportedly wrote while in various alters, and asked for my opinion."

"And you could tell from his handwriting that he really had multiple personalities?"

"I did some research and found some articles on how to identify it in handwriting. The first criteria is are the samples so dissimilar that they reflect totally different personalities? And the second is, are there enough subtle similarities to identify that they were all written by the same hand?

"When a person has Dissociative Identity Disorder, it's virtually always a response to extreme abuse or neglect before the age of five. The abuse is so appalling that the child can't deal with it, so pieces of their personality 'split off' and deal with the abuse for them. Those pieces are their defenders. When one of the 'defender' parts is active, the original personality—the host—usually doesn't know about it. The host sort of goes to sleep and the alter takes over."

Claudia could feel him paying close attention. "What's that mean, 'goes to sleep'?" he asked.

"The alters know about each other and about the host personality, but the host doesn't know about the alters unless they come out and make themselves known during therapy. Sometimes an alter comes out and takes over the host's body—could be for a few minutes, hours, days, sometimes even years." Claudia shook her head with a rueful smile. "Can you imagine how it would feel when the host wakes up one day and realizes she has no idea what she's been doing all that time? She could have been living a life altogether different from her own. Or *his* own. Blackouts like that are called 'losing time.' DID is pretty rare, but there are documented cases."

"You mean like in those old movies, *The Three Faces of Eve*, or *Sybil*?"

"Well, Sybil's been challenged. But, *When Rabbit Howls*, or..."

"Okay, I get the point. What happened in the case where you testified?"

"The defendant's handwriting samples met both criteria. Bottom line, the wrong guy was on trial. It *was* one of his alters who committed the crime. So the host personality, the guy sitting in jail grieving over the murder of his wife, was totally unaware of what he had done. It was as if somebody else really killed her. He was the 'somebody else' during the time of the murder. The rest of the time he was just a nice, quiet guy, nothing like the alter, who happened to have this brutal side."

"That's a lot to swallow, babe."

"The guy didn't get off. He was remanded to a mental institution, which is just about as bad as prison." Claudia twirled a strand of auburn hair around her finger and tugged on it thoughtfully. "I'm sure Zebediah must have considered the possibility. Jenna was with him when he called this afternoon, so he didn't say much, but she signed a release for him to talk to us and he's faxed it over. He's going to see her on Saturday. You and I will meet her at his office—" She broke off with a grin. "Assuming you agree, of course—and I'll get the new sample from her then. If I get the original sample from my client and a new one on Saturday, I'll be able to compare them and see if there have been any major changes. I'll also be able to see if there are signs of a head injury."

"I see you've got it all planned out," Jovanic said with a slight smile, and Claudia knew that the case had ignited his interest.

He continued, "I'll call a buddy over at Missing Persons and tell him we've got a Found Adult. Get me everything you can on her. Have Gold fax a copy of both driver's licenses and any other vitals, and we'll see what pops up. If she really did lose her memory, her family is going to be looking for her. There could be an MP report floating around out there. And if that doesn't generate something, I'll run her prints."

ELEVEN

Driving away from Dr. Gold's office, it felt to Jenna—she doggedly clung to the name—as if she was leaving the safety of an oasis. Her head was throbbing like a drum. No…more like an entire steel band.

Did the car accident cause the amnesia?

Of course it did. What else could it have been?

The psychologist's presence had been comforting, something solid to hold on to. Having already folded the scene into a tight little package and locked it away in the darkest recesses of her mind, she was grateful that he had not pressed her to talk about why she emerged from hypnosis shaking and sobbing, or why she refused to tell him what she had experienced. He'd simply handed her a box of tissues and a glass of water, assuring her that he would help her work through the events that had resulted in her memory loss.

Jenna was to return on Saturday to meet Claudia Rose and her detective friend. She was frankly curious to meet the woman who had analyzed her handwriting. Would she remember Claudia? Or would her face be as unknown to her as all the other faces in the world?

As she signed a release for Dr. Gold to discuss her case with the handwriting analyst, it seemed one more cruel twist that aside from the signatures on her driver's licenses and credit cards, Jenna had no idea what her own handwriting should look like. It was also downright spooky that after analyzing her handwriting, Claudia already knew more about her personality than Jenna herself did.

Driving back through Santa Monica and Pacific Palisades, traffic was rush-hour heavy.

At Chautauqua, Jenna was one vehicle behind a minivan when the light turned yellow. That vehicle's back wheels were already across the white line into the intersection when the driver changed his mind about running the light and hit the brakes.

Jenna's foot automatically hit the brake, too, burning rubber. The Nissan squealed to a halt, kissing distance from the minivan. The driver behind her laid on the horn.

And just like that she was back on the dark mountain road; Jessica, staring into the driver's malignant scowl; hearing the crying child; unbuckling her seatbelt and turning to comfort him. She felt the impact of slamming into the semi, the sensation of flying…

This time, there was no Dr. Gold to recall her to safety.

Someone was screaming.

Then, just as fast, she was back, clawing her way into the Nissan's backseat to rescue a child that did not exist. The screams registered as her own.

The traffic light had cycled to green; the blaring horns emanated from a line of impatient motorists backed up behind her. If a cop saw her, she would certainly get a ticket for obstructing traffic.

Or for being crazy.

Shut up. Shut up. Shut up!

She twisted back into her seat, hardly able to breathe, and hit the gas. A couple of miles down the road she pulled off the highway onto the dirt shoulder. Her throat was raw. She sat for a long time at the side of the road, a terrible sense of impotence tearing at her.

By the time she switched on the ignition again and got back on the road the moon had risen, a pall of misery had seeped into her bones, and it didn't matter whether she ever made it back to the apartment. She could not bring herself to think of it as home.

Hours later, Jenna lay in bed, staring at the ceiling long into the night, the accident scene looping endlessly in her head like a bad movie that wouldn't end: the car veering off the road, plunging down the mountainside. The soaking rain. The utter wretchedness of knowing that she was helpless to prevent what was going to happen next. She told herself that she should not have let Dr. Gold hypnotize her; that she would have been better off not seeing those images.

As he had promised, what she had witnessed in her trance state felt more like a dream, not something from a waking memory. Yet, somehow, it felt real, too.

How can it be both?

When exhaustion finally overcame her, she dropped into a troubled sleep, waking in a sweat hours later from a nightmare. The nightmare had not been about the accident. Despite the warm summer air, Jenna drew the covers up over her head and curled on her side like an unborn child in the darkness, trying to recall the dream.

Little by little, images developed: men in dark clothing grabbing at her; a hand covering her mouth, muffling her cries for help. Who were the men in the nightmare? Neither was the man in her hypnotic state.

If the car accident was the cause of the amnesia, as she had begun to believe, then what part did the men in her dream play? Or were they simply a creation of her imagination, a symbol of the sick fear that lived within her every moment, waking and sleeping? And what about the powerful person who wanted to kill her? Had she told Dr. Gold the truth about that?

Why would I lie?

Why don't you know who the hell you are?

Throwing back the covers, she rolled out of bed and washed her face, drank some water, and roamed around the apartment.

Outside the kitchen window the sky was a striped blanket of orange, red, and steel blue. Too early to get dressed, and with no TV to take her mind off thoughts that continued to chase each other like rats around a maze, she sat down at the computer and Googled BioNeutronics Laboratories where, according to the badge in her purse, she was employed.

Human biology figured prominently in the laboratory's

universe. Words like DNA, karyotyping (she was going to have to look that one up) sexually transmitted diseases, genetics and human behavior, made up the content.

Eventually, she fell back into bed and lay there unmoving, as if her immobility might generate the memories that refused to come. Counting backwards from one hundred, she dropped off to sleep, only to be jarred awake again and again.

Around the fourth awakening, Jenna came to a realization. Somewhere deep inside, among all the missing pieces she had discovered a stubborn streak of courage. And whether or not she ever recovered the life she had lost, she was not going to be beaten into submission by whatever, or whoever, had put her in this untenable position.

TWELVE

At six a.m. the bedside alarm made a rude intrusion into the seesaw between restless sleep and troubled wakefulness. But the loud reminder was necessary. Jenna's plan was to show up early at BioNeutronics Laboratories and try to get the lay of the land before the other workers arrived.

This would require going to an unfamiliar building that she should be accustomed to, and interacting with strangers she was supposed to know. Whether or not she could pull it off was the big question.

The neat-as-a-pin lineup of petite business suits in the closet showed good taste, and at least a hint of compulsiveness in the way they were hung according to color. Dressing in a navy skirt and jacket ensemble, Jenna looked in the mirror and tested out a tentative smile.

She was pleased to find the image that looked back at her was beginning to feel more familiar. Aiming the hair dryer at the short hair and fluffing it up, her fingers touched the scar. The questions started up again like a song you can't get out of your head.

Was there really a car wreck, or is my imagination filling in the gaps?

If there had been no accident, why would her mind have produced that particular scene under hypnosis? The pitiful cries of the child in the backseat echoed in her head.

"No! We're not going there." She spoke the words out loud to cover up the chilling sounds. Instinct told her it was more pain than she could manage.

You can't pretend forever.

Maybe I can.

Denial is not just a river in Egypt.

Why don't you just shut up?!

She stopped trying to figure it out. More urgent was getting ready for her job. According to the badge, she was known at BioNeutronics as Jenna Marcott.

Jenna. Jessica. Jessica. Jenna.

Which one am I? Both?

Just tell them you don't know.

No!

The strength of her reaction startled her. She thought about the nightmare; about the men attacking her in the dream. She wondered what had happened to Jessica Mack.

From the street, the BioNeutronics building was an anonymous concrete and glass facade. Uncertain at first whether she had found the right place, Jenna drove into the parking lot and double-checked the address on the entry doors at the rear of the building.

It was seven-fifteen when she parked next to a black Mercedes CLS. Hanging the employee ID badge around her neck, Jenna strode across the lot pretending to know where she was going, and entered the building.

The lobby was empty, which allowed her to bypass the vacant security desk and go straight to the wall directory.

BioNeutronics shared the building with financial advisors, lawyers, and therapists. The lab's offices comprised the second and third floors, the research lab was located in the basement.

Taking the elevator to the second floor, Jenna was still asking herself what she could hope to achieve with this insane gamble when the doors slid open onto a reception area. Behind a semicircular desk sat an attractive young woman with a mop of bronze Orphan Annie curls that made her look like a pixie. A nameplate identified her as Keisha Johnson.

The receptionist's manicured brows shot up, her mouth a big

'O' of surprise. "Look at you, girl! It's friggin' awesome!" She got up as Jenna came towards her and leaned her elbows on the counter, making a twirling motion with her index finger. "Turn around now; show me the back."

Jenna, remembering that Zach had said she had new haircut, pivoted in a slow circle.

"You *killed* it." Keisha said, dropping back into her chair. "Wait till Simon sees it. You know he's been trippin'. That man does not know how to function when you aren't here to hold his little hand."

Simon. Jenna's tension relaxed just a bit. Having what was clearly her boss's name answered an important question. But like the ball bearings in a pinball game, a dozen more caromed around her brain:

How will I know him? Where do I go? What am I supposed to do? And; *How could you be so stupid to think you could pull this off?*

"Is he here yet?" Jenna asked.

"Oh, yeah. He beat me in." Keisha lowered her voice and sent Jenna a wink. "He's in the lunchroom trying to figure out how to pour himself a cup of coffee. He—" She broke off as a door opened behind her. Tipping her head back, she flashed an innocent smile at the man who stepped into the reception area. "Oh, there you are, Dr. Lawrie. We were just talking about you. Look who's here."

The ground seemed to slip away. Of all the shocks Jenna had lived through in the past thirty-six hours, this one registered a 10 on her personal Richter Scale.

He was clean-shaven now, but the George Clooney looks, the sensuous lips, belonged to the man in the torn photo. The man whose size 42 Long suit hung in her bedroom closet.

This must be what an out of body experience felt like. The man Zach had referred to as 'Mr. Mystery'—her boss—was standing right in front of her. What did it mean that she read relief in his eyes?

"Jenna!" Simon Lawrie looked as stunned as Jenna felt. "I thought—I mean..." He quickly recovered his composure and a big smile lit his face. "I didn't expect to see you...today."

Jenna fought her way back into her head. Grappling to accept this stunning new piece of the puzzle, she found a weak smile for him. "Yay, I'm back."

Simon Lawrie turned to the receptionist, who was following the exchange with undisguised interest. "Coffee please, Keesh. My office." He turned back to Jenna, not quite meeting her gaze. "We've got a lot of catching up to do."

With a secret smirk, Keisha rose, smoothing down the tight skirt of her gunmetal grey suit, and exited through the same door Simon Lawrie had just entered. Simon held the door, looking at Jenna expectantly.

She rounded the reception desk and followed him into a long corridor. Simon fell into step beside her, his longer strides forcing her to hurry to keep up. She would like to have taken the time to study the series of framed posters on the walls that advertised the lab's accomplishments, but that would have to wait.

They boarded a smaller elevator at the end of the hallway. Simon swiped a card key to access the third floor. As if there was a tacit agreement between them to wait until they reached the privacy of his office to speak, the elevator rose in silence. He stared up at the floor indicator as if they were strangers, but from the torn photo, Jenna knew they were not.

If it were not so tragic, it might have been comical. Five minutes earlier her biggest worry had been how she would find her work area and whether she had dressed appropriately for her job. Now she was fretting over how she was supposed to deceive a man with whom it appeared she was intimately acquainted. And the bigger question—*why* did she feel compelled to deceive him?

The few inches between them yawned as wide as a football field, but her need to understand the torn photograph had gone from a slight tickle to an obsessive itch that demanded scratching.

What happened between us?

I should tell him that I don't remember him.

No!

Why not?

Just...no.

Simon stopped at a door bearing a brass plate with his name and the title, "Director." Jenna's name and "Assistant to the Director," marked the office right beside it.

He slid his card key through the reader and as he held the door for her, Jenna ducked past like a truant called to the principal's office.

Tasteful furnishings. Persian rug, a sofa that would have been at home in a luxury salon, polished cherry wood conference table. Floor-to-ceiling windows offered a panoramic view that terminated at the horizon over the Pacific Ocean.

Simon kicked the door shut behind him and closed the few feet that separated them, agitation crackling off him like an electrical current. Before Jenna could react, he grabbed her arms and pulled her into an embrace so tight she could feel his heart hammering against her own chest.

"Thank God," he murmured into her hair. "Thank God you're safe."

It struck her right away that her body was not responding to his touch. Shouldn't there at least have been a physiological response? They must have made love countless times. Shouldn't she feel *something*? Jenna pushed away from him. "You're hurting me."

Simon immediately relaxed his hold, but his hands stayed on her shoulders, as if afraid that she might disappear if he broke contact. "Jesus, baby, I'm sorry. I don't ever want to hurt you…I just—I didn't know—I was so scared."

Shrugging free of his grasp, she took another step back and looked up at him, searching his face. "What did you think?"

"What do you mean, what did I think? *Where have you been?*" His question held a fierce heat that hinted at a world of emotions seething barely below the surface.

The sharp 'click, click' of high-heeled shoes in the corridor came to a halt outside the door, saving Jenna from having to come up with an immediate answer. There was a knock and Keisha's voice called out, "Incoming."

With a muttered curse, Simon turned on his heel and strode to the big window at the rear of the office. Jenna took a deep breath to steady herself and opened the door.

Keisha came in holding a small tray with two mugs and accouterments. "Here you go, Jen. Tea with honey for you, 'cause you look like you could use it. And your coffee, Doc."

"Desk," Simon snapped, as if he'd forgotten that he had personally requested the coffee. Keisha placed the tray on his desk and gave Jenna a roll of the eyes before closing the door behind her.

What did he think happened to me?

As if she'd spoken her thoughts aloud, Simon turned and saw her looking at him. "Where *were* you, Jenna?" he asked again. "I was out of my mind with worry. I didn't know what—I thought—"

"What *did* you think?" He crossed the room towards her, but Jenna sat down in one of the guest chairs at his desk and picked up the mug of tea. Simon Lawrie was a stranger to her, and despite the intimate way he was looking at her, she could not pretend that she wanted his hands on her body.

Simon faltered. She could see that her resistance confused him. He must be accustomed to her going along with whatever he wanted.

Until I destroyed the photo?

Instead of going around his desk and taking the executive chair, he dropped into the one beside her, stretching out his long legs so the soles of their shoes almost touched. "I don't want to tell you what I thought," he sighed. "But *God*, I'm thankful to see you alive."

"You thought I was dead." The bald statement hung on the air between them.

Simon stared at her. "For the third time, Jen, where the hell were you?"

"Where do you think I've been?"

He slammed his hand on the desk, making her jump. "Don't fucking answer a question with a question! Where have you been for the past three days? And what did you do to your hair? You look like hell."

What part did this man really play in her life? She tried to convince herself that she recognized his woodsy cologne, but the faint scent of wild thyme and tangerines was foreign to her. She glanced back at him. "It's not nice to tell me I look like hell when you know I've been sick."

"Don't play with me, Jen. Why didn't you answer your phone?"

"The battery's dead."

The disbelief in his eyes made her want to laugh. He refused to believe the truth of a dead battery, but if she had come up with some sort of lie he would have accepted it.

Simon Lawrie glowered at her. "Baby, you've got to tell me what happened. Did they hurt you? Threaten you?"

"I don't know what you're talking about, Simon."

"What do you mean, you don't know?" His voice hardened in frustration. "You up and disappear and it had nothing to do—I accused Christine of—*What happened?*"

"I told you, I don't know!" She wondered who Christine was and what he had accused her of.

"You can't just pretend nothing happened. The way you stormed out of here, and then didn't answer the phone. I thought Christine—I went off on her—"

She followed his gaze to a portrait on the wall. There, an attractive woman dressed in a red power suit stood tall before the U.S. flag. Self-confidence and ambition shone on her face. Off to side, set just a few inches away from the portrait, was a grouping of family photos featuring the same woman with Simon Lawrie, joined by two handsome young men in cadet uniforms.

Jenna's stomach flipped.

An affair with your married boss, Jenna? Seriously? How stupid can one person be?

"Jen? Earth to Jenna." Simon was leaning into her space, snapping his fingers in her face.

She batted his hand away. "Stop that!"

"I've been worried sick about you and you're blowing it off like nothing happened."

"Why were you so worried, Simon? Why did you think she'd done something to me?"

Simon jumped to his feet and began pacing, enumerating on his fingers. "Friday, you freak out, then you just leave. Saturday, you don't show up at the hotel. Sunday, you don't answer the door." His voice continued to rise. "You've ignored my phone calls, emails, texts. Look, I know you were upset, but it's not like you to disappear that way. Just tell me where you've been."

"Do you have to always know where I am?"

She might as well have slapped his face. "Yes, Goddamn it, I do!"

"Maybe I just needed a break."

"I don't believe you."

"What were you so afraid of?" she pressed, believing that the key to her amnesia could well be in his answer.

"You *know* what. With her connections it'd be easy enough..." He stopped, a frown forming on the handsome face. "Wait a minute. You're not going to make trouble with my wife, are you?"

"Is *that* what you're really worried about?" She looked away from him, letting her eyes roam the hand-crafted Italian-made furnishings, the original LeRoy Neiman decorating a wall. Men like Dr. Simon Lawrie don't rock their comfortable boats, she thought. Her head ached with the effort of keeping up the pretense of knowing what he was talking about, but she had to hold it together. If she blacked out the way she had in Dr. Gold's office, the charade would be over...and Jenna wasn't ready for that.

Simon scrubbed his face with his hands. He shook his head as if trying to rid himself of an unwelcome idea. "I know you're still mad, but baby, I *can't* file for divorce now. She's just about to get the nod at the Convention. If we were in the middle of a divorce—or worse, a sex scandal— shit. My life wouldn't be worth a good goddamn nickel if she lost it because of my screw-up."

Convention? Nomination? Jenna's eyes returned to the official portrait and the penny dropped. *Holy Christ—his wife is running for President? This can't get any worse.*

"Shouldn't you have thought of that before?" Her tone was as sharp as the broken glass in the picture frame.

"Hey, it's not like you didn't know I was married."

"There are a lot of things about you that I don't know."

Simon leaned forward and grabbed her wrist, holding it tight. She tried to pull away but his grip was too strong.

"Right now, Jenna, I'm thinking that I don't know *you*. What the *hell* is going on? I ask you where you've been and you say you *don't know?* What kind of bullshit is that? What am I supposed to think?"

His petulance irked her. "Let go of me *now*, Simon, or you *will* regret it."

He blinked in surprise and she could almost hear him wondering who this person was in front of him. He let go of her wrist. "It's not like you to be secretive, Jen. Paranoid, maybe, but not secretive. What aren't you telling me?"

"Isn't it enough that I'm here?"

Simon's features softened; the lines around his eyes lost a little of their tension. "Ah, baby, you know I love you, don't you?"

For half a second Jenna was tempted to believe his sweet-talk, to allow her vulnerability to blind her to the facts. Then the harsh voice of reason chimed in: *Are you totally whack? He's married to a freaking presidential candidate and he thinks she did something to you!*

Not knowing what had happened between them was like walking blind without a cane. She had to proceed carefully. "Simon, you must have always known that this—thing between us was never going anywhere."

He threw up his hands and blew out a big sigh. "Why are you doing this, Jen? How many times have we had this conversation?"

She had no answer for that; nor why she had allowed herself to fall for a married man in the first place. His looks and social standing might be enough for some women, Jenna thought, but she knew that combination was not enough for her. Not who she was now, anyway.

"This isn't only about my marriage, is it?" Simon's words broke through her thoughts.

"What does that mean?"

"Oh, come on, Jen. All those questions you were asking last week about Project 42. Your *concerns*? the way you stormed out of here?" He pushed his fingers through his hair, leaving little tufts standing on end. "Listen, Jen, I've had a lot of time to think about it over the last few days. The thing is, you took that email out of context. You don't really understand what we're doing here."

That's for sure. What is Project 42? What email?

"I get it that you were upset," he continued. "But you weren't seeing the bigger picture."

"Which is what?"

"Once we've finished the clinical trials and get the results the client is looking for, it's going to improve so many lives."

"If it's so great, why would I be upset?"

Simon compressed his lips into a tight line as though trying to hang on to the last thread of his patience. "I don't know, Jenna. Maybe you resented having to deal with all the specs and the early experiments and all the rest of it, seeing how normally it would have been the word processor's job. But, honey, with the level of confidentiality on this project, you must know that you're the only one I could trust. I think the trouble is you misunderstood how the device works…that's all."

"Maybe you could explain it to me so I understand it better."

"I will, baby. Let's get together tonight at the apartment and we can talk. Right after some fantastic make-up sex, that is." He smiled, doing his best to charm her.

"And what about Christine's campaign?"

"We've always been careful. Nothing has to change."

Jenna gave him a thin smile of disgust. "You know, I'll bet a lot of work piled up while I was gone. I'd better get started on it."

"Dammit, Jen, why are you being so frigging stubborn?" She said nothing and he offered up a sigh. "Okay, you're still mad. Fine. For now. Just don't think this is over."

She rose from the chair. Simon rose, too, and moved close. Knowing he was going to kiss her, Jenna turned her face so that his lips grazed her ear. He spun her around and caught hold of her chin. Determined not to be denied, he turned her face and kissed her mouth with force, as if he owned her.

Jenna could not miss the triumphant gleam in his eyes just before he released her.

THIRTEEN

Jenna's office had the unique chill of a space that had been unoccupied for several days. Closing the door behind her, she leaned against it, thankful for the cool air on her flaming face. With a deep sense of shame, she had to admit that some perverse part of her had allowed that bruising kiss to happen...and even enjoyed it.

Muscle memory.

Whatever gets you through the day, dumbshit.

She glanced around the workspace. No photos graced the walls, no colorful mugs or silly gifts from friends decorated the desk. Nothing personal. Of course, Jenna thought, what photos would there be? It wouldn't do to advertise that you were sleeping with the boss.

Were *sleeping with the boss. No more.*

He's kind of old, but he's pretty hot.

He's a cheater. I hate cheaters.

How do you know what you hate?

Shut up.

You helped *him cheat, stupid.*

Shut up. Just shut up.

Moving around the desk, Jenna revised her earlier assessment. There was something personal after all. The smiling figure of a red-headed mermaid was propped against the computer monitor.

A flash of recognition.

Ariel.

The Little Mermaid, from an animated Disney film. She picked it up, wondering what special meaning it held for her. The rubber material felt hard and unfamiliar in her hand as she closed her eyes and waited, hoping for a memory that did not come.

Feeling let down, Jenna set the mermaid back against the monitor and turned to the stack of files on the desk.

Simon had left handwritten notes paper-clipped to the files explaining what he wanted her to do with them. His handwriting was difficult to read and it crossed her mind that Claudia Rose, the handwriting analyst Dr. Gold had told her about, might have some insights into the man.

Once she had figured out Simon's hieroglyphics, Jenna had no qualms about performing the tasks he had set her, which was reassuring. There were notes about interoffice memos he wanted her to correct, and emails galore: notes on items to be filed; notes about arranging meetings; and notes about a Powerpoint presentation she was to prepare for a conference coming up. A trip to DC with his wife that she was supposed to book with the company travel agent—how galling.

That's what you get for screwing around with a married man.

Leave me the hell alone.

As Jenna skimmed through the contents of the files she began to form an impression of the work handled at the BioNeutronics Laboratory. One thing she did not find, however, was any reference to something called, Project 42.

Simon's comment came back to her. He'd said she had stormed out of work on Friday due to something related to this project. The reverent way he spoke about Project 42 made it sound like the elixir that held the secret to eternal life was being created right here in this building. What had he said? It was going to improve the lives of many people.

The computer booted to a company splash screen with the BioNeutronics logo, a wire frame globe turning in the open palm of a disembodied hand. Encircling the globe, coiling itself through the frame like a ribbon, was a UPC bar code that morphed into a network user login form.

A cursory search of the desk drawers turned up paperclips and pens, odds and ends arranged with precision in plastic holders, but no handy hidden note containing the password. A locked file cabinet under the desk yielded to the small silver key on the ring in her purse.

It contained Simon Lawrie's personal correspondence: responses to fund-raising letters from the local symphony, correspondence related to a private jet and boat, and his estate in the upscale neighborhood of Montecito, thirty miles north of Oxnard.

At the back of the drawer Jenna struck gold with a file containing an administrator's list of user names and passwords for everyone in the lab. Her password was *!Ariel*. Glancing at the Disney character on her desk, Jenna quickly keyed in the strokes, relieved that her memory loss had not robbed her of her ability to handle electronics.

Navigating to the Windows Explorer icon, she found a folder titled 'Projects,' and began combing through the long list organized in numerical order: Project 41, Project 43, and so on. Project 42 was conspicuously absent. She tried a system-wide search. When that yielded nothing, she turned to the green hanging files in the top drawer of the file cabinet behind her desk, but…nothing.

The bottom file drawer offered up a pair of pink and white size five athletic shoes like the ones in her hypnotic trance. There was a small stack of three-ring binders containing diagrams and specifications with headings, like clinical pharmacology, clinical trials, contraindications, side effects, and more. On the front of each binder was a plastic holder containing a project name printed in a large font—but Project 42 was absent.

At eleven forty-five Simon entered her office without knocking and dropped a twenty dollar bill on her desk. "Kung Pao Chicken," he said, "and whatever you want."

Jenna walked through the corridors of BioNeutronics, running into a couple of people who complimented her on her haircut. The smile she produced still felt stiff, but with practice she figured she would get the hang of it.

Her confidence was growing, and the day was going far better than she had anticipated. Even though an affair with a married man—especially her boss—wasn't something she was proud of, at least she had learned something about her life while keeping her amnesia secret.

The heavy coastal marine layer would not lift until mid-afternoon, but despite the overcast it felt good to leave the hermetically-sealed laboratory office and its subtle smell of cleaning fluid.

On her drive in that morning, Jenna had noticed a strip mall across the street, which boasted several fast-food restaurants, including Chinese. Glad for the opportunity to stretch her legs, Jenna picked up Simon's order, then went to the Starbucks at the far end of the strip, where she ordered a mocha latté and a protein plate for herself. After yesterday's session with Dr. Gold, followed by the terrifying blackout on the road, food had been the last thing on her mind.

On her return, she found her office door open and a rolling cart in the hallway outside with a sign that read Oxnard Plant Care and Maintenance. A woman in a green and tan uniform was inside, polishing the leaves on the tall rubber tree in the corner.

Jenna tapped lightly at Simon's door and entered. He was working at his conference table, sleeves rolled up, tie loosened. He pushed aside an untidy array of papers and gave her a warm smile. "Stay and eat with me."

She shook her head. "I'm going to rest at my desk."

"Maybe you came back to work too soon."

"Maybe. It was a pretty bad flu." Having practiced the lie, it came easily now, but she wasn't so sure he bought it.

The plant caretaker was on her knees snipping dead leaves when Jenna entered. She turned with a shy smile and said in halting English, "I finishing soon."

Jenna returned the smile. "Thank you, it looks good."

She snapped the lid off her protein pack and went to work on the brie and crackers. After so many hours without eating, they tasted like ambrosia. She had just taken a bite of hardboiled egg when the other woman spoke up. "Uhn, lady?"

"Yes?"

"You wan' me to water these?" She pointed to the base of the rubber tree.

"Water it? I guess so."

"*No, aqui esta.*"

If Jenna had known Spanish before, the language had disappeared along with everything else. She shrugged. "I'm sorry, I don't know what you mean."

"Oh, okay." Apparently knowing little more English than Jenna did Spanish, the woman gave her a big smile. She picked up her clippers, and with a cheery "bye bye," left the office, closing the door behind her. She had not watered the plant.

Jenna got up and went to the rubber tree, curious to see what the woman was talking about. She knelt on the floor, parting the glossy leaves near the bottom of the plant. The corner of a plastic bag stuck up out of the soil. The bag was effectively hidden…unless you were looking for it. Her stomach tightened.

Oh, Jesus, am I a drug dealer and this is where I hide my stash?

Dealing drugs could explain the two driver's licenses, and all the rest of it, except for the amnesia. Heedless of the potting soil getting under her nails, she dug in. The baggie came out easily enough. She took it back to her desk and gazed at the contents in surprise.

Not drugs.

A flash drive, the type of small portable storage device that plugged into the USB port of a computer

It seemed logical to assume that since it was in her office, she must have been responsible for burying it. Getting on her knees, Jenna crawled under the desk and reached around the back of the CPU, feeling for open USB slots.

"Jen?"

Her head jerked up in surprise and banged against the underside of the desk drawer. "Do you ever knock?" she asked, exasperated.

Simon leaned over the desk, where her rear was sticking out. "Now there's a delectable sight. What are you doing under there?"

Feeling like a fool, she backed out and slid up onto her chair, keeping her dirt-caked fingernails hidden from his sight. "I dropped a grape."

Simon regarded the remnants of her protein pack with its hard-boiled egg, triangle of cheddar and handful of red grapes, in disfavor. "No wonder you're so skinny. All you eat is rabbit food."

"Something I can do for you, Simon?" she asked, acutely aware of the flash drive that she had left on top of the CPU under the desk.

"Have you set up my meeting with Dr. Kapur yet?"

Who is Dr. Kapur?

"I just got back from picking up lunch, remember?"

"Christ, Jenna, what did you do all morning?" He took the guest chair across from her desk and seemed prepared to stay a while.

"You left me a lot of projects, Simon, and I've been working my way through them."

"How're you feeling?"

"I have a slight headache," she said quickly, hoping it would discourage him from staying.

"Why don't you get something from Keisha's first-aid kit. I don't want you sitting here feeling like crap." He sounded sympathetic, and she took a moment to study the long, almost feminine lashes that framed his cobalt blue eyes. Her gaze dropped to the full lips, and her cheeks burned, remembering the rough, possessive way he had kissed her.

The words "Project 42" brought her attention back to what he was saying. "...probably noticed that the files have been removed from your work station while you were out sick."

"Of course I noticed. Who was in my computer?"

"I didn't mention it sooner because I wanted to give you a chance to get back into things gradually. Don't take it personally, babe, okay?"

"It *feels* personal."

Ignoring her remark, Simon continued, "Kapur is going to be sending a couple of the client's own employees to handle what's left of the project. Their people will be working here on site for this part of the operation. They'll be using the private lab you set up for the rest of the clinical trials, which means they won't need the same kind of hands-on participation from us from here on out. You won't have to deal with the admin tasks anymore."

"Well, that's convenient." Jenna didn't bother to hide her sarcasm, but she would have killed to know what he was talking about. Remembering what he had said to her that morning, she asked, "Did taking everything off my computer have anything to do with those questions I was asking last week?"

He was too quick to respond, "Of course not." The way he avoided her eyes convinced her that he was lying.

"Did you send someone to clean up the computer in my apartment, too?" she asked.

Simon stared at her as if she had just stepped off a UFO. "Your *apartment?* Please tell me you don't have any Project 42 files at home."

"Of course not. I was joking."

"Well, it's not funny. You almost gave me a heart attack." He shook his head as if clearing some frightening image. "Call Dr. Kapur and get the meeting set up as soon as possible. We've got a lot to discuss." Before she could stop him, Simon reached out and tipped her chin towards him. "Jen, I know I don't have to remind you that this project is still absolutely confidential. I can't emphasize enough that it has to stay that way. It's top security, regardless of how you feel about it."

She pulled away from his touch. "Of course, you don't have to remind me."

"Okay, good. I damn sure don't need any problems at this point in the game. Call Security and let Kevin Nguyen know about the changeover. He's a pain in the ass and he's going to make a fuss, so give him some time to get over it."

"When is the changeover scheduled?"

"Monday. Kevin's out this afternoon at a meeting, so you can call him tomorrow morning. Don't leave it on his voicemail."

"That doesn't give him a lot of time to get over it."

"I guess that's his problem, isn't it?"

Simon flashed a grin with such charm that Jenna couldn't help but smile back. "Okay, boss. I'll get right on it."

He rose, angling his tall frame across the desk for a kiss, but Jenna lowered her head and began writing herself a note to contact Kevin Nguyen. When the moment passed, she glanced up to see Simon leave her office, his shoulders slumped like a child who'd been denied ice cream for dessert. And for the first time in her short new life, Jenna felt powerful.

The feeling lasted only until she realized how close she had come to Simon seeing the flash drive she had unearthed from the rubber tree pot. Good thing she hadn't had time to pull up the files it contained. If he had come around the desk and found unauthorized data on her monitor she would be toast. As much as she wanted to see what was on the drive, it was too risky to do it at work.

As she scrubbed the dirt from under her nails in the ladies room, Jenna was quite sure that it was not a coincidence that all files referencing Project 42 had been removed from her computer...and that she had buried a flash drive in the rubber tree plant. She could think of no good reason to have hidden the drive unless her access to its contents was unauthorized. And could it be a coincidence that she had buried it just before something had happened to cause her memory loss? Or was she just being paranoid? That's how Simon had described her. Still, someone had done a thorough job of cleaning her office computer of any files that might be related to the mysterious Project 42.

As clean as the computer at the apartment.

The connection raised her suspicions. The strength of Simon's denial had felt plausible, but the question that burned in Jenna's mind was what had happened between her 'storming out' of BioNeutronics on Friday, and Sunday evening when she had awakened on the train with a blank memory? She wasn't being paranoid about that. It was a goddamned fact.

And just like that, the little demon was back, sharpening the pickaxe in her skull.

"Is he giving you a bad time?" Keisha asked, taking a first-aid kit from the drawer and handing over the painkillers Jenna asked for.

"A bad time?"

The receptionist gave her a knowing look and lowered her voice, "Hey, Jen, I haven't forgotten how pissed you were when you took off out of here on Friday. I could see with my own two little peepers that something really big happened between you guys. I'm guessing *that's* really why you didn't come in yesterday."

She made a gun finger and pointed it at Jenna. "Don't you let him get to you, girlfriend. By the way, the bitch was here on Monday." She gave a delicate shudder. "Do you think she might actually get elected? Imagine...Christine Palmer in the White House? Puke! There goes the country!"

"Simon's wife was here? What for?"

"Hell if I know. They went down to the lab and left her security goons up here. She told them she didn't need a security detail babysitting her in the lab, thank you very much, and to go sit in the lobby like good little boys and wait for her. You know that annoying snotty way she has. They weren't too happy, but you know how it is. When there's no cameras aimed at her, all that sugar and honey goes right out the window."

The phone lit up and Keisha got busy connecting calls. Jenna headed back to her office, disappointed that the conversation had to end there. She thought about what she had just learned: Keisha had confirmed Simon's remark about her storming out of here last Friday. And while Jenna was wandering around with no memory, Simon's wife—whose name was evidently Christine *Palmer*, not Lawrie—paid a visit to the lab. Was that another 'coincidence'?

Was "the bitch" aware of her husband's sexual indiscretion? If Palmer had a security detail of her own and she was about to become a presidential candidate, she must already be some kind of heavyweight.

By the time five o'clock rolled around, Jenna could hardly wait to examine the flash drive. The drive was tucked in an interior pocket of her purse, along with a building map she had found in her file cabinet. The map detailed an emergency evacuation plan and diagramed escape routes throughout the building. Each of the four floors in the building, plus the laboratory, had a page of its own. The names of each office occupant was printed in the relevant space, and Jenna intended to study it that evening to learn the names and locations of her co-workers.

After powering down and closing up her office, she knocked on Simon's door to let him know she was leaving. There was no response, and when she tried the knob, Jenna found it locked up tight.

The man at the back of the line of employees inching toward the lobby doors turned around when Jenna joined them. "Another goddamned surprise security check," he grumbled, his mouth set in a tight line of resentment. "They think they're the frigging TSA with their goddamned pat downs."

Jenna's heart skipped a beat. "What're they looking for?"

"Who the hell knows? Maybe they think we're stealing drugs, or trade secrets, or some other damned thing no one cares about. Wasn't Friday enough? This is ridiculous, I'm putting my resume on the street."

"Friday? I left early."

"Well, I guess you missed out on that one. It's like the friggin' Gestapo."

People in back of her were complaining, too, as others joined the line. Near the exit Jenna could see two security guards searching briefcases and purses, using their electronic wands to scan everyone before allowing them to leave. It had never crossed her mind that security at BioNeutronics might be that high.

She considered the possibility that the flash drive in her purse had nothing to do with the mysterious Project 42, but quickly discarded it. The chances of such a 'coincidence' were impossibly slim.

Only three people were left between her and the exit when one of the guards pointed at a middle-aged heavyset woman. He crooked his index finger, indicating that she should step out of line. The woman glared at him in outrage as he said something that made her cheeks flush bright crimson. He called to the female guard, who escorted the protesting employee behind a privacy screen at the rear of the lobby.

That single act made up Jenna's mind. She could not risk getting caught with the flash drive and losing it without knowing what it contained. Murmuring to no one in particular that she had forgotten something, she walked rapidly away from the line and went back to her office.

If she hadn't witnessed that woman being pulled out of line, she might have hidden the flash drive in her bra or underwear, but the all-too-real possibility of a strip search had turned that alternative into a losing proposition.

Jenna plopped down at her desk and addressed the little mermaid propped against the monitor. "What do you think, Ariel? How do I get that thing out of here without getting caught?"

Swiveling her chair in a slow circle, she gazed around the small office, looking for inspiration.

It came to her that if she dropped the flash drive out of the window, she could return later this evening and pick it up.

Stupid. If it falls into the plants, you'll never find it, especially at night.

But if I put it inside something bigger and easier to spot…

She scrabbled in the trash can under her desk and got out the Starbucks cup she'd tossed out earlier. She zipped the flash drive back into the baggie in which she'd buried it and stuffed it into the cup. A crumpled paper napkin kept it from rattling around. Snapping the lid on, she took it the window.

The window was sealed shut.

Damn!

Even the smallest things seemed beyond her reach. Jenna wanted to scream in frustration. She threw herself back in her chair and stared at the computer monitor feeling as though a dark cloud was following her.

For surreal moment the monitor came alive. People in motion. Like a fight scene in a movie, but blurred so she could not identify the actors. It took place in the blink of an eye, then the screen was blank again and she was no longer sure of what she had seen, or even whether she had seen anything.

Am I crazy after all? Is that why I'm pretending to be Jenna Marcott, when I'm really Jessica Mack? Or am I really someone else and haven't found my true identity yet?

I am Jenna.

No, you're not.

Something wanted to break through; some memory flitted around the edge of her consciousness. But like an irritating sneeze that tickles the back of the nose, the something refused to fulminate. There were more pressing issues to consider. Jenna studied the coffee cup in her hand.

The employees downstairs were already on the verge of mutiny. It seemed unlikely there would be another security check tomorrow. Maybe she should re-bury the drive in the rubber tree pot. She could walk it out the front door at lunchtime tomorrow and lock it in her car.

She went to the rubber tree plant and had started to remove the lid from the cup when her office door opened and Simon Lawrie strolled in.

"You drink too much caffeine," he observed. "Your hand's shaking."

"I thought you left."

Simon shook his head. "I was down in the lab."

There was no denying the man was some nice eye candy. A few years younger, and he could have modeled for *Maxim* magazine.

"Do you need me for something?" Jenna asked pointedly.

"I thought you could give me a lift over to Eric Ericsson's. I'm meeting some people there for drinks and I don't want to take my car."

Eric Ericsson's. Memory clicked. The restaurant on the pier near the Amtrak station. Jenna nodded. "Of course, no problem."

She started towards the door, but Simon reached out as she made to pass him and pulled her body against his.

The man never gave up. The tip of his tongue brushed tantalizingly across her lips. "Meet me later at the Crowne Plaza," he murmured. "We can have that make-up sex we talked about."

"You mean *you* talked about," Jenna said, pushing him away. "I guess we're supposed to show up here together tomorrow morning wearing the same clothes?"

"It wouldn't be the first time. We've always been discreet."

She thought of the suit hanging in the back of her bedroom closet, the razor and extra toothbrush in the medicine cabinet…and then, she thought of his wife, Christine Palmer, and remembered the torn photo in its smashed frame. Simon seemed to take for granted that everything was okay between them despite last Friday's argument. That photo said he could not be more wrong.

"It might not be the first time," she said. "But as it happens, I have other plans tonight."

"What plans?"

"Just...plans."

"But, Jen, you—"

"I'll give you a ride to Eric Ericsson's, but one of your drinking buddies can get you home, or there's always a taxi." He could certainly afford a thirty mile cab ride to Montecito. Or, he could take a room in the hotel. Without her. She continued past him, coffee cup in hand. During their exchange, Plan B had come together in her mind. She said, "I'll meet you downstairs. I need to make a pit stop."

Simon groaned. "You have to now?"

Jenna held up the cup. "Like you said, too much caffeine."

"Well, just don't take forever like you always do."

She gave him a falsely bright smile. "See you in the lobby."

The ladies room appeared unoccupied, but Jenna checked each of the stalls to make sure. It would be hard to explain what she was doing if someone came in needing the facilities in the next two minutes.

High up on the wall was an open window. Stepping out of her pumps, Jenna hiked her skirt high up on her thighs and after testing to make sure it would bear her weight, climbed up on the sink.

Now, if she could just catch a break, any stragglers in the parking lot would be too eager to get home after going through the security check to notice the Starbucks cup falling through the air.

The coffee cup sailed through the six-inch opening without a hitch. Step One was complete. Jenna jumped down from the sink thinking about Step Two: a return to BioNeutronics later that evening to retrieve the cup. She was smoothing her skirt when the door opened and a woman walked in.

Tall. Thin and angular. Nondescript brown hair scraped back in an old-fashioned Alice headband. The name "Raisa Polzin, MD" was embroidered in blue across the left breast of her white lab coat.

Dr. Polzin glanced down at Jenna's stocking feet, then at her shoes and said in a heavy eastern European accent, "Not very sanitary."

Jenna stepped back into her pumps and gave the woman a brief smile. "My feet were killing me."

The scientist raised a critical brow. “Toilet is not good place for bare feet.”

“Good point. Good night.”

Jenna’s hand was on the door when Polzin added with a hint of derision, “I see Dr. Lawrie standing outside in the hall waiting for you. Good night, Miss Marcott.”

FOURTEEN

"How late are your *'plans'* going to keep you out?" Simon asked, sulking as they headed to her car. "I can get one of the guys to drop me at the apartment. If you're asleep, I'll just let myself in and wake you up, just the way you like to be woken."

"No thanks, I still don't feel all that great."

Simon settled into the passenger seat of the Nissan and as she drove out of the lot, reached over and put his hand on her knee. Slowly moving up her inner thigh, he started to raise her skirt. "I can make you feel better, baby, you know I can."

She pushed his hand away. "Not now."

He shot her a sharp glance. "Hey, you're not ditching me for some young punk, are you?"

"That would be the smart thing to do. Have you already forgotten that fight we had last Friday?"

"I'd *like* to forget it. You know my marriage is just a sham. With the boys both at West Point, Chris only needs me as an escort at fundraisers, and the lab makes her look good with her billionaire pals." His voice turned bitter. "Twenty-five years, solid as a rock. What a crock. I'm stuck like a damned bug in a roach motel."

Jenna flicked a glance at him. A depressing sourness spread in the pit of her stomach because she had involved herself with such a man.

"That's such hypocrisy," she said. "You know you want to be

the First Gentleman, or whatever it is they'll call it. You want it as much as your wife wants to be President. Don't pretend you don't. If you wanted to be with me, you would have left her."

His jaw hardened. "Goddamn it, Jenna! How many more times do we have to go over this?"

"None. We're done with it right now." She turned onto Harbor Boulevard. "Where do you want me to drop you?"

"Where you always drop me."

Oh hell, where is that?

With neither of them willing to yield, the frigid silence stretched. As they neared the pier at Ventura beach, Jenna caught him looking at the Crowne Plaza. She hung a U-turn and braked at the curb in front of the parking garage, hoping she'd picked the right spot.

The moment she stopped the car, Simon climbed out and slammed the door behind him, making no attempt to hide his anger. He strode away without a word.

With each new memory Jenna built, the world was beginning to seem a little less alien. She tested herself constantly to make sure that she was retaining information—the names of streets; the co-workers she had met; her next appointment with Dr. Gold on Saturday. The new memories could never replace those she had lost, but it was some consolation that they were staying within easy reach.

One thing she had retained was the ability to find her way around town. After dropping off Simon, with a couple of hours to kill before returning to BioNeutronics under the cover of darkness, she gassed up the Nissan at the USA station next to the old Trader Joe's on Victoria, then went into TJ's and stocked up on groceries.

After packing the bags into the trunk, Jenna left the car in front of Trader Joe's and walked across the parking lot to the Batteries Plus store. There, she picked up a cell phone battery and charger. She also purchased a hefty MagLite flashlight.

Reaching for the exit, she noticed a familiar figure on the sidewalk outside. Zach stood there, a little more formal than she had seen him before in a shirt and slacks.

Jenna chewed her lip. She was in no mood to exchange

pleasantries that might lead to a discussion of her battery store purchases or where she was going that evening. Standing just inside the door, she pretended to be engrossed in a display of cell phone accessories and waited for him to leave.

A moment later, a black SUV pulled up. The passenger, a woman in a dark suit, got out and walked over to Zach. She handed him something small enough that Jenna couldn't make out what it was. After an exchange of a few words, she gave him a nod, then got back in the vehicle and drove away.

Huh.

Zach took a quick look around, though his gaze did not take in the store where Jenna stood, and then climbed into his truck and drove away.

She thought about it on her walk back to the Nissan, but with no way to satisfy her curiosity about what she had just witnessed, she let it go and concentrated on her plan to get the flash drive back.

There was nothing to do but return to the apartment and hunker down until darkness fell.

Jenna sat at the dining table and studied the emergency evacuation map over a bowl of ramen noodles. The third-floor ladies room was located at the southeast side of the building, which would put her out of the view of anyone driving by on the street.

She took a quick shower and dressed. In the dark clothing she had selected, and with a navy watch cap she'd found hiding her blonde hair, she looked like a wannabe Ninja.

In Jenna's jittery state the sun seemed to hover on the horizon for hours longer than normal, but by eight o'clock dusk was falling at last. After making sure the phone battery was plugged in and charging, Jenna hurried around to the carport.

Afternoon traffic had died down and the return journey to the Oxnard lab took a quick fifteen minutes. Her nerves were wound to a fever pitch as she drove to the rear of the building, pausing at the main doors to check out the guard station in the lobby. Unmanned. With any luck she would be in and out of the parking lot within five minutes.

She drove the Nissan into a dark area at the back of the lot and scanned the floors until she located the ladies room.

In and out. Go.

Hunched low and moving fast, Jenna crossed the parking lot, melting into the shadows at the edge of the building. She knelt in the grass, wet from the sprinklers, and switched on the MagLite, pointing it at the ground. If she had judged correctly, the coffee cup would have fallen straight down and should be in or behind the foliage.

She aimed the flashlight at the intersection of cement wall and ground and swept it from side to side, sending nocturnal creatures scuttling. The powerful beam lit up the tangle of branches at the bottom of the hedge, but no Starbucks cup.

Considering the possibility that the cup's trajectory had altered as it fell, Jenna crab-walked across the grass several feet to her left, pausing every few steps to point the beam at the base of the shrubbery. By the time she had reached the end of the building without find it, her mind was racing. It had never once crossed her mind that she might come up empty.

Back at her starting point, she stepped up on the low retaining wall that surrounded the hedge and started to walk along it, holding the light at an oblique angle that raked the top of the foliage. Her back was turned when a rough voice cut through the night and a second flashlight lit her up as if she was on stage. "Hey! What are you doing?"

Startled, Jenna slipped off the wall and stumbled on the grass, her mind grasping for a believable cover story. She could not clearly see the security guard until he lowered his flashlight. His right hand hovered over a holster. Not a rent-a-cop. His uniform buttons were taut against his broad chest. Grey hair buzz cut, military style. Even in the darkness Jenna could see the cruel set of his mouth.

Jenna made sure her hands were where he could see them. "Please don't shoot me," she said in a shaky voice, "You scared the crap out of me."

"I asked what you're doing here," the guard demanded coldly.

"I uh—I lost something. I—I work here—I—I think I dropped it out here at lunchtime." The words fell out of her mouth, choppy and disjointed.

"Lost what?"

Her ability to lie easily had deserted her. She cleared her throat nervously, still trying to come up with something reasonable. "Uh, it was a—a credit card. I think it fell out of my pocket."

"Yeah?" She could tell he wasn't buying it. He moved his hand away from the gun and extended his palm. "ID."

Jenna dug in her pocket with clumsy fingers, relieved that she had followed a gut instinct to bring her employee badge. The guard shone his light on it, studying it as thoroughly as if he were cramming for an exam. He pointed it back at her face, forcing her to squint against the glare.

Jenna read the name Nate Farley on the badge pinned to his shirt and tried for friendly. "Nothing to worry about, Nate, I work for the lab director, Dr. Lawrie—"

Farley pointed at the watch cap covering her head. "What's with the beanie?"

She pulled off the cap and ruffled her short locks. "I uh, didn't have time to dry my hair."

He gave a loud snort of disbelief. "Riiiiight. You come here at night dressed like a cat burglar and I'm supposed to believe you're looking for a credit card?"

"Well, I didn't *mean* to look like a cat burglar, and it's not really night, it's still early evening." She couldn't seem to stop babbling. "Listen, Nate, do you know if anyone turned in a credit card?"

"That's Mr. Farley to you."

"Fine, *Mr.* Farley. So, about my—"

"I'll be sure to make a note for the next shift to keep on the lookout," he broke in with obvious sarcasm.

That was the last thing she wanted. "Please don't bother. I'll ask around when I get to work tomorrow."

"You sure you lost your *credit card* over here?" He was looking at her with open contempt, letting her know he knew she was lying.

She had no choice but to brazen it out. "I think it was around here because I was sitting on the wall, eating lunch. Look, I know it was stupid to come back tonight, but I didn't want to wait in case someone picked it up. I'm always losing it and...don't tell anyone, okay?"

He cast a last look at her badge and handed it back to her.

"You oughta be more careful with your 'credit cards,' Ms. Marcott."

"I will. And I'm going now, so goodnight." The words were scarcely out of her mouth before she turned tail and sprinted to the Nissan. She didn't glance back until she was behind the wheel with the door locked. Farley was marching toward the area where she had been searching for the cup, the beam from his flashlight throwing a milky pool across the grass.

Jenna held her breath and sat there, watching him hunt around for a minute or so. When he gave up and let himself in the front door of the building, she drove slowly past. She could see him at the security desk through the big plate glass windows. He appeared to be writing something.

The back of her neck was clammy with perspiration. If her nighttime visit was reported to Simon he would know that she had eaten lunch at her desk, not on the brick wall. He would want to know why she had lied.

What were the chances that someone had already seen the cup and picked it up? The maintenance crew? Maybe someone had tossed it into the trash. Glancing in the rearview mirror she gave a moment's thought to where the dumpster might be located, and the possibility of her searching it.

You idiot. If that guard finds you dumpster diving, you'll be totally screwed.

I'm already totally screwed.

She wasn't sure which was worse—that someone might even now be accessing the files on the flash drive, or that the cup had been trashed, with its contents lost to her forever.

FIFTEEN

By the time Jenna returned to the apartment the phone battery was charged enough to install it in the phone. She snapped it into place, going went over and over the encounter with Nate Farley, thinking of all the things she should have said or done.

The welcome tone played when she switched on the phone, giving her a little zing of optimism. An envelope icon on the display indicated new voicemail. Punching buttons, she arrived at the access message and when prompted entered *1Ariel*, hoping it was her password for everything. But a recording informed her that the password she had entered was invalid and suggested she try again.

Just one more thing outside her control. Pretty much summed up her life as she knew it.

She didn't have the heart to call the service provider for a password reset. They would probably ask for her social security number or her mother's maiden name to verify her identity, and she would be SOL.

Do I even have a mother?

Let's not go there.

She scrolled to the texts sent and received mailboxes and found them empty. Simon had accused her of ignoring his voicemail and texts. Why would he lie about that?

Scrolling through the received calls, there were five of them all dated the previous week, originating from a number in the 310 area code. 310 was part of greater Los Angeles and included Marina del Rey. The name "Belle" was associated with the number.

Another two calls were from the 760 area code, which was around San Diego. That made sense, given that one of her driver's licenses had an address in Escondido, a San Diego suburb. No name or phone number was associated with either call.

In addition to the two phone numbers in the Received file, the Contact List contained a scant four items: Belle, clinic, hair, voicemail. Listings that held no meaning for Jenna Marcott. It seemed a sad indictment that her phonebook held no contact that might be a friend, except maybe Belle, whoever she was.

Something deep inside her stirred, shifted sideways.

Belle.

Ariel.

Two characters from Disney kids' movies: 'The Little Mermaid,' and 'Beauty and the Beast.' That couldn't be coincidence, could it?

What sort of reaction would she get from the person who answered if she called Belle's contact number and said; "Hi, do you recognize my voice or my name? Can you tell me anything about myself?"

She wasn't ready to do that…yet.

Praying fervently that Simon wouldn't show up shitfaced after an evening out with his buddies, Jenna undressed and got ready for bed. At eleven-thirty, when he had not appeared, she climbed under the covers, feeling as though she had been granted a reprieve. As hostile as they had both been when he'd left her at Eric Ericsson's, she hoped he understood that she had no intention of sharing her bed with him ever again.

For a long time she lay awake agonizing over the lost cup and its secret cargo. What information was so important, or perhaps so dangerous, that she had buried the flash drive in the planter? And where was it now?

In the end, unable to shut down the unanswered questions whirling in her head, Jenna got up and poured herself a glass of the "two buck Chuck" pinot noir she had picked up at Trader Joe's. Curled up in the big leather armchair drinking wine and fretting, she waited for exhaustion to knock her out.

That night brought an unwelcome rerun of the bad dreams, but Friday morning started out without incident. Jenna half-expected Nate Farley, the security guard, to be waiting at BioNeutronics, pointing an accusing finger at her. It was almost an anticlimax when he was not. To cover herself, she asked at the reception desk whether anything had been turned in at the lost and found.

"Not that anyone told me," Keisha said. "What'd you lose?"

Jenna repeated the story she had told the guard about the missing credit card.

"Damn, girl, how'd you do that?"

"Stupid, I guess."

Keisha gave a sympathetic shake of her head. "You'd better call and cancel that card. You know how it is. Somebody might've picked it up and kept it."

Simon had left a message that he would be out of the office until the afternoon. After the hostility of their parting she wasn't looking forward to seeing him again. The tension of working with him, pretending to know about their relationship but not remembering any part of it, was starting to wear on her.

For now, she needed the income the job provided and would have to make it work, at least until she created a new life for herself. Until that time, the unpredictable blackouts, the buzzing behind her ear when the stress became unbearable, not knowing anything about her past or what had happened to her memory—those things made it impossible to think about the future.

She checked the company directory on her office computer for Kevin Nguyen, the person in Security that Simon had told her to contact, and learned that he was BioNeutronics' chief of security. Clinging to the hope that her nocturnal visit had gone unreported, she punched up Nguyen's extension on the desk phone and relayed Simon's message that the Project 42 client was bringing in their own employees.

Nguyen's voice was that of an older man whose American accent still bore strong traces of his native Vietnam. When he made no mention regarding her being caught on the grounds the prior evening, Jenna breathed a little easier.

As Simon had predicted, Kevin Nguyen was cranky when she delivered his message.

"The clients are sending their own people? They have to go through background check, just like everybody else, you know. Nobody starts work here unless they get clearance first. You know that. *You* had to get clearance. Everybody gets clearance. You tell Simon Lawrie these people have to complete the paperwork. I am gonna email it to you, you get it over to them, and make damn sure they return it to me so I can review and approve these people."

He stopped to take a breath and Jenna broke in before he could renew his rant. "They're supposed to start on Monday, Kevin. Today is Friday. That doesn't leave much time to get their information."

"They can't start Monday. Too soon. They need clearance first."

"Simon said—"

"Why does he wait to the last minute to tell me this? How can I do my job if he works against me?"

"I don't know. Maybe it was a last minute thing. I'm sure he didn't mean to upset you."

Nguyen made a sound that could only be construed as disgust. "Never mind, I'll call him myself. I heard you were out sick."

"I had the flu."

"Now, don't you let him work you too hard." The security chief cackled as if he'd said something hilarious. Jenna felt her cheeks warm. She figured he was referring to her sexual relationship with her boss. Keisha clearly knew about it, too. Who else at BioNeutronics knew?

"What was up with the surprise search last night?" she asked, keen to change the subject.

"A surprise search is supposed to be a surprise," Nguyen said. "Random search, random times. If people know when they're going to happen, they would know when it's safe."

"Safe to do what?"

"How we gonna know, unless we do random check?" He laughed again. The sound was grating. "They think they're being clever. No worries, we'll get them. Sooner than you think."

Something about his tone worried her. What did he know?

"I saw someone get pulled out of line. Did you…catch anyone in the act?"

"You know better than to ask me that."

"Well, I just thought…as Simon's assistant…"

"Hah! Random search. Like the airport. What we are looking for and what we find is *our* business. Security department business. Not your business."

She hung up completely unsatisfied. Her gut told her that Kevin Nguyen knew something. She just wasn't sure what.

You're being paranoid.

Oh yeah, it's just a coincidence that they do a search on my first day back at work when I wanted to smuggle contraband out of the building.

Sometimes a cigar is just a cigar.

After lunch, Simon phoned. His tone was cool; it didn't take a psychic to hear his resentment. He asked Jenna to bring the security clearance paperwork for the new consultants down to the lab and rang off.

Jenna took the elevator to the basement, where she used her card key to open a door marked Laboratory. A young technician hunched over a microscope glanced up as she entered. "Hi Jen. Wow, Keisha was right, that haircut is awesome on you. Where'd you get it done?"

Jenna returned the smile and came up with the first lie that popped into her head. "A friend in Solana Beach did it for me."

"Well, she did a seriously awesome job." The tech cocked her head toward a door at the far end of the lab. "If you're looking for Dr. Lawrie, they're in the library."

The door led to a corridor lined on both sides with more doors. Each was marked: Lab 1, Data Center, Lab 2, Microscopy, Lab 3, Machinery, and so on. Long horizontal windows allowed someone in the corridor to watch technicians at work inside the rooms.

The library was a sizable, attractive room trimmed in ash veneer and lined on each side with bookcases containing numerous scientific magazines. Jenna thought it odd that there were relatively few books, until it struck her that due to the speed with which scientific advances were made, many works would be obsolete even before they hit the shelves, while periodicals could be rapidly updated.

Through the glass wall of a reading room at the back, she could see Simon seated at a round table with the woman she had encountered in the ladies room the previous evening—Dr. Raisa Polzin—and a distinguished-looking man in a jacket; his white dress shirt open at the neck. He wore wire-rimmed eyeglasses and sported a greying goatee.

"Oh, there you are," said Simon, rising when Jenna arrived at the open door. He beckoned her into the room and turned to the other man. "Dr. Kapur, you haven't met my assistant in person. This is Jenna."

Dr. Kapur rose and acknowledged her with a slight bow. "A pleasure indeed. We have spoken on the telephone so many times."

"It's good to meet you," Jenna said, as if she knew what they had spoken about. She turned with a small start of surprise to the other woman seated at the table. A woman she recognized from the photos in Simon's office. Yesterday, Simon had intimated that his wife had caused Jenna bodily harm. What was she doing here?

"Hi there, Jenna," Christine Palmer said. Her mouth smiled, but her eyes glittered with animosity. Jenna gave her a nod and returned an uncertain smile.

What do I call her? Mrs. Lawrie? Ms. Palmer? Christine?

Simon answered the unspoken question. "Chris brought Dr. Kapur out from DC with her to tour the lab before his people take over next week. You have the paperwork, Jen?"

He appeared perfectly at ease bringing his wife and his lover together in the same room, which made Jenna dislike him even more. She wondered how she had dealt with such meetings before her amnesia. She could not imagine ever feeling comfortable about it.

Setting the file folder containing the security clearance applications on the table in front of Dr. Kapur, she said, "Welcome to BioNeutronics, Doctor. If you would complete and return these to me today, I'll take them to our security chief so they can be processed right away."

Dr. Kapur thanked her and promised to handle it. His

speculative gaze flicked from Simon to her, lingering for a moment. His interest barely registered. For Jenna, Christine Palmer had sucked the air out of the room and it was all she could do to keep her hands steady. She was afraid her cheeks were bright red with embarrassment.

You should *feel guilty. Homewrecker.*

I'm not a homewrecker. The marriage was already over.

Whatever gets you through the day.

Although she was at the table, Raisa Polzin stayed quiet while the men discussed the security forms. Was it because she didn't like having Dr. Kapur's employees foisted upon her that she looked so sour, as if she'd been sucking on a lemon? Or, maybe she had been in charge of Project 42 and was resentful of having it removed from her control.

"Dr. Kapur's people will be working in the new lab," Simon said to Jenna. "I'll let Kevin Nguyen know about the additional clearance level they'll need." He returned his attention to the scientist. "Card key entry will be limited to those personnel and me. Information is strictly on a need-to-know basis until the clinical trials are complete. The reader will be installed on the door before Monday." Glancing over at Jenna, he seemed surprised to see her still there. "Thanks, Jen, that's it for now."

And just like that, she was dismissed, which irked her beyond words. She had hoped to learn more about Project 42 and the high level of security surrounding it.

She left the reading room and started back across the library, stopped by Christine Palmer's voice calling out her name.

"Jenna, could I have a moment?"

Simon's wife came over and slipped an arm through hers, as if they were the best of friends. From the distance of the reading room, no one would be able to see her gouge her fingernails into Jenna's arm. Nor could they spot the way she dug in mercilessly when Jenna tried to pull away. Christine Palmer moved in closer, as if she was about to share a secret. "We know what you're up to, you little scammer." Her hissed accusation was just loud enough for only Jenna to hear it. "Just don't think you're going to get away with it."

SIXTEEN

Simon did not appear for the rest of the day, which left Jenna's afternoon dominated by replays of Christine Palmer's threat. Was it possible that his wife knew something about the flash drive? Had it been found and somehow traced to Jenna's office computer? Who was the "we" she was talking about?

There was no security check that afternoon. If only she had left the damn flash drive buried in her office overnight, she could have walked it straight through the front door.

Dumbass.

Yep.

After a solitary dinner of salad and a carton of yogurt, Jenna checked the computer for new email. Along with the usual glut of spam, Zach had invited her to a party on Saturday. She replied with a "thanks but no thanks." Bluffing one person at a time was hard enough; mingling in a group of people unknown to her was out of the question.

Didn't she have any other friends? What about Belle, the one personal name in her phone's contact list? She considered calling the number, but thought better of it, afraid she would learn that aside from her neighbor, Zach, she had no friends at all.

For a few minutes, Jenna gave herself over to melancholy. Here she was, on a Friday night, twenty-seven years old and home alone with her computer. She could at least have had a cat. But that would be no good if she kept forgetting who she was and where she lived. The poor creature would never know when he would next be fed.

It occurred to Jenna that the entire day had passed without a headache or a blackout, no buzzing. Despite still having no memories of her life before Sunday night, it felt like some kind of progress.

Before powering down the computer she googled Christine Palmer and discovered that the man with whom she'd been having an affair was married to a United States senator.

Holy shit.

Scouring the web for information, she quickly learned that Palmer was a hardcore political animal whose presidential aspirations were well documented in articles that were rife with speculation about her ambitions. More than one reporter noted that, not since Sarah Palin's resignation as governor of Alaska had there been so much conjecture about a possible female bid for the presidency.

Jenna sat back and thought about it. What if Christine Palmer had just learned of her husband's affair? What steps might she take to keep it away from the likes of CNN or the Huffington Post? Simon was right. If the media got a whiff of scandal they would be on it like ravening dogs. How far would Palmer go to keep something like this quiet? Surely not far enough to cause her husband's paramour physical harm—or worse.

Simon believed she would *go that far.*

The faint crescent marks of Palmer's nails biting into her flesh were still visible. Jenna was convinced she would have drawn blood if she had thought she could get away with it. But something didn't make sense. If Palmer had engineered some kind of attack last weekend, how had Jenna escaped? And how had she ended up on a train to Ventura with no memory?

Then there was the question of the car accident. Simon was not the driver of the car in her hypnotic trance. Those dark, demented eyes that haunted her were definitely not his baby blues.

She typed Simon's name into the Google search engine, eager to read what Wikipedia had to say about Simon Willard Lawrie,

Ph.D.

There were far less entries than for his wife, but under 'Early life,' Jenna learned that Simon was eighteen years her senior, born and raised in a small Texas town. The only child of Willard Lawrie, Jr., a hardware store owner, and Janice Sweet Lawrie, a homemaker, Simon won a full scholarship to UCLA, where he studied biochemistry and met Christine Morelli Palmer, a Poli Sci major.

After graduation he earned his chops at a major pharmaceuticals company in Buffalo, while Christine gave birth to two sons and got herself elected to city council. The family moved back to California in the early 1990s and, partnering with a group of well-funded businessmen, Simon founded BioNeutronics Laboratories, which subsequently flourished. The article mentioned his pride in maintaining a private laboratory that was independent of government funding and therefore, government interference.

Independent of his wife's influential contacts?

The other articles detailed Bioneutronics' various research projects and accomplishments. There was no mention of Project 42, but given the level of secrecy Simon had impressed upon her, she had not really expected to find any.

Snippets and fragments of scenes and conversations over the past three days were spiraling through her brain. There must be some way to make sense of what she had come to learn about herself.

She went looking for a pen and paper. She might not be the super-organized Jenna that she had been B.A.—Before Amnesia—but she was certain that making a list of everything that had happened was a good start.

Jenna located a pen and steno notebook in the meticulously arranged kitchen junk drawer, then propped herself against a pile of pillows on the bed and began to summarize her life as she had come to know it:

Fact: Unconscious—how long?

Fact: Train from Solana Beach to Ventura

Fact: Three addresses: Marina del Rey, Ventura, Escondido

She noted that her handwriting was small; the printed letters squashed close together. Jenna wondered what the handwriting analyst would make of it.

Probably think I'm a psycho.

She'd be right.

Just keep writing!

Fact: Blackouts, headaches, buzzing noise in head

Fact: Asked Dr. Gold about betrayal on previous visit

Fact: Told Dr. Gold someone was going to kill me

Question: Hypnosis. Car accident?

Question: Crying—

Stop!

Jenna had started to write "crying child," but the act made her queasy and clammy all over. *So much for making progress.* She scribbled her pen over the letters, obliterating them as if that could erase the child's face from her mind, and kept writing.

Fact: Employed at BioNeutronics Laboratories

Fact: Affair with boss

Fact: Boss's wife a Senator

Fact: Buried flash drive

Question: flash drive data Project 42 info?

Question: why was Project 42 removed from computer?

Fact: Three days after amnesia, no additional memory loss

When she reviewed the list, it said a lot and nothing at all.

By now, utterly drained, she had no strength to fight her drooping eyelids. Her breathing gradually slowed and she turned onto her side. The pen and pad clattered to the tile floor.

Startled awake, Jenna jumped up without thinking. She groaned, realizing what had happened, and crouched on the cool tile, lifting the comforter to retrieve the pen.

A surprise awaited her under the bed.

SEVENTEEN

What's a cell phone doing under the bed?

It was a newer model than the old flip phone she'd found in the backpack. A much fancier, "there's an app for that," kind of phone.

She turned it on and slid an experimental fingertip across the icons, accessing the various menus. A string of text messages from Simon clogged the Inbox. So he had told the truth about trying to reach her.

What the hell *is going on?*

Two names. Two driver's licenses. Two phones.

Unlike the other phone, this one did not require a password. Simon had sent twenty-three texts over a span of three days, the first was received last Friday at seven p.m.; the final had arrived on Monday at eleven-forty-eight p.m., the tone increasing in urgency.

The texts started with a terse request for Jenna to call him, then went on to demand that she call, and finally…begging her to. The last one implied more than a hint of frustration: *G-d it, J, WTF are you??? Can't stand this!*

Was this a unit that she kept only for Simon's calls?

In the Contacts folder the first name on the list caught her by surprise: *Ariel*. 'The Little Mermaid' again.

Jenna tapped on the name and lifted the phone to her ear. The muffled music came from another Disney soundtrack—*Beauty and the Beast.*

Barreling into the living room, she reached the dining room table as the voicemail announcement began in her ear: "It's Jessica, leave a message."

Jessica.

Her voice sounded half-dead, as if attempting to find the strength to say the five words was an insurmountable task. With the phone in one hand, she grappled the purse open with the other, and read the name on the phone's LCD screen: Belle.

She clicked off before the beep and set the phone on the dining table, then navigated to the Contacts folder of the second phone. Selecting the name "Belle," she pressed Send.

Moments later, the first phone began to play a ring tone from *Part of Your World*, a song from *The Little Mermaid* soundtrack. After the fourth ring, the announcement began and her own cheerful voice said, "It's Jenna, leave a message."

***

"I want to make sure she feels safe," Zebediah Gold said into his cordless phone. "She's in a tremendously vulnerable place emotionally. We have to take it slowly, give her time to deal with what's happened to her."

On the other end of the line, Claudia Rose readily concurred. "So, how do you want to play it?"

"It might be best if you meet her first, then have Joel join us once she's comfortable. That would be less threatening than having to face two new people together, knowing they've got you under the microscope. I mean, darling, you may have met her at the convention, but with her amnesia, you're a new person."

"You're the shrink, dear doc. I'm just the humble handwriting analyst groveling at the feet of the master."

Gold gave a low huff of laughter. "Oh, darling, if only that were true."

"I'm prostrating myself as we speak," Claudia cracked, then got serious. "Do you think there's any possibility of Dissociative Identity Disorder?"

"It's too soon to make that kind of diagnosis. Right now I'm more concerned with helping her to verbalize what she's experiencing."

"Am I correct in assuming you want me to collect a new handwriting sample for analysis?"

"But of course, my sweet. When have your insights not helped in a case we've worked together? Anyway, you've met her before. I'd like to get your impressions of her now."

"It's an interesting case."

"It is that. The amnesia appears to extend to her entire personal past, but her cognitive functioning seems unimpaired, which leads me to think the amnesia is likely the result of a trauma rather than some sort of organic brain disease. She refused medical testing, so at this point that's guesswork from my own observations."

"You mentioned a hypnosis session?"

"Yes. She clearly experienced something under hypnosis that she refused to talk about. Whatever it was really shook her." He checked the wall clock. "I need to go, she should be here any minute."

"Okay, I'm on my way. I'll ask Joel to give us a fifteen minute head start."

Gold rang off and then began to prepare for his appointment with Jenna. Or Jessica. He wondered which one would show up. Claudia's question about Dissociative Identity Disorder as a possibility for her problems was an intriguing one that could not be adequately answered in just one or two sessions.

***

Jenna settled into the chair she'd taken before. "Was that statue there last time?" she asked, noticing a small bronze figurine on the table. "I don't remember it."

"I think you were a little preoccupied," Dr. Gold replied, taking his chair opposite her and laying his hands in his lap. "That's Green Tara."

"Green Tara?"

"In the Buddhist tradition, she's the Goddess of Compassion. You see how she's sitting in the half-lotus position with her right leg extended? That's because she's poised to get up quickly to help those who need it."

"I like that."

"The legend says that Green Tara was born from the tears of Avalokiteshvara, the bodhisattva of compassion," he explained.

"The bodhiswhat?"

Dr. Gold smiled. "Bodhisattva. A bodhisattva is someone who has achieved a state of enlightenment and is worthy of becoming a Buddha, but who postpones his own nirvana to help others. So, as the story goes, this particular bodhisattva looked upon the suffering of the world and wept so much over the trauma, his tears formed a lake.

"In that lake a lotus sprang up, and when it opened, there was Tara. Actually, there were *two* Taras. White Tara came from the tears of Avalokiteshvara's left eye and Green Tara from the right. It's said that Green Tara, this one here on my table, works day and night, endlessly striving to relieve our suffering. She is the fierce Mother Earth who saves us from danger."

"What does White Tara do?" asked Jenna, intrigued by the story.

"She *gently* protects, and brings about long life and peace."

His voice was melodic and deep, easy to listen to. Jenna thought she wouldn't mind hearing the tranquil tone all day. "*I* could use some protection," she mused aloud. "I think I'll look for a Green Tara for my apartment. Maybe after I leave here. There's that New Age store on Abbott Kinney that I passed last time..." she let her voice trail off. "Last time" she had blacked out on her way home.

It all came rushing back: the cold terror of becoming conscious and finding herself halfway into the backseat at the traffic light...

Had Dr. Gold seen her shudder? She thought there wasn't much those amber-flecked eyes missed.

"Have any memories returned since you were here?" he asked.

"Not exactly." She wanted to tell him, but hesitated. "When you hypnotized me I saw—I think I was in a car wreck."

He gave an encouraging nod. "The scar on your head could have resulted from a car accident."

"Do you think Ms. Rose's detective friend can find out whether it's really true? I mean, that I was in an accident?"

"We'll certainly ask him. They'll be joining us shortly." Dr.

Gold allowed several seconds to pass before he spoke again. "Are you ready to talk about what else you saw while you were in the trance state?"

"No! I mean, do I have to?"

"Only if you're ready, Jenna, but you might find talking about it makes it less threatening."

"How sure are you about that?"

"That's the way it usually works." He was relaxed in his chair, hands loose in his lap, not pushing or prodding, letting her decide for herself. Maybe he was right, but still she held back, undecided about what she was willing to share with him.

What if he was wrong? What if telling him made things worse?

What could be worse?

The hypnosis made it worse.

Did it really?

She was aware of Dr. Gold awaiting a response.

Tears prickled the back of her eyelids. Jenna pressed her hands to her face, struggling to contain the eddy of emotions welling up. If she didn't trust him, there was no way she would be able to progress.

Can I trust him?

Yes.

The moment she reached that conclusion, words rushed out like air from a popped balloon.

"I was in a car and it hit a truck—one of those big grocery haulers. We were at the top of a steep grade. It was *pouring* rain—really heavy—like a waterfall. We hit the truck. The car went over the embankment—we were flying, then we started rolling and my head hit the windshield, then the roof…" Jenna broke off. The buzzing was blocking out Dr. Gold's quiet voice and she had to concentrate to hear him.

"Were you wearing a seatbelt?" he asked.

"I was, but I had to unbuckle it to—" She broke off again. Trust had its limits. She could not talk about the child.

"Were you driving the vehicle?"

Bzzzzzzz.

Stop, dammit!

"No, a man was driving. He kept staring at me like he hated

me—" She broke off, remembering those malevolent eyes.

"Did you know him?" Dr. Gold asked gently.

"I think—so—I think—I think I did. Yes. I knew—"

"Did he say anything?"

Bzzzzzzz.

"Um...yes, he said..." The words were right there, the words she had heard over and over in her nightmares. She tried to slow her breathing. "He said—he said, 'I'll take you with me.'"

There was a long pause before Dr. Gold asked, "What do you think he meant by that?"

"He was going to kill us all." She spoke without thinking and Dr. Gold left her statement floating in the air. The silence grew and expanded until it filled the room.

When he spoke, his voice was deceptively soft. "Who else was in the car with you, Jenna?"

"What?"

"You said he was 'going to kill us *all*.'"

"I meant *both*. He was going to kill us both. Him and me. Just him and me."

His eyes probed her deepest secrets—penetrating all the way through to the ones she herself had forgotten. Or wanted to forget. "I think you meant 'all.' Can you tell me who else was in the car with you and the man?"

Jenna shook her head fiercely. "No one. I made a mistake. No one else was there." She pressed her fingertips against the scar behind her ear as though it were a volume control button that could reduce the horrid wasps. And then she told the big lie. "I don't remember."

"It sounds like someone else was with you and the man in the car, Jenna."

"What about the handwriting analyst?" Her voice sounded too loud. She dialed down the volume. "She's still coming, isn't she?"

"She'll be here shortly." Dr. Gold sat forward, relentless in his search for information. "Jenna, can you tell me who else was in the car with you and the driver?"

"Someone's coming." She rocked back and forth, her arms crossed protectively over her stomach. "Someone's at the door." Before she had finished speaking, there was a light knock.

Thank you, God. Thank you, thank you.

Clad in jeans and t-shirt, a mane of auburn hair tumbled over the shoulders of an off-white linen jacket. Claudia Rose didn't look intimidating. Jade-colored eyes sparkled with frank curiosity and good humor. She said, "Please, don't get up," as Jenna started to rise.

Claudia made her way around the coffee table and took a place on the couch, reaching out to offer her hand. "We met in San Diego." She said it matter-of-factly, not looking at Jenna as if she were a freak for having amnesia.

Jenna liked her for that. She said, "I'm sorry, I don't remember any of it—the convention, meeting you. I guess Dr. Gold told you my story." She glanced over at the psychologist who sat quietly in his chair, taking in their exchange.

"He's shared the basics," Claudia said. "It must be—well...I can't even begin to know how it must be, but I think it's beyond unimaginable."

"I've learned some things about my life over the past few days that have left me with a lot of questions about who I really am. I hope your friend has some news for me."

"He'll be joining us in a few minutes. In the meantime, I was wondering, Jenna, would you be willing to write a new handwriting sample for me?"

"What for?" Jenna heard the defensiveness spring up in her voice.

Claudia gave her a reassuring smile. "It's just to give us a baseline to compare the sample you wrote for me in San Diego, to see whether anything has changed."

"Like what?"

"If there's something physiological to be concerned about it might show up, like if you'd had a blow to the head, which seems to be the case. Plus, you've experienced emotional stress which could cause some changes, too."

"So, if you have a head injury it could make your handwriting change?"

"It could, yes."

"But what if you had an injury and it didn't affect you

physically?"

"Even then it might show up," Claudia replied. "Some types of concussion, for example, or a certain type of closed head injury, can cause behavioral changes and memory problems, even when you can't see anything wrong on the outside."

Jenna felt curiosity overtake her reluctance. "If you think it might help, I'll do it. What do I have to write?"

Claudia opened the briefcase she'd brought with her and reached inside for a clipboard with several sheets of blank paper already attached. "Do you have a special pen you like to use?"

"I don't know."

"That's fine; you can use this one." She handed Jenna a Uniball. "Are you right or left-handed?"

Jenna had to think about it before taking the pen in her left hand. "Um, I *think* I'm left-handed. Does it make a difference?"

"Handedness is just one of the things your handwriting doesn't tell about you. That, and age and gender."

"What do you want me to write?"

"It doesn't matter *what* you write, but it should be essay style. Don't make it a lyric or a poem because that changes your natural patterns and can make the handwriting artificial. You can write as much as you like, more is better, but at least five or six lines. When you're finished, sign your name."

"What if I only print?"

"Printing is writing, too."

Jenna noticed Claudia signal to Dr. Gold with an eyebrow lift. He rose from his chair. "We'll give you a few minutes alone so you can concentrate without having us looking over your shoulder. We'll be right outside in the garden if you need anything."

EIGHTEEN

The door closed behind them and Jenna looked down at the clipboard on her lap, intimidated by the blank paper waiting to be filled. All that white space seemed like an ocean…and she had a mere bucketful of words.

Her thoughts were jumping around like a monkey on a jungle vine:

What if they want to use my handwriting to prove I'm crazy?

Why would they do that?

What will the detective say about the two driver's licenses?

Maybe he'll take you to jail.

That's stupid, I haven't done anything wrong.

How do you know?

After several deep breaths to wrestle the monkey into submission, she managed to write a few bland lines about the drive from Ventura to Venice. Rereading what she had written, curiosity stirred. What would her handwriting reveal about her?

She was signing her name, which still felt awkward, when the office door opened and Dr. Gold entered with Claudia and another man who she assumed must be Claudia's detective friend.

He was more than a head taller than Claudia, who was about five-seven. Jenna guessed he was around forty. His salt-and-pepper hair was trimmed close to his skull, but it had a slight curl and looked as if it might get unruly if he allowed it to grow much longer. He was tanned and fit in a golf shirt and cargo pants, and she fancied the detective spent time working out at a gym.

For a moment she let her imagination run wild. An involuntary mental image of him sweating in shorts and nothing else, sent a hot flush to her face that made her glance away. It struck her as distinctly strange that she could experience this quiver of sexual interest in the detective when she felt nothing at all for Simon, who had been her lover.

The detective introduced himself as Joel Jovanic and shook her hand with a firm grip. "I work for the Los Angeles Police Department," he explained as they all sat down. "But I'm here off the book as a favor to Claudia."

Would he have a weapon concealed on his body the way off-duty detectives did in the movies? There was a toughness about him that made Jenna think he was not someone to cross. But his voice was calm and dispassionate, and gave her confidence in his ability to help her.

"I'm so grateful to you for doing this," she told him shyly. "I guess it means you're working on your day off. Thank you."

He gave her a brief nod. "I've already spoken with someone I know in Missing Persons. He checked the state and regional Missing Adult databases with the information on your two driver's licenses that Dr. Gold photocopied. There was nothing filed on a missing person for either Jenna Marcott or Jessica Mack."

"When I went to work on Wednesday, my—er, boss, told me he'd been trying to reach me since last Friday. That's a whole week ago now."

"I understand. But so far, there hasn't been a report filed."

"If no one's reported me missing, maybe it means I don't have any family."

Until this second, Jenna realized, she had not given any real thought to her family. If she allowed herself to admit it, she had deliberately pushed the subject aside, along with so many other things. But now, the idea that apparently nobody had noticed whether she was dead or alive was devastating.

Detective Jovanic shook his head. "That's not necessarily the case. Could be you've just not been in contact with your people for a few days. You were on a train, so maybe your family thought you were still away. It's not all that long for someone to be out of touch." He paused. "I understand you're staying in Ventura. What about the other addresses, the ones on the licenses in Marina del Rey and Escondido—have you checked them out?"

"No, I haven't."

"The first thing I suggest you do is visit those addresses and see if anything hits you. Knock on doors, talk to the neighbors, see if they know you."

"If they do know me, they'll think I'm crazy."

When he eased up on the serious expression, the detective had a nice smile that creased the corners of his eyes. "I have every confidence that you'll find a way to do it without them thinking you're crazy. And chances are, the mystery will be solved right there."

"And if it's not?"

"If it's not, I'll meet you at the division where I work and take your fingerprints. It's possible that running them through the system might produce something."

"I have a security clearance at work," Jenna said. "Doesn't that mean I would have been fingerprinted before?"

"Probably, but unless you've been arrested for engaging in some type of criminal activity, you wouldn't be in our databases. For that reason, let's hope you're not." The detective sat on the edge of the couch, elbows on his knees, leaning towards her. "Jenna, is there anything you can add to the information on the driver's licenses that might help me when I search?"

She told him about the possibility she had been injured in a car accident. "Would an accident show up in your database?"

"Only if there were criminal charges filed. I'll check it out."

"And if charges were filed—when will you know?"

"I'll call you Monday afternoon and let you know either way."

He asked for her cell phone number, which prompted her to tell him about the second cell she'd found under the bed.

She fished both phones out of her purse. "I hope I'm not a drug dealer or something like that. Who else would need two ID's and two cell phones?"

"There are many possible reasons for that." Detective Jovanic slid his finger across the screen of the newer phone like she had, checking the Contact list. "If you were dealing drugs, there would be a lot of names in the address book, which neither of these phones has. You might want to call the carrier and find out how long the accounts have been active." He handed her his business card. "If anything else comes up, or you remember anything over the weekend, give me a call."

"And if you need someone to talk to, whether anything new comes up or not, call me anytime," added Claudia, who had been sitting in the background listening quietly. She got out her card, too, and gave it to Jenna, who felt a little overwhelmed by the knowledge that she now had an entire team on her side.

***

Claudia picked up the handwriting sample and ran a practiced eye over the lines Jenna had written. She wasn't reading the words, but absorbing the layout on the page, the style, and hundreds of other elements. Jovanic observed over her shoulder without comment.

"So, what can you tell me?" Zebediah Gold asked.

Claudia gave him a light punch on the arm. "Give me time. You know I don't like doing quickies."

Gold faked indignation. "Did you see that, detective? She assaulted me."

"If you want to press charges, doc, I'll have to cuff her."

"She'd probably enjoy that, wouldn't she?"

Jovanic threw her a sly glance. "She might at that."

"Hey, guys," Claudia interjected. "I'm standing right here, remember? Do you want to know what I think of Jenna-Jessica's handwriting, or not?"

"Yes, darling, I certainly do," Zebediah said, without the least contrition. They had been friends for so long, he knew what he could get away with. "What does my client's handwriting tell you?"

Claudia got serious. "Of course, I want some time to look at it properly, but here's my first impression: The writing shows tremendous stress, which isn't surprising under the circumstances, but it's far more basic than that. This is a strongly introverted personality with a compromised ego. At her center, she's extremely insecure and uncertain. She's pretty fragile."

She gave them both a look of concern. "I'd say she's experienced emotional pain so deep that she can't begin to face it. She cuts it off, pushes it away, and pretends that it doesn't exist. Maybe *that's* the reason for the amnesia—the truth of her world is too much for her to face."

"She's definitely in denial about what happened to her," Zebediah said. He sketched out for them how Jenna had first indicated that more than two people had been in the car in her hypnotic state, then later had refused to admit it.

"So, there was someone she can't bear to think about," Claudia suggested. "Someone who—what?"

"That's something we don't know. It might take a long time for her to come to terms with whatever happened to her. I don't want to push her too far, too fast."

Jovanic looked unconvinced. "That doesn't explain the two identities, or the two cell phones."

"It might," Claudia said. "It looks like she's been living two separate lives without even being aware of it." She pointed a French tipped fingernail at a tiny dent in the ink line at the top of a letter 'l,' and at a similar dent on a 'b.'

"See these dents? Those are a physiological artifact. They indicate a possible blow to the head that could be causing cognitive problems related to the amnesia."

Zebediah added, "She *is* sporting a small scar on her head. We don't know for sure what caused it, but we're assuming it was possibly a result of the auto accident she saw under hypnosis. So, darling, how does this handwriting compare to the sample you saw before when you met her in San Diego? Any differences?"

She cocked a brow. "You're kidding, right? That was *months* ago and hers was one of about six hundred samples. The good news is, my client from the convention is going to ship them to me. I'll let you know on Monday when I get them."

"Darling, I'm in your debt."

"You are for sure," said Claudia. "But to answer your question without being a smartass, from what I remember, this handwriting is *very* different from the earlier one."

NINETEEN

After leaving Dr. Gold's office Jenna tapped the address from the Marina del Rey driver's license into the Nissan's GPS. The instrument calculated the distance at precisely one mile. Following the voice instructions, she drove to an apartment building on Washington Boulevard, one block east of the ocean to a large three story pink brick structure with beige trim and an external staircase.

No apartment number was listed on the driver's license, so she did a quick check of the names on a cluster of fifty mailboxes inside the foyer. There was no Jenna Marcott among the names printed on the boxes. Rentals in the beach town went fast, so she guessed that her unit had been rented to new tenants even before she'd moved to Ventura.

She toyed briefly with the idea of knocking on doors, but the thought of approaching strangers and asking if they knew her made her want to run back to her car.

Hanging out in the foyer for a brief spell produced nothing more than a generic nod from a few residents who passed through. When she left the building, she knew nothing more than when she had arrived.

On the way back to where she had parked the Nissan Jenna stopped at the Cow's End for lunch. Everyone at the little neighborhood café seemed to be acquainted with each other, and as she put in her order at the counter for chicken salad and a white mocha latté, she felt a wave of melancholy.

Waiting at her solitary table for her food, she studied the Jessica Mack driver's license. The Escondido address was a little over a hundred miles south of her current location. The voice started in on her.

You're halfway there.

It's a ninety minute drive from here.

It's three hours from Ventura.

The voice won.

She found a Norah Jones CD in the glove box and slipped it into the player, surprising herself with a sweet, husky voice, singing along to *Come Away With Me*. For the next sixty miles the music took her mind off whether the drive to Escondido would be a wild goose chase, but when the CD ended halfway to her destination, she could no longer avoid the latest spate of questions:

Why did I change my identity? Who is Jessica Mack? Why move from Escondido to Marina del Rey? Why go further north to Ventura? Why? Why? Why?

It dawned on her that she had forgotten to tell Detective Jovanic about the threat Christine Palmer had made. Jenna dug his card out of her pocket and started to punch in his number, but clicked off before the call connected. She had already intruded on his weekend more than enough.

It was close to four o'clock when she exited the freeway at Vista Way in Escondido.

The address on the driver's license led to the Casa Blanca Apartments, a series of modern two story buildings that took up two blocks in a quiet neighborhood. She walked up a nicely kept flower-bordered pathway with a nod of approval and entered the open front doors.

Scanning the names on the bank of mailboxes, after her disappointment in Marina del Rey, she felt a jolt of surprise at the name "J. Mack" on C207.

Her fingers traced the name on the mailbox as if that might somehow explain her connection to Jessica,. but it was just a name on a piece of paper. She debated turning around and walking right back to her car.

You want to know, don't you?

I'm not so sure anymore.

The second set of keys had been in her purse ever since Pigpen from the train had returned her backpack. It stood to reason that with this being the address on Jessica Mack's driver's license, those keys would gain her admittance to the apartment.

But reason is in pretty short supply these days.

It was only when the metal teeth of the keys bit into her palm that she realized she had taken them from her purse. The discomfort was an anchor to the material world, which felt very different from the surreal one in which she had been living. She chose the small silver key and inserted it into the slot on the mailbox.

Stuffed behind the metal door was a week's worth of circulars, a gas bill postmarked last Monday, and an envelope that bore the return address of the San Diego Police Department. That one made her heart race.

Tossing the junk mail into a trash can next to the mailboxes, she slipped the gas bill and the SDPD envelope into her purse. At the back of the foyer was a set of glass doors.

As she stood in front of them, the doors seemed to Jenna like a metaphor for her life. On this side, at least she knew she was Jenna Marcott, even though she knew precious little else. On the other side waited Jessica Mack and the greater unknown.

She could see across a hotel-sized swimming pool and a clubhouse bordered by palm trees to a building with a large letter "C" attached. With a quiver in her stomach, Jenna pushed open the door and stepped into Jessica's world.

After exiting the stairwell on the second floor of building C, Jenna began to walk along the balcony. She had reached 206 when the door opened, startling her.

A woman around her own age stepped out, pushing a jogging stroller. Firm-bodied with a deep tan, sun-streaked blonde ponytail, she was dressed in a bright pink halter top and black spandex bicycle shorts: the iconic California Girl.

"Jessica! You're back!" Big sparkling teeth showed extra white against skin the sun was tanning to leather. "Are you okay, hon?"

What's her name? She knows me, I must know her name.

Faking a return smile, Jenna kept her eyes averted from the baby in the stroller. "I'm fine, thanks."

"Well, after you lit out of here like a bat out of hell? Then I didn't see you again and now it's a week later—*hello?*"

"I had a—an emergency."

"No duh! I mean, come on, Jess. You may not be the most outgoing gal in the complex, but it's not like you to totally ignore me when I say something. What happened?"

"I'm sorry. I, er, I had to leave in a hurry."

What the hell is her name? Paula? Pauline? Patti?

"I guess so! You left in *such* a hurry I bet you didn't even know you left your front door hanging wide open, did you?"

"I did?"

Pam? Penny?

"Yeah, you did. That's what I was yelling, but you just ignored me and kept on going." She patted Jenna's arm. "Don't worry, hon, when you didn't come back by eleven o'clock I closed your door and locked it for you. Brad told me I shouldn't interfere, but *anyone* could have just walked in and stolen your stuff in the night, right? I didn't want some stranger messing around next door to my family, did I? Of course not. Then you didn't come back anyway, so it was the right thing to do, wasn't it?"

Peyton. Her name is Peyton Butler.

"Yes, of course it was. Thank you, Peyton, I appreciate it."

Peyton leaned down to coo at the baby, who had begun to fuss. "It's okay, Brandon boo boo, we're going." She glanced up at Jenna with an expression full of pitying condescension. "I know you don't have kids, but you gotta know they get cranky when they want their walkies."

She had no way of knowing that her baby's fussing had triggered Jenna's nightmare and the cries of the child in her hypnotic trance rang in her ears. Peyton Butler was unaware that it took every scrap of willpower Jenna could mobilize not to turn and flee from the whimpering infant.

"See you later," Jenna mumbled, starting to move past the stroller.

"Oh, wait, I forgot to tell you," Peyton called after her. "A police officer came looking for you a couple of days ago."

Jenna wheeled around. The San Diego Police Department envelope was a dead weight in her purse. "A—police officer?" she echoed faintly. "What did he want?"

"I think it was Wednesday," Peyton said, scrunching her face in concentration. "Lemme think. Yeah, Wednesday afternoon. I remember because Oprah was on, so it had to be between three and four. She had this old guy singer, Johnny Mathis, and Josh Groban. I just love Josh. He is so..."

Jenna thought for sure she was going to throw up. "*What about the cop?*"

Peyton's face registered surprise at the terse interruption. "Oh! I guess I got carried away. You know how I am. It's my ADHD. So, anyway, he was a small guy, bald, dressed by Sears or JC Penney, nothing nicer for sure. Said he was a detective. I heard him knock at your door so I thought someone must be selling something, so when he came to my door next, I was getting ready to tell him that no soliciting is allowed in here. Then he showed me his badge and asked if I knew where you were. I had no clue, of course. I mean, I'm your neighbor, right, not your keeper?"

Peyton lowered her voice to a stage whisper. "Don't worry, Jess, I didn't say a word about the way you took off that night. Are you in some kind of trouble, hon?"

"No! Everything's fine."

Her neighbor shrugged, but her expression was doubting. "Okayyy. If you say so. But hey, if you need someone to talk to..."

"There's nothing wrong, thanks. Everything's fine."

"He left a card in your door. It's still there."

The cream-colored business card in the doorframe was embossed with a gold-leaf star and imprinted with the name of the California Highway Patrol Commissioner, Central Division, Fresno Area Office. Sergeant Carl Galen was also printed on the front.

Fresno was three hundred miles north of Escondido.

On the back of the card, Sergeant Galen had printed in bold black ink: 'Please contact me ASAP.'

Asking herself what the hell she might have done to warrant

the attention of the Kern County CHP *and* San Diego PD, and whether it had anything to do with her amnesia, Jenna slipped the card into her purse and unlocked the door.

The lights were on in the apartment, the air as musty as an old shoe. With the automated response of habit, she dropped her purse and keys on a small table by the front door and went to open the vertical blinds and front windows to let in the fresh breeze.

For a Twilight Zone moment Jenna was sure she had stepped into an alternate reality. A garden gnome identical to the one on her front porch in Ventura stood beside the entry to the kitchen.

It's not the same *gnome, idiot.*

The realization came as a relief. Sweeping the room with her gaze, she took in the pile of laundry on the couch: a tangle of towels and undies waiting to be folded and put away. On the coffee table sat a stack of paperback mystery novels and a coffee-stained mug resting on the cover of a crossword puzzle magazine.

There were also several unopened envelopes with the same return address as the business card: California Highway Patrol, Fresno Area Office. *Fresno*. The postmarks indicated that some of them had been there a long time: March. April. May. June. July.

Her stomach flipped, remembering the road she had seen in her hypnotic trance. She had known right away it was in the Fresno area.

Adding the new gas bill to the pile, She plopped down on the couch and poked at the CHP envelopes as reluctantly as if they contained ricin. Even when she pushed them out of her line of sight, there was still the San Diego Police Department envelope.

It's probably not smart to ignore the SDPD.

I know.

Her fingers felt as thick as sausages as she opened the envelope and unfolded the single sheet of paper inside. The printed form notified Jessica Mack that a 2011 Honda Accord registered to her had been towed from the Solana Beach Amtrak Station last Monday. Ms. Mack would be required to pay a hefty fee to the City of San Diego to have the vehicle released to her.

All at once, the air felt heavy, as if she were trying to breathe at the bottom of a swimming pool. What had sent her rocketing out of here, according to Peyton Butler, like "*a bat out of hell,*" to take a train from Solana Beach to Ventura, leaving behind a car to get towed?

The CHP envelopes on the table invaded the corner of her vision.

Open them.

No freaking way.

It's got to be something important.

No!

She pushed off the couch and went to the kitchenette. A cereal bowl sat in the sink; the mushy granola on the bottom in rancid milk was as thick as yogurt. The trash under the sink smelled. A two-thirds full bottle of pinot noir stood on the counter, the cork next to it staining the white top purple.

Across the living room she could see through the bedroom door to the foot of an unmade bed. Her heart did a funny little bump. Was *this* where she would find the blood and gore she had been so sure she would discover in the Ventura apartment?

A simple box spring and mattress had been pushed against the wall to make room for a computer desk not unlike the one in Ventura. Once again, though, there was no blood staining the sheets, no brain matter splattering the walls. But there were fragments of a wine glass on the keyboard of a laptop computer, a mouthful of drying red wine pooled in the broken bowl.

First the smashed picture frame, now this. Sweeping up broken glass was becoming a habit in the life of Jenna Marcott.

Or Jessica Mack, depending on which apartment you're in.

She dumped the larger pieces of glass into a wastebasket under the desk, then fetched a hand towel from the bathroom and gently wiped the smaller fragments from the keyboard, removing what debris she could. Dark splash marks warned that the wine had probably soaked through to the motherboard.

Mentally crossing her fingers, she pressed the power button. The light came on and the hard drive gave a faint whir, but the screen stayed dark. With a sinking feeling, she removed the battery pack, counted to twenty and replaced it, then tried again. It *had* to work.

Nada. Zip. Zilch.

If Peyton Butler was to be believed—and there was ample

evidence to support her tale—the person known as Jessica Mack had bolted out of here on Friday night a week ago, upset enough to leave the front door wide open late in the evening. Upset enough to lob a glass at her laptop and leave it marinating in red wine?

Or had there been a physical confrontation and she'd dropped the glass while defending herself from—who?

What the hell happened here?

Jenna forced herself to sift through the facts as she knew them. The bottle of wine in the kitchen was more than half full. There was only one wine glass in evidence—the broken one that she had just cleaned up. From what she had gleaned from her neighbor, it sounded as though she had been alone at the time. So, *not* a physical confrontation.

A phone call? Had she been talking to Simon Lawrie?

As if on cue, a land line phone rang. Her heart was racing as she followed the sound to the kitchen counter and read the caller ID: Anonymous—a blocked number. She picked it up and said a tentative, "Hello?"

"Ms. Mack?" A deep male voice with a slight Texas twang asked.

"Who is this?"

"Detective Carl Galen here. I've been trying to reach you."

Oh hell.

"I—I just got here."

"You haven't answered any of my letters or returned my phone calls, so I stopped by your place the other day. Seems I missed you again."

Just "stopped by" three hundred miles south of Fresno?

"I've been out of town."

"Well, isn't it fortuitous that I found you just now. When could you be available for an interview, ma'am? I'll drive on back down there."

If he was prepared to make another six-hundred mile round trip to see her, it had to be serious.

Maybe he was coming to arrest her.

For what?

The silence filled up and spilled over. She cleared her throat, but her voice still sounded high and nervous. "Can't we just talk on the phone?"

Now it was her turn to wait for him to fill the void. In the end, he said, "I do believe it would be better if we do this in person, ma'am. We really need to talk about your husband."

TWENTY

"Ms. Mack? Ms. Mack? Hello—hello? Can you hear me? Are you there?"

My husband? I don't have—

Those baleful eyes staring back at her. The accident…Fresno.

Detective Galen was still talking when Jenna pressed the disconnect button and replaced the handset in its cradle. She raced around the apartment, closing windows and switching off lights, taking care to lock the door on her way out. She ran down the stairs propelled by one thought: *get away, get away, gotta get away.*

Heading back to the freeway she had a strong intuition—or maybe it was an actual memory—that her flight from Escondido today was scarcely less frenzied than the one a week ago that had been expunged from her memory.

What the hell happened that I needed so badly to forget it?

She darted a look at her bare left hand. If she had a husband, where was he? Why could she not remember him? Why wasn't she wearing a wedding ring? And why did a police detective from Fresno want to talk to her about him?

And what about Simon Lawrie?

Her mind staggered under the burden of what she didn't know. Oh God, what if she'd done something so awful that she'd wiped it from her memory along with everything else?

What if I killed him?

She drove with a lead foot, burning up the miles. By the time she reached the 405 junction, she thought she just might crack into a million pieces. Something told her if that happened she would never be able to recover.

The Venice Beach exits started to appear on the freeway signs and it crossed her mind to call Claudia Rose or Dr. Gold and confide in one of them. But after what she had learned this afternoon it seemed a monumentally bad idea to talk to anyone. When the Jefferson Boulevard exit came up, she kept driving.

Ventura was halfway between Kern County and Escondido. All day Sunday, Jenna stayed holed up in the apartment with the blinds drawn, petrified that Detective Galen would somehow uncover her whereabouts and come for her. Whatever he had to say, she knew she could not bear to hear it.

She contemplated googling Jessica Mack and her alleged husband. Even got as far as standing in front of the computer. The cold, dead eye of the monitor glared at her, daring her to switch it on and risk opening Pandora's box.

Now that she thought about it, the Greek myth made a good symbol for her situation. Pandora's box held all the evils of the world. When Pandora got too curious and disobeyed the order not to open the box under any circumstances, every bad thing flew out and contaminated the earth.

But hope was left at the bottom.

Better to leave the lid shut tight and keep it there.

Monday morning dawned after yet another restless night filled with spirits as hideous as Harry Potter's Dementors rising from a chest at the bottom of the ocean, coiling themselves like vines around her throat, dragging her down. She got out of bed weary and depressed. Her trip to Escondido had unearthed no new memories, but at least now she knew why the sight of a police uniform freaked her out: there was a detective in pursuit of her.

The face that looked back at her in the bathroom mirror that morning was as drawn and pale as the wraiths of her nightmares. Dark circles bruised the tissue under her eyes. *You can't remember anything that you'd like to*, she mocked her reflection, *but you'd like to* forget *Detective Galen, and there he is, right up front in your head.*

Shower, dress…the thought of eating made her ill. Drive to BioNeutronics. It was becoming routine.

Although he had not told her who he was going to see, Jenna knew that Simon was scheduled for a meeting that would last all morning. That was fine with her. It eased the pressure of fending off the unwelcome passes he insisted on making at her.

At nine-forty Keisha called on the office intercom and asked to be relieved at the switchboard while she took her coffee break. The employee who usually replaced her had a dental appointment and would be out of the office until after lunch. Jenna was her next backup.

They traded places at the reception desk and Keisha handed over her headset. "It's been totally dead. I'm falling asleep. Gonna run across the street for a triple."

"Starbucks?"

"Yeah, the coffee here just ain't cuttin' it. Want anything?"

"No, thanks. I'll go later."

"Okay, see you in twenty."

Jenna sat down and studied the console. Operating the system was easier than she had expected. The button next to each extension was marked with a printed name and she only disconnected one caller as she got to know her way around the switchboard.

She was starting to relax when a man in a gardener's tan uniform exited the elevator and came towards the reception desk. His eyes flicked around the lobby, as if fearing he might be accused of trespassing. He took off his hat as he approached the reception desk and Jenna read his name tag: Ramon Gutierrez.

Leaning his elbows on the high counter, he spoke in a low voice. "I gotta talk to somebody in Security."

Like a co-conspirator, Jenna lowered her voice, too. "What's the problem?"

"Uh, I think I should talk to *them*. Can you just call them?"

Her hand hovered over the telephone keypad, ready to punch in Kevin Nguyen's number. "Is it an emergency?"

"Well…not exactly."

"I'll have to tell them something before I ask someone to come up."

"You sure?" The gardener glanced around again, clearly nervous.

"Why do you need security?"

"Well…the other night, you know? I found something."

An instant premonition curdled in Jenna's stomach. "The other night?"

"Yeah, it was last Thursday. I was working late, finishin' up after everybody left. I got backed up, so I had to stay over. Then Friday I was at another facility, so this is the first chance I got to come and report it."

Jenna stood up. She knew without a doubt what Ramon Gutierrez was going to say next.

"Yeah, so, anyways. I saw this cup on top of one of the bushes right up next to the building? You know, a paper cup, not a real one—and I was gonna put it in the trash. But I dropped it on the ground and this lil gizmo fell out of it."

He seemed to forget his discomfort as he warmed to his story. "It was weird, you know? It was stuck in there like it was hidden? I figured I better bring it in."

Having resigned herself to the idea that it was irretrievably lost, Jenna had all but forgotten the flash drive. Now, she held out a hand. "Can I see it?"

Ramon Gutierrez dug into his pants pocket and took out the plastic baggie with the flash drive still sealed inside, just as she'd left it. Jenna glanced at the clock. Keisha was due back from her break. "You can leave this with me," she told him. "I'll make sure the right person gets it."

"But…you don't think I should talk to Security?" Ramon said, sounding disappointed.

"It's okay. I'm the Director's assistant. You can trust me; I'll take care of it."

"Well…okay, if you're sure. It's a computer thing, right? It was kinda weird, you know? It was just lying there on top of—"

"You did the right thing," Jenna broke in. "Just don't mention it to anyone else, okay? It's better if you don't talk to *anyone* about it in case Security wants to talk to you later."

"Wow, no kidding? Good thing I found it, huh?"

Across the lobby, Jenna saw the light come on above the elevator, and heard the 'ping' of the cab arriving. "Yes, it's a very good thing. You'd better get back to work before someone starts looking for you. Remember, don't say anything to anyone."

"Okay." He shrugged, turned and walked back to the elevator, avoiding looking at Keisha, who threw him a curious glance. Jenna quickly stuffed the plastic baggie in her jacket pocket.

"What'd *he* want?" Keisha asked, taking back the headset Jenna handed her.

"Just some aspirin."

Luckily, Keisha's mind was on other things and she didn't see through the thin answer. "I saw Raul Melendez over at Starbucks," she said with a sly grin. "You know, that guy in Accounting? He's pretty hot. I get the feeling that when he talks about having coffee, he doesn't mean just a Caramel Macchiato."

Jenna nodded and smiled in all the right places, but her mind was moving at warp speed. That she had been at the reception desk when Ramon Gutierrez showed up with the flash drive was an incredible break. It didn't bear thinking that if she had been in her own office, the drive would have ended up in the hands of the security department.

Simon seemed absent-minded when he arrived at Jenna's desk a few minutes before noon, entering, as usual, without knocking.

She looked up at him. "How was your meeting?"

He pulled his money clip out and peeled off a couple of tens, not answering her question. "Would you pick me up a broccoli beef bowl."

"So, it wasn't a good meeting?" she persisted, curious about where he had been.

He threw her a look that made her wonder. "It was a briefing with my wife and I don't want to talk about it. How about that lunch?"

Jenna stood in line at China Wok, contemplating the coldness of having to have a briefing with your spouse. Her stomach roiled. According to Detective Galen, *she* had a spouse. Was that why she and Simon had gravitated to one another? Because they were both in relationship denial? She didn't want to think about that any more than Simon wanted to talk about his 'briefing.'

He was on the phone when she dropped off his food, and she returned to her desk, glad that for once, he had not tried to detain her. An idea was forming to get the flash drive safely out of the building.

She downed a few forkfuls of vegetable and noodles, not ever tasting them, then created a well in middle of the noodles. Laying the baggie with the flash drive into it, she piled noodles and veggies on top and snapped the plastic lid into place, pleased with her solution.

As she was placing the bowl into the carry-out bag the door opened, and Simon entered. The man obviously had a sixth sense for exactly the wrong time to come looking for her.

"Smells like a Chinese restaurant in here," he said, closing the door behind him.

Jenna offered him a thin smile. "Maybe you should change your diet."

Simon smiled back, showing her the charm. "Maybe I will." Apparently having forgotten that they were still at odds with one another, he eased behind her chair and began to knead her shoulders with strong fingers. "You're really tense, baby. You need a massage."

She shrugged him off. "Stop it! You're hurting me. And anyone could walk—"

He bent down, his face close to hers, his warm breath soft as velvet against her ear. "Tomorrow," he interrupted smoothly. "Tomorrow, we'll take the afternoon off and go someplace nice. Think about where you'd like to go. Our favorite suite at the Crowne Plaza?"

"Why are you in here, Simon? Is there something you want from me?"

"There certainly is, Ms. Marcott, but there's not enough time for that right now." When she failed to respond, he straightened and huffed an irritated sigh. "Christ, Jen, you're *still* mad? How long are you going to hold a grudge? We'll talk about it all tomorrow, I promise."

"It's not holding a grudge, Simon. You're married."

He made an impatient sound, blowing off the important fact to which she had just called his attention. "The new Project 42 scientists are here. I need you to go down to reception and get them."

Jenna rose. "I'll bring them up."

When she stepped out of the elevator, the two people seated on the sofa in the reception area glanced over at her with expectant looks. Both were close to middle-aged, one male, one female, as matching as the briefcases at their feet.

They looked like stereotypical movie scientists: thin, pale, plain, serious. His hair was blond, trimmed very short; hers was medium brown, set in a fifties shoulder-length pageboy style brushed away from her face. Both wore iron-grey suits that were more suitable to an east coast winter than a couple of miles from the Pacific Ocean on a late August afternoon.

Jenna pasted on a welcoming smile and started across the lobby towards them.

"They no speaka de Engles," Keisha said *sotto voce*, as she neared the reception desk.

"None?"

"Nope. They came in with Simon's name written on a piece of paper. Dr. Paschke and Dr. Lessig."

Jenna raised a dubious brow. "Should be interesting."

She smiled at the pair again and said hello. She didn't know which was Dr. Paschke and which was Dr. Lessig, but each scientist acknowledged her with an unsmiling nod and rose to follow when she motioned them to come along.

In the elevator, the woman spoke to her colleague in a language unfamiliar to Jenna, but she guessed it might be something Eastern European. The man snapped back a sharp response, and the woman lowered her head and looked down at her shoes for the rest of the short ride.

Simon answered her knock with a call to enter. Toward the rear of the spacious corner office, the plush armchairs around the conference table were occupied by Simon, an Asian man with slicked-back grey hair and old-fashioned horn-rimmed glasses, and Dr. Raisa Polzin in her usual white lab coat.

A third man stood alone at the window. Easily six-five and as hefty as a quarterback, his shaved head was deeply tanned, as if he spent a great deal of time outdoors. Despite being indoors now, his eyes were hidden behind the kind of dark glasses she associated with Secret Service agents. One of Christine Palmer's security detail? The senator herself was not in evidence.

The man stood with his arms crossed like Mr. Clean in the old TV commercials from Jenna's childhood. Except that Mr. Clean wore an earring and a friendly smile. This man was not smiling and remained in the background, a mere shadow that nobody introduced or acknowledged.

Something about him spooked Jenna. She was quite certain that this was not the first time she had seen him, and equally certain that their acquaintance was not a friendly one.

Everyone but Mr. Clean tipped their heads at one another and Simon greeted the visitors Jenna had in tow. Raisa Polzin, the scientist, hurried forward, hand outstretched, speaking to the newcomers in German.

After introducing Simon Lawrie, Polzin indicated the Asian man, who rose from his chair and came forward. She said, "Kevin Nguyen," and something that sounded like "shefdersicherheight."

The security chief greeted them in heavily accented German that got the visitors grinning. Age lines carved in Nguyen's sallow face and the deep, droopy bags under his eyes gave him the look of an old basset hound. He turned to Jenna. "I've already taken care of their clearances. No need to inform Human Resources. They're acting as consultants, not on the payroll." He pursed his lips, his head cocked to one side in an appraising way. "I want to talk with you," he said. "Not today. Maybe tomorrow."

Something in Nguyen's tone worried her. The sooner she got the flash drive out of the building, the better.

Jenna was sorting Simon's afternoon mail when Detective Jovanic phoned.

"I have some information for you," he said.

"That was fast. What—?"

"Are you free this afternoon if I drive up to Ventura? I'd like to meet with you in person."

Her pulse started thrumming. "I get off work at five. Is something wrong? Is it something bad?"

"Let's wait and talk later. Can we meet at your place?"

Jenna gave him the address and they agreed to meet at five-thirty. She clicked off the call with a bad vibe. Maybe there was a good reason why she had forgotten her past. In truth, she was no longer sure she wanted to learn about it.

There was no surprise inspection at BioNeutronics that afternoon, but carrying the flash drive through the front doors concealed in the China Wok bag made Jenna feel less vulnerable. It still took all her self-control once she got out of the building not to run to the Nissan.

Waiting in line to turn out of the parking lot, she glanced in the rearview mirror and noticed a black SUV behind her. The upper area of the windshield was tinted, but she could see well enough to identify the driver as the big man from Simon Lawrie's office. Not knowing where had she seen him before, or under what circumstances, left her with a sour feeling in the pit of her stomach.

When she turned left, the SUV turned left and stayed behind her all the way up Vineyard. When she entered the freeway, the SUV did, too. Jenna glanced over at the takeout bag on the seat beside her. There was no way anyone could know about the flash drive hidden inside. *Was there?* And if they did, why was that worth tracking her movements?

With afternoon rush hour traffic clogging the roads, Jenna was unable to get more than a car length away from the SUV. She kept one eye on the rearview mirror, but quickly lost sight of it. Maybe she was just being paranoid after all.

TWENTY-ONE

A white vintage Jaguar was parked at the curb in front of Jenna's apartment building. She drove past and turned into the alleyway, her stomach twisting with anxiety. She had spotted Claudia Rose in the passenger seat. Why would Detective Jovanic bring Claudia with him, unless he needed help softening the blow of bad news?

She's his girlfriend, stupid. They're probably going to a romantic dinner at the beach later.

As Jenna shut off the engine, the thought crossed her mind to run and hide. But she had waited too long. By the time she walked around the back of the carport to her gate, her visitors were already halfway up the path from the front of the building.

Claudia gave her a warm smile. "Hi, Jenna. Good to see you again."

"I'm sorry the place is kind of a mess," Jenna mumbled, opening the front door. "I didn't know I was going to have company."

"Don't worry about it; we're not here to judge your housekeeping."

"I should have cleaned up yesterday, but..."

"Seriously," Claudia said. "Don't worry. Oh, look at the gnome, Joel. I love garden gnomes. My English grandmother always had them."

"There's a matching one in the Escondido apartment."

"So, you've been to Escondido," said Detective Jovanic,

following her inside.

"I went after I saw you on Saturday. It was a lot closer to go from Venice than from here. I went to the Marina del Rey apartment first, but that was a dead end."

Jenna set the China Wok takeout bag on the kitchen counter and hurried to snatch up the blanket and socks she had left in a heap on the couch the night before. She flung them in the bedroom and closed the door, collected dirty cups and glasses from the coffee table and dumped them in the sink.

Her visitors sat together on the loveseat. Both declined her offer of something to drink. "How did it go in Escondido?" Detective Jovanic asked.

Jenna removed her suit coat and took the armchair. "I found my—the Jessica Mack name on a mailbox. There was a tow notice from the San Diego police that says I left a Honda at the Amtrak station." She should tell him about Detective Galen, but she wouldn't. "I ran into a neighbor there who called me Jess. And I remembered her name; Peyton Butler."

"Did you learn anything from her?"

"Just that she said I left in a big hurry. I only talked to her for a minute."

"And you were able to get into the apartment?"

"I had a key."

"Did you recognize anything?"

"Just the gnome. Like I said, there was a matching one." Jenna began to fidget under the probing of the detective's laser sharp grey eyes. "Something had happened in the bedroom." She fumbled for the right words to describe the scene. "There was a broken wineglass on the laptop keyboard. It wouldn't boot up. The wine had spilled…"

"Did you happen to bring the laptop back with you? There are ways to recover information, even with liquid on the motherboard."

Remembering the hasty retreat she had beat from the apartment, Jenna shook her head. "No. I—I left without it. If you think it might be important, I could go back and get it."

"I don't think for our purposes that will be necessary." The detective adjusted his position on the loveseat and sat forward. "Jenna, as I told you over the phone, I have some information for you. First, let me ask you a question. Have you spoken with a Detective Galen from Fresno?"

There was no way to hide her look of guilt. "No—yes—I mean…" She cast her gaze past Detective Jovanic's shoulder, staring at the wall, the coffee table, the floor—anywhere but those penetrating eyes. He must know she had spoken with Galen. Maybe the two detectives had already conferred about her.

An iron band was squeezing her rib cage until she couldn't catch her breath. Once again, she experienced the peculiar sensation of floating outside her body, as if she were connected by little more than a thread to the young woman huddled in the armchair.

She heard kitchen cabinets being opened and closed; the faucet running, then Claudia put a glass in her hand. Keeping her own warm hand over Jenna's icy one, she said, "Breathe in through your nose and hold it for a couple of seconds. That's right. Now, exhale slowly and drink a little water." She turned to the detective. "We need a paper bag for her to breathe into."

Jenna shook her head. "No, I'm fine. I'm fine."

"We don't have to hurry this," Jovanic said. "Why don't you take it easy for a minute."

"Please. I need to know. I don't want to, but I *need* to know." She gulped water from the glass, almost choking in her haste. "Let's just get it over with. *Please*. What do you have to tell me?"

"Okay. You were correct that you were involved in a highway collision." Detective Jovanic removed a sheaf of papers from his jacket pocket and unfolded them. "This is the report of an automobile accident that occurred last February along the Grapevine in Kern County."

"The Grapevine! That's what I saw in the trance with Dr. Gold. It was the part where the highway goes through the mountains."

"Detective Galen is the investigator on the case. He's with the MAIT."

"What's that?"

"It's the Multidisciplinary Accident Investigation Team. They get involved in investigating major traffic collisions."

"But you said the accident would only be in your system if there was an arrest."

"Yes, that's correct. There *was* an arrest in your case."

"Who was arrested? Was it me?"

Jovanic took a pair of reading glasses from his pocket and after he'd put them on, bent his head and read from the report: "I'll just summarize: A motorist named Gregory Justin Mack was arrested by California Highway Patrol officers on February 19 of this year in the Grapevine section of Northbound Interstate 5. Mr. Mack was charged with reckless driving and second degree murder in a traffic collision that resulted in the severe injury of his wife, Jessica Mack." He glanced over, gauging her reaction, giving her time to digest what he had told her.

Detective Galen's voice rang in Jenna's head: '*...about your husband...*"

"Murder." she echoed in a faint voice.

Jovanic continued reading, "Second degree murder in the death of a minor child, Justin Mack."

Justin.

The name hammered at the door of her consciousness.

Let me in.

No! I can't.

Let me...

I can't. I'm sorry. I can't.

Mama, please...

"Jenna? Jenna, are you all right?" Claudia's voice came through the fog.

How can I be all right?

"Yes. I'm fine."

'...about *your husband...*"

"Would you like me to call someone for you?"

Who is there to call?

"No, thank you." The words were automatic, her voice robotic.

"Would you like me to stop?" Detective Jovanic asked.

"No."

He returned to reading the accident report in a gentle monotone, as though a calm voice could soften the poisonous blows he was raining down on her. "Ms. Mack, who was not wearing a seatbelt, was thrown from the car."

I was trying to stop him from crying.

No! Don't go there.

When Claudia reached over and took her hands again, Jenna realized that her mind was straying and tried to pull it back.

"...sustained a serious head injury and was in a coma for approximately two weeks. This was Mr. Mack's second DUI. His blood alcohol level was 2.0, which is, of course, well above the legal limit of .08." Jovanic glanced up again and said, "that's why it was charged as a homicide."

"What—what happened to—to him?"

"He's currently a guest of the California Penal System at the Pitchess Honor Rancho—that's the County Jail in Santa Clarita. He's awaiting trial, which is set to begin October 4. It seems Detective Galen has been trying to contact you to interview you about the accident. The district attorney would like you to testify as a witness but, of course, he can't legally *compel* you to testify against your spouse."

"No." What was the matter with her voice? She couldn't raise it above a whisper.

"I'm truly sorry for your loss," said the detective.

"No! This can't be right. You're telling me I'm Jessica Mack, but I'm not, I'm Jenna Marcott. I don't have a husband. I don't have a child. I don't believe you."

Don't believe the evidence on your own driver's license? Don't believe the evidence in your own hypnotic trance, your nightmares? The Escondido apartment? Peyton Butler? Jenna shook her head, trying to shut out the voice that only she could hear.

Claudia crouched beside her chair and put an arm around her shoulders. "Give yourself a few minutes, Jenna. Just take it slowly."

"You think I stole this woman's identification. That's what you think, isn't it? Because she's not me."

"No, sweetheart, that's not what we think. Remember the scar on your head that you showed Dr. Gold?"

Jenna's hand went up automatically and touched the ridge on her scalp. She snatched her hand back and put it under her thigh, as though it were guilty of creating the slight rope of scar tissue.

Claudia said, "This morning, Joel—Detective Jovanic—spoke with the neurosurgeon who took care of...Jessica after the accident. The surgeon said there was a two-inch incision behind her left ear as a result of the accident and then surgery."

Detective Jovanic added, "After leaving the hospital, Jessica was scheduled for a follow-up appointment, but she never showed. The doctor's office tried several times but was unable to contact her." He glanced over at her. "The address they had was the apartment in Marina del Rey, in care of Jenna Marcott. Their letters were returned, no forwarding order. Galen was able to trace her to the Escondido address. So you *are* Jessica Mack, and it seems that Jenna Marcott is the identity you adopted to—"

She covered her ears with her hands, resisting the words. "I want you to leave now."

"Jenna..." Claudia said.

"Thank you for everything you've done, but you have to leave." Jenna started to rise but her legs gave out and she dropped back into the armchair.

"I know this is tough news for you," Detective Jovanic began. "We—"

"Please," she said. "Just leave."

"You shouldn't be alone," Claudia said.

"I'm not alone. My upstairs neighbor is a friend. I'm fine."

"Would you like us to—"

"No. I don't want you to do anything except go. Thank you for coming all the way up here. I know you're trying to help me..." She knew she sounded angry. She *was* angry. Who were these people to tell her she had a dead child? "I told you to go."

It's your fault he's dead, Jessica.

No!

She jumped when Claudia touched her lightly on the shoulder. "You have our phone numbers," the handwriting analyst reminded her. "You can call either of us anytime, day or night."

Detective Jovanic gave Jenna's shoulder a reassuring pat. "When you're ready to talk about it," he said. "We'll be here."

After the door closed behind them she sat in the armchair for a time as ice formed in her veins. She thought she might never be warm again. Eventually, she changed into jeans and a sweatshirt, but the warm clothing did little for the goosebumps. It didn't matter. Nothing mattered.

Hugging her knees to her chest, she rocked back and forth like a small child. Her instincts had been right. Detective Jovanic had brought Claudia Rose to help deliver bad news. The worst of all possible news a person can receive.

For hours she sat there rocking, doing her damndest to retreat into the protective cocoon that the amnesia had provided. When that didn't work, she tested herself to see whether she could remember.

My baby boy.

My son.

Her conscious memory was still as empty as ever. But as much as she wanted to deny it, she knew in the depths of her soul that she and Jessica Mack were one and the same.

An aching sadness left her feeling as though she had bathed in Novocain. Shouldn't she be raging at the man whose careless drunken state was responsible for the death of their child?

Her eyes shifted to the stack of sealed moving cartons in the corner, before shifting away again. She no longer wanted the answers those boxes might hold, the answers she had been resisting.

Against her will, new questions started popping up like balloons held under water and released: *How long have I been Jenna Marcott? If the accident was in February, why have I only now developed amnesia?*

The voice in her head mocked her. Who said it was only now? For all she knew, this could be the latest in an entire series of episodes.

How did her job at BioNeutronics fit in? And her relationship with Simon, who didn't seem to think there was anything unusual about her? How long had she been carrying on a double life?

In just a few minutes, Detective Jovanic had ripped down the fragile walls she had built for herself, the illusion she had created over the past week, and now she had nothing left. No defenses. She considered death, but could not find the strength to get out of the chair and kill herself.

Eventually, like frostbitten nerve endings coming alive, the pain made its way to the surface, so fresh, so visceral, that every cell in her body protested the violence of it. How could something that did not originate from a physical cause hurt so much?

Jenna—no, *Jessica*—hauled herself out of the chair and gulped down a half-dozen ibuprofen with a slug of wine straight from the bottle she'd left on the counter. Pouring it into a glass took more effort than she was willing to expend. It didn't matter that it dribbled onto her sweatshirt; the neat freak had effectively disappeared. Jessica threw herself on the bed and prayed for dreamless sleep.

Her prayers went unanswered. The nightmares were more vivid than ever and she awoke sweating and feverish, with an awareness that, once again, these dreams were not about the car accident. Trying to recall the hazy scenes only made them evaporate faster, leaving her with no understanding of what had frightened her so badly.

Jessica's mouth was as dry as parchment. She had not cried a single tear, yet her eyes felt gritty and swollen, as if she'd wept an ocean. Lying atop the bedspread she was too depleted even to roll off the bed and get a glass of water.

The accident report had said that she had a husband who hated her enough to want to kill her. But they must have loved each other at one time. They'd made a beautiful baby boy together. What had made that love disappear so completely? His threat echoed: "I'll take you with me."

What kind of mother doesn't remember her own child?

What kind of man tries to kill his family?

What kind of woman stays with a man like that?

A woman named Jessica Mack.

She tried to shut out the voice's unbroken criticism of her every failure, every sin, but something outside her head penetrated. Something outside the apartment. The sound of a metallic clink of a latch engaging and a gate being closed with care.

Aside from her meeting with Zach Smith on the day she had begun this version of her life as Jenna Marcott, Jessica had yet to encounter anyone else in the apartment building. Each night over the past week she'd heard the next door neighbor coming and going at eleven forty-five and assumed that the person who lived there worked the graveyard shift. A glance at the bedside clock told her it was one fifty-four. Graveyard started at midnight. The neighbor must be very late for work.

Then her ears picked up a much closer sound. A scraping on the front porch, followed by the soft rattle of the doorknob…

Someone's breaking in.

TWENTY-TWO

Instantly alert, Jessica sat up in bed, listening hard. The faint sound of a pick scratched at the lock.

Need to call 911.

The phone was in her purse in the living room.

Quiet as a cat, she was on her feet, covering the few yards that took her to the doorway. Her gaze caught on the wooden knife block on the kitchen counter. It was cold comfort that the intruder didn't know she was awake and just ten feet from a weapon that could filet him. Jessica tiptoed forward, options clicking like a stop-action video in her head.

The lock sprang as she was crossing the entry. The door swung inward and the sharp metal weather stripping raked her bare toes. From the porch came a low grunt of surprise. Her involuntary yelp of pain had stolen any advantage she might have had.

Jessica dove for the knife block, but a hulking figure lunged across the threshold and snatched a fistful of her sweatshirt. He twirled her around with whiplash speed and clamped a heavy hand over her face, making it impossible to scream or even breathe.

Mindless fear mobilized her and she started squirming, kicking with her heels at her attacker's shins. But the way he had her pinned with her feet off the ground, she couldn't get purchase and her kicks landed far off the mark.

The man shook her like a rag doll. "Get in here," he rasped to a second person she had not seen. "Grab her legs, goddamn it!"

Some higher part of her brain that still functioned with clarity caught the sound of the front door closing and the lock sliding into place. It was the lower reptilian brain that mobilized her to keep bucking wildly. The man who held her was roughly the size of a mountain.

The second intruder seized her shins and banged her ankles together, holding on like a bronco rider determined to break a rowdy filly. "Jesus, she's a feisty little bitch," he said, with a tinge of admiration.

Desperate for air, Jessica tried to twist her head and get the massive hand off her nostrils, but the mountain's arm was a lead weight pinning her against his chest.

"If you ever want to breathe again," he said in her ear, "you'd better knock it off right now."

She forced herself to go limp and felt herself carried a few feet across the floor. Her back hit the padded arm hard as they dropped her into the armchair, but at least her mouth was free and she could fill her lungs.

Moonlight filtered through the half-closed vertical blinds on the sliding glass door at the back of the living room, not bright enough to see her captors' features. But Jessica did not have to see them to know who they were. Even before he ordered his flunky to shut the blinds and find a light she recognized the silent giant who had stood at the back of Simon's office.

It took an extra second to identify the other man as Nate Farley. The name came to her before she connected it to the security guard who had caught her poking around at BioNeutronics last Thursday night. He had replaced his guard uniform with a black turtleneck shirt that covered his arms, and black pants. His buzz cut was now concealed under a black watch cap like the one she had worn at their first meeting.

Jessica scrambled to right herself in the chair. The big man loomed over her. Without his Ray-Bans concealing them, his eyes had the cold detachment of a shark sizing up its prey. "You gonna keep your mouth shut," he snapped. "Or do I have to gag you?"

The adrenaline rush had subsided and her teeth were chattering. She wrapped her arms around her knees. "You—ffollowed me from the lab," she managed in a shaky voice.

He squatted in front of her, a fake smile pasted on a face as grim as Death. "Well, I had to know where you were staying so we could come and pay you this little visit. Imagine my surprise when you led me here."

"Wh-what do you want?"

The smile disappeared. "I want the files you stole."

Jessica had no doubt he was referring to the flash drive. Her eyes slid to the takeout bag on the kitchen counter, where the drive was still hidden under the noodles. In the face of the news that Detective Jovanic and Claudia Rose had dropped on her—that Jessica Mack was the grieving mother of a dead child—the flash drive and Project 42 had lost any significance.

Project 42 was significant to someone, though. Enough to send these thugs to break into her home and terrorize her in the middle of the night. What should she do? The familiar voice answered quickly: *Deny, deny, deny.*

Well, why not? She'd been denying her entire life for a while now.

"What are you talking about?" She asked, doing her best to sound indignant. "I haven't stolen anything."

She could see the man evaluating her, taking her measure. He shook his head. "Don't bother denying it. The network is configured to do send an alarm to security When privileged files are downloaded or copied."

"I don't know what you're talking about. I didn't download anything." It was easy enough to sound convincing when she couldn't remember having done it.

The mountain straightened to his full height. Even if he never opened his mouth, his size and his air of authority would put him in charge. He leveled a mean stare at her; his voice held the low rumble of thunder. "I'm warning you not to fuck with me."

"I'm not! I'm serious. I don't know how—"

"Who are you?"

The curt question took her aback. "You *know* who I am. Who sent you to break into my apartment?"

"*I'm* asking the questions here. Now, you *will* shut your smart mouth and answer me." He raised a fist the size of a ham hock.

Jessica recoiled into the crook of the armchair, waiting for the blow to strike. "I'm Jenna Marcott."

For an endless moment he looked down at her, the flat eyes unreadable. Then, with the speed of a much smaller man he cuffed the side of her head with an open palm, hard. "You are *not* Jenna Marcott."

Jessica's head snapped back. Her hand flew to her ear, which was hot and stinging from the slap. "Hitting me isn't going to change who I am!"

Through a glaze of tears she saw the moment when Farley spotted her purse. He grabbed it and started pawing through her things, holding her wallet aloft like a prize. "She's got two sets of ID, Mr. Bagshot," he said. "One in the Marcott name and an AKA—Jessica Mack, address in Escondido."

With a satisfied nod, the mountain, Bagshot, compressed his lips into a thin line. "Okay, Jessica Mack, who sent you to BioNeutronics?"

Jessica heard the words, but he might as well have been speaking a foreign language; the whistling in her head drowned him out. A mesh of black spots formed in front of her eyes and she began to fade.

She was viewing a familiar scene play out.

Seated at her computer in the bedroom, yet watching from afar. Her blonde hair, longer than it was now, pulled into a ragged ponytail. Bagshot at the bedroom door, arms crossed. Another man, not Farley, behind her. Bending to crook his arm around her throat. Her head jerks back, connects with his nose. A cloud of red spray hits the monitor, drips on the keyboard tray.

She was back in the armchair, panting and queasy, Bagshot crouched in front of her as if genuflecting. "Hey, Jessica!" His stale breath reeked of too much coffee and too many cigarettes. "Hey! Where'd you go?"

Her stomach roiling, she turned her face away, but Bagshot grasped the arms of her chair and leaned in closer until his hawkish nose was a couple of inches from hers.

"Answer me *now*, Jessica, who hired you?"

"Simon Lawrie hired me."

Bagshot cuffed her again, harder and she cried out in pain.

"Where are the files you took?" He gave her no time to reply before his knuckles connected with her cheekbone. Jessica understood, when there was no crunch of breaking bones, that he had pulled his punch, giving her just a taste of what was to come if she didn't supply the answer he wanted. Her hand went up to her cheek, fury making her foolhardy. "What kind of asshole hits a chick half his size?"

"The kind who's gonna snap that chick in half if she doesn't start cooperating."

"But I don't *know* about any files. Beating me up isn't going to change it."

Bagshot let out a sigh of exaggerated patience and nodded at Farley. "I guess we have to do this the hard way."

Farley unsnapped a leather sheath on his belt and withdrew a hunting knife with a blade that looked sharp enough to slit her throat in one quick swipe. The chilling thought came to Jessica that maybe her earlier certainty that there would be blood in the apartment had been a premonition of her own death. She shrank away, her mind spinning.

Farley leaned in and brought the knife close to her nose, touching the tip to her skin hard enough to draw a bead of blood. Seeing the sadistic pleasure on the security guard's face, Jessica was sure that he would not hesitate to follow through.

If she told them where the flash drive was, would they let her go? Probably not. The crazy thing was, even if Bagshot was telling the truth and she *was* an industrial spy, she had no clue who she might be working for.

The light glinted off the blade as Farley raised the knife high.

Jessica drew breath to blurt the truth. The words were still forming on her lips when Farley veered towards the loveseat. He raised his knife high. The leather cushion ruptured with a soft pop that denied the violence of the act. He dug into the cushions, ripping the knife from one edge to the other. Mounds of cotton batting littered the floor.

"Please, stop," Jessica whispered hoarsely. "You won't find anything in there."

Bagshot grabbed her chin and wrenched her face to look at him. "Where, then?"

"Nowhere! You've made a mistake."

His lip curled in derision. "You know, Jessica, I expected more professionalism from someone like you. Or is this your first job?"

"I'm *not* a spy!"

"Okay, then, explain to me what you've been doing masquerading as Jenna Marcott, and what you're doing in her apartment?"

"What—what are you talking about?"

"You don't seem to understand, *Jessica*. This isn't something that's going to be settled with lawyers and litigation. It's not one of those situations where your principal gets sued and you walk away. The stakes in this game are way too high for that penny-ante crap."

"Please—I don't know what you mean."

Bagshot flashed her a look of utter contempt, as if she had disappointed him. "You might look a lot like Jenna Marcott, but you'd better get this, Jessica Mack: your mission is a failure. Your mission is scrubbed." He turned to Farley. "Might as well check under the tables. See if she's got anything taped there."

"Yessir."

Farley tipped over the tables on either end of the loveseat and ran his meaty fingers inside the facings. Finding nothing, he knocked the small dining table onto its side with a clatter, scattering the contents of Jessica's purse across the floor.

"Goddammit," Bagshot snarled. "Are you *trying* to wake up her neighbors?" Giving Farley the stink eye, he ordered him to open the moving boxes still stacked in the corner; the boxes Jessica had instinctively avoided.

The security guard pulled down the top carton and sliced his knife through neat strips of packing tape. College textbooks, novels, and cookbooks came tumbling out on the floor as he tipped it on its side. Jessica looked on as he tore the covers off the books.

The second box held childhood keepsakes nested lovingly in newspaper cocoons. The first casualty was a crookedly formed ceramic cup that Jessica, watching, heartsick, guessed must be from the first or second grade. Blue glaze chips went skittering as Farley hurled it to the tile floor.

A china Belle figurine went next, ground to dust under his heel. He pulled out a miniature satin pillow, the lace trim sewn on with the big stitches of a small hand, and slashed it with his knife. A well-loved old teddy bear was not immune, either. There was an evil glee in his eyes as he ripped off the arms and tossed them aside. He went on until every item in the box was wrecked.

The remnants of a forgotten childhood—there was nothing she could do to save them. Left with an unutterable sadness, Jessica remembered none of these objects, but she recognized how much they must have meant to her, seeing that she had held on to them through the years.

When Farley started on the third box: photo albums, Jessica caught her breath. Surely photographs would jog her memory. She wanted to beg him to spare them, but knowing her pleas would only egg him on, held her tongue.

Before he could do more damage, though, Bagshot barked at Farley to let it go. "We've wasted enough time here." He clamped Jessica's shoulder in a crushing grip and yanked her off the chair.

"Get your shoes on, Jessica Mack. You're coming with us."

TWENTY-THREE

He warned her before they left the apartment that he would make her regret it if she made the slightest noise. Her face throbbed where he'd struck her, and she was in no hurry to test him. She was pretty sure Zach would come to her aid if she screamed for help, but she was afraid of what they would do to him. Her neighbor might be a tough guy when he was facing the pothead from the train, but he wouldn't stand a chance against these two brutes.

They hustled her out of the apartment and around to the carport where Bagshot's black Mercedes SUV was parked behind the Nissan.

Farley opened the back door to the SUV. He pushed her inside and climbed in after her. "Don't get any ideas," he warned. "Kid locks." His heavy arm pinned her against the seat as he reached across and rattled the door handle to prove his point.

Up front, Bagshot's muscular body filled the driver's seat. Glancing in the rearview mirror, he caught the look of cold hatred Jessica cast at him. Without a word, he reached into the glove box and took out a thick plastic strap that was looped in the middle. He threw it back to Farley. "Hook her up."

"No! You don't have to do that."

The security guard flipped her around with practiced skill and had her right wrist cuffed before she could finish her sentence. A half-second later both hands were locked behind her back.

She cried out at the plastic digging into her wrists. "Where are you taking me, you sonofabitch?"

"I think she needs a gag," Bagshot said.

"No!"

Farley peeled off his watch cap. Jessica tried to squirm away, but half-turned in his seat, Bagshot brought his fist back and caught the bridge of her nose with his knuckles.

Pain as harsh and blinding as a lightning strike hit her between the eyes. She was still trying to catch her breath when Farley pulled the knit cap over her head and face. Blood trickled from her nose and slid down her upper lip, leaving a salty taste in her mouth, but with her hands pinned behind her back there was nothing she could do about it.

"You want that cap stuffed in your smart mouth?" Bagshot snarled. "*Do* you, bitch? You'd better answer when I ask you a question."

"No."

"Then keep your fucking mouth shut and you *might* get out of this with all your teeth. Farley, get her out of sight."

"You got it, boss." The security guard pushed her down until she was sprawled, half-kneeling on the floor, her face pressed into his groin.

The watch cap was hot and itchy and smelled rancid. It made her want to retch. At least if she wiped her nose on his pants, maybe her DNA would identify her if her killers were ever caught. Her shoulders were already aching from being stuck in the unnatural position and her nose had quickly swollen, making it hard to breathe. She wondered whether it was broken. Not that it would matter if they were going to kill her, and she was pretty sure they were.

What did I stumble into?

What the hell is *Project 42?*

Where are they taking me?

When the SUV came to a halt about fifteen minutes later, Farley removed the hand that had kept her face buried in his bulging crotch. Still blinded by the watch cap, Jessica wrenched as far away from him as the space in the backseat allowed. She heard the driver's door open and the vehicle lifted as Bagshot exited.

"C'mon, *Jessica*." Farley's voice.

She could no longer feel her hands. Farley dragged her across the seat and out of the SUV into the chilly night air. She lurched forward and nearly fell. Heavy hands encircled her upper arms and caught her, setting her down hard on gravel.

She tried to see below the hem of the cap, but the wool had molded itself to her face and covered her mouth. She could not even see her own feet. In her head, she counted off thirty paces before they stopped walking and Bagshot told Farley to get the door. The click of a lock and the familiar 'swoosh' of power doors made her guess that they were at BioNeutronics.

Another twenty feet, another stop. Jessica heard the whir of an elevator and one of them prodded her forward. The floor shook slightly as they climbed aboard, then began to descend.

They bumped to a soft landing. She heard the door slide open and one of them led her out. She had counted fifteen paces before she was jerked to a halt and a heavy hand landed on the middle of her back. She flinched, just before a rough shove sent her down on her knees.

She tried to roll to one side but with her hands behind her back, the edge of her chin met the cement floor. Pain slammed through her entire body. Someone yanked her wrists up behind her, causing the plastic cuffs to bite deeper into her flesh. She hung there suspended, waiting for her arms to pop out of their sockets. Then the pressure on her wrists relaxed and she hit the floor again, the wind knocked out of her.

A door slammed shut. Then…nothing.

TWENTY-FOUR

Zebediah Gold opened the door to his guesthouse and ushered Claudia Rose inside. He gave her a long hug and pressed a kiss to her cheek before offering coffee, which she accepted.

Following him to the kitchenette, she took a manila folder from her briefcase and perched on one of the two stools at the breakfast bar. "I'm glad you were free this morning."

Zebediah shot her a grin as he went about the business of getting out coffee paraphernalia and pouring two steaming mugs. "I must admit I was amazed when you phoned at eight a.m. I didn't think you knew the world existed before ten."

Rolling her eyes, Claudia accepted the carton of soy milk he offered. "Let's see *you* work half the night and get up perky at the crack of dawn."

"No need to be cranky, darling. I know what a dedicated worker you are."

"I'm really worried about Jenna. I mean Jessica. She looked so *stricken* when Joel read her the accident report. Well, of course she did. She didn't even know she had a child, and we were telling her that she'd lost him." She poured milk into her coffee. "We didn't want to leave her like that, but she insisted. I was hoping she'd call me last night, but she didn't."

"She didn't pick up when I phoned her." Gold spooned several heaps of sugar into his coffee. "She's been in such profound denial about her child's death. After what she's gone through this past week, I hope the news didn't tip her over the edge."

Claudia stared at him, aghast. "Are you thinking she might have hurt herself?"

"It's more likely she blocked it all out again."

"You mean a whole new fugue state?"

"I don't see her as suicidal, but…"

"Should we call Ventura PD and ask them to do a welfare check?"

"That would scare her even more. She has a thing about uniformed policemen. I'm thinking about driving up there later and see if she'll talk to me. I've cleared my calendar for the afternoon."

"Do you want me to go with you?"

"I don't think so, darling. Right now, she would probably associate you with the bad news."

"All right, then let me show you what I found."

Zebediah took a sip of coffee and nodded. "I take it the handwriting samples were delivered from the client you worked for at the convention?"

"All six hundred of them." Claudia scooted her mug to one side. "The box was on the porch when Joel and I got back from Ventura last night. I started going through them right away. I figured Jenna's sample would be on the bottom, but wonders never cease—it was near the top of the stack."

From the folder she withdrew two sheets of paper, one of which she showed Zebediah. "This is the sample you've already seen; the one she wrote for me here last Saturday."

He took a long look at the small printed writing. "It *looks* lonely and shy," he said. "I remember you said it indicated insecurity and avoidance of reality."

"Yes. It's not the writing of a *weak* person, but there are some really deep problems with her ego. I would hazard a guess that she suffered some kind of abuse early in life. Not necessarily sexual, but her ego was battered. More like neglect or abandonment would be my guess." She offered him the second sheet. "This is the sample she wrote at the convention."

Zebediah Gold took the paper and looked at the two lines of

handwriting. He looked over at her, his eyebrows raised. "This is a completely different style."

"It certainly is, my dear doctor," Claudia replied. "Well-observed."

"I don't have to be a handwriting expert to see the obvious, sweetie. The one from the convention is larger, it's got loops, and the words are spaced close together."

She smiled. "Good job."

"You've taught me enough to know these differences indicate widely varying styles of functioning."

"They do indeed. The printed one—let's call it the Jessica sample—as I've said, shows an insecure loner. The cursive one, which we'll call the Jenna sample, is a more outgoing person with a strong need for love and affection. She's softer than what we see in Jessica. See how this t-cross bends in a cup shape? She's easily led and it's hard for her to say no if someone she looks up to, or perceives as being stronger, wants her to do something. Her writing is also quite neat and regular, a perfectionist. And she's more emotionally dependent. In its way, despite the ego problems, the Jessica sample is the stronger, firmer, more self-reliant one."

Zebediah scratched his beard, taking in Claudia's words. "In a fugue state where the patient has memory loss they may take on an entirely new identity, as Jessica seems to have done."

"And experience a complete personality change."

He nodded. "Like a mini case of Dissociative Identity Disorder. And if the personality changed, the handwriting would, too, wouldn't it?"

"Yes. But there are two other points of note that I haven't mentioned yet."

"Okay. What are they?"

"Jessica is left-handed. As you know, handedness can't be identified conclusively from handwriting, but there are some indicators. For example, she crosses her t's from right to left, as lefties often do. In the Jenna sample they're crossed from left to right. And look, it's noted on her sample that she's right-handed."

"I see," said Zebediah. "What's the other point?"

Claudia put the two handwriting samples side by side on the counter top and tapped them with a fingertip. "Where two very different-looking writings are done by the same hand, I would expect there to still be some subtle similarities." She looked over at Gold. "I don't see any here."

TWENTY-FIVE

A century or two passed while Jessica lay curled in a ball on the unforgiving floor, groaning from the pain in her right knee, her shoulders, and the nosebleed that would not stop.

Her hands, swollen and numb from the restricted circulation, were as unwieldy as boxing gloves. She rubbed the backs against each other, then the palms. It took a while for the blood to recirculate, and when the numbness began to wear off, the pins and needles started up, torturing the nerve endings. When at last she could make her fingers do what she wanted, Jessica reached up and tore off the watch cap.

Even without the woolen cap, she could see nothing in the cold, dark room but a faint sliver of light outlining the bottom of the door. The faint smell of pine cleaner burned the linings of her injured nose. Where was she? Some kind of janitorial closet?

"Hello?" she called in a thin whisper. "Is anyone here?"

The only sound that reached her ears was the distant hum of machinery. She had not expected a response, but when none came, fear, grief, and pain collided.

How does this nightmare end?

I don't want to die.

You don't remember your useless life anyway.

I could make a new life.

Not now, dumbshit.

The malignant voice carping at her was almost welcome. At least it was company.

So pathetic, talking to yourself.

Well, maybe I won't bother if you're going to be so damned critical.

Jessica sobbed for a while, until, having had her fill of feeling sad and powerless, she simply refused to cry anymore. Licking her fingers, she used her sweatshirt sleeve to rub away as much of the sticky blood smeared on her upper lip as she could. Her cleanup efforts didn't amount to much, but it made her feel a teeny bit better to be doing *something.*

When she had done the best she could manage, she scooted over to the door and stretched out flat, laying her cheek against the icy concrete. She pushed her face right up against the bottom of the door, where the half-inch of space gave her a limited view of unfinished flooring in a dimly lit hallway.

There must be a light somewhere in this room. Her knee protesting in agony with every flex, Jessica pulled herself to her feet. As she had expected, there was a wall switch next to the door, but when she flipped it nothing happened. Battering the door with the side of her fist, she yelled as loud as she could: "Let me out! Goddamn it, let me out of here!"

She yelled until her throat was sore, but nobody came to tell her to stop. Nobody came for any reason at all.

Where were her captors? Were they even now discussing her fate with whoever had sent them to take her? And who *was* giving the orders? Not Simon. He had been far too scared when he thought Christine Palmer had hurt Jenna. Palmer herself? How was she involved in Project 42?

As long as they didn't know where the Project 42 files were, maybe she could buy some time—but for what? She wasn't naive enough to believe she would be allowed to go free. Something on that flash drive was so important that she had risked her job, her life, and jeopardized her relationship with Simon for it.

To what lengths would they go to make her tell them what she knew—which, of course, was nothing. And once they got that truth out of her, what then? Whatever choice she made was going to be a no-win for Jessica Mack.

With the fingertips of one hand in contact with the wall and she stretched out the other arm and stepped into the dark area. Swinging her arm back and forth, she felt nothing but empty space. She limped four steps to the right and came to the first corner of the room. Continuing to pace the perimeter, she encountered nothing but cold concrete walls.

Get farther away from the wall.

I don't want to.

A memory: skinny blonde child, maybe four or five years old, shivering on the deck of a backyard swimming pool. Lowering clouds, a sharp breeze. Not a good day for a swim.

A tall, dark-haired woman yelling: "Go on, Jessie, jump in. Don't be so stupid, you big chicken." The little girl started crying that she was scared; she didn't know how to swim. She shrank away from the edge, but the woman laughed unkindly and gave her a push that sent her belly-flopping into the deep end. The water closed over little Jessica's head and she inhaled a big gulp of water. Gasping…suffocating…

Grown-up Jessica came crashing back to the present.

I'm still *afraid.*

So stay there hugging the wall, stupid. Just wait for them to come back and kill you.

I'm not *stupid! Stop saying I'm stupid.*

She repeated it out loud. "I'm not stupid. I'm Jessica Mack and I'm an adult now."

Her memories of her past were still missing, but with those words she knew something important had happened. She had accepted her identity and all that it meant. Like wrapping herself in a tattered old robe, the sensation was not particularly comfortable, but there was a familiarity about it.

Feeling her way back to the wall, she slid to the floor and sat on Farley's knit cap for a little insulation. She hugged her knees to her chest and fastened her eyes on that little sliver of light under the door, waiting.

How long would they leave her here? Were they going to come back for her at all? Or did they intend to let her starve to death and return one day to collect her remains? It shouldn't take all that long, she was already pretty thin.

She imagined what it would be like to slowly waste away. How long would it take? Two or three days for the onset of severe hunger pangs gnawing at your stomach. You could go without food for weeks, but you had to have water. How long before your flesh started to shrivel from lack of hydration, and your organs began to desiccate?

The grisly images helped her fend off the other thoughts scratching the edges of her consciousness. Thoughts of a beautiful little boy with curly black hair and mischievous eyes that reflected the fierce love she had felt for him.

A love that had not been fierce enough to save him.

Time was the enemy, sucking at her like quicksand, dragging at her, second by wretched second. She drifted in and out of a half-dream, impressions thrusting their way to the surface, fragments of memories coming alive inside her mind.

She was sitting in an old rocking chair, cradling a tiny bundle in her arms. Baby eyes gazed up at her as if they possessed some secret knowledge of a centuries-old connection to her soul. She had held him close to her heart and promised that she would always love and protect him. A promise too soon broken.

Her mind returned to the accident. Once again she was staring through the windshield into the emptiness that waited over the edge of the cliff. Rolling and rolling. Her son's whimpers were the last thing in her ears before she lost consciousness.

The first break-in. In the Escondido apartment, sitting at her computer talking to—no, wait, that wasn't right. Jessica snapped awake. Bagshot and his flunkies had invaded the *Ventura* apartment both times, not Escondido. And in none of her nightmares had she been talking to anyone. To whom had she been speaking? Someone on the phone?

Web cam.

She heard the words in her head as clearly as if they had been spoken aloud. That made no sense, though. She'd run out of the apartment "like a bat out of hell," according to her neighbor. Why go to the Ventura apartment and speak to someone there on the web cam? Who? Not her husband—the thought made her shudder—he was in jail. Simon? None of it jived with her waking up on the train. The more she thought about it, the more confused and agitated the questions left her.

Jessica pressed her hands to her temples. How long would it take to go crazy under these conditions? Would you starve first, or lose your mind? Left alone in the dark with nothing to do but imagine the gruesome things that were going to happen to you, she would put her money on losing your mind.

She considered saying a prayer, but even with her memory gone, something told her that she had not prayed in a long time. Why would she? If God had not heard her prayers to keep her baby safe, how could she expect Him to save Jessica Mack from this hell?

TWENTY-SIX

The sound of hydraulics brought Jessica to her feet. Pushing aside the pain of her injuries, she waited for the door to open.

Had she been in the dark place for ten minutes or forty? Two hours or twenty? The sensory deprivation gave her no means to gauge the passage of time, but she had decided that whatever they did to her, the least she could demand of herself was to go down fighting.

Footsteps in the hallway; the sound of a key turning. The door swung open. Jessica squinched her eyes against the bright light, trying to make out the shadowy figure standing in the rectangle of the door frame. Too small for either Bagshot or Farley.

"Why is it so dark in there? My God, what did you do to her? Are you people crazy or something?"

Jessica recognized the voice. As she moved closer to the door, Kevin Nguyen, the BioNeutronics Director of Security, drew a sharp breath. "Holy crap, what happened to her face?"

"She tripped," Bagshot lied.

"You idiot!" Nguyen turned to Jessica and spoke in a soft voice. "Are you all right?"

She stared at him in disbelief. "*Am I all right?*"

Like boiling lava, rage rushed up and exploded. Jessica launched herself at Nguyen. Hunching his shoulders, he raised his arms to protect his face against the fists that pummeled him anywhere she could land a blow. If only she were stronger, she would have broken bones.

It was over in seconds. Bagshot stepped in front of his boss and yanked him back. Then he reached out to grab Jessica. This time, though, she was too quick for him. Moving in close like a boxer, she rose on the balls of her feet and reached up. Her fingernails dug deep into the leathery skin, raking them from eyelid to chin.

Bagshot's hand went to his face and came away covered in his own blood. Taking advantage of his distraction, Jessica drove her knee into his crotch.

Bagshot spun on her, cold murder in his eyes. "You fucking—"

"Enough!" shouted Nguyen. "The young lady has a right to be upset." To Jessica's amazement, Bagshot obeyed the order.

Nguyen bent to pick up his eyeglasses, which had clattered to the ground. He flapped his hands at Bagshot like an old washerwoman shooing geese. "Now you go away. I need to speak with her. Wait for me outside the med suite."

Without a word, Bagshot turned on his heel and marched up the narrow corridor, his massive back stiff with anger.

Once the big man was out of earshot, Kevin Nguyen spoke in a quiet voice to Jessica, who was leaning against the wall, trembling all over, now that the adrenalin rush was subsiding. "Please. You must be calm now. I'm very sorry for what happened to you. Come with me."

Still vibrating with emotion, Jessica pulled away from the helping hand he tried to put under her elbow. "Come where?"

"Just to my office. It's along the hallway here. It's not very fancy, but..."

She had been right in her assumption; they were in BioNeutronics' basement. But this was a vastly different section than the one she had visited last week when Simon had called her down to the lab. The walls and floors were unfinished, galvanized air conditioning duct work ran overhead along the ceiling. Nobody would have ever looked for her here.

"Just get me out of here," Jessica snapped. "What time is it?"

He consulted his watch. "Seven twenty-three."

"Morning or night?"

"Morning."

"What day?"

He turned a curious look on her. "Tuesday."

She would not have been surprised if the security chief had told her it was Wednesday night. It seemed unfathomable that a scant five and a half hours ago she had been lying on her bed, trying to deny the news Detective Jovanic had brought her.

Nguyen's office was a windowless utilitarian room. Four computer monitors claimed most of the space on the wide metal desk. Jessica guessed the monitors allowed him to keep an eye on the comings and goings of employees around the building.

An old filing cabinet and a small refrigerator against the back wall were both stacked high with folders. The lone guest chair was piled with magazines and files, DVDs in handwritten jewel cases, and a video camera. Nguyen flashed tobacco-stained teeth at Jessica in a self-deprecating smile. "I'm getting too old for all of this. Maybe time for me to retire soon, eh?"

Jessica didn't bother to reply. He stooped with a grunt and dumped the contents of the guest chair onto the floor, making room for her. She sat down and glared at Nguyen. "What the hell is going on?"

"Ah." Nguyen rested his elbows on the desk, steepling gnarled hands under his chin. "You have my deepest apologies for my operative's behavior. Mr. Bagshot stepped far beyond the boundaries of his authority and his instructions."

"You think so? They broke into my apartment in the middle of the night, destroyed my things, *kidnapped* me, beat me up—" Jessica started getting worked up again. "Look at my face! My knee—"

"It was a terrible misunderstanding. I will see to it, of course, that you get medical attention, and anything that was broken will be fixed."

"Some things can't be fixed," she said angrily, thinking of the relics of her past that Farley had strewn across the living room. Maybe someday she would remember what they had meant to her and be able to properly mourn them.

"Don't worry, you will be compensated. However…" Nguyen's thin veneer of sympathy slid away, replaced by something far less agreeable. Alarms went off in Jessica's head as he sat back in his chair and clasped his hands together in front of him. He cleared his throat. “There is still the matter of missing files that Mr. Bagshot so overzealously attempted to recover. The fact is, you did download proprietary information from a workstation here at BioNeutronics. You can’t deny this.” He tapped the monitor closest to him. “The evidence is in here. Now, you must tell me what you did with the information that you acquired. Who did you sell it to?”

“I didn’t sell anything.”

His expression was deadpan. “Perhaps it’s a matter of my phrasing: What did you do with the information?”

“I didn’t do anything. I don’t have any information.”

“Who are you working for?” Nguyen pressed.

“You know I work here, for Simon Lawrie. Why are you asking me this?”

“Ah. I understand that was the story you told Mr. Bagshot, but you and I know it is not true. Don’t we, Ms. *Mack*?”

“You saw me here yesterday. You were in Simon’s office when I brought those scientists in. We talked on the phone last week.”

“Yes, I saw you here, but that does not explain what you were *doing* here.”

“What’s really going on here, Kevin? Why did your goons break into my apartment *twice*?”

Surprise flared in his face. “How do you know that?”

“Are you crazy? You know I was there!” Her voice rose with emotion. “What did they do to me that first time? You have to tell me!”

“What do you mean by that, Ms. Mack?”

“You *know* what I mean. They did something to my mind. I need to know what it was!”

Kevin Nguyen sat up straighter. “Your *mind*?”

Jessica jumped out of her chair, choking on emotion. She leaned forward, her hands splayed on his desk. “I don’t know what you sent those men to do to me. All I know is, I woke up on a train with no memory. I don’t know anything about my life. Why *can’t I remember anything*? Tell me what they did to me!”

Nguyen stared at her. “This is a very interesting story. Please tell me everything that has happened and I’ll see if I can help you.”

"It's not a story, it's the truth. I got off the train in Ventura. I ran into a neighbor who took me to my apartment. That's when I found out that my name was Jenna Marcott and I decided to show up at work and see if I could figure out what happened to me because, of course, I didn't know anything about your thugs then. I only found out last Saturday that I also used to be Jessica Mack. Was it a drug? What did they do to me? Why do I have amnesia?"

"This is true about the amnesia?"

"Of course it's true. Why would I make up something like that?"

"That, Ms. Mack, is an excellent question."

Jessica could see the wheels turning in his head as he pondered what she had told him. Was it possible that he really didn't know what had happened to her?

At length, Nguyen said, "Perhaps you will allow me to show you why I am puzzled about what you're telling me."

He rose and left the office, Jessica following close behind. Unlocking a heavy fire door, he pushed it open and waited for her to pass through.

They stepped into what appeared to be a reception area, where a petite Filipina nurse in blue scrubs sat behind a desk reading *People* magazine. The environment could not have been more different than the one they had just left.

Glancing up, the nurse started to nod a greeting at the security chief. Catching sight of Jessica, her face went slack with surprise.

"What—how—?" She looked toward a half-closed door across from her desk, then back at Jessica. Nguyen's stern glance silenced her. He crossed to the door, beckoning for Jessica to follow, and stepped inside.

Vital signs blipped silently on a digital monitor next to a hospital bed that was angled towards the door. Kevin Nguyen went over to the bedside and like Vanna White revealing the answer to a puzzle, spread his hands. "Allow me to introduce you to Jenna Marcott."

TWENTY-SEVEN

She might have been looking in a mirror.

Crazy thoughts surged through Jessica's mind: Was Project 42 a cloning experiment? Was this person in the bed an android? She shook her head slowly, denying what her eyes were telling her. "I don't understand. Why does she look so much like me?"

"You tell me," Kevin Nguyen said smugly.

Jessica's mental overload hit critical mass. Not knowing where she was headed, she turned and pushed past Nguyen, running blindly out of the room. She rounded the nursing station, and shouldered her way through a door marked 'EXIT' and ran right into Bagshot, who held a bloody handkerchief to his face. One massive hand closed reflexively around her wrist and with a vicious jerk, he bent her arm behind her until she was almost doubled over.

"Lemme go, you bastard!" Jessica screamed.

Nguyen had followed her. "Bring her back here," he ordered.

"I think—" Bagshot began, but Nguyen cut him off. "*Don't* think. That's not what you're paid for. Nurse Anna—"

Bagshot shoved Jessica back through the door so abruptly that she stumbled and almost fell. Her mind was reeling. Nguyen had identified the young woman in the bed as Jenna Marcott. But how could she be? *I'm* Jenna.

No, you're Jessica.

I'm both...Aren't I?

A hand on her arm was pushing her gently. The nurse's voice said, "Sit down here," and Jessica let herself be led to a chair. She plopped down and leaned forward, elbows on knees, trying to quell the muddleheaded feeling.

The wasps were back, droning loud enough to drown out the voices speaking around her. She clapped her hands over her ears, but Nguyen's voice pushed through the buzzing.

"What are you running from, Ms. Mack?" he asked. "Did you think we wouldn't figure it out?"

Jessica turned her head to look up at him, regretting it when vertigo swept over her. "Figure what out?"

"That you and Ms. Marcott were working together."

"Are you crazy? I'm not working with anyone. *I'm* Jenna Marcott."

"Clearly you are not."

"I don't understand. Why does that girl look so much like me?"

"'That 'girl' is Jenna Marcott," Nguyen insisted. "You still say you don't know her? I only let you go on pretending to be her for a few days so I could keep an eye you, but I admit, I'm still not sure of your game. So, now it's time to let me in on your secret."

"I already told you, I have *amnesia*," Jessica repeated. "If I have any secrets, *I don't frigging remember them*!"

Nguyen turned to the nurse, who was regarding the scene as it unfolded like a play, her dark eyes alight with interest. "Nurse Anna, please come." To Bagshot he said, "Escort Ms. Mack."

With Bagshot prodding Jessica from behind, they all trooped back into the hospital room where the patient, oblivious to the drama unfolding around her, slept on.

Blonde hair fanned out around a pale oval face that was a virtual duplicate of Jessica's. The only conspicuous difference was their hair length.

"It's time for Ms. Marcott to wake up," Nguyen said.

The nurse's eyes boomeranged from Jessica to the young woman in the bed, and back again. "But Dr. Kapur—"

"Is Dr. Kapur your employer, Nurse Anna?"

"No, sir, but..."

"Then do as you're told. Do it now."

To the left of the bed was an IV drip pole. Jessica could make out the word 'propofol,' printed on the label. The name sounded vaguely familiar until she remembered it was one of the drugs administered to the pop star, Michael Jackson, prior to his death. Media reports had said it was a drug used by anesthesiologists. The nurse edged around the security chief and reached up to turn off the valve on the bag.

"Who is she?" Jessica whispered again. She could not stop staring at the young woman Kevin Nguyen had identified as Jenna Marcott. "Why is she here?"

"Ms. Marcott is participating in a research experiment that requires in-patient care."

Nurse Anna, standing in a protective position next to the head of the bed, glanced over at Nguyen. Her expression was carefully neutral, but her body language radiated disapproval.

"What kind of experiment?" Jessica pressed.

"That will be a subject for later discussion. I admit I'm curious about the remarkable resemblance between the two of you. Although, seeing you standing next to her, I can detect some differences," Nguyen said. "If you weren't working with her, what were you doing posing as Ms. Marcott?"

"I wasn't *posing*. I told you. I thought that's who I was. Who I *am*. I—I don't understand what's happening."

The patient was beginning to stir. Her eyelids fluttered and her lips moved, but the sounds she emitted were slurred and jumbled together.

"Ms. Marcott?" Nguyen said loudly. The patient moved her head, mumbled something indistinct again, and gave a deep sigh.

"Mr. Nguyen, please give her some time to wake up," the nurse protested. "The sedation will make her groggy."

"How long?" Nguyen asked.

"About thirty minutes, maybe more."

A weak voice from the bed said, "*Jess?*"

"I'm here, Belle." Jessica answered without thinking. Then she realized what she had said.

I called her Belle...

"Ah!" Nguyen said triumphantly. "You do know each other."

"No," Jessica denied. She moved further into Jenna's line of sight.

"What—" Jenna Marcott's eyelids opened halfway and she yawned languidly. "Water."

Nurse Anna patted her hand. "I'll get you some." Pushing past the security chief, she went into the bathroom and returned with a wet washcloth, which she pressed to her patient's chapped lips. "She won't be able to drink just yet," she explained to Jessica, ignoring Nguyen. "She'll have to wait a little while."

Jenna licked the drops on her lips. "Wha' happ'n?" her words were slurred as if she were drunk, her thoughts mixing together. "Where'm I here?"

"You're in the medical suite," Kevin Nguyen said. "You've been asleep."

"Why'm—Where'd you say?"

Even the timbre of their voices was similar, Jessica realized, stunned.

Why did I call her Belle?

"Don't you remember?" said Nguyen. "You volunteered to participate in a research experiment."

A look of puzzlement passed over Jenna Marcott's face. She closed her eyes and turned onto her side. "Lemme sleep."

The nurse reached over to fix the hospital gown so that it covered Jenna Marcott's naked backside. "It's going to take a while for her to wake up properly," she reiterated. "You should wait outside. I need to remove the feeding tube and the catheter and get her ready for you. I cannot do that while you are in here, Mr. Nguyen."

"Feeding tube?" Jessica repeated. "How long has she been here?"

"I think you can figure that out," Nguyen said, guiding her back to the waiting area.

"You're telling me *she's* Jenna Marcott, and I'm not. You're implying she's been here at least since I showed up at BioNeutronics." Nothing made any sense and Jessica's bewilderment was growing with every new revelation. "Does Simon know about this?"

Kevin Nguyen shook his head. "Dr. Lawrie believes and accepts that *you* are his assistant and his—well, let's just leave it at that. He is unaware of Ms. Marcott's participation in the experiment."

It struck her with relief that Simon Lawrie was not her lover after all. It explained why she felt nothing for him.

"I *am* at least Jessica Mack, aren't I?"

Nguyen's thin lips compressed into an even tighter line. "That is a mystery I hope Jenna will be able to help us unravel."

Images spiraled through Jessica's head like tumbleweeds in a tornado: her flight from the Escondido apartment, the Ariel mermaid on her desk at work, the Belle figurine Farley had broken, the two names in the Contact list on the cell phones. The different voices on the two cell phone greetings, one bright and sunny, the other half-dead. Now Jessica understood why her voice on the one was so listless. It was after the accident…

But the door to her memory was still shut tight; locked as securely as the room where she had been held prisoner.

Close to an hour passed before Nurse Anna opened the door and invited them back inside. She had turned up the lights and raised the back of the bed. Jenna Marcott was sitting on top of the sheets, dressed in jeans and a sweatshirt very much like the ones Jessica was wearing. She looked more alert. Her face, still ghastly pale, lit up when they entered.

"Jess! You're really here! I thought I was dreaming you."

Jessica hung back, unsure how to respond to this stranger who was her mirror image.

"You appear to know Ms. Mack," said Nguyen to the young woman on the bed.

"Of course I know her," Jenna Marcott said. "She's my twin."

TWENTY-EIGHT

My twin...

Jenna Marcott's words acted like tumblers of a lock clicking into place. The door to Jessica's memory cracked open an inch. "I—I—" Her voice didn't want to work. She stepped forward into the light.

Jenna's mouth dropped open. "Ariel! Your face—Omigod, what happened to you? Will somebody please tell me what's going on?"

"I have amnesia," Jessica burst out, talking fast. "I met Zach and he thought I was you. He took me to your apartment and when I saw the gnome I knew there would be a key and when I got inside I found a purse with ID that looked like me, so I thought—and now you're saying—"

Jenna put up her hands, palms out. "Wait! Stop. Are you saying that right now you don't know who I am?"

Why didn't she sound surprised? Jessica bowed her head, shame burning her face that she did not remember her own twin. "I'm sorry, no."

Jenna reached out a hand to her, but she was still a stranger and Jessica was unsure how she felt about being so close to someone she didn't recognize, despite owning virtually the same face that stared out at her from every mirror.

"You were in a car accident a few months ago," Jenna began. "You had a head injury."

Jessica interrupted, "I know about that part. I mean, I don't exactly *remember* it, but I know about it. And I know about—about my—" Emotion welled up in her throat and choked off the words.

"Ah, Jess, we don't have to talk about that right now." Jenna reached out her hands again. This time, Jessica took them. An electric current passed between them, binding them in some primal way.

"Ever since the accident you've had little spells of forgetting, but only...certain things." Jenna's face scrunched in confusion. "Everything's so fuzzy. What am I doing here?"

"You've been here for over a week," Jessica said.

"A *week?* That can't be right. How—?"

Jessica turned on Kevin Nguyen, who was closely following their exchange. "You're the one behind all this. Tell her!"

He shrugged. "As I've already explained to you, Ms. Marcott volunteered to be an experimental subject in a research study. It's just the residual effects of the sedation. She'll remember later."

"What kind of research?"

"If you want to know about our experiments, you will need to see Dr. Polzin."

Another tumbler fell into place and the door to her memory opened a little wider. "The first time your men broke in, it was *Jenna* they kidnapped, not me. I saw it on the web cam!" The hazy memory from her dreams came into the sudden, sharp focus of déjà vu. A sob caught in her throat. "I thought they killed you, Belle!"

Jessica knew now why she had sought refuge in amnesia. Most of her past was still locked and stowed in the far reaches of her mind, but she knew with absolute certainty why she had shut down emotionally and ended up on the Amtrak Surfliner to Ventura. She had been coming to her sister's aid, but on the heels of her child's death and her own head injury, the belief that her twin had been murdered by Nguyen's thugs was more than she could bear and she had entered a fugue state.

"We were talking and you went to get a glass of wine," Jenna said slowly, filling in one more gap. Her eyes widened in remembered fear. "These men came into my apartment. One of them grabbed me from behind."

"You slammed your head back and hit him," Jessica said, recalling the scene that had come back under the pressure of Bagshot's questioning. "All I could see was the blood. I thought it was *yours.*"

Jenna clutched her hand tight. "I don't remember how I got here."

Jessica glared at Nguyen. "This is what you call 'volunteer' participation?"

He shrugged. "Ms. Marcott signed a consent form. She must have forgotten we were sending someone to pick her up."

"Oh for Christ's sake." Jessica wanted to punch him again. "*Seriously?*"

Jenna slumped back against the pillows, exhausted by the exchange. "You're lying, Kevin," she said faintly. "You did this because I was going to blow the whistle on Project 42."

"You have quite an imagination," Nguyen said in a patronizing tone. "I'm sure I don't know what you're referring to."

"What they're doing isn't right and you aren't going to shut me up."

Nguyen made a dismissive sound. "Jenna, Jenna. You've been watching too many episodes of Forensic Files on TV."

Jessica held her tongue. Jenna was unaware that whatever proof she had gathered was hidden under a pile of rotting noodles on her kitchen counter.

"What's next, Kevin? Are you going to have us killed?"

Nguyen gave an amused chuckle. "Such melodrama!"

"You think it's funny?" Jessica pointed to her bruised face, which was throbbing like a broken tooth. "*This* isn't melodrama." She turned to address Jenna, still trying to grasp the weirdness of looking at what was essentially her other half. "His thugs wrecked your living room, and they did this to my face."

"That was a regrettable mistake," Nguyen broke in smoothly. "But as I've explained, you will be well compensated. Call it…a bonus."

"You arrogant asshole," Jessica shouted, losing her temper. "Can you really pretend everything is okay?"

"Everything *is* okay," Nguyen responded. "Now, Jenna, if you're feeling up to a car ride, I'm going to ask Mr. Bagshot and

Mr. Farley to see you home."

"You're letting us go?" Jessica saw her own skepticism reflected in Jenna's face and realized that even their expressions and mannerisms were the same. It was an uncanny sensation, one that would take some time to get used to.

Nguyen shrugged. "You had a break-in. What are the authorities going to say? As you ladies just discussed, your sister suffered a head injury that causes memory problems. She's an unreliable witness."

"If we both tell them the same—"

"Sisters supporting each other with some outlandish story of kidnapping? Please be my guest, call the police."

"When they see these bruises and what those men did to Jenna's apartment, they'll have to take a report and investigate," Jessica said.

Nguyen's smile was so cold it sent shivers straight through her. "Ladies, feel free to blow whatever whistles you like. There is nothing for anyone to find."

TWENTY-NINE

Jenna entered the apartment first, hesitating on the threshold. Behind her, Jessica knew what she was seeing: tables upended, mementos shattered, cotton batting from the eviscerated loveseat clumped on the floor like piles of dirty snow. Her sister would need some time to absorb what had happened to her, as well as the damage to her possessions.

Taking a few steps inside, Jenna sank to her knees and gently scooped up the mutilated teddy bear, hugging it close. "Didn't they leave me *anything*, Ariel?"

"Well, *I'm* still here," Jessica said, nudging the broken Belle figurine under the loveseat so that her sister would not have to see it.

"Thank God for that." Jenna looked up at her with tear-filled eyes. "I almost lost you in the accident. I couldn't stand it if..." Her voice trailed off as she began to comprehend what Bagshot and Farley had done.

Jessica, who was still trying to process the fact that she had a twin sister, picked up the torn books and returned them to their box, then started right-ending the tables, restoring as much order to the room as she could. The fact that these were not her things after all made it no less gut-wrenching to witness Jenna's grief over their loss.

"I can't let those freaks get away with what they're doing."

Jenna said.

Although her voice was still weak, Jessica could hear the determination. For her part, she was more than ready to walk away from whatever experiments were being conducted at BioNeutronics and never look back. "We're kind of outgunned," she said. "What can we do?"

"I'm not going to let it go; I can't!"

"After what you've been through, you shouldn't make big decisions right now. You should lie down and I'll bring some tea and toast. I could use some, too."

"Okay, fine, but this isn't over."

After helping her sister get settled in bed, Jessica toasted some bread, nuked water and dunked chamomile tea bags in two mugs, adding a spoonful of honey to each. Performing the everyday domestic tasks, she could feel the ice inside her beginning to thaw as she drew comfort from the physical connection to the one person in the world who knew more about her life and history than anyone else—more, at this moment, than Jessica herself knew.

Her nose felt slightly less swollen, but it still hurt, and so did her cheek. Afraid to look in the mirror and see the damage Bagshot had done, she tore off a couple of paper towels and gingerly dabbed at her face in the kitchen sink. It felt good to get the blood washed away and feel clean again.

Balancing the toast plate on top of the mugs, she returned to the bedroom and found Jenna curled in a fetal position, looking very young and vulnerable.

Is that how I look, too?

An old cliché popped into her head: two peas in a pod. As Kevin Nguyen had pointed out, aside from the length of their hair, there were subtle differences, but the face on the pillow was remarkably like the one that looked back at Jessica from the mirror every day. Alike enough that she had mistaken her twin's driver's license photo for her own.

Jenna pulled herself to a sitting position and covered her face with her hands. "What the *hell* did they do to me? I feel so messed up."

"I don't know, Belle. I'm just glad you're alive."

"Me, too." Jenna's eyes filled with tears. "I can't stand that they beat you up like that. Your poor face must hurt like hell."

"It'll be okay. Tell me about the 'experiment' Kevin claimed you volunteered for."

"I didn't volunteer!"

"Of course you didn't." Jessica sat on the edge of the bed. "Eat some toast. You need to get those drugs out of your system."

Obediently, but without enthusiasm, Jenna nibbled at the toast. She pulled the comforter aside. "Climb in with me so we can talk."

"After sitting on that floor all night, I feel pretty gross. Do you mind if—"

"Take whatever you like." Jenna didn't need to hear the rest of the request. "We've always shared clothes."

"I've certainly been sharing yours for the last ten days." Jessica felt as though another puzzle piece had been neatly fitted into the whole. She unzipped her Levi's and let them drop, wincing in pain as she bent her knee to step out of them.

"My God, Jess!" Jenna cried out. "They did that to you, too?"

Jessica's right kneecap, which had taken the brunt of her fall, was red and swollen. "I hope it isn't fractured."

"There's an ice pack in the freezer. You need one for your knee and one for your face." Then, as Jessica headed to the kitchen, Jenna called after her to take some ibuprofen, too.

"I guess I'm lucky they didn't do worse," Jessica said on her return. She punched up a pillow and got into bed, pushing it behind her back, then balanced the ice pack on her knee.

"There's nothing lucky about what they did to your face," Jenna said. "Why do you think they let us go?"

"You mean you didn't buy Kevin's explanation?"

"I don't buy anything that little toad says."

"Me either."

"My head feels stuffed with oatmeal."

"Remember, you were in a drug-induced coma for about ten days. It's going to take a little while to get clear."

"I remember seeing blurry faces looking down at me and I know I heard voices, but I couldn't understand what they were saying. You know what's weird? That's exactly what you told me after you came out of the coma from the accident."

"That's one experience I wish we didn't have to share," Jessica said. "Tell me about Project 42, Jen. You told Nguyen you were going to blow the whistle."

"They wanted to stop me from talking about what they're doing."

"Simon took the project away from me. I mean you. He's—"

"What do you mean 'took it away'?" Jenna interrupted.

"When I went to work on Tuesday he said that I—*you*—were off the project. All the files were removed from your work station. They brought in two new scientists. Neither of them speaks English, so there's no problem with them saying the wrong thing to anyone. Plus, they're working in—"

"—the private lab," Jenna finished for her. "I set up that lab so it wouldn't have to go through the purchasing department. Okay, Jess, exactly what do you know about Project 42?"

"Exactly nothing."

"I've got to get to my office. I—"

"Downloaded the files," Jessica finished for her. Odd how she knew exactly what Jenna was going to say.

Her twin didn't seem surprised. "How did you know that?"

"I found where you hid the flash drive—"

"In the plant." Now it was Jenna's turn to finish the sentence.

Jessica explained how the woman from the plant maintenance company had found the baggie in the potting soil; about her own abortive attempt to get the flash drive out of the building, and her encounter with Farley that night.

"Why didn't you just wait until the next day and walk it out?"

"After that woman got pulled out of line for a strip search, I couldn't take the chance."

Jenna kicked the bedspread back and started to get up. "Well, we have to go back and get it. It's the only chance I have to prove—" She flopped back against the pillow with a groan. "I'm so dizzy."

"Chill, Jen, it's here."

"Here? The flash drive is *here*?"

Jessica told her how Ramon Gutierrez, the gardener, had returned the drive and she had hidden it under the Chinese food. "In fact, it's still on the kitchen counter in the takeout bag. Didn't you smell it when we came in?"

"Holy cow, Jess! Good thinking."

"I almost gave it up to those creeps last night. Now I'm glad I didn't."

"One day while Simon was out, I copied everything from the Project 42 directory off his computer. Then we had this huge fight about the project and I never got a chance to look through them."

"When you downloaded those files it set off an alarm."

"That's what I was afraid of. And that's why I buried it in the plant. I knew there was high security on the project, but I didn't know exactly how they had it set up. Simon and Kevin worked that out between them and didn't tell me."

"Kevin must have totally freaked when I showed up at work. Here comes someone who looks like you, says they *are* you, while he knew you were unconscious in the basement. He couldn't very well accuse me of being an imposter without exposing what he'd done."

Jenna grinned. "It's not the first time we've traded places. You took a math test for me in high school. Sometimes we traded dates, just for fun. I can't believe you actually thought you were me."

"What else could I think? I woke up on a train not knowing who I was. There's still so much that's not clear, but I can feel my memory trying to wake up. It started when Detective Jovanic was here yesterday."

"Who's that?"

"Dr. Gold introduced me to him. He's been trying to help me find out what happened to me."

"Dr. Gold? *My therapist*? Wow, you really did take over my life, Jess. That feels a little weird."

"Dr. Gold thinks I'm you. He hypnotized me to see if I could remember anything."

"Well, did you?"

"I saw the accident. Then Detective Jovanic brought me the accident report yesterday. He came with his girlfriend."

"His girlfriend?"

"Claudia Rose. She's the handwriting analyst you met."

"She was great." Jenna's expression softened. "Poor Jess, it must have been awful for you."

"When I got here, I just *knew* I was going to find blood all over. But there wasn't any, except for a little spot." Even though she now knew what had happened, the terrible fear Jessica had experienced upon first entering the apartment swept over her again.

"They must have cleaned up after they took me." Jenna squeezed her sister's hand. "Thank you for coming to look for me, Jess, even if you didn't know that's what you were doing. You've always looked out for me."

"I have?"

Jenna smiled. "You're ten minutes older and you never let me forget it. Don't worry, Ariel, I'll fill you in on everything."

Have we had those nicknames since we were kids?"

"We fought over them. You wanted to be Belle, but I started crying, so you gave in and let me have my way, as usual. I was always a spoiled brat."

Jessica listened intently, soaking up every detail. Every little tidbit seemed vitally important. She felt a spark of excitement that she would finally get the answers to her questions. One question pushed to the front. "I found the torn up picture of you and Simon in the drawer."

"It was the only picture I had of us together. I'd told him I didn't want to see him anymore, but he wouldn't listen." Jenna blinked several times as if to escape an unwanted image, but tears leaked through her lashes and rolled down her cheeks. "He kept calling that night, but I didn't answer. I ended up turning off the phone."

"I found it under the bed, full of his voicemails and texts." Jessica got up and limped to the bathroom for some tissues.

Jenna accepted the wad and blotted her wet face. "I'm done with him," she said in a tight voice.

"He was shocked when he saw me. He thought his wife had you killed."

"He's married to a senator who's running for president. How stupid am I?"

"I didn't know you were having an affair with him, did I?"

"It's all too humiliating. He was never going to leave her, I know that now."

"Why didn't you tell me?"

Like a little girl who'd dipped into her mother's blush, spots of color suffused Jenna's pale cheeks. "How could I tell you? I started seeing Simon right after your accident. Greg was in jail for murder.

You'd been in a coma, then you were grieving for Justin." Her voice rose. "I would have been as much of an asshole as the asshole you married if I'd dumped my problems on you, too."

Seeing anger rise in her sister's eyes, Jessica felt a little frisson of alarm. "It's okay," she said. "I get it."

"No, I don't think you do!"

"Why are you so mad?"

"Mad? Me? I don't *get* mad, remember? I clean."

"What?"

For the second time, Jenna threw back the comforter. This time she seemed to get a surge of energy. "Oh, that's right, you *don't* remember. I'm *OCD Jenna*." She rocketed out of bed and stormed into the kitchen.

Cabinet doors and drawers slammed open and shut. "You're such a slob. Look at this mess! It's not right to leave a place looking like this!" Jenna pulled a plastic garbage bag from a box under the sink and marched into the living room. She began furiously flinging her mangled possessions into the bag as though they were at fault for their own destruction. Without warning, she whirled on Jessica, her voice harsh and ragged. "How could you let them do this to me?"

Baffled and a little scared, Jessica felt as though she'd been slapped. "*Let them*? What do you think I could have done?"

"Something. Anything! What the *fuck's* wrong with you, Jessica?" Jenna hurled the trash bag across the room. Its contents spilled out onto the floor. "I'm gonna burn all this shit, I swear I am."

"We can deal with all this later," Jessica said, willing herself to stay calm, at least on the outside. "I think some of it can be fixed."

"No! It's no good now. Those people are evil. They've screwed up everything they touched. What do you care anyway? It's not *your* stuff! I'm going to burn it all, right here, right now." Jenna began scrabbling through the junk drawer. Her voice rose to a near-shriek. "Where are the matches? I can't find the matches. What have you done with my goddamn matches? Where are they?"

"Jenna, stop! You can't light a fire in here."

"I'm going to burn it. All of it."

Jessica stared at her in horror. She might not *remember*, but she knew instinctively that this was not the sister she had grown up with. Something was seriously wrong. Watching Jenna, her mirror image, slamming drawer after drawer in her search for matches was like viewing a demented movie of herself.

Jenna swung around, pointing an accusing finger. "You hid them, you bitch. What have you done with my matches?" Her hands curled into fists.

In that sickening instant, Jessica knew that her twin was going to physically attack her. She closed the space between them and grabbed Jenna's shoulders. She gave her a sharp shake. "*Stop it!* Do you hear me? *Jenna*!"

The slim body stiffened. Their faces were only inches apart and Jessica could feel her twin's shallow breaths on her face. She could sense the racing of her heart as if it were her own. Jenna's empty eyes stared back at her. Then gradually, the emptiness cleared, replaced by confusion. "What's wrong with me, Jess? Am I going crazy?" Her body went limp and she started to fall.

Jessica reached out to catch her, but the weight was too much for her injured knee and they crashed against the counter. Jenna pulled away first, burying her face in her hands. "Oh God, what did they do to me?"

THIRTY

Jessica closed the bedroom door behind her and began the sad task of sorting items that might be repaired from those that would have to be thrown away. She had coaxed Jenna back to bed with promises of tidying up.

As she worked, the echoes of Jenna's question hung in the air: *What did they do to me?* And her own question: *Why did they let us go?*

She set aside the damaged teddy bear, promising herself that she would mend it. The loveseat cushions would have to be re-upholstered. The Belle figurine was a total loss. Maybe she could find a replacement on eBay.

Still reeling from the past sixteen hours, Jessica numbly stuffed the cotton batting back inside the loveseat cushion. She had gone from knowing nothing about herself to learning she was a bereaved mother with a jailed husband awaiting trial, to being kidnapped and tortured, then discovering a twin sister. It was too much to take in.

She tried to pat down the ugly bulges in the leather, but the rip across the seat was a grim reminder of what had taken place here. Maybe she and Jenna would go furniture shopping together and they would eventually be able to forget.

Yeah. As if.

Forgetting might no longer be an option. Jessica could feel her memory starting to open up. She had a sinking feeling that once the dam burst there would be no going back.

The China Wok takeout bag with its secret cargo still sat on the counter. She removed the container from the bag and opened the lid, gagging at the pungent odor. Pushing aside the congealed food with a fork, she took out the baggie wiped the mess off the outside. The device inside was intact.

"Is that my flash drive?"

Jessica nearly jumped out of her skin at Jenna's voice right behind her. "You scared me!" She dumped the noodles into the garbage disposal. "Are you feeling better?"

"Yes, I feel a lot stronger. I'm sorry about before. I don't know what happened. I'm just not feeling like me."

Jessica handed her the flash drive. "Feel like booting up the computer?"

"Definitely. Let's see what we've got."

Jessica leaned over her sister's shoulder, waiting. "Is this a new computer?"

"No, I've had it for a while. Why?"

"So there should be some data files on it..."

Jenna looked up at her. "Yes, of course there should. Why?"

"There's nothing but programs. No emails, except for junk mail from this week, and one from Zach."

"Damn them. They must have thought they'd take care of it by erasing everything, in case I'd already uploaded the Project 42 files."

"But we've still got the files."

Jenna inserted the flash drive into a USB slot. "Cross your fingers, Ariel." A second later they were looking at a list of 431 files, the contents of a folder named P42. Jenna pumped her fist. "Yes, we win!"

"Sweet."

"Some of the Word files are specs Simon had me type up for the overall project. We can skip those. They're the objective, the scope of work, stuff like that. Those are the ones with my initials—JM at the front."

"What exactly *is* the objective?"

"It has something to do with stimulating certain parts of the brain to act like a Viagra-type drug."

"You mean Project 42 is something that gives horny old guys a hard-on?"

"Well, that's an elegant way of putting it."

"Oh, excuse me, I meant 'it treats erectile dysfunction.' You mean *that's* what all this hoopla about?"

"It's not just horny old guys who use those kinds of drugs, Jess. There's a *huge* market for them. Beside, Project 42 isn't a drug. It's some kind of electrical stimulation device."

"Sounds kinky."

"Not that kind of stimulation. Brain stimulation. And it's not just for men."

"Unisex brain stimulation? Why kidnap us over that?"

"That's not why they kidnapped us. They kidnapped us because they think I know what Project 42 *really* is."

"What is it *really*?"

"I'm not sure yet."

Jessica frowned. "If you were going to blow the whistle on it, you must know more than that."

"Some of the memos I saw between Simon and the client bothered me, but I didn't have enough information to go public."

"The client—Dr. Kapur?"

Jenna shook her head. "He's just a front man who's in charge of the project."

"Well, who *is* the client?"

"One of the subsidiaries of the Morton Brothers Foundation."

"Okay, I don't mean to sound uninformed, but I don't know who that is."

"It's an international conglomerate that owns companies up the wazoo. Hundreds of them. They pretty much run half the world."

"Half the world?" Jessica echoed.

"I'm not joking, Jess. WikiLeaks released some information on them a while back. Morton Brothers' entities pretty much run the governments of several smaller countries. I have a feeling they're aiming to do the same here in the U.S. eventually."

"With a sexual brain stimulant?"

"*No*. There's something else going on in Project 42. The volunteers in the clinical trials aren't being told the truth about the experiments—that's what I discovered from those emails. I asked Simon, hoping he would deny it, that he would convince me I was wrong, but he didn't. He just warned me to let it go."

Jessica remembered the note she'd found in Jenna's purse on her first night in the apartment: *I'm warning you, Jen, back off. Now! You have to give me more time.* She had later recognized the handwriting as belonging to Simon.

She said, "But if it's such a big deal, why a small lab like BioNeutronics? Or—do the Morton's own the lab?"

"That's what I asked Simon."

"What was his answer?"

"Basically, he patted me on the head and told me to be a good little girl. He said we'd just made love and he didn't want to talk about work."

"But you didn't let it go, did you?"

"Of course not. I kept ragging on him until we got into this huge fight. He tried to convince me that it's because BioNeutronics has such an *excellent* reputation and because we don't take government funding, so we're truly independent." Jenna gave her a sour look. "We may not take government funding, but remember who Simon is married to."

"A U.S. senator who's running for president."

"She's wrapped up in this whole thing somehow, I just know it."

"Dr. Kapur came from DC with her last week."

"See what I mean? Simon got way too quiet when I started asking him about his wife and the project. He shut right up and wouldn't say squat about it." Jenna got up, talking over her shoulder while she went to the kitchen and poured two glasses of apple juice. Her strength seemed to be making a rapid rebound.

"I've been working on a theory. I did some research on the company that brought the project to BioNeutronics. It's definitely a subsidiary of Mortons. I think they might be secretly funding Palmer's presidential campaign. It can't be a coincidence that twenty-four hours after I started voicing my concerns over the project and threatening to go public, that I ended up as some kind of guinea pig in the medical suite of the lab." Her voice cracked,

"Simon betrayed me."

"You think he told Palmer?"

"Of course he did, she has him totally whipped. I don't believe he sent those men after me—or you, but *she* would do anything to protect her own interests. I *know* she's involved up to her eyebrows."

"Do you have any proof?"

"Jess, are you listening to me? The Morton's own the company that's behind Project 42 and Palmer is running for president—they own *her*."

Jessica thought about that. It all seemed to add up. "Kevin Nguyen is working for the Morton people, then?"

"Or directly for Palmer."

"She threatened me."

"What did she say?"

Jessica had no difficulty remembering Christine Palmer's words. "She said: 'We know what you're up to, you little scammer. Don't think you're going to get away with it.' Do you think she meant that in reference to you blowing the whistle? Or did she mean me it, thinking I was an industrial spy like Nguyen believed? Because she must have known they were already holding you."

Jenna's face reflected her frustration. "It doesn't matter why. The fact is, she's evil and she threatened you—doesn't that tell you—?"

A loud rapping on the front door cut her off mid-sentence.

THIRTY-ONE

Zebediah Gold was worried. Despite what he had said to Claudia, he was deeply afraid that Jessica—he had to remind himself not to think of her as Jenna anymore—might have hurt herself.

The drive up from Venice had taken twice as long as it should have. He must have been nuts to think PCH would be faster than the 101 when there was road construction along the Santa Monica end, and the tourists and surfers were still clogging the Palisades and Malibu. He'd been two hours on the road, during which he hadn't much resembled the Zen therapist Jessica had seen in his office. He had fretted and fumed, second-guessing himself that he should have insisted on accompanying Joel Jovanic when he and Claudia brought Jessica the news of her child's death.

If Jessica didn't answer the door, he decided as he knocked, he would call Ventura PD and ask for a welfare check.

Hearing sounds inside the apartment, he let out the breath he had been holding. Then the door opened and a surprised face peeped out at him.

"Dr. Gold! What are you doing here?"

"Hello, Jessica. You weren't answering your phone, so I wanted to make sure you were okay."

"I'm Jenna," she said, which immediately put him on alert. He had been concerned that after learning about Jessica's car accident she would dissociate again and not recognize him. The door opened wider and for a startled moment Gold wondered if he was seeing double, except for the black eye and bruises that were a sick decoration on one of the faces.

"Look what I found out," the bruised version said. "I have a twin!"

Gold blinked in confusion. "*Not* what I was expecting. What—"

"Come in," they said in unison, and stepped back for him to enter. One of them offered him the armchair and both went to put on coffee, with promises to bring him up to date on everything that had happened.

Gold, thoroughly bemused at the turn of events, but thankful to have his concerns about Jessica allayed, wanted to know first about the rainbow of bruises on her face; the ruined love seat seemed ominous. What had happened here?

Jenna brought the coffee, while Jessica fixed a towel over the cushions. The two young women sat close together on the loveseat: Jenna, prim, with her hands folded in her lap, as she had done in his office, while Jessica fidgeted. Their looks were eerily alike, but the temperamental differences were conspicuous to a trained observer.

Jenna began, then Jessica took over the astonishing tale. They took turns until they had reached the end. "So, Kevin Nguyen says the police aren't going to believe us," Jessica said, wrapping up. "Do you think he's right?"

"Detective Jovanic could probably answer that better than I," said Gold. "But I'm sure he would agree that you should file a complaint with Ventura PD. This is all mind-boggling—and coming from me, that's saying a lot."

"You do believe us, don't you?" Jessica asked, clearly anxious. "I know it sounds crazy, but…"

"It's all so crazy we *couldn't* make it up," Jenna added.

"I believe what my own eyes are telling me," said Gold. "The two of you could be clones. It's easy to see how the people at your job might be fooled. *I* certainly believed she was you, Jenna."

He tugged his beard, contemplating what they had told him. "From what this Kevin Nguyen said, they've anticipated you reporting them. It sounds like they've removed or destroyed any physical evidence at BioNeutronics. But, at the very least, the police can open a vandalism investigation and start there."

"But what about the fact that Jen was kept under sedation all that time, not knowing what was happening to her?" Jessica said. "And what about my face? The bruises are evidence, aren't they?"

Gold nodded. "It shows you were assaulted, though I don't know how you can prove who did it. As for Jenna's situation, if Nguyen claims to have a signed consent form for whatever they did to Jenna, it might complicate matters, but that shouldn't stop you from filing a complaint."

"It *can't* be my signature," Jenna stated flatly. "I would never willingly have signed anything like that. And if they got me to sign something while I was drugged, that would be illegal. Couldn't I hire Claudia Rose to prove that I didn't sign it?"

"You could, but first you'll need to get a copy of the document."

"I'll get a copy."

Seeing the stubborn set of Jenna's jaw, Dr. Gold was convinced that she would do as she said. His glance went from one twin to the other. Looking at them side by side, Jessica had a slightly more delicate prettiness. But separate them, and anyone would be hard pressed to identify which was which.

"I must confess," he said, addressing Jenna, since Jessica wouldn't know the answer. "I'm curious about you two. Did you fool people a lot growing up?"

"We used to switch off at school and on dates," Jenna told him. "We switched off when one of us was getting punished, too, which was often. We shared the punishment."

Jessica had given very little thought to her family. It was as if finding Jenna—her other half—was enough for now.

"We were adopted at birth," Jenna continued. "What our parents really wanted was a pair of dolls to show around in public, and then put away in a closet until the next time we were required. They weren't particularly nice people."

"Was the mother very tall and thin with longish black hair?" Jessica asked.

"Yeah, that's Lorraine," Jenna said, getting excited. "Do you remember her?"

"While I was locked in that room last night I had a flash. I think she pushed me into the deep end of a swimming pool when

I was pretty small."

"She did. You were crying bloody murder because you couldn't swim. She thought it was funny. The gardener had to drag you out. I was scared to death you'd drowned. You never wanted to go near the water after that."

"Yet, we both live near the beach."

"We were raised in Ventura. You moved to Escondido after the accident. There was an insurance settlement—"

"What about the father?" Jessica interrupted.

"Parker. He's a big shot in banking, way too busy at the office to notice what his wife was doing, which was mostly lying in bed, drugged up to her eyeballs, or at the bar with her girlfriends. Until we were about twelve and started rebelling, she used to bring us out in matching dresses that the nanny picked out for us, with disgusting big pink bows in our hair. She pretty much ignored us the rest of the time."

"That feels familiar," Jessica said. "No wonder I didn't want to remember her."

"We left home the minute we could and never looked back. We had each other, and that was always enough." A scowl clouded Jenna's face. "Until you married that piece of crap Greg, anyway."

"Stop. I'm not ready to go there."

"You'll have to face it sometime."

"Not now, okay? I don't want to think about it."

"Sticking your head in the sand won't make it go away."

"Yes, it did."

Seeing an argument brewing, Zebediah Gold, who had been paying close attention, fascinated by the way the two sisters interacted, cut in, "I can see that you two have different ways of operating. It might be a good idea to slow down and take some time to get to know each other again."

Jenna glared at him with a level of antagonism that seemed not at all to fit with the impression he had formed of her. It was Jessica who spoke up. "You're right, Dr. Gold. It was really nice of you to come all the way up here to check on us—although you didn't know there was an 'us.'

"We appreciate your concern, but as you can see, we're fine," Jenna added stiffly.

Gold smiled. "Well, you're safe for now, but after all you've both been through, 'fine' may be stretching it."

"We'll handle it," Jenna said, standing up and extending her hand in a formal dismissal. "Thank you for coming. We've got a lot of files to look through on the computer, so…"

Gold rose from his seat. "I'm glad you have each other to lean on. Is there anything I can do to help you through this?"

Jenna spoke up quickly. "No. The questions we need answers to are on that flash drive."

"Are you sure you still want to be involved in that?" Dr. Gold asked pointedly. "It's already proved dangerous to both of you. Maybe you should consider letting it go."

"I've already suggested that," Jessica said.

"Thank you for coming, Doctor Gold," Jenna said, walking to the door and opening it. "We'll think about it and let you know if we need your help."

THIRTY-TWO

"That was rude," Jessica said, as Jenna locked the door behind Dr. Gold with a decisive click. "He drove a long way to see if we were okay."

"He was going to try and talk us into giving up on Project 42, and that's not happening. What those people are doing is wrong."

"Of course it is, but like he said, are you totally certain you still want to try and fight them?"

"*Especially* after everything that's happened. If they get away with what they're doing I could never live with myself."

"But you're not even sure what it is they're doing."

"I'm sure they're experimenting on people without telling them the truth about it. I just don't know *specifically* why. I don't even know what they did to *me*. Now, are you with me or not? I was doing it alone before you got here, so I can finish it alone."

"No," Jessica said, with more than a twinge of misgiving. "I can't let you get into any more trouble by yourself."

After sharing a quick lunch, Jenna sat back at the computer desk, and Jessica stretched out on her stomach on the bed. "What was in the email that got you thinking something was wrong?" Jessica asked.

"It was from Dr. Kapur—a printout of an email was stuck in some papers Simon gave me to file. He obviously didn't know it was there."

"What did it say?"

"I'd already read some of the memos about advertising for subjects with sexual dysfunctions, and also normal people who would like to boost their sexual prowess, male and female—like, who wouldn't? We were advertising at colleges and sex clinics, places like that." She paused and went through a series of mouse clicks that brought up an email on the screen. "I'd typed up all those specs, so when I found this printout, I read it. But then... here it is, the original email."

Jessica got up and leaned over Jenna's shoulder to read the monitor.

Venerated Dr. Lawrie:

"Kind of an odd way to address him, don't you think?"

"No, he's from Bangalore. They're much more formal than we are."

"Okay." Jessica continued reading aloud.

"The first rounds of animal testing have been a rousing success—pun intended. We are now ready to begin testing human subjects. The subject will, of course, be able to fully control the main device. The sub-device, which the subject will be completely unaware of, will piggyback off it. Currently, it has a range of about 1-plus miles."

Frowning, Jessica re-read the words out loud. "Am I reading this right? There are *two* devices and one is unknown to the person who gets it?"

"That's what got my attention. The way I read it, the volunteers are getting something they didn't agree to."

"So, if the sexual stimulant is the secondary device, what does the *main* device do?"

"My point exactly! And whatever it is, if they don't know about it, it needs to be exposed. Maybe if we keep digging through all these files we'll find the answer. When I call the FDA, or whatever 3-letter organization controls things like this, I don't want to look like some wacko.

"I didn't want Simon to get into trouble, so before I did anything, I needed to see what else he might have been hiding from me. That's why I downloaded everything about the project I could find from his computer. I hid it in the planter and planned to go back for it on the weekend. I was going to come up with some excuse to go to the office."

"Like I did with the coffee cup," Jessica said.

"Twin minds think alike," Jenna said, scrolling down the monitor. "There's a whole batch of emails here. Let's see what they say."

Most of the emails proved to be nothing more enlightening than routine scheduling issues. After reading through a long series of dry communications between Simon Lawrie and Dr. Kapur, Jessica covered a wide yawn. "This is really boring."

"Take a break," Jenna suggested. "I'm going to keep going."

Jessica closed her eyes and was dozing on the bed when Jenna's excited voice roused her. "Holy crap, Jess, look at this."

My Dear Dr. Lawrie,

Another test subject—not the one we discussed last week—has been experiencing unanticipated side effects. The pulse generator has become unstable and he needs to be immediately removed from the trial.

"I wonder what the side effects were," Jessica said. "And whether it's the primary or the secondary device that gave him the problem."

"*That's* a very important question. We need to know who the test subjects were that experienced problems."

Lowering herself flat on the floor, Jessica began to slowly bicycle her legs to keep her bruised knee from stiffening up. She felt like a creaky old woman. "Are there any spreadsheets or database files that would list the people participating?"

"How would that help? We don't know who the subjects are that Kapur is referring to. He said "another" test subject."

"Wouldn't they have to record it when someone was booted from the trial?"

"Good point. If we can find out who they are, we can call and pretend to be following up for the lab."

Jenna sorted the computer list by file type and browsed through it. One file had an .xls extension, which designated it as a spreadsheet. She double-clicked on the file to open it. Rows and columns of data filled the screen.

"It's got names, code numbers, contact information, everything!" Jessica said, excited. "How many people are in the study?"

Jenna tapped the Ctrl and End keys, which took her to the bottom of the spreadsheet. "Two-hundred forty-seven."

"Go to the top of the document and look at the column headings. Is there one for rejects?"

"There's a column titled 'Dismissed.'"

Jenna sorted by the column she had pointed to. When the sort was complete, the top four cells had a date entry in the column. The following rows in that column were blank, which they took to mean that four people had been removed from the study. The dates in the cells for the blank named entries were within the previous two months. Following the row back to column A with a fingertip, Jenna pointed out that three of the subjects who had been dismissed were male, one female.

"Read me the names and phone numbers," Jessica said.

After Jessica had recorded the numbers, Jenna set her cell phone so caller ID would not identify her name or number, and dialed the female subject.

Candace Childers, age 36, lived in Moorpark, only a few miles from the BioNeutronics lab. An automated message came on, informing them that Childers' mailbox was full.

"Let's google her," said Jenna. She pulled up a browser and typed in the woman's name and town.

"She's on Facebook," Jessica said, pointing over Jenna's shoulder to the top Google result. The link took them to Childers' Facebook profile. "Jeez, why would *she* need a sexual stimulant? Anyone would call her a hottie."

Candace Childers' profile picture portrayed an attractive woman in black leather pants with an emerald green tank top. Head thrown back, her copper hair cascaded over her shoulder as she stretched on a lounge chair in a provocative pose, offering up a seductive smile.

"Oh hell," Jenna said. She was pointing to several posts left by Childers' Facebook friends:

"We miss you, Candy."
"Wish there were more like you."
"When will it stop hurting?"
"RIP, Candace."
"Today, I heard that song you used to love and I cried."

—

Jenna scrubbed her hands over her face. "Does that sound to you like it does to me?"

"If it sounds to you like she's someplace we're never gonna get to talk to her then, yes, it does."

"I wonder what happened. Car accident? She was only 36."

"It doesn't say. We're out of luck on that one. What's the next number?"

"Tyrone Spence, age 48, lives in Goleta. That's a forty mile drive to the lab." Jessica read out the phone number and Jenna punched it into her cell phone, counting off the rings—two, three…

"Hello, is Mr. Spence available?" There was a pause before she continued, "This is um, Mary Jones with BioNeutronics Laboratories. I'm calling to follow up on—excuse me?"

Jenna's eyes widened. A raised voice sounded through the phone. Jessica couldn't make out the words, but she knew it wasn't good news.

"I—yes, I—I'm really sorry to hear—can you tell me—oh, I see. Thank you, Mrs. Spence. I'm so sorry to have disturbed you." Ending the call, she turned to Jessica with a troubled expression. "Tyrone is in a psychiatric hospital and his wife blames it on the study."

"What happened?"

"A couple of weeks after he got into the study he started having extreme headaches and acting like a crazy dude—her words. She said he was having wild mood swings and then he got violent—which he never had before. It was bad enough for her to call the cops and have him picked up on a three-day hold. He's still there."

The sisters exchanged an uneasy glance. "Could be a coincidence," Jessica said. "Maybe Tyrone was already a crazy dude when he went into the study."

"Uh, uh. The specs called for all subjects to be very carefully screened for psych problems before they could be accepted. We have to assume the research people followed the protocol. Who's next on the list?"

"Matthew Casey, age 42. Lives in Venice."

Jenna punched up the number. "Hello, is this Mr. Casey?" She nodded at Jessica and gave her a thumbs-up. "Mr. Casey, this is Mary Jones with BioNeutronics Laboratories, calling to follow up on your—I—what's that? Well, okay, sure. When would be a good time? Are you still at your Venice address? Good. How's tomorrow at 1:30? I'll see you then. Thank you."

"He asked for a meeting?"

Jenna nodded. "He actually sounded kind of spooked; said he didn't want to talk on the phone. So, it looks like we've got a road trip tomorrow."

"Do you think he'll call the lab and check your creds?"

"No, it wasn't like that. He didn't seem suspicious, just nervous. Who's next on the list?"

"Sean Gilchrist," Jessica read from her paper. "Woodland Hills."

"That's another 80 mile round trip. These guys are pretty motivated." Jenna punched in Gilchrist's number and put the phone to her ear. A moment later, she signaled Jessica that someone was answering the call.

"Could I speak to Sean Gilchrist, please? Mary Jones with BioNeutronics Laboratories to—he what?" The color leached from her face. "Oh, I—I see. I had no idea." Jenna listened for what seemed a long time. Then she said, "Oh, yes, uh, I guess some wires got crossed. I apologize for—" As she was cut off, she stared at Jessica. "Gilchrist is dead. He had what she called a 'psychotic episode' and killed himself three weeks ago."

"Oh—my—God. What else did she say?"

"I quote: 'What do you want from me? Should I thank you for the money? I want my husband back. Can you give me that?'"

"They paid her off? Isn't that an admission of wrongdoing?"

"She probably had to sign a confidentiality agreement when she accepted the money—that's how those things normally work."

Jessica stared at her sister in growing alarm. Even after all that had happened, the implications were too much to grasp. "Jen, what are the chances it's a coincidence that two of the four people thrown out of the study are dead, and a third is in a psych ward?"

"Slim and none."

"At least Matthew Casey is okay. And he's willing to talk to you."

"I wonder what he wants to talk about. He sounded really uptight." Jenna's turned troubled eyes on her. "What the hell did they do to all those people—*and me*?"

THIRTY-THREE

Jessica woke with a start from her first dreamless sleep since falling into the black hole of amnesia. The room was dark, and for a terrified instant she was back locked in the basement at BioNeutronics. It took a moment to get her bearings and realize she was alone in her sister's bed. And that an alarm was bawling.

Then she smelled the smoke.

Jessica raced to the bedroom door. She touched her hands to the wooden surface, relieved to find it cool, and opened it a crack. The acrid smell of burning paper instantly filled her nose.

Wisps of smoke rose from a small bonfire in the center of the living room floor. Through the haze, Jessica could see the slight form of her twin bending over the fire, her arms filled with books Farley had delighted in ripping apart. Jenna was dropping them, one by one, onto the flames.

Jessica flew across the room. Smoke curled into her nose and seared her palate. Fighting panic, she tried to remember where she had left her phone. She had to call 911 and get some help. Blinking against the smoke, she shouted to her twin. "Jen! Get away from there! Jenna, can you hear me?"

Her words had no effect. The flames were starting to take hold and grow, devouring the dry paper like a hungry beast. Jenna's eyes, eerily illuminated in the flickering light, were enormous, the pupils dilated to the edge of each blue iris as she stared across the flames without comprehension.

As Jessica's fingers closed around her arm, she cried out, "No! I have to burn it all. I have to—"

"Stop it!" Not caring that it meant Jenna dropped her armload, Jessica wrestled her sister away from the scorching heat of the flames. With an anguished sob, Jenna fell to her knees, scrambling for the scattered books.

Over the noise of the smoke alarm, Jessica heard a pounding on the front door, and the voice of the neighbor, Zach. "Jen! Jen! Are you okay? Jenna?"

Zach pushed past her as soon as she opened the door. To Jessica's relief, he was carrying an industrial sized fire extinguisher. At the sight of Jenna, he halted mid-stride and did a double take on Jessica. The obvious question was on his face, but he didn't waste time asking it, just told her to bring some water.

Jenna had crawled back to the fire and seemed to be fixated on feeding the flames. With a muttered oath, Zach forcibly pulled her behind him. He aimed the big fire extinguisher at the base of the fire, blanketing the burning books with a plume of white powder.

Filling the biggest cooking pot she could find, Jessica could hear him yelling at her sister. "What the hell's wrong with you?"

"I don't think she can hear you," Jessica said, carrying the heavy pot to the smoldering embers. If the floor had not been ceramic tile she figured the whole room would have been in flames by now. She dumped the water and stepped away as hot steam hissed into the air.

Before Zach could ask his question, a fat man in striped pajamas appeared at the front door. "Hey dude," he called from the front step. "The fuck's going on? You people okay in here?"

"Yeah, man." It was Zach who replied. "We got it, thanks; we got it covered."

"You call 911?"

"We're okay. Don't worry, I'll make sure it's all out."

"What the hell, man? I can smell smoke up in my place. What happened? It's three a.m.; I gotta work in the morning."

Jessica fetched a dish towel and began fanning the smoke detector, which was wailing loud enough to pierce alligator hide. She spoke over her shoulder. "I'm sorry, I'm really sorry. It was an accident."

The neighbor snorted in disbelief. "Doesn't look like an accident to me." He pointed at Jenna who was on her knees, staring blankly into space. Her lips were moving silently, as if in prayer. "Looks like goddamn arson. What the hell is up with her?"

Jessica continued fanning the alarm. "Can we talk about it tomorrow? I need to take care of my sister."

The fat man scowled, and she thought he was going to argue with her. Not that she could fault him for being bent out of shape. Instead, he simply shook a warning finger. "Okay, fine, but I *will* be back. I hope you have renter's insurance."

Renter's insurance? We'll be lucky if we don't get arrested.

A knot of neighbors in various states of undress had flocked to the gate of Jenna's unit and were chattering among themselves. Jessica heard the fat man advise them that the show was over, followed by the sound of his heavy footsteps on the stairs. A door slammed.

Zach climbed on a chair and removed the battery from the smoke detector. The sudden hush was as deafening as the wail of the alarm. "I didn't know you had a sister," he said to Jessica.

"Actually, *I'm* the sister. I'm Jessica." She held out an unsteady hand.

"Jesus. What—"

"It's a long story, Zach. Too long for right now. If you hadn't brought that fire extinguisher—" With the crisis averted, she was shaking all over.

Zach tipped his head at Jenna. "What's wrong with her?"

"I don't know." That was only half a lie. Jessica wrapped her arm around her twin's shoulders and drew her to her feet. "Are you sure we don't need to call the fire department?"

He shook his head. "Leave it to me; I'll open up everything, get the smoke out, and put the burned shit on the patio."

Jessica gave him a tremulous smile. "Zach to the rescue yet again." Pulling Jenna to her feet, she guided her sister like a life-size doll, walking her past the sodden lump of books—now a filthy, stinking mess soaking up water that had pooled on the tile.

She sat her unresisting twin on the edge of the bathtub. Like a mother caring for a young child, she wiped away the streaks of soot from her sister's face and hands and feet, murmuring to her that everything would be okay, even though she didn't believe it for a moment.

And all the while Jessica worked, Jenna chanted in a whisper, "Burn it down. Burn it all. Burn it all down."

THIRTY-FOUR

They were separated in age by only ten minutes, but Jessica had always felt like the much older sibling. She knew this because during the night, while she had kept vigil over her twin, important chunks of her memory had re-emerged from the black hole into which they had disappeared. But for all the painful facts and details she could now recall with aching clarity, nothing in Jessica's past could have prepared her for the situation in which she now found herself.

Looking down at the features so very like her own, Jessica pondered her sister's bizarre behavior. What had Raisa Polzin and her comrades done to her during her ten day imprisonment at the lab?

Jenna had always been the good twin, eager to please and do what it took to gain approval and acceptance, especially where men were concerned—older men, like Simon Lawrie. Her sudden changes of emotion, the way she had attacked Jessica, were completely out of character. Jessica had assumed it was the aftereffects of the trauma and the drugs Jenna had been given. But setting the fire had taken her behavior to a whole new bizarre level.

Jenna fell into a deep sleep as soon as her head hit the pillow. Worn out and tense, Jessica was too afraid to relax and go to sleep, scared of what Jenna might do next. She sat on the bed beside her as the hours passed, listening to the cleaning noises in the living room.

There was no way she could have handled Jenna without Zach and his fire extinguisher. He seemed to have a talent for being there when she needed him.

When she heard the front door close behind him, Jessica got up and tiptoed out of the bedroom. He had done as he'd promised and hauled the mess out to the patio, leaving the kitchen window and the sliding glass door to the tiny patio open to allow the noxious fumes to escape. Even so, the place reeked of smoke and wet pulp.

The damage was relatively minor and confined to the living room. Charcoal burn marks blackened the ceramic flooring and the leather skirt of the loveseat was scorched. Thank God no one had been hurt.

Except Jenna.

Jenna woke at seven, complaining about the awful smell. Beside her, half-dozing, Jessica came awake. "You don't remember?"

"Remember what?"

"Setting fire to the living room."

Jenna stared at her with wide, uncomprehending eyes. "What do you mean?"

"You. Set. The. Living room. On. Fire. You don't remember that?"

"I remember being really tired last night. We went to sleep and I just woke up...you're serious?"

"As serious as a heart attack. Zach heard the smoke alarm and brought a fire extinguisher."

"Holy shit. I set fire to—*what the hell's wrong with me*?"

"Isn't it obvious...they did something to you. Look, Jen, we can't fight BioNeutronics on our own when we have no idea what they did to you. We need to talk to Dr. Gold. He'll help us."

"You're right, but I—" Jenna stopped mid-sentence. She scrambled out of bed and dove for the bathroom. Seconds later, the sounds of her vomiting made Jessica turn a little green.

Jenna came back, waxy-faced and shivering. "My head hurts. My stomach feels like hell." She fell back into bed and pulled the covers up to her chin.

"It's a reaction to the anesthetic, and the smoke, I think."

Jenna buried her face in her pillow, her words muffled in the soft down. "I feel horrible."

"Ah, Belle, I'm sorry. Do you want me to brush your hair like when we were kids? You always said it made you feel better." How comforting it was to have an old memory to call on, Jessica thought.

"Yes, please." Jenna curled on her side, pulling her knees up to her chest. "I'm so scared, Ariel. I don't know what's happening to me. Something's wrong inside my head."

Jessica fetched a brush from the bathroom and knelt on the bed, drawing it gently through her twin's hair. "We've got to get out of here this morning. We can drive down to my place. I want you as far from BioNeutronics as possible so I can get you some medical help."

"We still have to go see that guy who left the study—Matthew Casey. All the other people who dropped out are dead."

"We can stop in and see him on the way to Escondido, and Dr. Gold, too."

"Ouch!"

Jessica stopped brushing. "What's wrong? Did I hurt you?"

Jenna reached up and touched a spot near the top of her skull. "It's tender here. It feels like a bruise. Can you see anything?"

With a spooky sense of déjà vu, remembering how she had asked Dr. Gold to do exactly the same thing, Jessica knelt on the bed and parted the hair on her sister's scalp. Her stomach dropped at what she saw.

"There's a little shaved spot. The hair is starting to grow back, but it almost looks like an insect bite in the center. I mean, it's not, but it's sort of a pinpoint red spot."

Dread widened Jenna's eyes. "Oh my God; oh my God, Jessica! The experiment Kevin Nguyen was talking about—they've implanted the device in *me!* They made me act crazy. They made me set the fire." Tears streamed down her face. "We have to get this thing out of me." She seized her head with both hands as if she would like to rip it off her neck. "What are they going to make me do next?"

In reply, Jessica limped over to the closet and pulled out

her backpack and a small suitcase, tossed them onto the bed. "Pack some clothes, Belle. We're leaving right now. We can finish checking out the Project 42 files at my apartment."

First, they would have to buy a new laptop to replace her wine-soaked one, but that was of little consequence compared with what was facing them. She added, "Maybe we should call Detective Jovanic."

Jenna, feverishly plucking clothes out of the dresser, gave no argument. "We can call him from the road. Let's just get out of here."

Jessica was in the kitchen, packing food into a bag to take with them when a moan from the bedroom sent her rushing back. "Belle, what's wrong?"

Halfway into a pair of Levi's, Jenna was doubled over on the bed, clutching her stomach. "Ah man…it hurts." The pain held on for thirty seconds. When it released, Jenna's face was pinched with pain.

Jessica said, "When we get away from here, we'll find a hospital and…"

"And do what? Tell them I've been implanted with some kind of microchip without my permission and it's making me act like a wacko? Might as well say I was abducted by aliens. We don't even know what the device is supposed to do. It's sure as hell not programmed to make me have better sex."

"The implant will show up on a scan."

"No! The specs said a CT scanner or MRI could cause severe burns around the implant." Another cramp overtook her and she rolled into a ball on the floor.

Jessica felt helpless, the way she had while she'd been imprisoned in the basement, and she hated the feeling. Unplugging the flash drive from Jenna's computer, she dropped it into her backpack. The sooner they got on the road, the better.

With Jessica driving, they took the 101 south, driving fast, eager to get out of Ventura County and closer to their destination. No meandering along the Coast Highway today. The cramps were getting worse with every mile. Whether Jenna wanted to go or not, Jessica intended to take her sister to a hospital as soon as they got to Venice.

A couple of times she glanced in the rearview mirror, but the car she thought might be following them hung back, making it impossible to know for sure. She didn't tell Jenna that she had noticed the same white sedan a few cars behind them almost from the time they had left the apartment. It was probably coincidence, but she kept a careful eye on the vehicle until it exited at Van Ness Avenue in Sherman Oaks.

They were merging onto the 405 when Jenna's cell phone rang. *Just Can't Get Enough* by The Black Eyed Peas, filled the car. "It's Simon," Jenna said, ducking her head in shame.

"Don't tell him anything. Remember, he thinks you've been at the lab for the last two weeks."

Jenna answered the phone. "I'm not coming in today, I'm sick. Simon, I couldn't get to the phone..." Her face crumpled, as if hearing his voice was too painful for her to bear. "I'll find another job...why don't you listen? I told you I don't want to see you anymore. I can't do this, I—" She broke the connection and set the phone in the cup holder between them. Fumbling for a tissue from her purse, she sobbed into it.

"I'm sorry, Jess. I'm such a screwup. I know I should never have gotten involved—" She broke off with a groan, rocking her body back and forth.

Glancing over, Jessica saw a dark stain spreading high up on the leg of Jenna's Levi's, confirming a suspicion that had been forming in her mind over the last hour. "Oh, Belle, you're pregnant, aren't you?"

"Only two months. I wasn't sure, but—"

Jessica finished the sentence in her head. *You're not anymore.*

By the time they arrived at the emergency room at St. John's Medical Center in Santa Monica, Jenna was hemorrhaging. Against her protests, the on-call doctor admitted her for observation. He had wanted to examine the injuries to Jessica's chin and cheekbone, too. She looked like somebody's punching bag, with bruises every color of the rainbow, but she ignored his pointed inquiry and suggested he stick to taking care of her sister.

Jenna's cold hand squeezed hers. "You have to keep the

appointment with Matthew Casey. You have to go as me."

Jessica squeezed back to remind her that they were together in this, wherever it led. "Okay, Belle, if you want me to, I'll keep the appointment."

"Find out what happened to him, *please*?"

The hospital was less than ten miles from where Matthew Casey lived. After leaving Jenna a change of clothes, Jessica entered Matthew Casey's address into the GPS and headed south on Lincoln Boulevard.

On the way, she left a voicemail for Detective Jovanic to call her, then stopped at a CVS drugstore and purchased some heavy pancake make-up designed to camouflage serious blemishes. It wouldn't do to scare Matthew Casey with her bruised face.

Everything about Casey was average—build, hair color, looks. He was the type you passed on the street and never noticed. Even his modest house was indistinguishable from its neighbors, which was saying a lot since homes in Venice tended to be unique.

Jessica's first glimpse of him was one brown eye, peering out at her with suspicion through a small grate in his door. He just stared at her, waiting for her to speak.

She had practiced aloud the alias Jenna had given him over the phone the day before so that it would come out smoothly, but she was nervous anyway. Reminding herself that she had proved to be a good liar, she gave him a bright smile. "Mr. Casey? I'm Mary Jones from BioNeutronics. We spoke on the phone yesterday."

Casey spoke almost in a whisper. "Show me some identification. Hold it up so's I can see it."

That was something she hadn't counted on. Luckily the employee ID badge was still in her purse. She fished it out and flashed it at him, making sure to cover the name 'Jenna Marcott' with her finger.

Casey flicked a glance at the photo of Jenna, then looked at Jessica. "Your hair's different," he said.

"I had it cut a couple of weeks ago."

Apparently satisfied with her answer he opened the front door a crack and stuck his head around it. Gazing over her shoulder, he looked up and down the street, until, apparently not seeing anything that raised his suspicions, Casey opened the door just wide enough for her to push past him. As soon as she was inside, he locked it behind her.

His clothing was as average as he was: off the rack light blue Oxford shirt, neatly tucked in; tan slacks, and brown loafers. His skin was pallid, as if, despite living close to the beach, he didn't get much sun.

Jessica followed him down a short hall to an office-cum-den at the rear of the house. The small room, which had probably been a second bedroom in a previous incarnation, had the appearance of a solitary man's abode. Forty-six-inch TV, red plaid sofa, well-worn recliner, and a laptop that sat open on an ottoman in front of the chair.

"We can't be seen from the street back here," Matthew Casey said in a low voice that sent a shiver up Jessica's spine.

"Are you worried about being seen?" she asked.

"They've been watching me." Casey went over and closed the laptop so Jessica couldn't see the website he had been viewing. He indicated that she should sit on the sofa while he took the recliner.

Had his eyes always darted around the room the way they did now, as if he were on high alert for danger? Or was it his experience with BioNeutronics that had left him hyper-vigilant?

Jessica perched on the edge of the sofa. "What makes you think you're being watched?"

Casey stopped his surveillance of the den and tapped the top of his head. "I can feel it here." He zeroed in on her. "Why are you here, Ms. Jones? What do you want from me?"

Jessica, already suspecting that she had just entered the presence of a nut job, gave him the warmest smile she could summon up. "We like to follow up on people who are released from the study to see how they're doing."

"I already signed all your papers. I took your damn payoff." Casey's eyes narrowed. "I've signed that I'm not going to complain to any authorities about what happened to me. So what I want to know is, why would you care how I'm doing now?"

"We do care, Mr. Casey. Can you tell me about your experiences with our lab? This interview is completely confidential and independent of the research project. I don't have your records. I only know that you left the study early." Jessica knew she was taking a chance with this approach, but something in his face told her it had been the right thing to say.

"You don't know what happened to me?"

"No, I'd like to hear your story. How long did you participate in the study?"

He hesitated. "I lasted three weeks."

"Can you tell me what happened?" Jessica prompted when he didn't continue.

"I—I—" Casey's breathing had quickened. "After the implant—"

"Was there a problem with the, er—insertion?" She couldn't think of what else to call it, but he shook his head.

"No, that was totally painless. For a few days, I even thought I might be one of the placebo subjects—you know, where they didn't really do anything? They told me that was a possibility when I signed up."

Jessica understood that in pharmaceutical research a certain number of anonymous subjects were administered a placebo instead of the genuine drug. "Did you meet with a psychologist at the lab before entering the study?" she asked.

"Oh yeah, I sailed right through that." There was a certain degree of self-satisfaction in the way he said it. "No problems there. I never had any of those kinds of problems *before*."

His forehead had broken out in a fine sheen of perspiration. He took a folded paper towel from his shirt pocket and patted his forehead.

"Are you okay, Mr. Casey?" Jessica asked.

"Call me Matt."

"Okay, Matt. Would you like me to get you a glass of water?"

He dabbed the paper towel against his neck. "Let's just get this over with."

"Okay, you were telling me about your experience after the implant." Jessica said. She waited expectantly, but Matthew Casey gave no response.

The seconds stretched. Casey's unblinking eyes were as vacant as a hologram on pause, the way Jenna's had been during the fire.

Jessica leaned forward. "Matt?"

Casey seemed to catch himself. "Uh, why am I talking to you again?"

What the hell is going on here?

"I'm following up on the BioNeutronics study."

"Oh, yes. The study. Um, they said if I got the real device it would help me with—well, you know…" He lowered his voice. "I had prostate surgery a while back, and it left me—"

"I understand," Jessica interrupted, not eager to hear the details of his operation. "So you had a procedure to implant the device in your brain…and—?"

"Yeah, it was quick, easy. Overnight stay at the lab and I was back home." He covered his mouth with his hand and gave a girlish giggle. "I have to say, it worked great. I felt wonderful; my girlfriend was *very happy.*"

"But you left the study."

Casey glanced away, shifting uncomfortably in his chair. Then, moving so fast that Jessica nearly jumped out of her skin, he sat forward on the edge of his seat, tilting his body closer to her. "Who wants to know about this? Who are you reporting to?"

"As I mentioned, it's an independent follow-up. Completely confidential, Matt. Nobody will know what you tell me." Jessica justified the lie to herself. She would certainly share what Casey told her with Detective Jovanic and anyone else if she thought it would help Jenna.

"You're not with *them*? The ones who are watching?"

"No, I'm *definitely* not with them."

Casey leaned further, apparently trusting the conviction in her voice. He dropped his voice to a near-whisper. "About a week after I got the implant my girlfriend started accusing me of doing things I didn't remember doing."

Jessica felt a chill. "What kinds of things?"

"She said I got *violent*. That's crazy. I'm not a violent person. Why would she make that up? And then she showed me a big bruise on her arm; she told me I'd knocked her down and she fell against the dresser. I would never hurt her. Why would she say something like that?"

"I don't know, Matt. What do you think happened?"

"She *must* have made it up. I have no memory of doing anything like that, and I would remember something like that, wouldn't I?" His voice rose, becoming agitated. "I'm not a violent person. I'm *not*!"

Jessica put her hands out to calm him down. "It's okay, I believe you."

"There were other times when she'd say I was much more loving than usual and that I'd do nice things—you know, sexual things, and—"

"Do you remember doing the nice things?" Jessica broke in before he could get graphic.

Matthew Casey cocked his head to the side, a smile curving his thin lips. "What I do remember is a feeling of extreme pleasure, like I was floating on a cloud and nothing could bring me down. What it must feel like to be high on heroin or cocaine. Of course, I don't know for sure, as I've never been one to do drugs, but I really—"

"So it wasn't all bad?"

"Oh, no. Sometimes it was *fantastic*. That's why I didn't want to give it up when they made me leave the study—it felt so good. At least the money is helping tide me over until I can get back to work."

"You're not working?"

Casey scowled. "I lost my job over it. My boss lied, too. Accused me of acting crazy, having mood swings. Isn't it against the law to fire somebody for that? I mean, it's not my fault, right?"

"Do you mind if I ask you how much the lab offered you?"

"Seventy-five thousand—a year's pay."

"So, you signed some papers that said..." Jessica trailed off, giving him room to finish her sentence.

"Yeah, yeah. I signed away my right to complain if I continued having problems. But besides the money, there were the psych benefits. They cover my therapy forever, so all in all, it was a pretty good deal."

"And are you continuing to have problems?"

"The only problems I have are those people out there watching me. Why are they doing that? Do they think I'm going to go back on my word? Do they think I'm stupid?"

"Relax, Matt, nobody thinks you're stupid. Have you actually seen somebody spying on you?"

"Of course not. They're too clever to let me see them. But I can *feel* them." He tapped his head again. "I can feel them in here."

"Have you thought about having the implant removed?"

"The lab people said it can't be removed, but I forget why. You know, I liked the way it made me feel—the good feeling, I mean. I don't remember the bad feeling. What's weird is, it didn't seem to have anything to do with whether I activated the device or not. It just happened randomly. Sometimes I'd realize that I didn't know what had happened until maybe fifteen minutes after."

Like Jessica having no memory of setting the fire.

"How is the device activated, Matt?"

"Wait here; I'll show you." He jumped up and left the room, back a moment later with a small plastic case that looked like an electronic tablet. "This is the transmitter. I just had to press a couple of keys and it would happen like magic. Look—"

"Uh, that's okay, you don't have to demonstrate."

Casey flushed bright red. "Well, of course I'm not going to demonstrate it! You think I'm some kind of pervert? Anyway, they deactivated the transmitter when I left the program. I was supposed to return it, but...hey, what the hell kind of person do you think I am, anyway?"

"Sorry, I didn't mean to offend you." Jessica stood up and extended her hand. She'd gotten what she came for, and the way his paranoia seemed to be heightening, she was more than ready to go. "Thank you, Matt. I appreciate you taking the time to talk to me."

Matthew Casey looked down at Jessica's outstretched hand as if it were something foreign attached to her arm. She saw his pupils dilate, his jaw slacken. With memories of her encounter with Bagshot and Farley still fresh in her mind, she knew she had to go.

"Who *are* you?" Casey said. "What do you *really* want?"

"Thanks for your time, Matt," Jessica said breathlessly. She hurried into the hallway, getting out her keys and pushing them between her fingers—a method of self defense she had learned. She had no desire for a confrontation with Casey, but she wouldn't hesitate to use the keys as a weapon if she had to.

"You're with *them*." Casey grabbed her shoulder and squeezed hard. "You're trying to hurt me."

Jessica wheeled around and slammed into him, knocking him on his butt, almost losing her own balance in her haste to get out of the house. She threw herself at the front door, tackling the unfamiliar lock as Casey picked himself up and came at her with a low growl.

The lock gave. Jessica wrenched open the door, hitting Casey with it as she ran outside. She had the Nissan unlocked with the key fob well before she reached the curb. Sprinting across the lawn, she flung herself into the car and locked the door, but when she turned back to look, Casey wasn't chasing her. His fear of the 'watchers' held him hostage in his home.

Accelerating away, Jessica could hear him shouting after her from his doorway. She had almost reached the end of the block when she caught sight of a familiar white sedan parked on the street.

THIRTY-FIVE

It was the same car she had seen before, Jessica was sure of it. Whether it was driven by Farley, Bagshot, or someone else, she had no idea. The windows were tinted, the visor down, preventing her from seeing who was in the driver's seat, but she had no doubt that Kevin Nguyen had set a tail on her. There must have been at least two of them switching off, like on TV cop shows. When the white car exited the freeway in Sherman Oaks, she had let down her guard, not noticing a second tail ready to take up pursuit. The white car must have picked them up again later when she was not paying attention.

Of course Nguyen was not about to let them go as easily as he had pretended.

Jessica phoned the hospital and was told that Jenna was being prepped for a D&C after the miscarriage and would not be able to speak to her for several hours. At least she knew that her sister was safe…for the time being.

"Changed your mind, doll baby?" Simon said, when he answered Jessica's call from Jenna's cell phone on her way back north. "Ready to make up?"

The lightness of his tone enraged her. Because of him her twin was in excruciating physical and emotional pain. And what affected her twin affected Jessica.

"This *is not* Jenna," Jessica answered in a tight, cold tone. "My name is Jessica Mack. I'm Jenna's sister."

"What the hell are you talking about? She's never mentioned a sister."

"Did you ever *ask* if she had a sister, Simon? No, I didn't think so. You kept her busy taking care of *your* needs, you arrogant asshole. We're identical twins, and *I'm* the one you've been working with for the past couple of weeks. Remember, the one with the haircut?"

"*What the—*"

"Surprise, surprise. Want to know why? Because Kevin Nguyen had Jenna kidnapped over your goddamned precious Project 42, and—"

"I don't know what you're talking about," Simon cut in swiftly. "But don't say anything more on that subject. This line is not secure."

Something made her want to keep digging at him. "Fine. I'm on my way to see you right now. But you need to know something. Right this minute, my sister is in a hospital after having a miscarriage. I'll give you one guess as to who the father was."

There was a long pause, then, "I'm sorry to hear that."

"Yeah, I just bet you are. Where do you want to meet? Not in the office. Someplace public."

He hesitated. "Starbucks across the street from the lab. When?"

"I'll be there in an hour."

Simon's voice was strained. "I'll see you there."

The speedometer needle held steady between seventy-five and eighty until Jessica started to hit the Camarillo exits. By the time she reached Las Posas, just a few miles before her off-ramp, every lane had slowed to a crawl. Traffic news said a fender bender at Rose Avenue in Oxnard was the cause of the slowdown, and the final few miles were stop and go.

It crossed Jessica's mind to phone Simon back and let him know she was stuck in traffic and would be a few minutes late, but she was too busy building a head of steam, saving up all the angry words she wanted to spew at him for their in-person meeting.

Exiting at Vineyard, she considered for a moment that what

she was about to do might not be wise. But the machinations at BioNeutronics revolted her, and she was sick at heart at what had happened to her, to Jenna, to all the people who had been suckered into the Project 42 study, not knowing what they were letting themselves in for. Confronting Simon Lawrie was a step towards taking her life back.

Turning onto Oxnard Blvd, she headed for Fifth Street. A block away from the lab, traffic came to a dead stop. A crowd was gathered on the corner, mostly disregarding the police officer who stood in the middle of the road directing traffic. Jessica craned her neck, which allowed her to see the red and white cab of a fire engine blocking the intersection, flanked by a paramedic van and several police cars. She could not see any smashed vehicles, and assumed they had already been cleared away.

The cop was letting a few vehicles through the intersection at a time. When her turn came, Jessica glanced to her left and immediately regretted the impulse. A sheet-covered form lay in the crosswalk.

Visions of the small sheet-covered form of her son taunted her.

Justin.

Not now. Not yet.

There would be time later to grieve.

Turning into the shopping center across from BioNeutronics, Jessica parked behind the oddly pink-painted Starbucks and climbed out of the Nissan, picturing Simon waiting impatiently inside, wondering what she wanted from him. That was fine with her. The more anxious he was, the better she liked it. And he'd sounded pretty anxious when she mentioned Project 42. Jessica had plenty to say.

She was walking toward Starbucks when she heard a voice call out to her. "Jenna! Oh my God, Jen!"

Jessica whirled and saw Keisha Johnson running directly at her. She saw the red-rimmed eyes, the streaks of mascara running down her cheeks…and *knew*. Her heart started racing. "What, Keisha? What? *Tell me.*"

"I can't believe it. I can't—" Keisha's face was a mask of shock. "Simon—ohmigod—I can't" she gasped. "I was coming back from Starbucks. I passed him in the crosswalk. The guy didn't even stop—*I was right there!*"

Oh my God.

Simon was the form under the sheet. Simon was dead at the hands of a hit and run driver.

Jessica could see Keisha's mouth moving, but the words refused to penetrate her ears. Images hurtled across her vision: Simon implying that his wife had done something to hurt Jenna. Christine Palmer's fingernails digging into her arm. Jenna's theory that the obscenely wealthy Morton brothers were bankrolling Project 42, and possibly, secretly, Palmer's presidential campaign.

The flash drive was in her backpack.

Not trusting herself to speak, Jessica turned and climbed back into the Nissan. She drove across the shopping center parking lot, leaving Keisha staring after her, and exited on the far side, away from BioNeutronics and Simon's body lying dead in the street.

Jessica checked into the Crowne Plaza. She had kept a sharp eye on the rearview, her hands gripping the wheel tight enough for her knuckles to whiten as she drove across town. She was reasonably sure she had not been followed, but having missed the tail to Venice, she intended to stay alert.

Her return to the Crowne Plaza seemed to symbolize coming full circle—it was the first place she had seen upon arriving in Ventura. But it was only as she was signing her name to the form the reservationist handed her that the full impact of the irony hit: she had chosen Jenna and Simon's trysting place as a refuge.

She had briefly weighed the idea of using Jenna's computer at the apartment, but the possibility that Kevin Nguyen would send his thugs for another run at her cemented her decision to go to the hotel. Besides, even if Nguyen was somehow able to track her transactions, her credit card would not be processed until she checked out in the morning, and by then she would be on her way to collect Jenna from the hospital.

The hotel's business center had two computer stations. The lone man who sat at one of them did not even look up when Jessica took the other chair. As long as no one wanted to print a boarding pass, she figured she ought to be okay for a while.

The knowledge that Simon's death was a direct result of her phone call plagued her. He had warned that the line was not secure. There was no doubt in her mind that someone had been listening in and heard their arrangements.

Jessica plugged the flash drive into the USB port and scrolled to where they had left off the day before. She began opening files, skimming through mind-numbing articles about technology that used radio frequency identification (RFID), and even satellite mapping technology to link tiny microchips embedded in silicate glass to a database containing the recipient's contact information.

She learned that a law had already been passed in California, and several other states, barring employers from requiring their employees to have microchips implanted in their arm for security purposes. Some senators had actually argued that such a requirement related to a reference in the Bible, Book of Revelation, about: "the Mark of the Beast." Christine Palmer had been in the small minority of senators voting against the law.

After a time, a boy stuck his head in the door telling the man at the other computer it was time to go. Later, a woman came in and plopped down, quickly complaining about how long the printer was taking to spit out her boarding pass. Jessica ignored her and decided to change her tactics. Instead of analyzing the files alphabetically, she would start by reading emails addressed to Simon Lawrie. Soon, engrossed in what she was reading, she stopped paying attention to the activity of the hotel guests who came and went.

Simon, this really has to stop. It didn't matter when it was just a piece of tail you were chasing, but this one is seriously interfering with my plans. Either you do something about it or I'll have to.

The return address was Napalm@yahoo.com. With a name like that, the author of the email had to be Christine Palmer referring to Jenna. Jessica printed it and turned it face down on the computer desk.

Then came an email from Dr. Kapur:

My Dear Dr. Lawrie,

A new issue has arisen that we need to address. The implant is being absorbed by the system which makes it difficult, if not impossible, to remove later if necessary. Further testing is to be scheduled using a newly developed type of silicon. I will keep you posted.

No wonder Matthew Casey had been told that the implant could not be removed. Did "absorbed by the system" mean that brain tissue was growing around it? Jessica's heart filled with dread. Was Jenna stuck with the chip in her head forever?

Another email from NaPalm@yahoo.com, dated two weeks earlier.

I'm getting worried about you, Simon. You're turning namby-pamby and we can't afford to have you getting squeamish now. Think of the future. Soon you can build a bigger, better lab and play scientist to your heart's content. Right now, you've got *to stay on target. Once the device is up and running the way it's intended, we'll give some of our targets the opportunity to try it out–LOL. Those horny old devils on* both *sides of the aisle will jump at the chance to keep it up all night and not have to worry about their dicks falling off from those little blue pills. They'll be begging for it. They'll never put it together. Now buck up Si! For god's sake grow a pair. I want to see the stud I married, not some wimpy asshole.*

"Are you going to be much longer? I need to use one of those computers."

Startled, Jessica glanced up at a woman in a loud striped beach cover-up standing behind her. "You've been here over an hour," the woman said pointedly. "I've come by several times and didn't say anything, but I really have to—"

"Of course, sure. I'm so sorry." Jessica selected Print, closed the file she was reading, and unplugged the flash drive, her head whirling with what she'd read. She collected the printouts of the emails she had thought were worth saving and edged past the woman.

Leaving the relative safety of the hotel, Jessica began to walk up the strand along the beach, sorting through the facts she'd accumulated from reading Simon's emails. If she understood correctly, Project 42 was intended to be used on unsuspecting members of Congress—but for what purpose?

She thought about it for a while. The microchip they had implanted in Jenna's brain had caused a literal brainstorm that resulted in her setting a fire, leaving no memory of doing so. Matt Casey had been violent without being aware of it. The other people who had left the study ended up dead.

What good did any of that do Raisa Polzin, Dr. Kapur, and whoever they were working for? Were these intended consequences, or were they just playing with their guinea pigs to see what would happen? And were they sending direct messages, or just randomly scrambling their emotions?

As she walked, Jessica tried calling Detective Jovanic again, leaving another message when he did not pick up, then Zebediah Gold, who did. She told him about the fire and Jenna's miscarriage. She told him about her meeting with Matthew Casey; about what she had discovered on the flash drive and her suspicions about the potential uses of the microchip.

"I know it all sounds far-fetched, Dr. Gold, but can you think of anything else that hangs together?"

"I'm perfectly willing to entertain the idea of a conspiracy to control the minds of politicians, Jess. God knows, some of them could use better direction. The question is what you should do with this information. Phoning the FBI or the CIA and telling them that a presidential candidate is plotting against Congress likely wouldn't get you very far, though with the files you have on that flash drive..."

"Simon was *killed* because he was coming to talk to me. It sounds to me like he already suspected that Project 42 was something other than it appeared to be. Jenna certainly raised the suspicion."

Simon Lawrie's sudden brutal death hit her again and she stopped in her tracks, her breath coming in sharp little gasps.

"Jessica?"

"Yeah."

"Are you all right?"

"If you mean am I going to go into another fugue? No, Dr. G., I'm still here. It might be easier if I could, but Jen needs me. *I* need me."

Thanks to his wife's status as a U.S. Senator, Simon Lawrie's untimely death was splashed across the six o'clock news. Sitting on the bed in her hotel room, Jessica watched video of a grim-faced Senator Christine Palmer being driven through the gates of an estate in upscale Montecito near Santa Barbara. According to the reporter covering the story, Palmer had flown home from DC in a private jet as soon as word of the tragedy had reached her.

Eyewitnesses described a big black SUV, but no one was able to provide a description of the driver, leaving police with few leads. Anyone with information about the hit and run was requested to contact the Oxnard Police Department. Jessica had a sinking feeling that she knew who had driven the SUV—Bagshot. But the police weren't going to take her 'feeling' as evidence.

"Poor guy didn't stand a chance," a witness said to the reporter. "That SUV plowed right into him."

Another: "He must have gone fifty feet in the air; came down, boom. The guy didn't even slow down."

"Are you sure the driver was male?" the reporter asked.

"Nuh uh; I just figured, you know? That's cold. A woman wouldn't do something like that."

THIRTY-SIX

"I haven't seen her yet," the charge nurse said, consulting her computer monitor. "I just came on shift. But from the notes, it looks like she's doing fine this morning. Once the doctor comes by for rounds and gives the okay, you'll be able to take her home. She's in room 432. Go on and wait with her."

Jessica thanked her and navigated the maze of hallways leading to Jenna's room. It took less than the flick of an eyelash to register the empty bed, and the swing-arm table cleared of personal items. A discarded IV line lay on the crumpled sheets; the adhesive tape that had fastened the needle to Jenna's hand was still attached to it. The clean clothes on the chair where Jessica had placed them the previous afternoon were gone. A blue and white hospital gown lay in a small heap on the floor.

Jessica rushed back to the nurse's station. "My sister isn't in her room. Where is she?"

The nurse looked up at her, startled. "What?"

"Was she moved to another room? Jenna Marcott."

"Let me check. No, she should be in 432. Are you sure that's where you went?"

"Yes, I'm sure. Her clothes are gone—"

"What would she be wearing?"

"Levis and a black t-shirt, running shoes. You've got to find her!"

"You need to calm down, honey. She probably got dressed and she's taking a walk around the floor, or she's gone down to the cafeteria for coffee. She certainly was here before shift change because they noted her meds. That was about," The nurse consulted her watch, "forty minutes ago. She can't have gone far."

"You don't get it—she may have been kidnapped!"

The nurse picked up the desk phone and paged Security.

After thirty minutes of pacing the waiting room while they searched the hospital, Jessica extracted a promise from the nurse to call her if they found any trace of her sister, then got back on the highway. The invisible antenna that kept her connected to her twin was drawing her back to Ventura.

A ripple of anxiety had started in her chest and was swelling towards full-blown hysteria. Was Jenna experiencing it, too? Is that where this throat-choking anxiety came from? Identical twins shared DNA; they were two halves of the same person. How could one not know what the other was thinking, experiencing? If you stubbed your toe, your whole body knew it.

So, where are you Jenna?

As she drove, Jessica checked her phone, furious with herself when she saw that she had missed a call from Jenna's number at eight o'clock that morning. No message. She had been in the shower and failed to hear the phone ring. She should have checked it earlier.

Her return call went straight to voicemail. Either her twin was on the phone or her phone was turned off. Jessica left an urgent message: *Call me!*

Five minutes later when Jessica's phone rang it was Detective Jovanic on the line. Dr. Gold had brought him up to date on what they'd uncovered on the flash drive and her visit to Matthew Casey. To that, Jessica added the information that Jenna was missing from the hospital.

The detective made no bones about his opinion. "Listen, Jessica, I strongly advise you to stop playing investigator and stay *away* from Ventura. Chances are she left under her own steam, but if she didn't, it's too big a risk for you to involve yourself in finding her."

"But I *am* involved. And how could she have left under her own steam? I've got her car."

"Call Venice PD and report her missing. Let them do their job."

"Do you really think they'd take me seriously?" Jessica pulled into a gas station, arguing with Jovanic while she filled the tank. "Can you get someone at the FBI to listen?"

"Better than *you're* listening, Jessica. You're asking for my help; you need to take my advice."

She replaced the nozzle, screwed on the gas cap, and got back on the road. "I'm sorry, Detective, but if I didn't follow my intuition and something else happened to her I would never forgive myself." Her voice cracked. "She doesn't even know that Simon is dead."

Jessica heard him release an irritated sigh. "I'll meet you after I get off work. Where will you be?"

"I'm going to Jenna's apartment to see if she's there."

"Text me if you find her."

"Of course. And, thank you." Jessica knew he was annoyed with her failure to heed his warning and she felt bad about it, but it could not be helped. She knew in every cell of her body that her twin had returned to Ventura. She just didn't know how.

Jessica's cell phone rang again. The hospital.

"What color hair does your sister have?" the security officer asked.

"Blonde, like mine, only longer. Why?"

"There's a bunch of blonde hair in the trash can in her room."

THIRTY-SEVEN

Jenna Marcott climbed into the big black truck and pulled the door shut behind her. She dumped her bundle of soiled clothes onto the floorboard and turned to the driver. "I was afraid you wouldn't come after the other night—the fire—"

Zach Smith gave her a wink. "You think I'd leave you stranded, chicklet?" He checked traffic and pulled into the flow on Venice Boulevard. He had not quizzed her when she'd asked him to drive the sixty-five miles to come get her; he just wanted to know where to find her. And slightly more than an hour later, there he was in his pickup.

She had seen the curiosity in his face when she flagged him down on the street instead of having him come to the front of the hospital, but he had not asked why. Jenna felt a warm rush of gratitude for her neighbor.

When Zach had phoned right after she'd unsuccessfully tried to reach Jess, it seemed providential. He had not known Jenna was in the hospital, of course, and she told him only that she was there for a minor procedure. If he wondered why she needed to drive all the way to Santa Monica for a minor procedure, he refrained from asking that, too.

"You really did cut your hair," Zach observed as Jenna buckled herself in. "Or, don't tell me, you're actually Jessica?"

"No, it's really me. They weren't going to release me until Jess got here and she didn't answer her phone. I figured if I looked like her, I could just walk out the front door. I found some surgical scissors on a cart in the hallway." She didn't tell him that she had another reason for the new hairstyle.

Zach threw her an admiring glance. "That was pretty resourceful."

"Pretty desperate," she corrected.

"I have to admit, it was a big surprise that you had an identical twin."

"Jess has been going through a rough time the last few months. There wasn't any reason to mention it before, and now…" The fear that had shadowed her all morning slammed her in the chest. "I wish I knew why she didn't answer the phone."

"Did you leave a voicemail?"

"I was afraid to." Fighting the urge to wring her hands as she always did when she was anxious, Jenna made herself hold them still in her lap. "I know this is going to be hard to believe, but…the other night—the fire—I don't remember anything. I only know what Jess told me happened."

She hesitated, unsure of how much she ought to share with him. "At the lab where I work, they're doing research on—on behavior control. I know this is going to sound crazy, but they kidnapped me and implanted a microchip in my brain. And then, when they thought Jess was me, they kidnapped her, too…" Jenna broke off, realizing just how deranged her story sounded. "It's all true, Zach, I swear. After they let us both go, they made me start the fire and…"

"Wait, back up. Did you just say you were *kidnapped*?"

"Yes! Two men broke into my apartment and took me. When I woke up, it was ten days later and Jess was there." She expelled a long huff of frustration. "It's a long, complicated story, and believe me, you're better off not knowing the details. You don't need to be involved."

Zach's eyebrows shot up. "It kinda feels like I'm already involved."

"I'm sorry. I shouldn't have asked you to come. I didn't know what else to do."

"It's okay, Jen, I'm just trying to understand what the hell's going on here."

"I need you to get me to the lab, Zach. I think they might have taken Jess again. I'm afraid they're going to implant the microchip in her, too. You can just drop me at the door. I'll get myself home from there. Please?"

"And you're going to do what—rush in and rescue her?"

"I don't know what I'm going to do, but I have to find out if they've got her. I have to call my—my boss, and make him…what are you doing?"

Zach pulled over to the curb and turned off the engine.

"Why are we stopping? I need to get to Oxnard."

He was staring straight ahead through the windshield, but she got the impression that he wasn't looking at anything particular. She could feel his reluctance as strongly as if it were some physical barrier between them. A nasty little frisson crawled over her.

"There's something I gotta tell you, Jen. It's bad."

Jenna's heart stopped. "About Jess?"

"No, I haven't seen Jessica since the other night. It's about the lab—your boss." He shifted in his seat and looked at her with eyes softened by sympathy. "There was an accident yesterday afternoon."

Jenna's pulse roared in her ears. "What kind of accident? Is Simon okay?"

"No, babe, he's not okay." Zach paused. "I'm sorry."

"I don't understand. What happened?"

"Dr. Lawrie was crossing the street. It was a hit and run."

"You're not saying—he's not…" Jenna shook her head, refusing to accept what Zach was telling her. She wanted to call him a liar, to rail at him. She wrapped her arms around herself and held on tight, shaking her head as if her denial would change the facts. "You have to say it, Zach! I won't believe it unless you say it."

Zach reached across her into the glove box. He plucked a couple of paper napkins from a stack and pushed them into her hand. "Ah, hell, chicklet, I'm sorry."

"Say it! You have to say it."

"Okay, I'll say it. Simon Lawrie is dead."

She thought of the last night they had spent in each other's arms. For all his arrogance and chauvinistic ways, Simon had made Jenna feel safe. She had foolishly believed the sweet words he poured into her ear, until she found that memo and realized that he knew what was going on with Project 42.

"He was your secret guy, wasn't he?" said Zach, breaking into her spell.

Jenna nodded automatically, unable to speak. What did it matter now if Zach, or anyone else knew the truth? "He wouldn't leave her. He—"

"It's okay, Jenna, I'm here for you."

"It was his wife," she sobbed against his chest, wetting his shirt. "She did this."

"What do you mean?"

"It was no accident, Zach." Her voice hardened and she sat up straight, narrowing her eyes. "Christine Palmer wants to rule the whole damn world and the Mortons are going to help her do it."

"Okay, Jen, now you're scaring me. This is beginning to sound way crazy. You're in shock."

"Don't patronize me, Zach. She's a power-hungry, ambitious bitch. She'd do *anything* to get what she wants, and what she wants is the White House. If Simon was standing in her way, she wouldn't hesitate for—oh God. Simon is *dead!*"

The BioNeutronics parking lot was empty when they arrived. It was mid-morning and no security guard was on duty. Zach wanted to go in with her, but Jenna asked him to wait outside. That way, if she got caught, he would have deniability and could go for help.

A handwritten sign had been taped to the glass door: *Due to the sudden tragic passing of the Director, the building will remain closed until Monday.*

Reading those words gave her a chill—as if a ghost had walked through her. She wondered where Simon was now; whether he had suffered on his way there. She'd never had strong opinions about an afterlife, and Jess had pretty much stopped believing in God after Justin's death. But Jenna decided right then that if she survived her attempts to expose the evil that was being perpetrated at BioNeutronics, she was going to have to give the afterlife some serious thought.

For a weird moment, catching sight of herself in the glass

door as she entered, Jenna thought she was looking at her twin. She had done a reasonably good job, chopping off her long hair with the surgical scissors, good enough to pass for Jessica. But the sacrifice of her hair had been for nothing. There was no one at BioNeutronics to fool.

Emptiness echoed through the lobby as she cut across to the elevator. She took out her cell phone and listened to Jessica's terse voicemail: "Call me."

Jessica answered her callback immediately. "Where the hell are you? Are you okay?"

As okay as I can be after a miscarriage and the news Zach just dropped on me.

"Yeah. How about you?"

"I went to the hospital—why didn't you wait for me? You scared the crap out of me."

"Jess, I'm sorry. Zach called—he came and got me."

"Zach picked you up?"

"You didn't answer your phone. I thought something happened to you." Jenna paused. "I'm at the lab. It's all closed up."

Jessica's tone softened. "Then I guess you know—"

"—about Simon. Zach told me." Jenna's voice broke. "Ariel, I can't believe it."

"He was on his way to meet me at Starbucks."

"*What?*"

Jenna stepped into the elevator, biting her lip to keep from crying. She did not want Jessica to hear her suffocating in grief. But they were two halves of the same person; how could she not know?

"He said his line wasn't secure, so we arranged to meet. Now he's dead."

"Oh my God."

"We'll get through it together, Belle."

Who would know that better than Jess? She was the expert at grieving, although she had tried to hide it from Jenna, even from herself.

Maybe like me she waits to be alone, looking in the mirror before she lets herself cry.

Jenna pushed the button for the third floor and stood with her back against the wall, dashing away tears with the heel of her hand. "You think his phone was bugged—that someone heard him talking to you." It was not a question.

"Don't you?"

"Yes."

Jessica quickly summarized all that had happened while Jenna was hospitalized—the visit with Matthew Casey; checking into the hotel after learning of Simon's death; what she had learned from the flash drive. "I know it was them, sitting right down the block from Casey's house. They were controlling his behavior from their car. I saw the moment he changed—it had to be when they activated the device. All of a sudden, I looked in his eyes and there was nobody home."

Jenna left the elevator and headed for Simon's office. "You mean, like me the other night, the fire."

"Just like that," Jessica acknowledged. "He went blank, then he exploded and came after me."

"Now I know that you're safe, I'm going down to the Project 42 lab and look for proof of what they're doing."

"No, Jen! We've got the flash drive; don't be a hero. I'm on my way back to Ventura. Stay out of the lab and wait for the cops to handle it."

"Okay, sure."

"Don't give me 'okay, sure.' Promise you'll leave there right now. Get Zach to take you home. I'll be there in less than an hour. Detective Jovanic is going to call when he gets off work."

"I've got to find out what's here. I can't just leave this—*thing* in my head and wait to see what the cops think about it."

"Some of those emails were incriminating enough to get an investigation going," Jessica pleaded. "We can just hand over the flash drive and let Detective Jovanic take it from there. He'll have more credibility than we do. The FBI will listen to him."

Jenna knew she ought to be happy that the detective was going to help them, but her insides were as hollow as the chocolate bunnies she and Jess used to find in their Easter baskets: wrapped in shiny foil on the outside, but under the thin shell, nothing but empty air.

Her voice was low and terse in the empty corridor. "Look, Ariel, they haven't messed with my head yet today, but you can't expect me to hang around waiting to see what they'll do next. I'll see you at home. I love you."

She ended the call and powered down the phone. It was weird how she and Jessica could look so alike, but be at opposite ends of the universe in so many other ways. She knew she was being unfair, but in some capricious corner of her mind Jenna felt betrayed that her twin had no way to fully understand how it felt, having a microscopic silicone chip was buried in her brain, programmed to interfere with her emotions and behavior without her knowledge or control.

She slid her card key across the reader on Simon's office door, rerunning their final encounter in her mind.

After finding the appalling memo he had inadvertently left in the file, Jenna had issued an ultimatum: Put a stop to it, or I will. They had very nearly come to blows over her threat to expose Project 42.

Simon's handsome face had gone dark with anger as he warned her to let it go. He'd said she had no idea of what she was meddling in. But her sense of morality was too deeply outraged by what was so clearly unethical and illegal.

She had lost her temper and shouted at him that she could not be with a man who found the concept of 'informed consent' unimportant; that it was somehow acceptable to experiment on a subject without their knowledge. She had told him the relationship was over.

At first, Simon had mocked the permeable walls of her morality, reminding her that she was engaged in an illicit affair with a married man. Then, when he saw she was serious, he had started pleading with her, saying that he couldn't bear the thought of losing her. He was still trying to persuade her when she brushed off his attempts to change her mind and locked herself in her own office.

After their confrontation, Jenna had feared that Simon, not knowing she had already downloaded all the Project 42 files onto the flash drive, would do something to limit her access. That was when she decided to bury it in the rubber tree plant to recover later.

Now Simon was dead. The enormity was more than she could

absorb.

Was it only her imagination that his scent lingered in the room? Could she really detect the wild thyme and tangerines of the cologne he ordered from a company in Argentina? She did what she could to barricade herself against the memories, but all she really wanted was to sit in Simon's chair and pretend to nestle into him, the way she used to sit in his lap in her armchair at the apartment he'd found for her.

Despite knowing he was married, Jenna had fallen in love the moment they met. She had tried to kill her feelings. Then he took her with him to San Diego to the pharmaceutical convention and declared his love for her, and she had foolishly allowed herself to be carried along on the wave of emotion. What a freaking cliché she was.

She knew all his faults—he could be arrogant and thoughtless. Lovesick and stupid, she had believed his lies about leaving his wife. She discovered a softer side that she believed Simon revealed to no one else. The side that had allowed her to overlook his unhappy union with Christine Palmer.

Jenna's body shook with the effort to contain her grief. Indulging in those memories was a luxury she could not afford. Not now, not ever. She clenched her hands tight, digging the nails into her palms. She was here to get Simon's spare card key, which offered access levels in the building that her own card did not. That's what she must focus on.

Holding her breath, she opened the center desk drawer and let out a sigh of relief that the card was there. Another gift of providence.

When the elevator door opened at the basement laboratory, Jenna stood on the threshold, weighing whether to return to the lobby and get the hell away from BioNeutronics as Jessica had urged her to. But as the door started to close, she thrust her arm out and interrupted the sensor beam.

Raising a defiant middle finger to the security cameras she knew were hidden near the ceiling, she sped past the data center, the biochemist's office, the chem lab, the biohazard room, the prep room, the PCR lab, the microscopy room, and around the corner at the end of the hallway.

The mini blinds over the lab windows were closed, preventing Jenna from seeing if there was anyone inside. But the empty parking lot made her believe she was alone in the building. Simon's card key slid across the newly installed reader on the door. On the reader, a red light flashed on.

Oh hell, have they already changed the code?

Get a grip, Jen.

She turned the card over and wanted to kick herself for stupidity. She was holding it with the magnetic stripe on the wrong side. Her nerves were playing havoc with her ability to hold the damn thing steady. When she flipped it around and swiped it again the light flashed green and she pushed open the door, hit the light switch.

Jenna had been the one to order the equipment that would furnish the place, but this was the first time she had seen the private section of the lab since it was set up. The Project 42 lab measured about twelve by fifteen feet. At one end, two computer work stations stood opposite each other. At the other end, a metal fume hood allowed technicians to work safely with noxious chemicals. Along the center, a large black laminated island lined with cabinets provided the scientists a place to perform experiments. Glass tubes, slides, and other laboratory supplies were stacked on shelves and in glass-fronted wall cabinets.

Her eyes swept the long black laminate work tops and cabinets that ran the length of the room. Jessica had described the transmitter Matt Casey showed her; something that looked like a mini tablet. That's what she was looking for.

She recognized some of the equipment from the requisitions she had filled out under Simon's direction—gas chromatography autosampler, centrifuge, stereo microscope with camera attachment, and the hideously expensive scanning electron microscope that was so powerful it could display an entire universe in a speck of dirt. Apart from those items, the work tops were bare.

Jessica's voice echoed as clearly as if her twin lived inside her head: *What did you think, Belle? You'd just walk in and there it would be, lying on the counter, so obvious that you couldn't mistake it?*

"That would have been considerate of them," Jenna murmured. She checked the wall clock. Her plan was to get in and out as expeditiously as possible. She'd promised Zach she would return within fifteen minutes, max, and she had already used up half of those.

She began trying drawers. Locked. Locked. Locked. Cabinet doors, locked. Of course they were locked, she berated herself. What did she expect?

Check the clock: four minutes down. Nearly time to leave.

The cabinets in the center island were her last hope. She reached out a hand to the drawer pull, reluctant, not wanting to be disappointed again.

Jenna stiffened, sure that she had heard a voice out in the corridor. Yes, she heard it again. Her gaze swung around the lab, desperate for a place to hide, but the straight lines and angles scrapped any hope of easy concealment. And there was no time to run across the room and turn off the lights.

The card key reader on the door made an audible 'click.' Jenna ducked behind the island and folded herself into the smallest package she could manage.

The voice, a familiar one, was apparently speaking on a phone. "…leave lights on in Project 42 lab?" said Raisa Polzin. She paused. "…well, I am saying somebody did. I am right now in 42 lab, and…" Polzin broke into a language Jenna didn't recognize.

What would the scientist do if she discovered Jenna hiding in the private laboratory? Everyone at BioNeutronics knew that Raisa Polzin had the hots for Simon. Her hatred for Jenna had floated between them like the odor of rotten eggs from day one. Project 42 had only upped the ante.

Did Polzin know about the twins? Was she aware of their separate detentions in the basement? Jenna hunkered lower behind the island, hardly daring to breathe.

She heard the jingle of keys, then, from the changing timbre of her voice, it seemed Polzin was bending down. A lock clicked on the other side of the island; then, the sound of well-oiled ball bearings rattled in the slides of a drawer being opened and closed.

Polzin switched back to English. "Yes, our Mr. Casey is becoming quite a problem. Needs to be handled immediately. I will bring the new RC1 device with me. The higher range frequencies will put him over the edge. Will be good test. Where do you want to meet?"

Behind the island, Jenna crouched absolutely still, listening to the woman speak about Matt Casey as if he were merely a lab rat. What she had just eavesdropped only confirmed what she and Jess had come to believe: Polzin and her cohorts were causing the Project 42 dropouts to kill themselves.

"I need to pick up a journal from the library," Polzin said. "I want to show you an article..." She switched languages again as she left the lab. Seconds later, the squeaky sound of the scientist's shoes faded, along with her voice.

Jenna let out a long, shaky breath. After what she had just heard, finding the transmitter had just dropped in priority. If she could reach Detective Jovanic in time, she might be able to save Matt Casey, and herself. She had no doubt that a similar fate was being planned for her, too.

She rose slowly on rubbery legs and started for the door, stopping short. The black surface of the work top had been bare before Polzin's visit to the lab. Now, an electronic tablet sat there—the device she had been discussing on the phone? It was somewhat larger than what Jessica had described, but...

It can't be that easy. Can it?

There was only one vehicle in the parking lot and it was not a Dodge Ram truck.

Where the hell is Zach?

Jenna tore around to the front of the building and out to the main road where there was foot traffic in the intersection and plenty of vehicles. If Raisa Polzin came chasing after her there would be witnesses—to what? She doubted the scientist would tackle her in public, especially right after Simon's death.

Simon.

Across the street, Starbucks' pink awning fluttered in the breeze like a waving hand. He had stood in this spot less than twenty-four hours ago, preparing to meet Jess, just before he was mowed down and left to die in the street like roadkill.

The short blast of a horn caught her attention. Zach's truck was up the block, backing up towards her. Jenna climbed into the cab. "Where were you?"

"Starbucks." He indicated the cup holder, which held two cups with the familiar logo. "When I got back, a woman was driving into the BioNeutronics lot, so I parked down the street. I didn't think you'd want her to see me."

"Good move. She's one of the scientists on the project I told you about." Jenna took one of the cups and wrapped her hands around it, trying to soak up its warmth. The outside temperature was in the upper seventies, but her emotions were deadened, her thoughts still tethered to the kill spot in the road.

"I tried to call and warn you," Zach said. "But it went to voicemail. What happened in there?"

Jenna closed her eyes and allowed a self-congratulatory moment for her successful escape. "Lucky for me, she was talking on the phone and I heard her coming." She held the tablet up for him to see. "It was actually an awesome piece of luck that she was there. I couldn't believe she left this out. I snagged it and hoofed it out of there. I wonder what she thought when she got back and it was missing."

"What is it?"

"I *hope* it's a transmitter. There won't be any going back there after this."

"Are you going to turn it on?"

"No way. I don't want to risk messing up my brain worse than it already is. I'm turning it over to a detective from L.A.P.D. this afternoon."

THIRTY-EIGHT

"Nice haircut," Jessica said drily. "Suits you." She dropped into the chair across from Jenna at the dining table, who sat staring at the electronic tablet.

"I cut it because I thought I was going to the lab as you…as me—you know what I mean. Then Zach told me about Simon." Her voice caught on a sob. "I decided to go anyway."

"What happened in there?"

Jenna handed her the tablet. "I stole this. It think it's the transmitter."

"You *what?*"

"Yeah, I know. Not like me to be a lawbreaker, but I'm freaking out here, Jess." Jenna told her how close she had come to being caught.

Jessica shook her head. "I can't believe you did that. Not that you *stole* it—though that's pretty huge for someone who won't even pick up a penny off the street. But, Jesus, Jen, you took an insane risk going there." She turned the device over in her hand, examining it from all sides. It seemed preposterous that something so banal was capable of doing such great harm.

"I had to," Jenna said simply. "And it's a good thing I did if they're going to make Matt Casey kill himself. Can you think of any reason why I won't be next on the list?"

Jessica gave her a skeptical look. "If this *is* the transmitter—and it's not like the one Casey had—it can't be the only one. Think of those guys parked near his house. They must have had one, too."

"From what Polzin said, the signal they used on him wasn't as strong as this one. Maybe this one lets them send out commands from further away. Anyway, if Detective Jovanic gives it to the FBI, they can take it apart and figure it out."

Jessica thought about it. Her twin's reasoning made sense. Or maybe she was just so done with all the stress that she couldn't be bothered to argue anymore.

"Zach wants us to wait at his place for Detective Jovanic to call," Jenna told her. "Nguyen's assholes won't look for us up there."

As if it was planned, there was a knock on the front door and Zach stuck his head around. "Hey, Jen, what time—wow!" His eyes went back and forth between them. "You *are* Jenna, aren't you?" he said, looking at Jessica, whose bruises were concealed under the make-up she had bought for her visit to Matt Casey.

"What do you think?"

He entered the living room and studied the two of them sitting at the table. Jenna had showered and changed clothes, tidied up her haircut. Both twins were similarly clad in black. They had not planned it, but neither was surprised to see that the other had chosen the same outfit.

Zach's eyes fixed on Jessica. "Hmm…I'm not totally sure, but—yeah, I think you're Jen. Am I right?"

They didn't answer, just showed him matching grins. He gave up with a resigned shrug. "Now that we're all here, c'mon up to my place. I ordered pizza."

For a bachelor, Zach kept his apartment remarkably neat, Jessica noticed. It didn't smell like a locker room. No papers or magazines laying around, and no dirty dishes or clothes on the furniture. No wonder Jenna liked him, neat freak that she was, Jessica thought. She had been that way since childhood. Could never abide mess of any kind. Her toys and clothes were never strewn across the floor the way Jessica's were. She insisted on keeping her most prized possessions in their original boxes, as fresh and new-looking as the day they were purchased. A speck of dirt on one of her dolls would spark a panic attack.

According to the shrinks their parents had taken them to, Jenna's behavior did not rise to the level of OCD, but was a lesser sign of anxiety manifested by a need to be in control…to 'do the right thing.' Which also explained her insistence on exposing the truth about Project 42 without regard to her personal safety.

Jessica handled her emotions differently. She simply bulldozed stressful experiences aside and denied the problem. This time, though, her denial had gone to a frightening extreme. Witnessing the attack on Jenna via web cam had triggered the vulnerability created by the head injury she had suffered in the car accident, and sent Jessica into a fugue state.

The three of them shared space on Zach's couch, eating pizza and drinking Coors, making fun of Jerry Springer's guests, and avoiding any serious conversation; marking time until they heard from Detective Jovanic. Every once in a while Jenna would burst into fresh tears. Jessica hugged her and let her cry.

Zach was flipping through channels, when Jenna stopped him at a news conference with Senator Christine Palmer. She stood at a bank of microphones, answering questions. "I want to know what she's saying," Jenna insisted when both Zach and Jessica objected. She snatched the remote and increased the volume.

"…late husband would want me to go on with my candidacy. He believed in me, and he believed that…"

"She's so full of crap," Jenna's voice rose in anger. "Did you hear that speech she gave a couple of weeks ago about Almighty God backing her? Simon laughed about it."

Zach took the remote out of her hand and switched the TV off. "No sense in torturing yourself, Jen."

"The only reason she's even running is because she's got those billionaires behind her. Does she really think they'll let her do what she wants if she gets elected? Doesn't she understand they've got their own agenda?"

"Once we get the information to Detective Jovanic, he'll figure out what to do with it," Jessica assured her. "She won't get elected to the city council, let alone president."

The short outburst had left Jenna out of steam. She curled into a corner of the couch and closed her eyes, shutting out the world.

Zach ambled off to his bedroom. Jessica, worn out, dozed off.

Sometime later they were startled awake by Zach's cell phone, which he had left on the coffee table. He came rushing out and snatched up the phone, apologizing, and took it back into his room, closing the door behind him.

"What time is it?" Jessica asked, hiding a wide yawn behind her hand.

Jenna got up off the couch and stretched out the kinks. "It's nearly four o'clock. My mouth tastes like a sandbox." She started carrying the empty bottles and napkins out to the small kitchen.

"Detective Jovanic should be calling soon," Jessica said. She smashed the pizza box and jammed it into the kitchen trash, then found some glasses and filled them from the faucet. "Let's tell him we'll meet him in Venice. That way he won't have to drive all the way up here. We can go on to Escondido from there, like we planned yesterday before you ended up in the hospital."

Jenna agreed. "Okay, let's tell Zach and we'll hit the road right now. You can call Detective Jovanic from the car."

"I'm afraid that's not gonna work," Zach said, entering the living room.

"Why not?" Jenna asked, surprised.

"There's someplace else you need to be."

"What are you talking about? Where do we need to be?"

Something about Zach was different. Jessica tried to decide what it was. He had changed out of the surfer shorts and Hawaiian shirt he'd been wearing earlier and put on dark khaki pants and a black t-shirt, which made him look more grown up. But it wasn't just his clothing that changed him. Something in his face looked serious, older. He even seemed to stand taller.

Jessica remembered the time she had seen him from the doorway of the Batteries Plus store. She remembered the SUV that had pulled up next to him in the street and the woman who got out and gave him something, then drove away. Something tingled in the back of her head and it was not the buzzing from her injury.

Looking at him now she was seeing not the easygoing, slightly goofy neighbor who had befriended her, but the tough guy who had faced down Pigpen from the train when he tried to ransom her backpack.

In all their encounters, Jessica realized, this was the first time she was really seeing how muscular his arms were, and the way his t-shirt clung to his hard body.

"What's going on, Zach?" she asked pointedly.

He dropped his phone into the pocket of his jeans and ran a hand through his hair so that it stood up in little spikes on top. "That call I just got? I've been instructed to take you for a ride."

Jenna searched his face, her wide blue eyes perplexed. "I don't understand. Why would you get a call about us?"

"Instructed by whom?" Jessica wanted to know.

He gave them both a wry smile and a shrug. "It'll all be clear soon."

"Wait a minute," Jessica said. "Just wait! We're not going anywhere until you explain what you're talking about."

"I'm afraid you are." Zach made a small gesture with his right hand, which had been down at his side. It was then she saw that he held a gun.

"What the hell, Zach—what—?"

"Sorry, chicklet."

"You're going to shoot us if we say no?"

He hiked a mocking brow, looking for just a second more like the friendly neighbor they knew. "You're not gonna make me do anything that drastic, are you?"

The truth dawned in Jenna's face. "Wait—you're on *their* side?"

"I'm not on anybody's side. I'm just an employee doing a job."

"What job?" said Jessica. "What the *hell* is going on?"

"My assignment was to keep an eye on Dr. Lawrie for the past few months, and you, of course. Now that he's out of the picture, I seem to have a new assignment."

Jenna's face paled. "Did you kill Simon?"

"Of course not." Zach sounded genuinely affronted. "I'm not a hired killer."

"Forgive us if we have trouble believing that when you're holding a gun on us," Jessica said with snort of disbelief. "You freaking traitor. We thought you were our friend!"

"I *am* your friend. More than you can know."

"Are you working for Kevin Nguyen?" Jenna wanted to know.

"We'll take your car, Jen," Zach said, ignoring the question.

"Get your keys."

Jessica dug the keys out of her sister's purse.

Zach held out his hand. "I'll take your cell phones."

"I left mine in the car," Jessica said.

"Turn out your pockets, please."

After assuring himself that she was not hiding a phone in her Levis, Zach took the one Jenna handed him and tossed it on the kitchen counter. Jessica made to pick up her backpack, and he remarked, "You won't need that. Leave it here."

"But why, Zach?" Jenna blurted. "Why did you take me to the lab this morning? The transmitter—"

He waved his free hand at her, indicating that she should stop talking. "That's information above my pay grade. I was told to take you where you wanted to go. You wanted to go to the lab, so we went to the lab." He gestured with the gun towards the door. "Let's go, ladies. The neighbors are all at work, so don't bother making a fuss."

"We're expecting a call from a police detective," Jessica said. "If he can't reach us he'll come looking."

Zach shrugged and opened the front door for them. "I guess you won't be here for him to find then, will you?"

Jessica tucked her sister's arm in hers and stalked past him, her mind zooming in a dozen directions. Trying to run was out of the question. He might do something to Jen, and from her twin's ashen face, Jessica really didn't think she was up to handling anything physical.

Besides, there was the gun.

THIRTY-NINE

At Zach's direction, Jessica got behind the wheel of the Nissan. He took the front passenger seat and Jenna folded herself into the small backseat. After shutting Jessica's cell phone in the glove compartment, he sat at an angle that allowed him to keep an eye on both sisters. The gun lay across his lap, his hand loosely covering it.

When he directed her to take the 101 North, Jessica knew immediately, without a single doubt, where he was taking them. Glancing in the rearview mirror, she caught sight of her twin's strained face and knew that Jenna had twigged to it, too. North was the direction of Montecito, where Simon Lawrie had lived with his wife.

Everything came back to Senator Christine Palmer, presidential candidate.

Remembering the painful bite of the senator's fingernails gouging her arm, Jessica asked herself to what lengths Palmer would go to wreak her personal revenge on Jenna.

Jessica could not fault her sister for her affair with Simon Lawrie, when in raw honesty, she had to admit that her own relationship had been every bit as damaging in its own way. Her husband, now awaiting trial, had caused the death of their precious little boy and nearly killed her, too. Both twins had paid the highest price for the choices they had made.

They followed the coastline north. Overhead the sky was an expanse of pure, cloudless blue. To their left, the ocean shimmered like silk, to their right, rolling green hills. Under other conditions it would have been a perfect day for a drive. Jessica wondered whether she was seeing it for the last time.

"So, what are you really," Jenna demanded. "Some kind of private muscle?"

Zach twisted to look at her over the seat. "You might call it private security, but my job description is flexible."

"I can't believe you've been spying on me—on *us*… since I moved in?"

Zach didn't bother to respond.

"I saw you at Batteries Plus," Jessica said.

"What? When?"

"I was in the store and I saw you outside. A black SUV pulled up and a woman got out and gave you something. I should have been suspicious then. She didn't look like your type."

"Don't believe everything you think you see," Zach said, as the Summerland exit appeared. "Get in the right lane and exit at Sheffield."

He directed her to make a sharp turn at the end of the off-ramp. They started up a narrow, heavily tree-lined road that curved as they climbed the bluff, offering occasional glimpses of luxury homes hidden behind iron gates and high hedges.

Soon they were driving through white mist. Her foot close to the brake, Jessica strained forward, as if angling her body closer to the windshield would improve visibility in the increasing elevation.

"Santa Ynez mountains, chicklet," Zach said, responding to her complaint that she couldn't see through the fog that swirled across the road. "Daytime fog most days of the year. Just drive slow."

"Maybe *you* should drive if you know the area so well."

"You're doing fine. Hey, did you know Oprah lives around here? Rob Lowe, too. They say there's more millionaires in one square mile here than anywhere else in the U.S.."

"Thank you so much for that vital piece of information," Jessica spat with contempt. "What are you, the frigging Chamber of Commerce?" She canted her body forward again, trying to peer through the spectral patches of mist that kept appearing and disappearing in front of them.

"Tsk tsk," Zach said. "Sarcasm doesn't become you."

"Well that gun doesn't become *you*."

He pointed to a narrow break in the road. "Turn there."

Jessica mashed her foot on the brake and made Zach's body jerk as she took the sharp turn. Her hope that he would drop the gun was a pipe dream. He quickly recovered and warned her to slow down.

Now they were above cloud level, entering a less-developed area, where the stilts of a new mansion under construction jutted out of the barren red dirt hillside. The wooden skeleton of the house stretched over thousands of square feet. As they drove past, she could see that the site was vacant, no workmen raising drywall or installing cabinetry.

On one side, a sheer drop into the canyon brought a lump into Jessica's throat. As if she needed reminding of the accident. Greg's drunken driving had plunged them over a similar drop. She slowed the vehicle, battling the memories that snaked in and trampled her already raw emotions. A birthday cake, two candles and a little red plastic car on top. Jessica, Jenna, and a couple of moms who had brought Justin's little playmates for his party. Everyone was smiling, singing Happy Birthday. Except for Greg, who was passed out in the bedroom.

Zach's voice interrupted her thoughts, instructing her to park at the top of the bluff. Jessica eyed the desolate terrain. Across the next ridge she could see an immense compound sprawled out on the crest of a hill—maybe Oprah's place. There were no other structures in sight of where they sat; just eucalyptus and citrus trees. Nobody to hear them scream.

From the backseat, alarm tightened Jenna's voice. "What are you going to do with us?"

Zach glanced at her over his shoulder. "We're gonna walk down the hill to the house. You can't see it from up here." He climbed out of the car and pushed the passenger seat forward, giving Jenna a hand. When Jessica came around from the driver's side to join them, he held out his hand for the keys, putting an end to her fantasy that he would forget to ask.

It seemed inconceivable that Zach was the enemy. He was older than her and Jenna by several years, but with his surfer dude manner and dress, she had viewed him as an overgrown kid. Which was exactly how he had conned both of them and wormed his way into their confidence.

Zach pointed them to a dirt path through a small clearing in the trees and told them to take it. A shower of pebbles and loose dirt cascaded down the slope as the twins started the descent, clinging to each other as much for balance as for comfort. Zach never threatened them with his weapon. He must know how acutely aware they were of its presence behind them.

Neither twin needed to verbalize her thoughts for one to hear what was in the other's mind. When the blue slate roof of an elegant French country house became visible below, Jessica could easily divine what Jenna was thinking: *Simon built and lived in this house, but he will never return here.* The painful grip Jenna kept on Jessica's hand said more than if she had shouted what she felt out loud.

A wall formed of river rock blocked their way at the bottom of the path. Zach punched a code on a keypad on the gate and led them, restrained and businesslike, into the garden. They filed past a swimming pool lined with chaise lounges dappled with late afternoon sunshine, past manicured flower beds, past a silver Bentley Continental standing on the circular driveway, ending up at the back door of the house.

Seeming to be in familiar territory, Zach led them into a sizeable utility room that opened onto an expansive country kitchen, then through a family room that was larger than both twins' apartments combined. The voice of a local news anchor blathered from a big screen television, replaying Christine Palmer's press conference.

They followed a glass-walled outer corridor that gave onto views of the heavily-wooded canyon and ended at a private study. Rich ox-blood walls, big leather armchairs and sofa, rough-hewn beams across the ceiling. Studding the wall behind the fireplace mantel, photographs showed Simon Lawrie and his wife hobnobbing with celebrities and dignitaries. French doors led out to a flagstone terrace.

"You can wait in here," Zach said, speaking for the first time since they had entered the gate. Jessica thought he seemed tense. "The patio doors are locked and this one will be, too, so plan on sticking around." As he closed the door behind him the muted click of a bolt slid into place, confirming his words.

Jenna went to the French doors and shook the handle anyway. "Do you think they're watching us?" she asked, her face taut with fear. Little beads of sweat showed at her hairline.

Jessica cupped her hands around her mouth and pressed her lips to Jenna's ear. "Probably. Be careful what you say." A visual sweep of the room had produced nothing she could identify as a camera, but it had to be assumed that surveillance equipment in a house like this one would be sophisticated enough to require an electronic 'sniffer' to locate.

Jenna dropped her voice to a barely audible whisper. "There's a spare key in the driver's side wheel well. If you get a chance, go. Promise."

"You too."

They linked arms and stood side by side, waiting for what was to come, as if banding together as a unit made them stronger. Jessica had a feeling they would need all the strength they could rally.

FORTY

The woman who entered the study was a pale imitation of the powerful senator in the photographs. Her eyes were as puffy and red-rimmed, her face as pasty and strained, as one might expect of any grief-stricken widow. She wore a smart black designer suit and spike-heeled shoes that seemed to indicate her recent arrival at the house, no doubt in the Bentley.

Senator Christine Palmer closed the study door behind her and regarded the twins from across the room. Her eyes rested first on one, then the other in silent appraisal. "Well, well," she said at length. "If it isn't the Doublemint Twins. Which one is the slut that was screwing my husband? Or did you take turns? A threesome, perhaps? Simon would enjoy that."

Beside her, Jessica felt her twin stiffen. She pressed her arm tighter, a warning to say nothing, and said, "*I'm* Jenna Marcott."

Palmer nodded, the full red lips pursed in contempt. "I learned long ago to live with Simon's flings—God knows there were plenty of them, but he really robbed the cradle this time."

Her words stabbed Jessica's heart on her sister's behalf. Had Jenna been canny enough to realize that their affair wasn't the first time Simon had cheated on his wife? Even at twenty-seven and with a track record of bad relationships, there was a guilelessness about Jen that had always led her to believe the lies of the men she attracted.

"You didn't have to kill him," Jenna said in a voice that trembled with emotion.

Palmer turned the sneer in her direction. "*I* didn't kill him, you sniveling bitch. And that's exactly why I had you brought here—to make you understand that what's going on is far bigger than this. It's bigger than me and it's certainly bigger than the two of you. This is our last chance." She threaded her way around the furniture and dropped into one of the big leather armchairs. Crossing one knee over the other, she kicked with the toe of her shoe toward the sofa. "Sit. Over there."

They complied and Palmer continued, "I don't care if you believe it or not, but I tried to save Simon. I *did* save *your* worthless lives. You didn't know that, did you? My..." She broke off, searching for the word she wanted.

"When you started asking the wrong questions, threatening to go public, my backers had every intention of silencing you right then. But I knew that if something happened to my husband's 'executive assistant,' it would have inevitably brought the spotlight onto me, which is a very bad idea for a candidate. The goddamned media is more thorough than the FBI and the CIA combined, and your little *affair de coeur* would have absolutely been exposed. So instead, we let you volunteer for the clinical trial of our very special device." Palmer paused again, appraising the twins with an unpleasant smirk. "I hear it worked out quite well, too. Much smoke damage, dear?"

Jenna jumped up. "How dare you screw around with people's lives! You aren't God. You can't get away with playing this kind of game!"

"Oh sit down, you tiresome little girl. The people I'm dealing with don't 'play games.' They have some very specific goals, and believe me, they *will* meet them, one way or another." Palmer gave a fatalistic shrug. "You could say I'm just a pawn in all this, too. What happened to Simon was because he was weak. He was about to cave."

"But now, the spotlight, as you put it, will be pointed at you anyway," Jessica said, drawing Palmer's focus away from Jenna, who had resumed her place on the sofa. "It doesn't sound like your backers planned very well, does it?"

"Collateral damage. Now it comes down to damage control."

"Nice way to think of your husband—collateral damage."

Palmer's expression remained indifferent. "Your precious sister insisted on discussing the project with him. Blame her. That's why he's dead."

Jessica tried to contain her disgust. How could this woman live with herself? "What is it you want with us, Senator?" she asked. "Why are we really here?"

"You are here for one reason. I've been given one last opportunity to appeal to your common sense." Palmer reached over to a side table next to her chair, where a crystal decanter and a lowball glass had been set out on a tray. She poured herself two fingers of Scotch and threw back a hefty swallow, then closed her eyes and released a long sigh. After a moment, she gave the twins a bold stare, her tight-lipped smile mocking them. "Not that I wouldn't love to see the two of you with matching bullets through your heads."

She allowed a moment for her words to sink in. "The trouble is, my campaign has to be free of innuendo of any kind. After the funeral, when I return to Washington, I will not allow Simon's death to distract the people from the importance of my message. When I'm President, we *will* bring this country back around to the way it used to be."

"And Project 42?" Jessica asked.

"Nothing changes there. The clinical trials are working very well."

"Let me guess," said Jenna. "You've come up with a way to get handpicked members of Congress to try the sexual enhancement device; but the truth is, your people will be controlling them with the secondary device, getting them to vote the way you want them to. Am I close?"

"Close enough."

"What else...the Supreme Court?"

"The Supreme Court and anyone we deem could use a little persuasion on certain issues. All for the benefit of the people, of course. It's going to take some more experimentation and tweaking, but we're getting there."

The Senator's smug self-satisfaction was driving Jessica crazy.

The woman had obviously drunk her backers' Kool-Aid. "How can you possibly justify what you're doing?" she challenged.

Palmer raised her glass if in a toast. "Because I'm doing God's work. This country has been going down the wrong road for a long time now. The people need help thinking the right way again."

"The *right* way? You mean *your* way. The Morton brothers' way," Jenna said sourly.

"Ah. You *have* done your homework," Palmer said. "I can see that they were right to rein you in. But whatever you *think* is going on doesn't matter, does it? Here's the bottom line, and it's your only chance. You will call off your detective and tell him it was all a misunderstanding, and we'll let bygones be bygones. That's it."

"Why would we agree to back off?" Jessica asked. "You just said you can't afford to kill us. The media would be on the story in a hot minute after Simon's death."

"Oh, we don't have to do anything so Draconian as to kill you. There's still another option. One where your mind, dear Jenna, ends up mush." Christine Palmer downed the rest of her drink and set the glass back on the tray. She weighed her upturned palms as if they were a scale. "Hmm, let's see. Back off and keep my cognitive powers intact, or end up in a straitjacket? Which would *I* choose?"

The senator's easy confidence gave Jessica a fresh prickle of alarm. "What's to stop us from having the device removed?" she asked.

"It's not that simple, darlin'." Palmer reached into her jacket pocket for a cell phone and punched in a number. "Would you come to the study, please," she said into the phone.

The door opened a few seconds later to admit Dr. Kapur.

"Tariq, I believe you've already met Ms. Mack," said Christine Palmer, though she was indicating Jenna. "At the time you were introduced, she was masquerading as Ms. Marcott."

Under other circumstances, Jessica would have laughed at the paradox.

"It's quite remarkable!" Kapur exclaimed. "I can see why there was confusion about Ms. Mack's identity. You do present a most interesting problem, but I must say I appreciate your participation in our test process."

"As if we were given a choice," Jenna said dully.

"Doctor," said Palmer, ignoring her. "Would you please explain the disadvantages of attempting to remove the microchip."

"I would be delighted, my dear." When Kapur smiled, Jessica could see his transparent pleasure at the opportunity to hold forth about his pet project. It showed in the lightness of his step as he went to stand in front of the big window; in the way he clasped his hands behind his back, taking up a lecturing posture, like a professor about to address a class.

"We have found that the device becomes rapidly assimilated into the body. Fibrous tissue begins to grow around it so that it actually becomes part of the host's brain. What this means to you, Ms. Marcott, is that since your procedure was nearly two weeks ago, tissue growth is assumed to already be well established. Admittedly, assimilation was an unintended side effect of the implant, but it's one that actually works out well for us. It makes the microchip virtually impossible to detect."

Kapur's gloating gaze went from one twin to the other—did he actually expect approval? Jessica's gut roiled. She took a covert glance at her twin. Jenna's eyes were fixed on a marble horse head on the cocktail table, her gaze boring into the object as if she could shut out the utter hopelessness of their situation.

Kapur went on. "Any attempt to excise the microchip would entail significant risk, as surrounding brain structures could easily be harmed in the process. You see, the implant is placed close to the amygdala, which, among other things, affects the emotions, and the hippocampus, which affects memory. Thus, removal of the microchip could severely impact memory functions. And from what I've heard, Ms. Mack can tell you something about how it feels to be without a memory."

Christine Palmer poured herself another drink while Kapur droned on. "Since the device is microscopic, once tissue overgrowth has become established, even if you were looking for it, it would not easily be seen on an MRI or CT Scan. And magnetic imaging would cause traumatic burns to the brain." He paused for breath. "If you read the specifications you stole, you will know that we use a very fine cathode needle, tracing its path through a computer screen to implant the microchip exactly where it needs to be to produce the electrical impulse to stimulate the appropriate area.

Because every brain is a little different, you see, it takes a great deal of skill to place it precisely in the cerebral cortex—"

"Thank you, Doctor," Palmer interrupted at last with an impatient wave of her hand. "I think they now understand the problem."

Jenna sat silent, her gaze still on the marble horse head. Her drooping shoulders said she had already given up hope. "Let me get this right," Jessica said, still acting as Jenna. "You're threatening to turn me into a zombie if we don't cooperate?"

Kapur frowned. "'Zombie' is so inelegant."

"Yes, more like stark raving lunatic," Palmer interjected with a malicious smile. "I know you're still tweaking it, Tariq, but maybe a little reminder is called for to help them make their decision."

"Of course, my dear." Kapur dug his hand into his jacket pocket. Pride shone in his face as he removed a tablet similar to the one Jenna had taken from BioNeutronics. The difference was, this one was half the size. He smirked at Jessica. "I understand you helped yourself to one of the early test transmitters from the lab. Wasn't it kind of Dr. Polzin to leave it out for you to find?"

"What do you mean?"

"Zach reported in when you entered the lab," Palmer said. "Luckily, Raisa was able to run over and help you out with the transmitter."

"But—why?"

"*Why?*" Christine Palmer echoed. "It gave you something to play with while the lab was being cleaned up."

Jessica would not give Palmer the satisfaction of seeing how close to despair she was. If the evidence of Project 42's secondary device had already been removed from the lab, there would be nothing for Detective Jovanic or his FBI contact to find.

The flash drive was in her backpack at Zach's apartment, and so was the transmitter. He would find and destroy both. Jenna gave no outward reaction, but Jessica could sense her deflate even further as any fight she'd had left seeped away.

"We've vastly improved its functions over the version you stole," Dr. Kapur was saying. "This beta version has its own app, too. Of course, the app can't go on the market right away. There's a lot of testing to be done yet."

As he spoke, he started tapping out commands on the screen. "Let's see what we can get out of Ms. Marcott today. With this version I may even be able to stimulate more precise emotions."

"Can you make her choke her sister?" Senator Palmer asked lightly, as if the whole thing were a joke. Knowing that she was deadly serious, the question made Jessica's mouth go dry.

"We are not quite at a stage where we can give specific commands. For now, it's a matter of stimulating a certain *type* of emotion. How the subject expresses the emotion is, unfortunately, random. Hence, the fire she set."

At his words, Jessica's pulse kicked into high gear. The knowledge that the scientist had been poking surgical instruments around in her twin's brain already made her want to beat the shit out of him. Watching him tap out commands designed to deliberately harm Jenna unleashed a rage that surpassed even her hatred for Kevin Nguyen and his minions. She shouted at Kapur to stop.

The distraction was enough to arrest the rapid movement of the scientist's fingers. Jessica's heart was thumping like a rock band's amp as she sprang off the sofa and raced across the room, arms outstretched, hands reaching for the transmitter.

Christine Palmer was ready for her. As she made to pass, Palmer aimed a vicious kick with her spike heel and connected with Jessica's injured knee. A searing pain shot through her leg and she went down, crashing into the glass cocktail table.

She was struggling to get up when Palmer dove into her and rode her back to the floor, forcing the air out of her lungs. The pressure against her diaphragm made it impossible to breathe. Thick pile carpet fibers clogged her nose and mouth, suffocating her.

Jessica fought to stay conscious, but her head was spinning and the familiar whistling pierced her ears. The world was turning to black and white…

"What are you—don't—" Dr. Kapur's strangled cry reached her fading awareness.

"Hey!" Palmer yelled simultaneously. Then the weight lifted off her torso and Jessica was back, fighting for air. Like a marionette whose strings are rudely cut, Tariq Kapur dropped to the floor in front of her.

Palmer was screaming for Zach. The sound of breaking glass shocked her into silence.

Still sucking oxygen, Jessica rolled onto her side and found herself face-to-face with scientist's body. One dull brown eye stared back at her. The other was closed.

The study door slammed open. Zach, weapon extended, rapidly swept the room. Swiveling his gaze back to the senator, he snapped, "Where's the other one?"

FORTY-ONE

Jenna Marcott stopped running and sat down on the dusty path. She hated dirt, but her head felt fuzzy, as if her blood sugar was in the basement. She pressed her hands to her temples, trying to remember.

How did I get here?

What happened?

Where's Jess?

Bits of memories floated, particles of images: Dr. Kapur typing on a tablet…a pleasant tingling across her scalp. Then, chaos. Literally, a brain storm.

Jenna could remember nothing else. Like a sleepwalker waking confused in the middle of a nightmare, she gazed down at the blue tiled roof some thirty feet below and recognized Simon Lawrie's home from photos he had shown her.

Why is Simon's house down there?

From her vantage point she could see across the wall surrounding the property to the flagstone terrace at the rear of the house. The French doors stood open. Jenna picked absently at the glass splinters dotting the back of her hand, wondering where they had come from.

Simon is dead.

She shut her eyes, puzzling over what had happened and what she was doing here. When she looked again, a dark patch in the glass of the French doors resolved into a jagged hole.

Why is there a hole in the door?

More memory fragments: Jessica, flying across the room at the doctor. Christine Palmer viciously kicking out at her. Jenna herself, consumed with a terrible, killing rage. She had taken the horse head statue from the cocktail table and...the memory abruptly ended there.

Jenna extended her hands in front of her, staring at the bloody fingers and palms as if the appendages belonged to someone else.

She remembered the question Christine Palmer had asked Dr. Kapur: "Can you make her choke her sister?"

Oh Jess, what did he make me do?

She could not have used these hands to harm her twin. Could she?

You set a fire while she was asleep.

Oh my God.

It *couldn't* be Jessica's blood. The idea was too abhorrent to even consider. But Kapur had sent an electronic command and she, Jenna, had picked up the horse's head...

She rolled onto her knees and emptied her stomach in the scrub.

When there was nothing left to vomit, Jenna scrubbed her hands against the dirt path. She scrubbed until the bloodstains were covered and caked with clay earth. She scoured and rubbed until finally, the only blood that remained was her own.

The blistering pain of palms scraped raw helped to clear her mind, but still, she found no conscious recollection of how the blood had come to stain her hands. But she remembered the promise she and Jess had made to each other in Christine Palmer's study: if one of them got away, she would run for help. She owed it to her twin to keep that promise.

Jenna climbed slowly to her feet and resumed her climb up the hill. She was within a few feet of the Nissan when the sharp crack of a gunshot echoed across the canyon.

FORTY-TWO

"Where's the other one?"

Jessica dragged herself to a sitting position, taking note of the gaping hole in the French doors, the scattering of glass on the floor. She saw the horse's head, its marble surface streaked with blood.

Where is Jenna? Did she escape?

Christine Palmer was bending over Kapur's still form, holding a wad of cocktail napkins. Blood from a wide gash above his eyebrow was rapidly absorbing into the white carpet. Jessica wondered if her twin had killed him.

"It's going to be hell to get this stain out," Palmer grumbled, wedging napkins under his head. "We have to get him out of here."

Kapur groaned. Not dead. In Jessica's opinion, the scientist deserved no better than he had gotten, but the senator's callous disregard for her confederate's life sickened her. "I guess your little device still needs work," she taunted.

Christine Palmer's teeth bared like a rabid dog. "You and your sister just used up your last chance."

"This is who she is, Zach," Jessica said, pulling herself to her feet with difficulty. Her knee felt like it had been worked over with a crowbar. "Can't you see, all she cares about is getting elected? It doesn't matter who gets destroyed along the way."

"Don't worry, Jessica, I see it."

Palmer swung around on Zach, who had lowered his gun

and taken out his cell phone. "What the hell do you think you're doing?"

"Calling for an ambulance."

"Put it down. I can't have him found here in this condition. We'll get him out to your car and you can take him to a discreet doctor. I'm sure you can come up with someone."

"This man has a head wound, Senator. He can't be moved until medical personnel check him out."

"He can't stay here, do you hear me, Zach?" Palmer's voice rose. "He can't stay in this house! Get him the hell out of here."

Jessica glared at her with loathing. "How could you involve yourself in something so evil as mind control? What made you willing to take this road?"

Palmer's brittle laugh held no humor. "I've sold my soul. It's not me who's calling the shots. I *have* to be elected—God wants me to be President; it's a Divine Calling. These people—my backers—they're just a means to get there."

"Do you know how little sense that makes? You can't serve two masters, Senator."

"I do what I have to do." Christine Palmer spoke to Zach. "You. Go find the sister and drag her back here by the hair if you have to. And if you're too squeamish, I'll get someone else to do the cleanup. By the way, you're fired."

"I'm afraid not," Zach said. "This is where it ends, senator." He straightened and once again, as Jessica had witnessed at his apartment, something indefinable had changed in the way he carried himself.

"You seem to have forgotten who's been paying your very nice salary," Palmer's lip curled into a sneer. "Don't tell me you're suddenly a starry-eyed idealist."

"No, ma'am, I'm a special agent with the FBI."

A look of shock froze on Christine Palmer's face the instant before she lunged for his gun.

An unwitting onlooker might have thought they were dancing as they swayed and twisted, their bodies pressed as close as lovers. Zach caught hold of Palmer's wrist with his free hand and tried to force her to let go.

"Watch out, Zach!"

Jessica's warning came too late. Palmer brought up a foot and raked his leg with her spike heel. Instinct bent Zach forward just long enough for her to grab his gun hand and pull the weapon down between them.

The shot was a deafening explosion.

Zach went down on his knees, clutching at his throat.

"You shot him!" Jessica cried, her ears ringing. "Are you crazy?"

"He shot himself." Palmer whipped around and backhanded Zach hard across the face. "I hired a fucking FBI agent? You sonofabitch."

Blood was streaming through his fingers, running down his arm in a river. His face had already turned paper white. With his hand pressed to the wound, Zach grabbed the gun, which he had dropped, and struggled to get to his feet.

If they didn't quickly stem the flow of blood, Jessica knew he would lose consciousness and it would be all over for Zach. She grabbed his cell phone from the floor where it had fallen and started to tap in 911.

"*Freeze*!"

The sudden loud shout came from the patio. "*FBI*! *FBI*! *Drop the weapon*!"

The sound of running feet followed the command and agents in tactical vests swarmed into the room, weapons drawn, yelling orders: "Everyone on the floor! Get down! Get down!"

Doors slammed in other parts of the house. For the third time in five minutes, Jessica found herself face down on the floor. A flurry of activity around her: Agents moving fast, yelling to each other, identifying their targets. Exchanges by phone with paramedics intertwined with rapidly fired questions: "Who else is in the house? Are there any other weapons? Anyone else injured?"

Then Jessica heard a voice that made her go limp with relief.

"That's my sister," Jenna said. "Let her up. She didn't do anything wrong."

Strong hands reached down and encircled Jessica's arms, pulling her to her feet.

FORTY-THREE

FBI Special Agent Zachary Smith woke up in a hospital bed with Jenna Marcott on one side and Jessica Mack on the other. He did not know which twin was which, but he did know that the man standing at the foot of his bed was Case Agent Roland Sparks, his boss.

Sparks had already explained to the sisters how relatively lucky Special Agent Smith had been. The round fired from his service weapon had missed his spine by a fraction of an inch, cleanly exiting the back of his neck. The bullet had struck the trachea just below the larynx, requiring surgical repairs to muscle and tissues. Zach was going to be out of commission for a while.

The doctor said it might take a week or more before he healed well enough for removal of the trach tube, and only then would they know whether his voice would return to normal. For the moment, he was unable to speak at all.

"But why did he have to spy on us?" Jenna wanted to know after being assured that Zach was going to recover.

"Think of it more as keeping watch over you," Sparks said with a touch of cynicism.

"By kidnapping us?" Jessica was beyond furious.

Frustrated by his inability to communicate verbally, Zach moved restlessly in the bed. Jenna lightly covered his hand with hers to calm him.

"He knew our emergency team would be monitoring the situation," Sparks said with an almost-smile. "When Special Agent Smith picked up Ms. Marcott from the hospital and she told him about being kidnapped and implanted with a behavior control device, it instantly changed the direction of our investigation. We were suddenly looking at a very different matter from diversion of campaign contributions and illegal use of funds, which is what we had been investigating for several months. He called me for instructions, then brought you up to his apartment to keep you out of harm's way until we could get our operation in place."

"You mean you had your people up on that hill already when we got there?" Jessica asked.

"No, they were right behind you, waiting for Agent Smith's signal. He was wearing a wire and we were listening in the car. Having a U.S. senator involved made it a highly sensitive situation."

Jessica couldn't help noticing how different Roland Sparks looked in his dark grey suit and crisp white shirt with silver silk tie. She had not had time to think about his looks when the five-person emergency rescue team had burst into the study, guns drawn. Leading his team into Senator Palmer's home, Sparks had been wearing a bulletproof tactical vest over his shirt; FBI was emblazoned across it in large yellow letters. He cleaned up pretty nicely, she decided.

Being laid out and handcuffed by the FBI, even for just a few minutes, was an experience Jessica would like to forget. Senator Palmer and each twin had been quickly separated and removed to other locations in the house until the agents had questioned them and sorted out who was who.

As a U.S. senator, Palmer had been accorded greater deference than the run-of-the-mill arrestee would receive, but she suffered the same indignity—on the floor, cuffed, patted down. She immediately lawyered up and clammed up.

Later, Jessica and Jenna wondered aloud whether the senator, with the backing of the Morton Brothers, would manage to slide out of whatever federal charges might be lodged against her. More likely, since she was no longer of any use to them—her presidential campaign in tatters—she would be left twisting in the wind.

Then, there was the urgent matter of the device in Jenna's

head. The sisters had spent long hours being interviewed—or interrogated, as Jessica thought of it—on what they each knew about Project 42. Jenna's flash drive had been confiscated, but Roland Sparks' superiors were pressing for more.

"You want *what*?" Jenna cried, appalled when he made his proposal. "You think I'm going to leave this thing in my head so your people can experiment on me?"

Sparks had the grace to look sheepish. "That's not exactly what I meant, Ms. Marcott."

"Then what *exactly* did you mean?"

"It's just that the scientists we've been talking to are viewing it as an incredible opportunity to study the effects of the microchip, and since it's *already* implanted…hey, don't kill the messenger."

She stared at him, trying to figure out whether he was serious. Were FBI agents ever *not* serious? She couldn't tell.

"You saw what I did to Dr. Kapur. He might have permanent brain damage—not that he doesn't deserve it—but the effects of the device are totally unpredictable. You know about me setting a fire. Matthew Casey attacked my sister. Why don't you go experiment on him?"

SAC Sparks was shaking his head. "We will be talking to him, and all the other people that were in the study, too. Look, I'm not saying you should do it, but you do have a rare perspective, considering your former relationship with BioNeutronics."

"Are you completely out of your mind? You must think I'm out of mine. This thing is gone as soon as I can find a neurosurgeon to dig it out of my head. Now, am I under arrest for something, or do I get to leave?"

Sparks shrugged. "We don't have any reason to hold you."

Jenna snatched up her purse and headed for the door.

FORTY-FOUR

Jessica Mack gazed through the window at the Pacific Ocean, remembering her last trip aboard the Amtrak Surfliner. A scant month ago—a lifetime—she had awakened terrified to find herself traveling north with no idea of who she was or where she was headed.

Her memory still had some holes, but her past was being restored piece by piece. She was confident that with the help of Dr. Gold, everything would eventually be restored. Meanwhile, she was returning to her apartment in Escondido to file for divorce and prepare herself for her husband's trial. Though it meant once again reliving the death of her child, Jessica had come to understand that the pain of remembering Justin was more bearable than the pain of forgetting.

On this trip, the twins were traveling together. Jenna had her own demons to face, her own grieving to do, but this time they would grieve together and decide what they wanted the future to look like.

They had learned that Senator Palmer bailed out of federal custody. If a trial ever actually happened, considering her resources and all the high-priced lawyers at her disposal, it would be a long time coming and the results seemed dubious. Meanwhile, the media were salivating over the juicy story, with the political channels' talking heads exploring every angle 24/7.

Zach remained in the hospital, recovering from his injury. The sisters had stayed at his bedside the first night and day, leaving only after making a solemn promise to stay in touch. There had been something in his eyes when he looked at Jenna—something that made Jessica believe that once her twin gained some distance from Simon Lawrie's death, love could find her again. She had not mentioned this, didn't need to; they were identical twins—two halves of the same whole.

"I couldn't believe Agent Sparks thought I would agree to be their guinea pig." Jenna pulled her sister's attention from the scenery outside the window. "As if I would leave this thing in my brain until they figure out how it works."

"Maybe he should have one implanted in *his* head," Jessica agreed. "Though, he was actually kind of hot."

"Yeah, Ariel, I saw how you were looking at him."

Jessica had to admit that she would not be averse to putting Roland Sparks back in the frame. She got that it would be unprofessional for him to say anything while she was involved in the case, but she had definitely sensed a return of her interest. "Maybe I can transmit some thoughts to him *without* an implant," she said with a grin.

They both laughed at that and made a pact: for just a few hours they would set aside their fears about the microchip in Jenna's head and pretend to be nothing more than twin sisters, happy to be riding the rails to Solana Beach.

ABOUT THE AUTHOR

Like Claudia Rose, Sheila Lowe is a court-qualified handwriting expert who testifies in forensic cases. She has more than thirty years' experience in the field of handwriting analysis and holds a Bachelor of Science degree in Psychology. The author of the award-winning *Forensic Handwriting Mysteries*, *Handwriting of the Famous & Infamous*, and *The Complete Idiot's Guide to Handwriting Analysis*, her comments on celebrity handwritings have appeared in such publications as *Time*, *Teen People*, and *Mademoiselle*. Her articles on Personality Profiling and Handwriting Analysis for the *Attorney* have been published in bar association magazines, and she is a blog contributor at www.algonquinredux.

www.claudiaroseseries.com

POISON PEN

BOOK 1: *A FORENSIC HANDWRITING MYSTERY*

Sheila Lowe "wins readers over with her well-developed heroine and the wealth of fascinating detail" (*Booklist*) in this captivating mystery set in Hollywood, where forensic handwriting expert Claudia Rose knows that despite the words it forms, a pen will always write the truth.

Before her body is found floating in her Jacuzzi, publicist to the stars, Lindsey Alexander, had few friends, but plenty of lovers. To her ex-friend Claudia, she was a ruthless, backstabbing manipulator. But even Claudia is shocked by Lindsey's startling final note: *It was fun while it lasted.*

It would be easier on the police—and Claudia—to write off Lindsey's death as suicide, but Claudia's instincts push her to investigate further, and she quickly finds herself entangled in a far darker scenario than she had anticipated. Racing to identify the killer, Claudia soon has a price on her head. Unless she can read the handwriting on the wall, she will become the next victim.

"The well—paced plot develops from uneasy suspicions to tightly wound action."
—*Front Street*

WRITTEN IN BLOOD

BOOK 2: *A FORENSIC HANDWRITING MYSTERY*

(Top ten pick of Independent Booksellers)

Sheila Lowe's Poison Pen was hailed as a "fast-paced, crisp...novel that penetrates the world of celebrity." (*Armchair Interviews*) And Hollywood forensic handwriting expert Claudia Rose is about to prove once more that no matter what words it forms, a pen will always write the truth.

Claudia Rose's latest client is a dime-a-dozen type. The widow of a rich older man, Paige Sorensen is younger than—and hated by—her stepchildren. And they're dead set on proving that Paige forged their father's signature on his Will, which left his entire estate, including the Sorensen Academy, to her.

Intrigued by this real-life soap opera, Claudia soon breaks one of the cardinal rules of business: Never get personally involved. But Claudia has grown attached to a troubled Sorensen student, and when disaster strikes, she'll realize that reading between the lines can mean the difference between life and death.

"[Claudia's] sharper, tougher, and more tenacious than ever."
—*American Chronicle*

DEAD WRITE

BOOK 3: *A FORENSIC HANDWRITING MYSTERY*

Sheila Lowe's mysteries "just keep getting better," (*American Chronicle*) thanks to feisty forensic handwriting expert Claudia Rose, who knows that when it comes to solving a murder, sometimes the pen can be mightier than the sword.

Claudia heads to the Big Apple at the behest of Grusha Olinetsky, the notorious founder of an elite dating service whose members are mysteriously dying. The assignment puts Claudia at odds with her boyfriend, LAPD detective Joel Jovanic, who suspects Grusha is trouble.

Drawn into the feckless lives of the rich and single, Claudia finds herself enmeshed in a twisted world of love and lies fueled by desperation. But desperate enough to kill? Clues in the suspects' handwriting might help Claudia save Grusha's already dubious reputation, before the names of more victims are scribbled into someone's little black book.

"Sheila Lowe is the Kathy Reichs of forensic handwriting—a rip-roaring read."
—Deborah Crombie, National Bestselling Author of *Necessary as Blood*

LAST WRITES

BOOK 4: *A FORENSIC HANDWRITING MYSTERY*

Claudia's friend, Kelly, learns that she's an aunt when her estranged half-sister, Erin, shows up at her home in desperate need of help. Erin and her husband have been living quiet lives in an isolated compound as members of the 'Temple of Brighter Light.' But now her husband and young child have disappeared, leaving behind a cryptic note with a terrifying message.

Seizing an opportunity to use her special skills as a forensic handwriting expert, Claudia becomes one of the few outsiders ever to be invited inside the mysterious compound. She has only a few days to uncover the truth about Kelly's missing niece before the prophecy of a secret ancient parchment can be fulfilled, and an innocent child's life is written off for good.

"A fascinating view into the world of handwriting analysis…captivating."
—Robin Burcell, Author of *The Bone Chamber*

INKSLINGERS BALL

BOOK 5: *A FORENSIC HANDWRITING MYSTERY*

A teenage girl, brutally murdered and left in a trash dumpster; a young tattoo artist, killed in a firebomb attack; a soccer mom, shot in the living room of her home; vicious thugs whose job it is to protect a suspected criminal…Just another week on rotation for LAPD detective Joel Jovanic. That is, until he uncovers a connection between the disturbing series of vicious crimes and Annabelle Giordano, who is in the temporary custody of his soulmate, Claudia Rose.

"With vivid characters, smooth writing, and a twisty plot, Sheila Lowe has crafted a mystery that will keep you guessing to the very end."
—Boyd Morrison, International Bestselling Author

THE COMPLETE IDIOT'S GUIDE TO HANDWRITING ANALYSIS

SECOND EDITION

Space-Form-Movement: A basic course introducing the gestalt method of handwriting analysis. Using hundreds of famous people's handwritings, the CIG2HWA shows you how to understand the core personality of a writer without having to take dozens of measurements. Learn what spatial arrangement reveals about how you arrange your life and time, what writing style says about your ego, and what writing movement reveals about your energy and how you use it.

HANDWRITING OF THE FAMOUS & INFAMOUS

SECOND EDITION

Handwriting communicates much more than what is committed to paper. A quick note, a carefully composed letter, an autograph or a scribble also reveals a great deal about the personality of the writer. What are the clues to look for in a person's writing and what do they reveal? What do they tell experts that the writer might prefer to keep hidden? This fascinating book is a collection of handwriting samples of some of the most influential and notorious people of the past and present.

Made in the USA
Charleston, SC
29 July 2016